ARRIVED

# ARRIVED

# JERRY B. JENKINS
# TIM LAHAYE
## with CHRIS FABRY

TYNDALE HOUSE PUBLISHERS, INC.
WHEATON, ILLINOIS

Visit Tyndale's exciting Web site at www.tyndale.com.

*TYNDALE* is a registered trademark of Tyndale House Publishers, Inc.

Tyndale's quill logo is a trademark of Tyndale House Publishers, Inc.

*Left Behind* is a registered trademark of Tyndale House Publishers, Inc.

Discover the latest Left Behind news at www.leftbehind.com

*Arrived* is a special edition compilation of the following Left Behind: The Kids titles:

*#38: The Perils of Love* copyright © 2004 by Jerry B. Jenkins and Tim LaHaye. All rights reserved.

*#39: The Road to War* copyright © 2004 by Jerry B. Jenkins and Tim LaHaye. All rights reserved.

*#40: Triumphant Return* copyright © 2004 by Jerry B. Jenkins and Tim LaHaye. All rights reserved.

Cover photographs copyright © by Punchstock. All rights reserved.

Authors' photograph copyright © 1998 by Reg Francklyn. All rights reserved.

Published in association with the literary agency of Alive Communications, Inc., 7680 Goddard Street, Suite 200, Colorado Springs, CO 80920.

Scripture quotations are taken from the *Holy Bible,* New Living Translation, copyright © 1996, 2004 by Tyndale Charitable Trust. Used by permission of Tyndale House Publishers, Inc., Wheaton, Illinois 60189. All rights reserved.

Some Scripture taken from the New King James Version. Copyright © 1979, 1980, 1982 by Thomas Nelson, Inc. Used by permission. All rights reserved.

Characters in this novel sometimes speak words that are adapted from various versions of the Bible, including the King James Version and the New King James Version.

Designed by Jessie McGrath

**Library of Congress Cataloging-in-publication data**

Jenkins, Jerry B.
    Arrived / Jerry B. Jenkins, Tim LaHaye, with Chris Fabry.
       p. cm. — (Left behind—the kids ; #38-#40)
    This is a special combined edition of three previously published Left behind: the kids titles.
    Summary: Four teens battle the forces of evil when they are left behind after the Rapture.
    ISBN 1-4143-0273-8 (hardcover)
    1. Children's stories, American. [1. End of the world—Fiction. 2. Christian life—Fiction.]
I. LaHaye, TIm F.   II. Fabry, Chris, 1961-   III. Title.
    PZ7.J4138Ar 2005
[Fic]dc22                                  2004028728

Printed in the United States of America

10   09   08   07   06   05
8   7   6   5   4   3   2   1

**JUDD** Thompson Jr. fell into a chair and gasped for breath. It felt like the air had been sucked out of his lungs. He couldn't believe he was trapped in New Babylon, the headquarters of the Global Community.

Judd spoke with Chang Wong for a few more minutes, and Chang said he would call with any information that might help Judd and pilot Westin Jakes escape.

Then Judd joined the others gathered around several computers. Some monitored cameras set up near their safe house, while others watched the latest from the Global Community News Network.

Rainer Kurtzmann, the German leader of this small group, took Judd aside. "I'm sorry you're trapped. I feel responsible for not getting you back to your plane last night."

Judd frowned. "It's not your fault. Westin and I made a bad choice."

"Whatever we can do to help, we will do."

A woman pointed to a tiny laptop computer. "Take a look at this."

Judd watched as a temperature gauge on the right side showed things were back to normal. The woman moved a remote camera slightly to the left, and several people crawled out of an underground bunker. Their skin was pale, and they looked like they hadn't eaten in weeks.

The woman zoomed in on a smiling group. A young man ran to a burned-out area and lay down, scissor-kicking as if making a snow angel. The others with him laughed.

The mood inside the safe house wasn't cheerful. They would no longer be able to move around during the day. Westin grumbled about his plane, wondering if the GC would find it.

"We have to prepare for possible inspections by Peacekeepers," Rainer said. "They'll be going from building to building soon."

A live shot of Carpathia's palace showed open windows and people streaming out of the building. Judd wondered if the GC would ever estimate how many had died from the heat.

Leon Fortunato appeared at a press conference, and Judd was shocked at the way the reporters looked. The normal crowd of men and women covering international news was down to only a few people in ragged clothes. Even makeup couldn't hide their gaunt faces.

Fortunato was dressed in his usual gaudy clothing, but Judd could tell the past few weeks had taken their toll. There were dark circles under Leon's eyes, and his clothes seemed to sag.

"I'm pleased to say that your potentate will speak just before noon today to give an update on the world situation," Fortunato said. "But I am happy to report that it appears this quirk of nature is over. We have reports from everywhere the sun is up that the heat is gone. Let us give thanks to the giver of all good things, Nicolae Carpathia."

———

Vicki awoke with a gasp and sat up in bed. The rhythmic breathing of the others in the cabin calmed her, but something didn't feel right. She listened for any noise outside but heard nothing. The heat wave had done many things to help believers, even zapping insects. Rivers and lakes had boiled for so long that frogs were nonexistent. Crickets, cicadas, and other bugs had either gone into hiding or had been burned to a crisp. Vicki was glad she could go out during the day because walking at night was so quiet it was eerie.

Vicki had awakened at other times and sensed a need to pray for friends. Perhaps this was such a time. Could someone be in trouble? Judd?

She closed her eyes and lay back on the pillow, whispering a prayer. Vicki found it better to pray aloud because when she prayed silently, she got distracted and sometimes simply fell asleep.

When Vicki had first become a believer, prayer had seemed like a duty. She ticked off a list of things she needed God to do, made sure she confessed her sins, got in the right amount of praise and worship, and went on with her life. But it had been six years now, and her view of prayer had changed. Just like she looked forward to talking with Judd and spending time with him, she looked forward to her times alone with God. In fact, speaking with her heavenly Father didn't feel stiff and formal—it felt natural.

Vicki discovered what had been missing from her prayer life a few years earlier: listening. She had always thought that prayer meant *saying* things *to* God. Now she remained silent for a few minutes, letting God bring back passages she had memorized or bits of verses.

At first, she had been unsure of how to address God. Should she talk to Jesus, call out to God, Father, heavenly Father, or say something else? She finally realized that God was more concerned with her simply coming to him, but she had found calling him "Father" a comforting way to begin.

"Father," Vicki prayed, "I don't know if something is wrong or if I'm up because of something I ate, but I want to listen now. I pray for Judd and the plans he has for the wedding and where we'll live once I get to Petra. Keep him safe, Father. . . ."

Vicki paused, suddenly thinking of a verse Marshall had quoted a few days before. The words she recalled were *perfect peace*, but she couldn't think of the rest. She flipped on a flashlight and grabbed her Bible from the floor. Shelly said something in her sleep and rolled over in the bed next to Vicki's.

Vicki remembered the passage was from Isaiah and

turned to chapter 26, the one Marshall had been speaking about. She found her answer in the third verse.

> *You will keep in perfect peace all who trust in you,*
>> *whose thoughts are fixed on you!*

Is God telling me something? Vicki thought. Is something about to happen?

She continued reading the passage.

> *Trust in the Lord always, for the Lord God is the eternal Rock.*
>
> *He humbles the proud and brings the arrogant city to the dust.*
>
> *Its walls come crashing down!*
>
> *The poor and oppressed trample it under-foot.*
>
> *But for those who are righteous, the path is not steep and rough. You are a God of justice, and you smooth out the road ahead of them.*
>
> *Lord, we love to obey your laws; our heart's desire is to glorify your name.*
>
> *All night long I search for you; earnestly I seek for God. For only when you come to judge the earth will people turn from wickedness and do what is right.*
>
> *Your kindness to the wicked does not make them do good. They keep doing wrong and take no notice of the Lord's majesty.*
>
> *O Lord, they do not listen when you threaten. They do not see your upraised fist. Show them your eagerness to defend your people. Perhaps then they will be ashamed. Let your fire consume your enemies.*

> *Lord, you will grant us peace, for all we have accomplished is really from you.*

Vicki shook her head at the timeless words. She couldn't wait to meet the writers of the Bible and hear what they had been going through when they penned words like these. She smiled as she read the end of the twelfth verse again: *". . . for all we have accomplished is really from you."*

Footsteps sounded on the path outside. Vicki switched off the flashlight and sat up in bed. The door creaked open, and Vicki's heart pounded as she squinted to see who was coming.

"Vicki?" Mark whispered. "You awake?"

"Yeah," Vicki said, leaning back on her pillow. She knew Mark had been on duty in the main cabin keeping watch for the night.

"Better come with me," Mark said.

Vicki was dressed in seconds and ran up the path, catching up to Mark just before he entered the main cabin.

"What is it?" Vicki said.

"Phone call. Bad news."

---

Judd waited for Vicki to come to the phone, visualizing the cabins she would pass. He cringed when she answered, sounding out of breath and worried.

"I'm sorry to call so late," Judd said. "I wanted you to hear this from me instead of something over GCNN."

"What's wrong?"

Judd told her the heat wave had lifted in New Babylon and that it was expected to do the same throughout the world. Vicki gasped when Judd told her where he was.

"What are you going to do?" Vicki said.

"We're keeping a watch on the place until sundown. Westin and I are hoping to make it back to the plane and head for Petra."

Vicki paused, and Judd thought she was crying. Instead, Vicki shared a verse she had just looked up and told Judd to read it as well.

"You're not mad at me?" Judd said.

"I'm terrified the GC will find you and I'll see you on some newscast. But we've been through this before."

"I'll let you know as soon as anything changes," Judd said.

The two prayed and this time Vicki did cry.

When he hung up, he went to the computer and composed an e-mail, telling Vicki all the things he couldn't say over the phone. He marked the message "private" and sent it.

As promised, Nicolae Carpathia addressed the world from the rooftop of the palace. For some reason God had spared the building. Judd noticed someone had set up fake plants and trees behind Nicolae to make it look like things were back to normal. A well-placed group of smiling GC workers stood behind him, as if the deaths of millions around the world meant nothing.

Nicolae beamed as he strutted toward the microphone. His hair fluffed in the wind. "As we prepare to partake of our noonday meal here in New Babylon, it is a festive atmosphere. We are all celebrating the end of the curious heat wave that enveloped the planet, and we look forward to the days ahead where we expect peace to rain down on us like a waterfall.

"For those who are in time zones where the sun has not yet risen, rest assured that I have taken care of this problem, with the help of my scientists, who have been working around the clock."

"Right," Rainer said. "Nicolae has been able to stop the heat wave with his injured little mind."

"The heating of the earth has actually caused the waterways to heal themselves, but there is more work to do," Carpathia said. "Those who are without homes will see them constructed in the quickest manner possible.

"In the past when we have faced hardships, we have pulled together as a Global Community, and that is what will happen now. Let us use this trouble to unite our hearts and minds for one common goal of peace. And let the enemies of peace beware, for we are more committed than ever to reaching our goal."

With his eyes flashing, Nicolae spoke in several different languages, telling people of the world that he was in control and that he had plans for the good of every person alive.

Hours later, Chang Wong phoned Judd and played part of a conversation Chang had recorded. "This is Nicolae behind closed doors with all of his top people. They spent most of the day just trying to settle people in their offices, but once the directors were there . . . well, listen."

Judd heard Nicolae rub his hands together as he said, "For the first time in a long time, we play on an even field. The waterways are healing themselves, and we have rebuilding to do in the infrastructure. Let us work at getting all our loyal citizens back onto the same page with us. Director Akbar and I have some special surprises in store for dissidents on various levels. We are back in business, people. It is time to recoup our losses and start delivering a few."

"What does that mean?" Judd said.

"I'm not sure, but I'd bet the GC knows something about what we've been doing the last few weeks, moving supplies and people. They want to hurt us."

"Anything new from the Trib Force?" Judd said.

"Everybody's back in hiding. Captain Steele says we have to pick our spots and strategize for the new night schedule. Which brings me to my other news."

"What's that?"

"Westin's plane."

Judd took a breath. "You think it's safe for us to make a run for it after dark?"

"I wish I had better news. I tapped into one of the local security channels a little earlier. The GC spotted the plane and somehow pulled it near one of the burned-out hangars at the airfield."

"So we might have to fight them to get it back?"

"No. All the fighting in the world won't help. They planted a bomb on board thinking it was a Judah-ite aircraft."

Judd clenched his teeth. "So we'll have to disarm—"

"Judd, listen—"

"No, Chang. If Westin and I can get to the plane tonight and get in the air, won't God protect us like he has protected all the other planes?"

"Judd, something went wrong with the detonator. The bomb exploded. There is no plane left to fly."

**WHEN** Judd told Westin about the plane, Westin cursed and slammed a fist on the table. "Forgive me," he said. "This whole thing is so messed up."

"It's understandable," Rainer said. "You wouldn't be human if you didn't show emotion about this."

Westin stroked a few days' growth of beard. "I guess I should be glad the plague didn't end while we were on our way to the plane." He glanced at Judd. "Guess your wedding plans are on hold."

"We're going to get out of here," Judd said.

Rainer nodded. "We're all hoping that's true because of the prophecy."

"What prophecy?" Judd said.

Rainer took a Bible from the middle of the table. "We came here to fight the GC and live right under Carpathia's nose. But the Bible motivated us."

"What's the Bible got to do with it?" Westin said.

"One of my friends—at least he used to be a friend—was studying the book of Revelation one day and came across an interesting verse."

Rainer flipped toward the end of the Bible and found chapter 18 and began reading. " 'After all this I saw another angel come down from heaven with great authority, and the earth grew bright with his splendor. He gave a mighty shout, "Babylon is fallen—that great city is fallen! She has become the hideout of demons and evil spirits, a nest for filthy buzzards, and a den for dreadful beasts." ' "

"Filthy buzzards, dreadful beasts, that's the New Babylon I know," Westin said.

"Here's where things get interesting," Rainer said. " 'Then I heard another voice calling from heaven, "Come away from her, my people. Do not take part in her sins, or you will be punished with her. For her sins are piled as high as heaven, and God is ready to judge her for her evil deeds. Do to her as she has done to your people. Give her a double penalty for all her evil deeds. She brewed a cup of terror for others, so give her twice as much as she gave out. She has lived in luxury and pleasure, so match it now with torments and sorrows. She boasts, 'I am queen on my throne. I am no helpless widow. I will not experience sorrow.' Therefore, the sorrows of death and mourning and famine will overtake her in a single day. She will be utterly consumed by fire, for the Lord God who judges her is mighty." ' "

"I don't get it," Westin said. "I mean, I understand the city is going to be destroyed by God, but why would that make you want to come here?"

Rainer smiled. "When it says, 'Come away from her,

12

my people,' we believe that means there will be true followers of God right in New Babylon. We couldn't imagine who they would be, and then God placed a desire on our hearts to come here and either *join* this band of brave fighters or *become* a part of the biblical history."

"How many of you came?" Judd said.

"There were thirty-eight altogether," Rainer said.

Judd had asked Rainer earlier if any members of his group had been killed. Rainer hadn't wanted to talk about it.

"Those verses beg some questions," Westin said. "If God's people are supposed to come out, how are they supposed to do it, and where do they go?"

Rainer nodded. "I have been thinking about that. It's clear God has had enough of the lies and killing of New Babylon, so he's going to destroy this evil city. But there must be something coming that will signal that it's time for us to leave. That's what we've been waiting for."

"Is it possible to talk with someone else?" Judd said. "What's the leader's name again?"

"You mean Otto Weser?"

"Yeah, he might have some ideas."

Rainer pursed his lips. "We have had no contact since . . . for quite a while. It's one of our unwritten rules. No one talks with Otto."

Judd glanced at Westin. There was something behind this Otto business, and Judd wanted to find out what it was.

---

Vicki and a few others had gone outside to watch the sun rise early the next morning. As it peeked over the hills in the distance, Vicki could tell the heat and humidity were gone, along with most of the smoke that had hovered over the valley.

At noon, Vicki ventured to the knoll above the campground. There was a lot of excitement with the weather change, more news from the Global Community, and activity on the kids' Web site. But the news of Judd made Vicki want to be alone.

It was spring, and the trees in the distance should have been covered with buds and new leaves. Instead, the countryside looked like some burned scar.

Something skittered along the ground and startled her. A half-burned tail flicked back and forth on the side of a tree. A squirrel. How he had survived the heat and fires, Vicki didn't know, but here he was, scampering up a tree with his charred tail.

"How many friends have you lost in the last few years, little fella?" Vicki whispered. She brought her knees up to her chest. She and her friends were like this squirrel, foraging, darting into hiding places, hoping to stay alive just one more day.

Vicki recalled the verse about God knowing even when a sparrow fell from the sky. But did God know every squirrel, raccoon, and deer that died in the heat plague? Did he see the death and devastation and hear the cries of believers who had been killed? Already the Global Community News Network reported arrests and beheadings.

*Will Judd be next?*

Vicki knew it was against the group's rules to be

outside at this time of day, so she stood and started for her cabin. Something was bothering her, and she couldn't put a finger on it.

She paused near a burned tree and heard movement at the bottom of the knoll. Someone was coming up the hill.

---

A few minutes later Judd found Rainer sitting alone in a room set aside for prayer. Several chairs sat in an empty circle, and Judd took one directly across from the German. Someone had painted a man kneeling in prayer on the wall. On the opposite wall was a painting, torn and weathered, of an old man with a piece of bread in front of him. The old man's hands were folded, and his eyes were shut tightly. Judd thought the picture looked familiar, then realized it was the same one that hung in his grandparents' kitchen.

Rainer looked up, his eyes cloudy. "I suppose you want to know what happened between Otto and me."

Judd nodded. "You don't have to tell me, but it might help me understand."

Rainer put his head back and closed his eyes. His face was strong and handsome, and his hair reached his shoulders. Judd knew he had been an actor in Germany, but what kind?

With his eyes still closed, Rainer spoke. "When light and dark collide and ignorance takes up the sword against understanding, what is left for weary men to do?" He paused, opened his eyes. "We, the weary, pick up pieces from the battlefield and live."

"What's that from?" Judd said.

"A play I was writing at the time of the disappearances. It wasn't very good."

"Sounded good to me."

Rainer smiled. "Do you know what an understudy is?"

"A person who's there in case the lead gets sick?"

"Yes. Before the vanishings, I was just an understudy at life. I knew all the lines and where to move and what to do onstage, but I was watching from behind some curtain. It took the most terrible situation in the world to bring me out of the shadows."

"You're talking about your relationship with God, right?"

Rainer nodded.

"Had you heard about God before the disappearances?"

"Many times. I had an aunt who told my brothers and sisters and me Bible stories. She was very dramatic. I think it was because of her that I wanted to become an actor."

"Were your parents believers?"

"No. They were killed in the earthquake. On a cruise down the Rhine River, the ship capsized and all but a few drowned."

"I'm sorry."

Rainer sighed. "So am I. I went to my aunt's house not long after she disappeared and relived some of those stories she used to tell. I still have her Bible. But I didn't make my decision to follow God until I stumbled onto Tsion Ben-Judah's Web site. My wife and I prayed the night after we discovered it."

"And your wife is back in Germany?"

Rainer closed his eyes. "No, she is waiting for me on the other side. Sometimes I dream that Gretchen and I are together on a beach somewhere. Talking. Laughing. Then I wake up and face this." He put his head in his hands. "I wish I could go back and talk to the people we were before the disappearances. I would convince us of the truth before any of this happened."

Rainer looked at Judd with tears in his eyes. "Sometimes I wonder if I'm here in New Babylon because it's God's will for me, or if I'm on a mission of death. One mistake and I'd be reunited with my wife forever."

"What happened to her?" Judd said.

---

Vicki moved behind the tree and watched as Lionel made his way toward the knoll. She thought about jumping out and scaring him but decided against it.

"Marshall sent me up here to see about you," Lionel said when he had caught his breath. "You okay?"

Vicki asked Lionel to sit. "I was up here thinking. I like this place. I'm going to miss it when I go to Petra."

Lionel bit his lower lip. "Vicki, I've always appreciated what a friend you've been, and I couldn't be happier for you and Judd . . ."

"But what?"

Lionel shook his head. "I don't know. Maybe God's trying to tell you something. Maybe you shouldn't go to Petra. Maybe Judd shouldn't have gone to New Babylon." Vicki slipped an arm around Lionel, and the young man hung his head. "He's the best friend I've ever had. I just wish he would be more careful."

Vicki looked at the sky. It had been weeks since she had seen any real clouds. Now some dark ones moved in and threatened rain. "I've been thinking a lot about what happens after the Glorious Appearing," she said. "Wondering if we'll know each other, if people will get married. If those who were married before the Rapture will be reunited."

"And what about people like Captain Steele?" Lionel said. "He was married to Mrs. Steele and then married Amanda. What about that?"

"I've been looking at Scripture, but I can't figure it out. There's got to be an answer."

"Why not go right to the top?" Lionel stood. "Let's get back. You can write Dr. Ben-Judah."

---

Judd listened as Rainer's story unfolded. The man described how he had met Otto Weser at a secret Bible study. Their first fight with Global Community forces had been in Stuttgart. It was Otto's idea to come into the heart of Carpathia territory, and thirty-seven others had followed.

"Otto is a verbose man. He rattles on and on. Well, we finally found a way to fly into the desert and take a slow route in separate vehicles. Otto didn't like it. He thought we should all go together, pretending to be GC recruits. There was such a disagreement that many split from the group. About a dozen decided to go a different way."

"And you went with Otto?" Judd said.

"Yes. Everything seemed fine during the trip. Our plane landed, and we bought an old school bus and started the journey across the desert. Otto was sure God was leading us. We huddled in the back of the bus, praying. My wife and I broke away from the others at one point and had our own prayer time."

Rainer pulled out his wallet and opened to a picture of a woman with long, dark hair. She looked like a famous actress Judd had seen. "She's very beautiful."

"Yes, she was." Rainer folded his wallet and put it away. "We were carrying some sophisticated heat weapons, along with machine guns and old AK-47s. It was our plan, if we were stopped, to take out any GC force before they could report us.

"We came to an unexpected checkpoint, a surprise from the Global Community. Before we could react, several Peacekeepers had surrounded the bus. We took our positions as Otto got out. We fired all of the heat weapons and the Peacekeepers rolled on the ground, but one of them managed to lob a grenade at the back of the bus. If we had seen it, we would have been able to react, but no one did."

"And the explosion killed your wife?" Judd said.

"It was a chest wound. She was in much pain. She said that I should carry on the fight without her. The last thing she said was that she would be waiting for me on the other side."

Judd sat back and shook his head. He couldn't imagine the man's pain at seeing his wife die. "How many died?"

"My brother, his best friend, and the man's wife were killed in the attack. There was no time to bury them. We simply took the GC squad cars and split up."

"What about the other group?"

"They made it with no problems," Rainer said.

"Did you ever talk with Otto about what happened?"

"I was so angry that I couldn't. I said I would never speak to him again." Rainer put his elbows on his knees and leaned forward. "This is why I say I might be on a mission of death. It is better for me to leave this place than stay."

"You really think your wife would want you to do that?"

Rainer smiled. "She was such a tough lady." He slapped his knees and stood. "I'll tell you my new mission. To get you and this Vicki girl of yours back togeth—"

One of the other members of the group rushed into the room. "It's the GC. They're on this block and headed our way. House to house."

**3**

**JUDD** watched the people in the hideout go into crisis mode. He and Westin stood back as the group sealed doors and tried to make it impossible for the GC to enter.

"They've placed booby traps around the house, but they're not activated yet," Westin said.

"What kind of booby traps?"

"Explosives. Mines."

"We need everyone quiet and in your places," Rainer called. "Judd, you and Westin come with me."

In the lowest point of the basement was a row of computers and machines. The chief technical person, a woman Judd knew only as Helga, manipulated a mechanical arm on the first floor. With a few quick movements she pushed some charred debris over the trapdoor, pulled a tarp over the whole mess, and made the mechanical arm disappear into the floor.

A silence fell over the room as the monitor showed a GC squad car making its way down the street. Peacekeepers carrying rifles followed.

"Are they looking for bodies?" Judd whispered.

"With rifles?" Rainer said. "They may find bodies in the rubble around here, but they're looking for anyone alive without the mark of Carpathia."

The squad car finally pulled in front of the safe house, and several Peacekeepers approached.

Helga turned to Rainer, who was scribbling something on paper. "Wait for my signal."

The Peacekeepers knocked on the sides of the house and called out. A Peacekeeper walked up to the porch and banged the door.

Judd could feel his heart beating as he watched. The room grew hotter with all the bodies and equipment.

Judd had felt unnerved by Rainer and the others talking about war and killing. There was quite a difference in being against the Global Community—escaping from them and fighting for the souls of people who had not yet taken the mark—and actually killing Carpathia followers. On the other hand, God was going to judge evil. Judd wanted to hear what Tribulation Force leaders would say. Would they actually shoot to kill and be a part of the final battle?

Judd noticed a panel filled with buttons and knobs. Underneath each was a piece of tape with writing. Judd pointed to it and Westin leaned over. "Helga told me those activate the bombs. And those over there are for guns hidden in a burned-out part of the roof."

"They can actually shoot by remote control?"

Westin nodded. "But once we start shooting, we give away our position. The GC can come in and wipe us out."

Rainer pushed his way through the gathering and into the hall. He paused when he came to Judd and handed him an envelope. "Take this."

Nothing was written on the envelope. Judd shoved it in his pocket.

Rainer tapped another man on the shoulder and they were gone.

"Is there any other way out of here?" Judd said to Westin.

Westin shrugged.

A man beside him leaned over. "There is an air lock on the other side of the basement that leads into the sewers. That's only to be used as a last resort."

"There are more officers coming," Helga said, looking around. "Where's Rainer?"

A buzzer pierced the small room, and a red light blinked on the computer.

Helga turned the alarm off. "The air lock is open. Someone's going outside."

*Rainer*, Judd thought.

Several men rushed out of the room. Judd kept his eyes on the monitor showing the roving Peacekeepers. They poked and prodded through the rubble above. One man pulled the tarp back and noticed the scattered debris.

Minutes seemed like hours. A man returned. "Rainer and Klaus are gone. They've taken several weapons."

"What could he be doing?" Judd said.

Westin pointed at the screen. "Watch."

———————————————————

Vicki waited for an answer from Tsion Ben-Judah as the others watched the latest news from GCNN. Because of the intense heat, many television transmissions had been interrupted. During the plague, the kids had usually seen coverage only at night. Now that the plague was over, it was clear the Global Community in the United North American States wanted to show they were back in control.

The sight of Kruno Fulcire turned Vicki's stomach. He had been the man responsible for her friend Pete's death, as well as hundreds of other believers who had fallen into the man's clutches. It was almost as if the military and political leaders around the world were having a contest to see who could kill believers faster.

Fulcire had chosen to be photographed near a small lake behind one of the many GC headquarters. A fountain sprayed water into the air, and Vicki couldn't help smirking as he beamed at the applause of the press corps.

"Looks like he's got water shooting out his head," Zeke said.

"Wouldn't hurt his brain any," Conrad said. "He probably doesn't have one."

"Let's keep it quiet," Marshall said.

Fulcire had no notes, charts, or graphs. He simply stood at the podium and smiled. "What a beautiful day." Laughter rippled through the crowd. "And every day is a great day to serve the risen lord Carpathia."

There were enough followers of Nicolae present to break into a hearty rendition of "Hail Carpathia," but Fulcire sang off-key.

When they finished, Fulcire grabbed the microphone and began pacing. "The end of this unnatural weather phenomenon comes at a most important time. We believe the United North American States can and will become the most loyal region in all the world. And to do that, we need the help of citizens who have already given so much."

"I think I know what he's leading up to." Janie smirked. "And it won't be good for believers."

Fulcire beamed, as if Carpathia were watching. "Since we can once again move around in daylight hours, we would like you to report any citizen who has not yet complied with receiving the mark of our lord and risen king. Anyone discovering an unmarked civilian will receive triple the reward previously offered."

"Great, the price for our heads just went up," Conrad said.

"Think of all the Nicks we could make if we turned everybody here in," Zeke said.

Mark stuck his head in the room and motioned for Vicki. "You have an answer to your message to Tsion."

Vicki hurried to the computer on the other side of the room and pulled up Tsion's e-mail. That the man would answer her personally excited Vicki.

*Vicki,*

*Thank you for your question about what will happen in the coming kingdom. As we draw nearer to that time,*

*now only a year away, many people have the same
concerns, so you have spurred me to teach more about
this here in Petra.*

*Let me quickly give you some thoughts. Jesus said that
people would be "marrying and giving in marriage"
during the Tribulation just as they did during the days
before the Flood. See Matthew 24:37-39. But as you
know, many who become believers after the Rapture will
be martyred for the cause of Christ and will be resurrected after the Glorious Appearing. Many others will
survive the Tribulation and be "the sheep" Jesus referred
to in Matthew 25:31-40 who go into the kingdom to
populate the Millennium, or thousand-year reign of
Christ. These, of course, will raise their children and possibly help with the raising of other children who survive
but are under the age of accountability when Christ
returns.*

*The story of the rich man in hell and Lazarus who
was a believer—see Luke 16:19-31—is quite clear. In the
next life we will still recognize not only those we knew on
earth, but as Lazarus, he recognized Abraham who had
lived hundreds of years before him. Even those in torment recognized those in paradise. That would indicate
we all will recognize one another in the next life. Remember, Paul said, "For me to depart and be with Christ is
far better." So we will have an even better relationship
then than we do now.*

*I know you still have Judd on your mind, and believe
me, we are praying for you both. Whether God allows you
to marry or not isn't the question. The question is, will*

*you trust him for your future? God can use you in the kingdom after his second coming, or he can use you in heaven. Trust him to be faithful.*

*Yours in Christ,*
*Tsion Ben-Judah*

As Kruno Fulcire finished his press conference, a wave of hope washed over Vicki like a waterfall. Judd was in God's hands. Their possible marriage was too. And all believers from Wisconsin to the remote parts of the world. No matter how much money the Global Community offered or how creative the GC could get trying to catch unmarked civilians, the believers still had God's protection.

———————————

Judd watched the screens carefully for any sign of Rainer and Klaus. He hoped they would come to their senses and turn around, but Judd gasped when a manhole cover moved in the middle of the street a block away. Weapons plopped on the ground, and Rainer and Klaus crawled onto the street.

Helga gritted her teeth. "What in the world are they doing?"

A man to Judd's left shook his head. "Rainer likes to say, 'Life is a temporary assignment.' "

"He's going to make it a lot more temporary if he doesn't get out of there quickly," Helga said.

Rainer and Klaus moved behind a burned-out car.

Automatic weapons fire sounded, and the two were up and running. The GC squad, at least a dozen officers strong, rounded the corner. Rainer fired over their heads.

"He could have killed several of them," Judd said. "Why didn't he?"

"Maybe he's not trying to kill them," Westin said. "Maybe he's trying to get them away from us."

Helga quickly switched to another camera showing that the area around the safe house was clear. She pointed to Judd and Westin and looked at the older man to her left. "Take them to number two."

"We're not leaving," Westin said. "We'll stay and fight with the rest of you."

She looked hard at him. "I'm not arguing. You're the only pilot here and this guy—" she pointed to Judd— "has a fiancée waiting. Go."

The older man led them to the secret exit, and they climbed into a large tunnel. The man stuck out his hand. "Gunther Carr."

They walked west, away from the house, through stagnant water. Gunfire erupted again above them, and GC officers' yells echoed in the cavern.

"What's number two?" Judd whispered.

"An underground bunker," Gunther said. "It's dark and stinks down there, but at least you'll be safe."

More gunfire. Judd prayed for Rainer and Klaus. He had no idea if he would ever see them again.

**JUDD** and Westin spent the night alone in the underground chamber. They were anxious to know what had happened to their friends but didn't dare go into the tunnel. The maze of pipes leading from their area made it nearly impossible to go back without someone leading them.

"What happens if the GC find the house and everybody's killed?" Judd said.

Westin shrugged and paced the room like a nervous animal. Gunther had shown them where to find food and flashlights, but they felt trapped with no contact with the outside world. Judd's phone didn't work in the enclosed space, and there was no computer hookup. Westin found a small television stashed in a cabinet, but it didn't work.

"Great, we can't even hear the GC's lies," Westin said.

After spending the evening praying for their new friends, Judd tried to get some sleep. Finally he sat up.

Westin was reading something by the fading glow of a flashlight. "What do you think about our chances of getting out of New Babylon alive?"

Westin yawned. "We improved our chances by coming in here, but I don't like the fact that we let those people fight for us."

"What are you reading?"

Westin held up a weathered New Testament and Psalms he had discovered. "I found this psalm about how God heals the brokenhearted, counts the stars, supports the humble, and feeds the animals. Then I came to this:

"*The strength of a horse does not impress him;*
*how puny in his sight is the strength of a man.*
*Rather, the Lord's delight is in those who honor him,*
*those who put their hope in his unfailing love.*"

"That's good," Judd said.

Westin ran a hand through his hair. "You know, when I believed what you and Lionel told me, there was part of me that thought I was pretty hot stuff. Being a pilot for the rich and famous, able to get you guys access wherever I wanted . . . Even when I started working with the Tribulation Force, I sort of felt like I was doing God a favor."

Judd smiled. "I know what you mean."

"And then I read a passage like this. If I really want to make God happy, I'll just trust him and let him use me however he wants. If it means I'm flying supplies, that's great. If it means I'm holed up in this dark, stinky septic tank, that's okay."

Judd nodded. "The biggest hurdle is believing God is real. Then you have to believe he really loves you and died to forgive you. Once I got that through my head, it was a lot easier to trust him, though it's not always easy."

It was after midnight when Judd heard footsteps echo in the tunnel. The door opened and Gunther entered with the rest of the group. One by one they crowded inside, some collapsing on the floor. Rainer and Klaus weren't with them.

"We need to stay here for a while," Gunther said. "The Peacekeepers are back, but we're hoping they won't find our hideout."

"What about Rainer and Klaus?" Westin said.

"They're dead."

"But not before they took a half dozen GC with them," a younger man said.

"What happened?" Judd said.

"Rainer and Klaus tried to get the GC to chase them away from the safe house," Gunther said. "It worked for a while, but then the GC surrounded them. After a firefight, the GC won."

"We're kicking ourselves for not going to their rescue," Helga said. "We should have at least used the remote guns."

"You know that wouldn't have done any good," Gunther said.

Judd thought of Rainer's wife. They were together now, reunited in heaven.

"Why didn't you set off the booby traps?" Westin said.

Helga sat forward and took some beef jerky from a

tin. "We left the entrance on automatic. If the GC find it and crawl inside, the whole place will go up. All the evidence will be destroyed."

---

Vicki waited for word from Judd and agonized when she didn't hear anything. She spent the entire night waiting by the computer, dialing Judd's number, but getting nothing.

As the sun rose the next morning, she lay in bed, thinking of Tsion's e-mail. Something he had said was running around in her head. Between that and news of Judd, she knew she wouldn't be able to sleep.

"Thinking about Judd?" Shelly whispered from the cot next to Vicki's.

"I'm thinking about a lot of stuff," Vicki said.

"It's good to see *you* tied up for a change. You always have your stuff together."

"If you only knew."

"So what is it?" Shelly said, sitting up.

"I'll tell you if you tell me what happened between you and Conrad. You guys were close, and then everything went south."

"I wouldn't want to jinx you and Judd," Shelly said.

"What do you mean?"

Shelly sighed. "Conrad's sweet. He's a little younger than me but really mature in a lot of ways. The closer we got and the more time we spent together, the more serious things became."

"He popped the question and you said no?"

"Not exactly." Shelly opened her mouth like she wanted to say something but looked at the floor. "This is really hard."

"Shel, what is it?"

She paused a moment more, then looked at Vicki. "We were fixing up one of the cabins with Charlie—this was before the heat wave and before Judd came back. Charlie ran for some supplies, and Conrad asked if he could kiss me. I got kind of uncomfortable. We had both said we wouldn't put ourselves in a situation where we were alone together, you know, so we wouldn't be tempted. When I hesitated, he thought I didn't like him anymore. Then I tried to explain and things really got bad. I know it was only a kiss, but I just didn't feel right."

"You guys talked after that, right?"

"Shouted is more like it. He said if I didn't trust him that we should break things off and just be friends. But we haven't been, and I don't see that changing anytime soon."

"Maybe if you brought Marshall or Becky in on it, they could help resolve it."

"I feel so hurt by the whole thing, and I know he's hurt too."

"I think you did the right thing saying no," Vicki said. "Something in your gut told you it didn't feel right."

"But Conrad's nice. He would never do anything—"

"Doesn't matter," Vicki said. "If you feel something's not good and you push that down, you stop listening to the voice God gave you."

"What do you mean, 'voice'?"

"I think God gives us something inside that tells us when things don't feel right. The times when I got into the most trouble, before I became a believer, were times when I didn't listen to that feeling, that voice that was telling me to watch out. And I know a lot of other girls who've had those same feelings but didn't listen to them because they were afraid they'd hurt somebody's feelings."

"So I wasn't crazy to say no?"

"I don't think so. And if Conrad loved you, he'd understand. Maybe he feels just as bad about it as you do. You won't know until you talk."

Shelly nodded and stared into the darkness. "Maybe I will." She turned to Vicki. "Now your turn."

Vicki waved a hand. "It's nothing compared to—"

"No fair, you promised."

Vicki rolled her eyes. "Well, the main thing is Judd. I don't understand why he hasn't called. If he's hurt or something I'll understand, but . . ."

"Judd wouldn't leave you hanging if he didn't have a good reason."

"You're right. But there's something else. Tsion wrote back and told me what he thought would happen after the Glorious Appearing. I mean, if Judd and I do get married, will we still be married after Jesus comes back? Could we have children? There's all kinds of questions, and the return of Christ is only a year away."

Shelly bit her lip. "Does make you think, doesn't it?"

Vicki pulled out a copy of Tsion's e-mail she had printed and turned on her flashlight. "He's talking about people who will go into the Millennium alive—"

"What's the mill . . . milla . . . what you said?"

"A millennium is a thousand years. When Jesus comes back at the Glorious Appearing, he's going to reign a thousand years before the time of judgment."

"And the thousand years starts after the battle of Armageddon, right?"

"Exactly."

"So what did he say?"

"Listen to this. 'These, of course, will raise their children and possibly help with the raising of other children who survive but are under the age of accountability when he returns.' "

Shelly leaned forward. "I don't get it. What's the accountability thing?"

"Tsion believes there will be kids alive who aren't believers but are too young to really understand the gospel."

"Okay."

"I had a dream once before we found the schoolhouse. I wanted to take in as many people as we could and teach them. Even unbelievers. We were able to take in quite a few—Melinda, Lenore, and the others—but I always felt drawn to kids."

"And you want to do that after Jesus comes back?"

Vicki frowned. "I don't know how it would happen or even where, but wouldn't it be exciting to take care of kids who don't have parents? Kids who were just like we were after the Rapture?"

Shelly raised her eyebrows. "You think you can get Judd to sign off on the idea?"

"It's probably just stupid—"

"Don't say that," Shelly said. "You've always said if God plants an idea in your head, no matter what other people think, he can help you accomplish it."

Vicki lay back on the bed. "I wish I could talk about it with Judd."

---

For two more days Judd and the others stayed holed up in the underground compartment because of GC activity above. Many in the group wept for Rainer and Klaus, blaming themselves for not going after them.

Judd thought of Chang. If he could get word to him about their trouble, Chang could do something. But Judd hadn't told anyone he knew a believer inside the palace, and he feared that he might endanger Chang by dragging him into their problem. Judd decided he would only bring up Chang as a last resort.

Judd recalled the envelope Rainer had given him, and he opened it while the others were asleep. Inside was another envelope and a note attached to it.

> *Judd,*
>
> *I wrote this to Otto after we talked. Klaus and I are going to try to lure the GC away. Please give this letter to Otto if you can. And tell Vicki about me when you see her.*
>
> *In Christ,*
> *Rainer*

After dark, on the third day, Judd followed the others through the sewers to the safe house. They had heard no explosions, so they figured the GC hadn't discovered the hideout.

One by one they crawled through the secret opening and entered the house. Everyone tried to squeeze into the computer room, though some had to remain in the hall. The computers were off, and Helga guessed there had been a power outage.

She fired up the computer with the biggest monitor and clicked on the security cameras. "That's strange. I can't get any of them to work."

"Maybe the outage affected the cameras and they have to be reset," someone said.

Helga scratched her head. "Something seems different."

"Work on it and we'll get some food," Gunther said. "Depending on how long the power was off, some of it may be spoiled."

Helga tried to pull up the Global Community News Network, but it wouldn't work. "Judd, do me a favor and open the secret entrance, then close it and come right back."

Judd hurried and did what he was told.

When he returned, Helga had a strange look on her face. "You opened it all the way, right?"

"Yeah. What's wrong?"

"The alarm isn't working on the computer."

A group rushed down the hall, and Judd thought someone was coming with food. Then he heard the click of rifles and shouts from the kitchen. Helga jumped up and darted for the hall but stopped dead in her tracks.

A GC Peacekeeper stuck a gun through the door. "On the floor! Now!"

# 5

JUDD was stunned at the sight of uniformed Peacekeepers running through the hideout. He hit the floor and watched black boots surround him and Helga. An officer patted them down and took Judd's cell phone. "On your feet and up the stairs."

The moon shone brightly as Judd climbed out and joined the others. Several squad cars with their lights on were parked in front of the house, illuminating the line of prisoners. A Peacekeeper ordered them to sit, then pointed a flashlight at their foreheads and their right hands, checking for the mark of Carpathia.

Judd knew he should feel scared, but a sense of peace came over him. He almost felt relieved that the running and hiding were over.

He thought of Vicki and regretted risking this trip. He had been trying to call her since they had gone into hiding, but his phone didn't work underground. Now he would never again tell her he loved her. He wondered if the GC would make examples of them and show their executions on television. Or would the GC just get things over right here? The believers were outnumbered, and the GC had so many weapons.

A man with several military medals pinned to his uniform stepped forward, hands clasped behind his back. "I suppose you're wondering why your little operation didn't explode when we entered, hmm?"

When no one answered, the man gave a fake smile and continued. "Well, I'll tell you. After your two friends gave us trouble, we found your guns." He motioned overhead. "When we uncovered your entrance, instead of barging in, we called in the bomb squad." He pointed to the side of the house, and Judd saw a gaping hole. "We made a new entrance—hope you don't mind—found your little bomb, defused it, and waited. What a shock when we heard you enter through the sewers."

Judd wondered if anyone would stand up to the officer, and he didn't have to wait long. Westin shook his head, and the man in charge kicked Westin hard. "Wipe that silly grin off your face!"

"You're going to lose," Westin said.

The officer squinted. "You have no guns, you have no contact with other rebels, and you have no chance of escape." He held up a small computer device. "And in this tiny drive I have all the information from your computers. Your contacts, your plans. Everything."

Helga gave the man a worried look. "Our files are encrypted. You'll never be able to—"

"With the resources of the Global Community? I'm sure our tech crew will have this figured out by my morning coffee." He turned to Westin. "You're crazy to think you can defeat us."

"You can kill us, but you're not going to win," Westin said.

"Ah, a Judah-ite, eh?" The man turned and spoke to the men holding guns on the group. "Followers of Tsion Ben-Judah. They believe in the God of the Bible and that he is punishing us for our sins. That sums it up, doesn't it, Judah-ite?"

"I believe one day every knee will bow and every tongue will confess that Jesus Christ is Lord."

"Amen," a few people whispered.

"Jesus Christ?" The officer tapped his lips with his index finger and looked at the other Peacekeepers. "Haven't seen him, have you?"

The others laughed.

"But I have seen someone come back from the dead. With my own eyes—not some fairy tale written thousands of years ago."

"One day you will kneel and admit that Jesus—"

The man punched Westin in the face. Westin slumped over and Judd reached out to help him, but the officer pushed Judd away with his boot. "Cuff them! Anybody so much as breathes, shoot them."

Peacekeepers moved behind the group and put plastic zip cuffs on each prisoner. Judd wondered if anyone would put up a fight or try to escape, but everyone seemed to submit to the procedure.

The lead officer spoke by radio to someone at head-quarters. After a head count, he relayed how many they were bringing in and that GCNN cameras should be waiting for them.

"You think your superiors will be proud of the fact that we were living right here under your noses?" Westin said.

The man glared at Westin. "I promise you, today I will dance in your blood."

The group had all been cuffed except for Judd and Gunther when the lights went out. Literally. Peacekeepers dropped their weapons and reached to rub their eyes as headlights on the GC cars went dark. Flashlights were useless to the officers. Streetlights disappeared. Judd had seen power outages before. Once his parents had been away and the power went out while he was watching a scary movie in the basement. It had taken him several minutes to find his way upstairs, and it had terrified him.

But this was different. Lights on phones, radios, the dashboards of the squad cars—everything was dark. The incredible thing was, Judd could still see. Everything was a hazy brown, and he could only see about twenty feet, but he could see.

*This must be what a cat sees in the dark,* Judd thought.

Some of the Peacekeepers still had their guns pointed toward the prisoners, but Judd could tell they were disoriented. One tapped his watch and punched a button, trying to see the time, but even the lighted display on his watch had gone dark.

"This is really weird," Westin whispered to Judd. "Can you see?"

"I can, but I don't think they can."

"What's going on?" a frantic Peacekeeper called out.

"Everybody hold your position and keep the prisoners where they are," the leader said.

"Did the lights go out or is it just me?" another Peacekeeper whispered.

If the situation weren't so serious, Judd would have laughed. As soon as the leader mentioned the prisoners, the Peacekeepers aimed their guns at where they thought Judd and the others were standing. It was like a military version of pin-the-tail-on-the-donkey, with men pointing guns in every direction.

The leader pulled out his cell phone but couldn't see the keypad. He reached for his radio microphone three times before he grabbed the cord and worked his way to the mike. "We have a situation here, Base, an electrical blackout."

A few seconds pause, then the dispatcher's stressed voice came on. It was clear things were just as bad at headquarters as they were here. "We have power here, but no visual—" Judd couldn't make out the rest because people at headquarters were screaming in the background.

Gunther lifted a hand and motioned the prisoners to the right. As one they crept past the puzzled Peacekeepers. Judd stopped a few feet away from a Peacekeeper and spotted a pair of pliers on the man's belt. He inched closer and grasped the tool, slowly lifting it from the man's belt. As Judd grabbed, the Peacekeeper whirled around and fired. The shot went over Judd's head and ricocheted off the burned-out safe house.

Judd jammed the pliers in his pocket, hit the ground, and put his hands over his ears. Other Peacekeepers opened fire on where they thought the prisoners were standing, but they either fired into the safe house or actually shot each other. Judd counted three Peacekeepers on the ground, writhing in pain.

"Hold your fire!" the leader said, pulling out his pistol and gingerly stepping forward. He felt the ground with each step, as if he were going to plunge off a cliff. "Prisoners, stay where you are!"

Judd rolled his eyes and tried to still his breathing. The leader was only a few feet away and inching toward Judd like a blind man.

Judd glanced at the sky. The moon had been out earlier, but now it was as if God had pulled down a shade on the heavens. Judd wondered what would happen the next morning when the sun came up. Would everyone in the world experience this?

Someone on the edge of the line screamed, dropped his weapon, and clawed at his eyes. "I can't see anything! Somebody do something!"

Judd used the noise to quietly sneak away, backing down the hill toward the GC squad cars. He put his hand through an open window and pressed the horn, which sent the Peacekeepers jumping. Judd leaped behind the cruiser as a volley of gunfire came his way, flattening a tire and crashing through a windshield.

Gunther motioned Judd over, and Judd crawled to the group and pulled out the pliers.

"Let's get out of here," someone said.

"We have to get that computer drive from the leader before we go," Helga said.

Judd snipped the plastic cuffs from Westin's hands. "I saw where the guy put it," Judd said. "I'll go."

"I'll go with you," Westin said.

When Judd and Westin returned, the Peacekeepers were in even worse shape. Some were on their hands and knees, trying to find their way back to their cars.

Within a few minutes these arrogant, cocky men were like frightened schoolchildren. They flicked flashlights, fumbled for lighters, and held their hands as close to their faces as they could, all in a vain attempt to see. But nothing helped.

Judd recalled the verses about Jesus being the light of the world and felt pity for these foolish people who had chosen Nicolae over the true God. If there had been a fire in front of these people, they would have walked right through it, so great was their darkness.

Westin pointed to the lead officer, and Judd angled toward the man who sat mumbling on a smoldering piece of wood. He had put his pistol back in its holster and was staring into the darkness.

Westin grabbed the gun and Judd expected the man to lunge or shout, but he just kept mumbling. "My wife. She doesn't know where I am. We should get word to the others not to come out, not to go into the dark."

Judd took out his pocketknife and carefully cut a hole in the man's right front pocket. The computer drive fell out. The Peacekeeper reached for his holster, but the gun was gone.

"You looking for this?" Westin whispered, cocking the gun close to the man's face. "Not dancing in any blood now, are you?"

"Please," the man cried, "don't take my gun."

Judd picked up the computer drive and took a few steps back. Westin joined him, emptying the gun and tossing it back at the feet of the Peacekeeper. The man picked it up, pointed it at his own head, and pulled the trigger. He pulled again and again, until the clicking of the gun mocked him. The man broke down, falling to the ground and jerking with sobs.

"These people sure are scared of the dark, aren't they?" Westin said.

"It's not just the dark," Judd said. "They're separated from everybody else. It's like God has put them in their own little world."

Judd and Westin rejoined the group, and Gunther handed Judd his cell phone. They had decided to reenter the safe house and get as many supplies as they could.

Judd helped move food and water into the second hideout through the sewer. He was surprised to find he could see belowground just as he could above.

Helga destroyed the computers and cameras, saving one laptop for use in their next location. Gunther said they had a couple of options of where to go if the plague of darkness continued.

In moving and sifting through supplies, Judd found a Bible and stuffed it in his back pocket. He had studied Revelation intensely and vaguely remembered something about darkness but couldn't remember the reference.

He climbed upstairs for one last look before they headed for the sewer. Gunther and a few others had rigged up some explosives to destroy the safe house.

Judd pulled out his cell phone and dialed Vicki. When she answered on the first ring, he could tell by the emotion in her voice that she had been crying.

"I can't tell you everything right now, but I'm all right," Judd said. "Everything's going to be all right."

"What's that noise in the background?" Vicki said.

Judd looked at the Peacekeepers, many of whom were on the ground, screaming and cursing God. They scratched at unseen sores and rubbed their aching bodies. The pain that began as an itch soon turned so intense that the Peacekeepers crawled beside rocks or cars and tried to rub up against them for relief. Men chewed their tongues until blood ran down their chins. Some found rifles on the ground and turned them on themselves, hoping to end their agony.

"It's awful here, Vick," Judd said. He explained briefly what had happened. "Is it happening there too?"

"No, this is just supposed to occur in New Babylon."

"How do you know that?"

Judd heard a click of computer keys. "Here it is. It's in Revelation, chapter 16." Vicki read the verses, her voice trembling. " 'Then the fifth angel poured out his bowl on the throne of the beast, and his kingdom was plunged into darkness. And his subjects ground their teeth in anguish, and they cursed the God of heaven for their pains and sores. But they refused to repent of all their evil deeds.' "

"That's exactly what's happening," Judd said.

"Then get out of there," Vicki said, "and go back to Petra as fast as you can."

**6**

JUDD and Westin jumped into the back of a squad car as Gunther and another member of the group got in the front. The rest of the group used the other vehicles.

Gunther had to drive slowly because he couldn't see very far. "Either of you know how long this is supposed to last?" Gunther said, looking in the rearview mirror.

Judd shook his head. "A friend of mine just read me the prophecy. From the stuff it says about people suffering, it sounds to me like it could be a while."

Gunther nodded. "That's what I think. Rainer and I talked about this. We both agreed when it happened, the end wasn't far away."

"What do you mean, 'the end'?" Westin said.

Gunther explained the prophecy about believers coming out of New Babylon. "The Lord predicts death and mourning and famine. Then it says he will destroy the city with fire. Rainer and I always thought that would be nuclear."

"If God's dropping his heavy artillery, we should get out," Westin said. "Maybe we could find a plane—"

Gunther held up a hand. "If Judd's right—and I think he is—we still have time to do some good here."

"What do you have in mind?" Judd said.

"Radios and computers are working," Gunther said. "We might be able to communicate with other locations and get the GC to release prisoners, maybe foul up their system. Plus, there's a holding facility not far from here. Captured Jews are sent to concentration camps from there. Since the heat wave ended, they've probably brought new people there."

"How do we know when to leave?" Judd said.

"The Lord will warn us. It's part of the prophecy. I know you two want to get back to Petra, but we could use the help."

Westin looked at Judd and shrugged. "If we can do some damage, I'm all for it."

Judd glanced at Gunther. "I need to make a phone call."

––––––––––––

Vicki told the others about her conversation with Judd, and no sooner had they begun their prayer meeting for him than the phone rang. It was Judd again.

"Where are you?" Vicki said. "Tell me you've already gotten out of there."

"We're heading for another safe house, or at least where we think one is. It's pretty slow going."

"But you said—"

"Vick, Westin's plane was destroyed. I assume most of the GC planes were burned in the heat wave, though they probably have some stored somewhere. There's no way we're flying out of here today. The thing is—"

Vicki put a hand to her chest, feeling her heart suddenly drop. "Judd, you're not thinking of staying, are you?"

"Just hear me out." Judd explained what he knew about Gunther's plan. "There's a chance we might meet some unbelievers, those who haven't taken the mark yet."

"How?"

Judd explained the information about the holding facility. In the past few months, Vicki had heard more and more reports about rebels around the world, mostly Jews, who were transported to concentration camps rather than being put to death. The Global Community wanted to make them suffer for not taking Carpathia's mark and for simply being part of God's chosen people. The camps gave prisoners just enough food to keep them alive and tortured them daily. Vicki and Judd had talked about wanting to help these people, but she didn't think they would ever have the opportunity. But Vicki's first concern was Judd and getting him safely to Petra.

"What happens if the lights come back on?" Vicki said. "The GC will kill you and anyone else with you."

"I don't know if this is what I should do or not, but . . ." Judd's voice trailed off, and Vicki heard brakes squeal. Then someone said something, and car doors opened and closed.

"What's happening?" Vicki said.

51

"We're at one of the mark application centers," Judd said. "The others are going to see if they can destroy some equipment. It's not much, but every little bit helps."

Vicki closed her eyes tightly. "Judd, if God's leading you into this, you know I wouldn't want to stop you, but I'm scared."

"Believe me, the last thing I want to do is risk being separated from you. I found the perfect spot in Petra. You should see it. It's just that . . ." Judd's voice trailed off again. When he could talk, he said, "I keep thinking about somebody out there crying out to God, behind bars or wherever, asking God for help, pleading with him to send someone. Maybe there's nobody there, but while this place is dark, I feel like I need to try."

Everything inside Vicki screamed for Judd to get to safety, but she knew if she were in the same position, she would want Judd's support. Finally, she said, "Go. Set as many captives free as you can. That's what we're supposed to be doing anyway, right?"

"Vick, I love you."

---

When Judd hung up, Gunther and the others were returning to the car.

Westin hopped in with a smile and slammed the door. "They won't be doing any marking of citizens in that place for a long time."

"Were there any people in there?" Judd said.

"Lots of them on the ground, screaming. Must have scared them half to death when we came waltzing in and smashed their equipment and took that head chopper apart." Westin looked at Judd. "You square things up with the little woman?"

Judd smiled. "She told me to go for it. When do we head that way?"

"Right now," Gunther said. He radioed the others, speaking in code, and told them where they were going.

"Why don't we just go to the palace?" Judd said.

Gunther shook his head. "We have no idea what kind of power Carpathia might have over this plague. Let's stick to trying to wreak havoc out here and maybe set a few people free."

The drive took longer than any of them expected. After three hours of navigating the streets at a slow speed, Gunther stopped outside a restaurant. "Nicolae himself is said to have eaten here with a few of his advisors. Come on."

Judd stepped out of the car and felt his flesh crawl. He had been to haunted houses as a kid and had heard the screams of frightened trick-or-treaters around Halloween, but he had never heard anything this eerie. People in torment had collapsed on the sidewalk. Some called from inside houses or businesses, pleading for help.

"Oh, Nicolae, you have all power," an older woman cried from across the street. "You bring light and peace and hope. Please, Nicolae, save us!"

"Shut up, woman!" a young man said. He was sitting with his back against the wall of a building next to the restaurant. "Neither Nicolae nor Fortunato can save you from this."

"Blasphemer!" an older man yelled. "You let Nicolae or any of his Peacekeepers hear you say that and you're a dead man."

The young man scratched at a bloody scab on his neck. "Death would be welcomed right now."

"I'm so hungry!" the old woman shouted. "Can someone bring me something?"

"Come on," Gunther said. "Don't pay attention to them."

"Who is that?" the young man said. "How can you drive a car when you can't even see?"

Gunther and the others went inside the restaurant, stepping over two bodies of people who had killed themselves. Judd stayed behind and inspected the young man's forehead. No mark. But when Judd leaned down and caught a glimpse of the man's right hand, he saw the clear mark of Carpathia.

The young man took a swipe at the air, missing Judd's head by inches. "Who are you? What do you want?" He had pulled his shirt up and was rubbing up against the coarse brick, trying to get some relief. His back was bleeding.

"I'm a friend," Judd said softly. "You don't have to be afraid."

"Do you have a gun?"

"No."

"Can you get one?"

"What for?"

The young man laughed wildly. "How long has it been since this darkness came? A week? Two?"

"It's only been a few hours," Judd said.

The man put a finger in his mouth and bit down hard. Blood poured from the wound and gushed down his lips. "I can't see to take a step, and I don't have the energy if I could. I just want to die. I know this is the end."

Judd stood and took a step toward the restaurant door.

"Please, I beg you. Hit me with something, knock me out. I can't stand this itching, and my head feels like it's about to burst!"

"I can't help you," Judd said. "I wish you'd have responded to God before it was too—"

"God?" the man screamed. "Jesus? I hate them! I hate everyone who talks about God!"

Judd walked away as the man cursed God, chewed his tongue, and smacked his head against the brick wall. Judd stepped over bodies and went inside the restaurant. Some people had been inside when the plague of darkness hit, and they were still moaning and wailing on the floor, under tables, and lying on booths.

Judd found Gunther and the others in the kitchen, cooking meat on the grill. The cook lay in the back, not moving. Some people had crawled inside the back door searching for food. One man near the grill had burned both his hands, not seeing the fire.

While Gunther cooked the meat, Judd and Westin gathered bread and drinks and headed for the car. Judd looked for the young man by the wall, but he had moved away.

When they were all inside the car, Judd tore off a

piece of French bread and grabbed one of the still-sizzling pieces of meat from Gunther. The smell of the food made Judd's mouth water.

Gunther put the car in gear, and they rolled over something. At first Judd thought they had been too close to the curb, but when he looked through the back window, he saw the young man lying on the street. He had crawled under the tires and now lay lifeless on the road.

Everywhere they drove, Judd heard howls from people in pain. It seemed to be getting worse by the hour. When people heard the car's engine, they ran into the street, reaching out like blind zombies, trying anything to relieve their pain. Judd hated ignoring them, but what could they do? These people had chosen against God and were now paying the price.

Judd wondered what it was about the darkness that made things so much worse. Simply turning out the lights on the world was one thing, but there was something supernatural about this that caused people enough pain to want to kill themselves.

The car stopped a half hour later in front of a guard hut. Judd couldn't see the building inside, but security fences with razor wire on top ran as far as he could see.

"I can't guarantee your safety in there," Gunther said.

"No way I'm missing this," Westin said.

"Me either," Judd said.

"Then let's go."

Gunther pulled up to the gate and opened his door. Someone inside the guard shack yelled, "Halt! Who goes there?"

Gunther didn't respond but went into a crouch and stuck his head into the doorway.

"Identify yourself or I'll shoot!" the guard said.

Gunther waved at Westin, and the pilot got out and went to the front of the car. "Why would you want to shoot—?"

*Blam!*

The gun's explosion sent Westin to the ground. The guard hobbled out of the shack like a drunken man, waving the gun and threatening to shoot again. With a swift movement, Gunther jumped, kicked, and the gun clattered on concrete.

The guard screamed in pain and fell in a heap. "Who are you? What do you want here?"

Judd got out as Gunther stepped toward the guard and said, "Where are the rebels you're holding?"

The guard's eyes widened. "I don't know what you're talking about."

"Right," Gunther said, picking up the gun. He walked into the shack and flipped a lever, opening the gate.

"You can see?" the guard said.

"Do you want me to shoot you?" Gunther said.

A wide grin spread across the man's face. "Yes. I'd like that. Please go ahead."

Gunther frowned and looked at Judd. "Help me tie him up. We'll find them ourselves."

7

JUDD followed the others through the fence and toward a huge building. The stone structure had survived the heat wave, and by the numbers of burned-out cars nearby, Judd guessed some had survived the heat by running inside.

They met two guards at the front entrance who were writhing on the floor, scratching their bodies, and moaning in pain. Instead of tying or cuffing them, Gunther and Westin retrieved their guns and proceeded down the hall.

"How are we ever going to find where they're holding the prisoners?" Westin said.

Gunther placed a finger to his lips and pointed at a female guard with her head on a desk at the end of the hall. As they approached, the woman sat up and looked wildly in their direction. "Who's there?"

"It's all right, Sergeant. Don't be afraid."

"How can you see me?"

Gunther ignored the question. "We come on a mission

from the potentate. There have been several rebels arrested in the past few days. They are awaiting transport?"

The woman grimaced and grabbed the back of her neck in pain. "Most of them were taken yesterday. There are seven left in the holding cell downstairs."

"I would like to see them."

"You have to have authorization. I don't even know who you are."

"Believe me, this request comes from the highest levels—from the potentate himself." Paper rattled and Gunther handed the sergeant something.

"I can't see this," she said. "How do I know you're telling the truth?"

"I could have disarmed you the moment I came in. You must trust me. Now if you will point me in the right direction—"

"I don't know which direction the stairs are. I'm all turned around."

"Hand me your key card and I'll let myself in."

"I'm not supposed to give that to anyone," she said.

"We both agree—these are extraordinary circumstances," Gunther said. "I'll be back."

The woman hesitated, then took off her plastic card and held it out.

Gunther motioned Judd and the others toward the stairwell, and they crept along as quietly as possible.

"What are you going to do to those prisoners?" she said. "They're just Jews."

"I want to talk with them. To see if I can't persuade them to come over to our way of thinking."

As Judd reached the door, the woman tilted her head and scratched her neck. "If you ask me, we should just kill them now and get it over. They're going to die one way or another."

"Yes, thank you for that advice."

"Wait. Does the potentate know when this darkness will stop?"

"We don't know when things will return to normal, but you can be sure the potentate only has your best interests at heart." Gunther walked toward the door and inserted the card.

Going down the stairs was like walking through a dense cloud. After going through several doors and walking down a narrow hallway, Judd pointed to his right, toward a series of cells. At the end was a large cell Judd thought would hold at least a hundred prisoners. Only seven men lay on cots or on the floor. Judd looked for the mark of the believer but saw none. But only three of the men had the mark of Carpathia.

"When will you turn on the lights?" a man yelled. "This is cruel and unusual."

The others in the cell shouted at the man to be quiet.

Gunther spoke calmly and without emotion. "Gentlemen, we are not with the Global Community. We represent the true potentate of the universe."

"Were you the ones who turned out the lights?" a younger man said.

"No. In fact we were about to be arrested by Peacekeepers when this plague of darkness began. God has enabled us to see, while those without his protection cannot."

"I am a religious man," another said. "Why would God give you special treatment?"

Another man grabbed the cell bars and pulled himself up. He had scratch marks about his face and neck. "Stop all this talking and let us out. You know what the GC will do to us if we're kept here."

Gunther asked Westin to find out how to release the cell door, then pulled a chair close to the cell. The men inside grew impatient. One with long hair stayed back, wary of Gunther's voice.

"How do we know you're not the GC with more of your tricks?" Longhair said.

"We come in the name of the Prince of Peace, the King of kings, the one who was called the Light of the World."

"Who is this light?" a bearded man said. "And when can he come down here?"

Gunther chuckled. "I will tell you about this light. In the beginning the Word already existed. He was with God, and he was God. He was in the beginning with God. He created everything there is. Nothing exists that he didn't make. Life itself was in him, and this life gives light to everyone. The light shines through the darkness, and the darkness can never extinguish it."

"Don't talk to us of light and life when we are locked away in darkness so thick you can taste it," a man said.

Others shushed him and asked Gunther to continue.

"We come on behalf of this light to ask you to gain

true freedom, true sight. There is a reason why we can
see—"

"You can't see any more than we can."

"Then how can I tell you're wearing a pendant around
your neck? And that your hair is down to your shoulders—and you're closing your eyes—no, opening."

"None of us can see. Do you have special glasses or
something?"

The man at the back stood. "Let us out of here and
we'll listen to you."

"Soon," Gunther said. "But first let me tell you that
the one who sent us made the world, but when he came,
the world didn't recognize him. Even in his own land and
among his own people, he was not accepted. But to all
who believed him and accepted him, he gave the right to
become children of God. They are reborn! This is not a
physical birth—this rebirth comes from God."

"I've heard these words before from that traitor
Tsion Ben-Judah," the bearded man said. "It was his
fault the Global Community came after us in the first
place."

The cell door began to move, and the men jumped to
their feet. Westin came back as the men groped toward
the opening, falling over cots and each other.

"We can show you the true light," Gunther said while
the men poured out of the cell. "If you don't receive this
gift God is offering, you are destined to live in darkness
forever."

"I'll take my chances," the bearded man said.

The three with the mark of Carpathia left immediately. The four others held out their hands, searching for a wall or anything that could guide them.

A young man stopped near Gunther and Judd. "You say there's a way for us to see, even in this blackness?"

Judd touched Gunther's arm. "Can I talk to him?"

Gunther smiled and nodded.

"My name's Judd. Put out your hand." The man did and Judd shook it. "I'll lead you out of here. We'll talk outside."

As they went through the hallways and up the stairs, Judd learned the man's name was Zvi Zeidman.

"When the mark of Carpathia came, I went underground with some friends," Zvi said. "We could sense hostility toward Israelis. When the heat wave hit, others joined us, but someone gave us up for the reward."

Judd paused at the top of the stairs and noticed the female guard was not at her post. They walked to the front of the building and heard gunfire. The few guards left were hunkered down, firing at any noise.

"It'll be best to stay here until they run out of ammunition," Judd said. He found an open office and sat Zvi on a cushioned chair.

"I don't know why I feel better having someone who can see," Zvi said. "In the cell I had started to itch and get a tremendous headache."

Judd got the man some water and sat behind the desk. Though Zvi was in his twenties, he looked much older and had dark, curly hair and deep-set eyes.

Zvi put his head back. "How can you see?"

"I don't see fully," Judd said. "Everything's kind of

brown. But I can see this computer screen and . . ." Judd studied the screen closely. He clicked on an e-mail message and pulled it up.

"What is it?" Zvi said.

"This office must belong to one of the prison directors."

About halfway into the message Judd spotted an interesting paragraph.

> *Regarding the latest Jewish camp on the Island, I wish to relate good news. The transport you sent arrived fine with only two dead prisoners. We have experienced great success in keeping the inmates alive and, at the same time, miserable. The camp doctor has come up with a concoction that we have to feed only once a day, and it sustains the prisoners for twenty-four hours.*

Judd read on, discovering this mysterious "Island" had more than two thousand housed there. A chill ran down his back. He wondered if the camp was under the plague of darkness, and if so, what people were doing.

"What are you reading?" Zvi said.

"Have you heard of the Island?"

"Yes. It's on the Tigris. I have heard horror stories of Jews being taken there. I'm not sure which is worse, being taken to the Island or facing the guillotine. At least with the blade, the suffering is over."

"What else have you heard about the camps?" Judd said.

Zvi put his hands behind his head and leaned back.

"It's worse than the Nazis in the 1930s and 1940s. The GC torture their prisoners to the point of death but don't allow them the decency of dying. I've even heard they take videos of the beatings and torture and send them to Carpathia."

Judd shook his head. He wished he could do something for people on the Island, but he decided he had to focus on Zvi. Random gunfire echoed through the hallway, and Judd moved closer. "You don't have to stay in the dark. God can open your eyes."

"You going to preach now? Like that guy did back in the cell?"

"We've risked our lives to come here because we thought there might still be someone who needed to accept God's forgiveness."

Zvi rolled his eyes and bit his lip, then seemed to remember that Judd could see his face. He put his head in his hands.

Judd paused, then continued. "Before I found out about God, I used to hate it when people would preach or act like they knew something I didn't. I don't want to come across that way. There was a time when I felt really nervous about talking about God, and I tried to figure out all kinds of ways to convince people without making them feel bad."

"And what do you do now?"

"The world's gone so crazy that there's no time to tiptoe. I just lay it out before people as plainly as I can and let them make their decision."

"Okay, so lay it out."

"Basically, God loves you and wants you to be his child. He wants to adopt you into his family, but he won't do that unless you want to be a part of it."

"What do you mean?"

"God's perfect. He can't allow anything near him that's imperfect. And you and I are both sinful. We've done bad things."

"I've been taught since I was young that the path to God was through obeying his commands."

"True, but you know as well as I do that you haven't lived up to every command. And if you break even one, you're out of the program. That's why God had to provide a sacrifice, so we could be forgiven."

"This is the part where you tell me about Jesus, how he is the Messiah, and if I'll just get baptized or pray some prayer—"

"Zvi, have you ever considered the possibility that you've been living in darkness your whole life? Do you know God's peace, feel his forgiveness, his love?"

"You can't know those things in this life."

"Yes, you can. Again, I'm not trying to preach, and this is your decision, but God is real and he wants to come into your life right now and make a difference. He wants to show you mercy, but you have to accept it. I've met a lot of people in the past few years who've been raised exactly like you, and when they see the truth, they can't believe they were blind to it for so long."

Zvi sighed. "And you guarantee relief from the darkness?"

Judd smiled. "It's one of the perks. Back when the

stinging locusts came—" Judd stopped as someone approached in the hall.

"I heard you talking," a woman said. A gun clicked. "Tell me where you are! Come out now or I'll shoot!"

**JUDD** sat still as the female guard stumbled down the
hall, her gun held in the air, the other hand out to guide
her. Judd leaned close to Zvi and whispered, "Don't make
a sound." But when Judd leaned back, the chair
squeaked.

The woman pointed the gun at him. "I heard that!
Come out of the director's office, hands up!"

Judd studied the angle of the gun. She was aiming
about three feet over their heads. He thought of rushing
the woman or hiding behind the desk, but neither of the
options seemed good.

Judd turned and picked up a beautiful glass paper-
weight from the desk. The delicate piece was about the
size of a baseball and had been created in the likeness of
Nicolae Carpathia. Judd carefully brought the object
behind his head and threw it over the woman's head. It
crashed against the wall, shattering into a million pieces.

The woman screamed and turned, firing at the wall. The bullet pinged through the hallway. Judd jumped up, lunged for the door, and slammed it. He turned the lock and dived for the ground as another bullet punctured the wall above his head. Judd hit the floor and pulled Zvi down with him.

Zvi was panicking now, breathing heavily and shaking. "A friend told me he saw a man appear at one of the mass beheadings of Judah-ites. Right out of thin air. He wasn't there, and then he was. Do you think that was from God?"

"What did the man say?"

"He talked about God's forgiveness, like you."

"I've seen angels do the same thing," Judd said. "They come as God's messengers to warn people about not taking Carpathia's mark. And they plead with the undecided to choose Christ. It's another display of God's love."

"I won't take Carpathia's mark."

"It's not enough to be against Nicolae. Jesus said those who are not for him are against him. That puts you in some pretty awful company."

Judd could tell by the look on Zvi's face that there was a fierce battle raging. He had seen the same look many times before. Those who rejected Christ seldom struggled like this. They simply threw their hands in the air and walked away. But Zvi was different.

The woman outside cried and moaned. The gun clicked over and over. Judd opened the door to find her lying on the floor, her face buried in her arms. She had pointed the gun at her head and was pulling the trigger.

"I'll be right back," Judd whispered to Zvi.

Judd crawled on the tile floor, scooting on his knees and pulling himself forward with his hands.

The woman looked wild, clawing at her skin until it bled. Big patches of hair were gone from her head. "Oh, God, help me. I don't want to go through another one of these!" She finally stopped and put out a hand toward Judd. "Who are you?"

"A friend. Don't be afraid. I'm not going to hurt you."

"You're one of them, aren't you? One of the Judah-ites."

Judd didn't answer. He simply stared at the -6 on her forehead, signifying that she was from the United North American States.

"Before the disappearances, before any of the bad things started happening, I went to one of those big meet-ings," she said. "The kind they used to have in stadiums." Saliva ran down the woman's lips and onto her chin. She was sobbing as she talked, reaching out, then pulling her hand back.

"A man sang and then another one stood up and talked about the Bible. I didn't want any part of it. My friends and I were there to make fun of the meeting. And then I saw some people from my neighborhood going forward. I almost went with them, just to see what would happen. I almost did."

"Why didn't you?" Judd said.

"I thought religion was for weak people. I thought I had plenty of time to decide. I wanted to have fun with my life. But . . ."

With this, the woman flew into a frenzy of scratching and wailing. Her eyes flew open and Judd saw how hollow they looked, as if he could see all the way to her soul.

When she settled, Judd came closer. "Let me help you to a safe place."

"Where can I go in this blackness that's safe?" she spat. "I might as well throw myself off the side of the building. There's no hope!"

Judd wanted to tell her she could call out to God and be forgiven, but he couldn't. The best he could do for her was ease her pain a little.

"I know what I've done!" the woman yelled. "I had a lot of chances to say yes to God, but I kept putting it off. Kept saying no. And now look what happened."

Judd sat back, drained of emotion. How many other people on earth could say the same thing? How many had hardened their hearts toward God, making jokes of the message or saying they would get around to it later? Judd had been one of them. He had ignored the truth for so long, but God had given him a second chance.

Judd scampered back to the office and helped Zvi to his feet. "Come on. We have to help this lady."

Judd pulled him into the hall, and they both helped the guard to her feet. Judd found a lunchroom down the hall and put the woman in a chair. "There's a refrigerator behind you, to your right. Looked like there were some sandwiches in there. And here's a drink in case you're thirsty."

The woman reached out and nearly knocked the can

of soda over. She took a sip, sat back, and mumbled something.

"What did you say?"

"I know he tried to reach me," the woman whispered. "I watched them bring people through here and treat them like dogs, then talk about peace and love and good-will. I knew in my heart it was fake and the other message was true." She looked up and opened her mouth. Her chin quivered as she tried to form the words. Then tears welled in her eyes.

Judd guessed what she was trying to say. She wanted to know if there was any hope, if God would somehow give her one more chance. But the woman must have known the answer. She put her head on the table and sobbed.

Judd put an arm around Zvi and guided him to the door. As they walked down the long hall, the woman's wails and cries nearly tore Judd's heart out.

When they reached the police cruiser and the others, Judd found Gunther and explained what he had seen on the computer in the director's office. Gunther and Westin went back inside to investigate while Judd and Zvi climbed into the GC cruiser.

"How could you have compassion for that woman when she wanted to kill you?" Zvi said.

"Because I was exactly like her before the disappearances. For some reason, God gave me mercy and allowed me to call on him before it was too late."

"Why do I still have a chance when that woman doesn't?"

"I don't know the full answer, but I do know that if God has given you one more opportunity to respond, do it."

Zvi turned his head toward the window, deep in thought. "Tell me why you think Jesus is the Messiah."

Judd began in the Old Testament and from memory shared many prophecies that looked forward to the Messiah. "In Genesis, God curses the serpent and says that a descendent of Eve will crush the serpent's head. Jesus won the victory over the devil on the cross. In Isaiah it's predicted that a virgin will conceive a child and give birth to a son. Mary, Jesus' mother, was a virgin.

"In one of the little books, Micah, I think, it says that out of Bethlehem will come a ruler over Israel whose origins are from ancient times. Jesus was born in Bethlehem."

"But wasn't Jesus just a good teacher? He never really claimed to be the Messiah, did he?"

"That was the reason the Jewish leaders were so angry. He called God his Father. He said, 'I existed before Abraham was even born,' which is how God referred to himself to Moses. It drove them wild. They wanted to kill him."

"But did Jesus actually say he was the Messiah?"

"In one of the Gospels, John the Baptist sent someone to ask that very question. It was something like, 'John wants to know if you're the one who was to come, or if we should expect somebody else.' "

"What did Jesus say?"

"I'm going from memory here, but it was something

74

like, 'Go back and tell John that the blind can see, the lame can walk, the deaf hear, and the good news—' "

" '—is preached to the poor,' " Zvi finished. "I know that passage. Isaiah 61." He closed his eyes. " 'The Spirit of the Sovereign Lord is upon me, because the Lord has appointed me to bring good news to the poor. He has sent me to comfort the brokenhearted and to announce that captives will be released and prisoners will be freed. . . .' "

"It's exactly what he's done for you today, Zvi. God has freed you from your prison so you can respond to him. So you can know him. So you can be forgiven."

Zvi stared into the darkness. "Give me a moment."

Judd nodded. "I'll be right back."

Judd stepped out of the car and said a prayer for Zvi, then dialed Chang Wong's secure phone and reached him at his apartment.

"Judd, your worries are over," Chang said. "I've finally decided it's time for me to get out of here. Captain Steele and a couple others are coming for me as soon as possible. They're taking me to Petra!"

"That's great news."

Chang told Judd what had happened at the palace during the last few hours, and Judd relayed his story about the guards and the building they raided.

"You're right in the thick of things," Chang said. "There's supposed to be some kind of emergency meeting there tomorrow morning. Nicolae was supposed to come, but with the plague of darkness, I'm not sure."

"We're following a lead on a concentration camp," Judd said.

"I've felt so bad that I haven't been able to do much about that. I've tried to slow things down with shipments and computer glitches, but they've even constructed a camp here on an island."

"Is there any way to tell if the darkness has affected it?"

"I'm sure it has, but let me check. Look, you and your friend must come with us to Petra."

"Right," Judd said. "Get back with the time of the flight as soon as you know."

Judd started to dial Vicki to give her the good news, but Zvi tapped on the window. "I think I'm ready."

"You are?"

"I've actually read Dr. Ben-Judah's Web site more than once. When he came on television and said that all the prophecies pointed to Jesus of Nazareth as Messiah, I laughed. My whole family scoffed at his statement. But God brought back much of what he said while you were talking. I can't believe I've been so blind."

"You can give your life to God right now and live for him the rest of your life."

"That's what I want to do."

"I'll pray with you."

"Yes, please."

"God, I thank you for my new friend, and right now we come to you with grateful hearts that you've helped us live through these terrible days. And I thank you that you've called Zvi to be your child."

Zvi picked up the prayer. "Lord God, I'm sorry for rejecting you and your Son for so long. I know that I've sinned and I've gone my own way. But now I want to choose your path. I believe Jesus died for me, that he was the Lamb of God—I just remembered that from Dr. Ben-Judah. You are the Lamb who took my sins and paid my debt. And I believe you did rise from the dead, not like Carpathia, but you came back to give life. Lord God, change me. Help me to live for you. Help me to tell others about you and follow you for the rest of my days."

"Amen," Judd said.

"Yes, amen."

Zvi opened his eyes and gasped. "I can see! I can finally see!"

# 9

AFTER Judd gave Westin and Gunther the good news about Zvi, the group rejoiced. Judd also told them about the meeting the next morning.

"I'd like to sit in on that," Gunther said.

Westin smiled. "No reason we can't."

It was late and everyone was tired. Westin suggested they backtrack to a hotel he had seen on the way and get some sleep.

While they drove to the hotel, Judd phoned Vicki and explained what had happened. She was overjoyed that Judd was safe and that they had helped a new believer, but she hesitated when Judd told her about the meeting the next morning.

"Why aren't you trying to get out of there?" Vicki said.

"Vick, listen—"

"No, you don't seem to care about what I think."

"I do care. It's just that it's so clear. I don't know why
God has turned out the lights in New Babylon. I don't
understand everything about the prophecies. But I do
know that we might have a chance to save a bunch of
lives and help them come to know God."

Vicki was silent on the other end.

"Vick, put yourself in my place."

"I'm trying."

"This doesn't mean I love you any less. And your
support means so much."

"I'll pray. I can do that much. But I can't hide the fact
that I'm ticked at you."

"Ticked at me, or ticked that God would put me in
this place?"

Vicki paused. "I guess I'm ticked at both you and God."

"Then I'm in good company."

Vicki chuckled and sighed. "Be careful, Judd."

"I love you."

Judd's car was the last of the group to pull up to the
hotel. New Babylon was half ghost town, half freak show.
There were people on the street, crying and moaning,
looking for some relief from their pain. Others seemed to
have hidden away.

Westin grabbed Judd, and they ran to the hotel office.
"We need a bunch of rooms. Okay if I put Zvi with you?"

"Sure," Judd said.

The lobby of the hotel was plush, with thick leather
chairs and expensive rugs. Westin stepped to the front
desk, looked around, then vaulted it with one leap. He
rubbed his hands together. "Let's get some rooms."

"What do you think you're doing?" a Middle Eastern man said. Judd turned and saw a nicely dressed man in a doorway by the front desk. His eyes were wild. "Who are you?"

"Sir, we're with the Global Community," Westin said. "There's a big meeting tomorrow morning near here, and we need a few hours of sleep."

The manager sighed with relief. "And you are able to see?"

"Special optical lenses. It's another one of those solar things. The potentate anticipated this, but we weren't able to outfit the population. Hopefully we'll be handing these out if the darkness continues."

A look of hope came over the man and he walked forward. "I was afraid this was some kind of . . . well, let me try to help you. We have many guests. How many rooms do you need?"

Westin told him.

"I can't see the computer, but most of our top floor is empty. If I gave you a master key . . ."

"That would be fine. We'll just slip in and get some rest and be gone by morning. When the lights come back on you can bill us."

"We have had many GC guests stay with us in the past."

"Good. Then you know the billing procedure."

The man hesitated.

"What's wrong?" Westin said.

"Nothing. It's just that you don't sound like any Peacekeepers I know."

"No, we're actually escaped Judah-ites from the local facility."

The manager laughed. "Yes, I suppose if you weren't GC, you wouldn't be staying here. And you wouldn't have those special lenses to help you see."

The man gave Westin two master keys, and Judd helped lead the group quietly to the elevators.

Judd had never seen such luxurious rooms. The room he and Zvi found was so big it even had a grand piano in it. A television screen took up most of one wall.

Judd fell asleep quickly and minutes later, or so it seemed, Westin and Gunther were standing over him, telling him to wake up.

"You've got time for a quick shower," Westin said.

Judd showered, dressed, and met them downstairs where the same manager was still on duty. They tiptoed out the entrance and headed for the meeting.

Something had bothered Judd about Westin since they had teamed up to rescue the people in the Indiana library. He seemed to have no problem lying to the GC or to members of the Tribulation Force. Judd tried to bring up the subject.

Westin frowned. "Look, this is war. Life or death. These people will chop our heads off. And pretty soon they'll be gunning for us with nukes."

"The GC is one thing, but to lie to Rayford Steele about me—"

"I was trying to do you a favor and keep you out of trouble."

"I know, and I'm grateful you wanted to look out for me—"

"Then drop it. If you have a problem with it, let me go my way and you go yours."

Judd felt frustrated that the conversation had turned into a fight, but he still felt bad about Westin's lies.

Gunther got them focused on the task ahead and explained that the meeting would most likely be in the first floor conference room they had passed the night before.

Not wanting to arouse suspicion, they parked a few blocks away and headed for the facility on foot. The streets looked the same as the night before. They passed several bodies. Those who were alive were in agony.

The ones who could walk looked like they were drunk, tipping one way, then the other. Judd noticed one man walking quickly toward a building, heading straight for a descending stairway. Judd called out, but it was too late. The man fell like a rag doll to the bottom. Judd shouted and raced down the stairs.

"Who is that?" someone said behind him. "Are you with the Global Community?"

Judd kept quiet and felt the man's neck for a pulse but found none. He guessed the man had broken his neck on the way down.

Then he heard it.

The sound began as a soft, crackling noise wafting through the streets. As Judd reached the top of the steps he made out the strains of a recorded version of "Hail Carpathia," sung by the 500-voice Carpathianism Chorale:

*Hail Carpathia, our lord and risen king;*
*Hail Carpathia, rules o'er everything.*
*We'll worship him until we die;*
*He's our beloved Nicolae.*
*Hail Carpathia, our lord and risen king.*

Judd's stomach turned when he heard the song. Then a voice Judd didn't recognize came over the loudspeakers. The man sounded like he was in pain as he said, "Loyal subjects of the Global Community, please move toward the sound you're hearing for food and water. We have a supply station nearby where you can find rations.

"Also, for those attending the joint staff meeting, please come to the aid station and move directly up the stairs to the conference room. The meeting will begin in ten minutes."

Westin came up beside Judd. "You notice anything about these people?"

"They're in a lot of pain," Judd said.

"Yeah, but they're not singing along. Usually they'd be chirping with the choir, praising Carpathia."

Westin was right. Some were even grumbling against the potentate. "Carpathia's always told people the big advantage of worshiping him was that he was a god you could see," Westin said. "I guess the real God took care of that for a while."

Judd found the aid station, which was a couple of tables set up with water bottles and premade sandwiches. Those who found the tables grabbed food and ate hungrily.

Others cried out in the distance. "What's happening here? Why can't we see?"

"How long will this darkness last?"

"Why am I in such pain?"

The aid workers, who were GC Peacekeepers pulled into service, were in just as bad of shape as those on the street. They had no answers.

No one blocked Judd's path as he walked up the steps. He passed a man in uniform crawling. The man had several stars on his shoulders, and medals clinked against the steps.

Gunther motioned them silently past an armed Peace-keeper. The Peacekeeper clutched his stomach and was nearly doubled over in pain. Despite his anguish, he repeated a phrase every few seconds. "Only authorized GC personnel past this point. Joint Chiefs meet directly across the hall."

Judd moved to the conference room where several people sipped at water bottles and moaned. Judd, Westin, and Gunther spread out around the room.

The man who had been crawling walked into the room, stopped, and announced, "General Showalter!"

The people around the table tried to stand and salute, but only half of them could make it out of their chairs. Judd wondered what difference it made, since none of them could see each other.

The general staggered to the table and sat.

The others collapsed in their chairs, and a woman pushed a weird-looking phone forward. "Chief Akbar wants us to call as soon as the meeting begins."

"Yes, I know. The potentate won't be here?"

"In this blackness?" a man to his right said. "We're lucky to have found our way from only a few blocks away."

The general punched the numbers slowly, and Judd recognized Suhail Akbar's voice on the speakerphone.

"Chief Akbar, can you give us an update on the situation?" the general said.

"I just returned from a meeting with the potentate. It appears that he is the only one we've found who can see in this most recent . . . phenomenon. You'll be pleased to know his presence actually provides a glow."

"How much of a glow?"

"Only about three feet around him, but it is quite comforting to know he has this situation under control. You will be encouraged to know that New Babylon is, at the moment, the only area affected by this blackout. Other countries have reported no loss of light, so it appears this is an isolated incident."

"Does anyone at the palace know why this happened?" someone said.

Akbar paused. "It may be a side effect of the heat wave, or it could be another electromagnetic phenomenon. No matter what the cause, the potentate assures us that it will pass very soon."

"Does the potentate know about the suicides?" another man said. "We can't work in this cursed darkness. It took me two hours just to find my way here, and it's only a ten-minute walk. And the pain. Are we to believe the pain we feel is caused by leftover effects of the sun?"

"I understand your concerns, and believe me, everyone at the palace is doing their best to provide relief. We are using your idea of loudspeakers here near the palace and should have a message from the Most High Reverend Father to calm the fears of those who have been affected."

Akbar cleared his throat. "The current concern is with the Island facility. As you know, the potentate has considered closing this, and now he is anxious about the prisoners there."

"Why is he anxious?" the general said.

"The Island is the only camp for Jews in the blacked-out area. He is requesting that you go ahead with extermination plans of all prisoners immediately."

Judd glanced at Westin and Gunther who both looked horrified.

"How do you propose we do that since we can't even see the prisoners?" a man in front of Judd said.

"We have every confidence that you will find a way. Shoot them. Gas them. Burn them. The potentate doesn't care how you accomplish this, just that it gets done."

"If that is the potentate's wish, we shall oblige," the general said. "We will communicate with the guards there and inform them of our plan."

The phone clicked and went dead. The general dialed the number again, but there was no response. Judd noticed Gunther had knelt and was doing something at the wall. He motioned for Judd and Westin and held up the phone cord he had pulled from the wall. Then he held up his cell phone and pointed toward the group at the table.

*He wants us to take all the cell phones!* Judd thought.

Judd moved to the end of the room and began collecting the phones placed on the table.

There was a flurry of activity in the room as they tried to get Akbar back on the line.

"Someone just took my cell phone," a woman said.

"Mine's gone too," a man shouted.

Gunther motioned to the door, and Judd and Westin moved quickly toward it. The general dialed his cell phone, but before Suhail Akbar answered, Gunther grabbed the phone from the general. Gunther raced outside and closed the door. "Terribly sorry about the technical difficulty, Chief Akbar. We'll get on the Island operation right away."

"Good," Akbar said as Gunther held the phone out for Judd to hear. "I'll inform the potentate that this matter will be cared for today."

"It certainly will," Gunther said.

# 10

**WHILE** Westin returned to the hotel, Judd and Gunther
blocked the conference room door. The general screamed
and two Peacekeepers came fumbling toward them, their
guns raised, but Gunther disarmed them quickly and sent
them running.

Gunther returned with a hammer, nails, and blocks of
wood he had found in a workshop area. "That should
give us some time."

Judd followed Gunther to an electrical box a floor
below, and the two spent a few minutes tearing out all of
the phone wires. When they were through, they raced
upstairs and locked the front door. A crowd had gathered
at the aid station below as people pushed and jockeyed
for food and water.

An hour later Westin returned, and Judd squeezed
into a squad car with Gunther and the others headed for
the Island. Judd dialed Chang Wong and told him their
plan.

"I support your efforts," Chang said, "but I'm worried you won't get back in time for our flight to Petra. Captain Steele is on his way now."

"I'll have to take my chances," Judd said. "This mission we're on is a matter of life and death."

Gunther made a phone call of his own, informing their other contact in New Babylon, Otto Weser, about the deaths of Rainer and Klaus. Judd could tell Gunther was trying to smooth over the rift the group had had with Otto.

"Let us know when you and the others are planning to get out of here," Gunther said.

Because of the distance to the Island and the fact that they had to drive so slowly, it took them a few hours to make it to the concentration camp. They drove by an open field, and Judd noticed towers that seemed to reach into the sky. "Is this thing surrounded by razor wire?"

Gunther stopped the car, stepped out, and picked up a stick. "Worse than that. Watch."

He heaved the stick toward the field and it stopped in midair, sizzling, crackling, and falling to the ground.

"It's a new kind of electric fence. Anyone who runs past the checkpoints and heads for this thing is toast."

"So there's only one way in?" Judd said.

Gunther nodded. "And one way out."

The car stopped and the group got out. Zvi asked to join the rescue since he had known some of the men inside.

Gunther pursed his lips and nodded. "First we go in and disarm the guards. Hopefully they know nothing about the order from Carpathia. Stay calm and let me do the talking."

Judd's heart pounded like a freight train as he and the others quietly walked the perimeter to the front gate. Two guards, one tall and lanky, the other shorter and smoking a cigarette, stood near the gate.

"Wonder when our relief will get here," the tall one said, scratching his head. "I can't see my watch, but we've had to have been here more than eight hours."

"I don't know how they can expect us to work in this," the shorter one moaned.

"Attention!" Gunther yelled.

One guard pointed his rifle toward Gunther's voice, and the other stood straight.

"General Showalter and his group are here for the inspection. You did get the message from the palace, did you not?" Gunther shoved an ID card into the man's hand and the guard looked down, a puzzled look on his face.

"We haven't heard a thing, sir," the short one said, flinging his cigarette to the ground. Judd wondered how the man had lit it without being able to see the flame. "We've had some communication problems, General, my apology."

Westin took up the ruse and lowered his voice. "I understand. You boys are doing a good job out here." He patted the short one on the back. "Prisoners are still here, right? You haven't let them get away?"

"No, sir," the short one said. "We've been right here all night . . . or day. Whichever. I can't tell anymore." He paused. "Uh, sir, are you able to see?"

THE YOUNG TRIB FORCE

"New goggles," Westin said. "We should have a ship-
ment for you in a day or two."

"Where's the motor pool?" Gunther said. "You still
have transport vehicles here, right?"

"Yes, sir," the tall one said. He started to point, then
bit his lip. "They're at the north end of the compound.
Outside the fence."

"Good," Gunther said, grabbing a radio from the
guard shack. "Radio us immediately if there's any kind of
problem."

"Yes, sir," the tall one said. "Do you want us to
notify—?"

"No, this is a surprise inspection. Not a word to
anyone."

"Yes, sir. Not a word, sir."

"You, come with us," Westin said.

"Me, sir?" the short one said.

"Yes. We'll need you to show us around."

"But, sir, I can't see."

"No problem. Just give me your gun so you don't trip
and kill us all, and tell me where to go."

Judd squeezed past the other guard and followed
Westin, Gunther, and the guard down the paved road
that led to the prison. Zvi followed.

The entrance to the camp was a looming, creepy arch-
way with a likeness of Nicolae carved into it. Climbing up
a few steps, they faced a series of doors.

"How do we get inside without announcing our
arrival?" Westin said.

"I can use my key, sir," the guard said.

"Let me have it," Gunther said.

He put the key in and the doors clicked. A few paces and they were inside. "Looks like your friends in here aren't as alert as you are," Gunther said.

"The others are probably near the prisoners, sir."

"Take us to them. Are they all in one area?"

"The cells run in a horseshoe shape around the outside of the building. In the middle is the common area where the prisoners are now. And then there's the . . . well . . ."

"The torture area?" Westin said. "Come on, man. You're not used to that yet?"

"No, sir, I can't get used to the screaming. That's one reason why they put me outside."

"Take us to this common area then," Westin barked.

The guard told them which way to go, and Westin and Gunther led the way. As far as Judd knew, the guard didn't know he and Zvi were there.

Through thick Plexiglas, Judd spotted the common area. There were no chairs or benches, basketball hoops, or anything he would have normally thought of as being in a prison yard. It was simply an area filled with dirt. Men stood leaning against the building, some lying down. He noticed some scratching and moaning in pain.

With Westin's help, the guard led them down a flight of stairs and through a security area. Two more guards stopped them.

Westin put on his General Showalter act again. "I want you to round up all the guards who are inside and have them meet us in the torture room."

"Yes, sir."

Within ten minutes all the guards had gathered near a door. At Westin's request they put their guns down outside the room and went inside. Judd couldn't believe how easily the men gave up their weapons.

When Westin had the door locked, they went into the common area and walked through the prisoners. Judd saw no one with the mark of the believer and only a few with the mark of Carpathia.

Gunther turned to Judd. "You did such a good job with Zvi, I'm going to give you the opportunity to speak with these men."

"Me?" Judd said.

"Westin and I are going to try and get the juice turned off on that electric fence. Gather them up and do your thing."

———————————————

Vicki awoke and looked around the room. They were back to sleeping during the day and staying up at night, and Vicki hadn't adjusted yet. She had finally fallen asleep after her conversation with Judd, but now she was wide awake.

The first person who came to mind was Chloe Williams. Odd. With Judd in New Babylon and going into such a dangerous situation, why would she think of Chloe? Was God trying to tell her something?

She lay back on her bed and tried to get to sleep, but Chloe's face kept coming to mind. Vicki prayed for her, for little Kenny, for Buck, and for the others who were living underground in San Diego.

Before she fell asleep, she prayed again that Judd would receive wisdom from God about what to do in New Babylon.

---

"Gentlemen, if I could have your attention," Judd yelled. He had moved to the end of the horseshoe-shaped area. Zvi stood nearby. "Walk toward me. I have something important to say."

The men hobbled forward, some tripping over those on the ground. A few fell to the ground and crawled. Judd wondered how these men had kept from being burned during the heat wave. Most looked like walking skeletons, with hair falling out, and wearing ragged clothes.

"What will you do to us next?" a toothless man shouted. "Haven't you tortured us enough?"

"I'm not here to torture you," Judd said. "I come with good news. Your cries have been heard. This day you will have your freedom."

The men stared into the darkness, unable to understand what Judd was saying.

Finally, the toothless man spoke again. "Do you mean you will finally let us die?"

Judd took a breath. "My friends and I aren't with the Global Community. We heard about your struggle and have taken advantage of the plague of darkness. We come to offer you sight, both physical and spiritual."

A murmur rose from the gathering. Some didn't believe Judd and thought it was another GC trick. "They're going to kill us all!" a man said.

"That's what you've been begging them to do for weeks," another said. "Shut up and listen."

"The God of Abraham, Isaac, and Jacob has caused this blackout," Judd continued. "He foretold this day in his holy Word, warning people about the leader who would rise and come against his people, the Jews. That leader is Nicolae Carpathia, and he's persecuting you because of your Jewish blood.

"God caused everything from the disappearances, to the earthquake, to the stinging locusts, and all the rest, including this plague. It's one of his final acts to get you to repent of your sins and come to him through his Son, the Messiah."

"This is another Judah-ite!" a man yelled. "We've had your kind in our midst before, trying to get us to pray to Jesus."

"We don't want your religion," the toothless man said, turning his back.

"Listen to me," Judd screamed. The men calmed as the hum of the electric fence shut off. "This may be your last chance. We are trying to get people to safety, but we won't force you. If you want to hear more about the God who loves you and gave his life for you, please stay. We'll provide you with food and shelter and safe passage to Petra when we can."

"And if we don't want to listen?"

"You're free to go," Judd shouted. "But I beg you not to squander this chance."

To Judd's astonishment, hundreds of men scurried forward past him. They clawed at each other, cursed and spat upon those who fell in their way, and rushed away in a panic.

When he turned back, only forty or fifty remained. Judd wondered how many of these were simply too scared to walk into the darkness.

Judd gave the same message he had heard from Tsion Ben-Judah and Bruce Barnes. It was the same one he had seen transform old and young alike. He spoke of the prophecies that foretold the coming of the Messiah and how Jesus had fulfilled these verses. His heart welled up as he looked at the gaunt faces of the men.

Zvi stepped forward and told his story. Before he had finished, several men asked, "What do we have to do?"

Judd led them in a prayer, much like the one he had prayed with Zvi the day before. Several received the mark of the believer. They were shaking hands with each other, slapping each other's backs, and praising God. Others who stood nearby asked why they were so happy, and the men told them they could see.

Westin walked up to Judd and pointed to the transport trucks. Judd told the new believers to follow Westin and said if any more were interested, they should grab on to him and follow. Like a winding kindergarten group, the men trudged through the darkness clinging to Judd.

*If only Vicki could see this*, Judd thought.

**JUDD** stared at the odd mix of believers in the parking lot of the hotel. It was morning and they were all together now. Those who weren't believers when they left the prison had since become convinced of the claims of Jesus. Judd wandered through the group while they ate breakfast or rested, catching the smiles of the men he had helped.

Westin and Gunther knelt together by the front of the transport truck. Judd walked up as Gunther patted Westin on the shoulder. "It's decided then."

"What's decided?" Judd said.

"We're going to take advantage of this new manpower and put the Global Community on its heels," Gunther said.

"What are you talking about?" Judd said. "We have to get back to the airport and get to Petra."

Gunther stood and put an arm on Judd's shoulder. "I understand, but we have pressing matters here."

Westin stood. "There are a lot more guillotines to destroy, and if we can get in Nicolae's palace before this darkness lifts—"

"But you can't do that," Judd said. "You might destroy valuable stuff the Trib Force needs."

"I don't understand," Gunther said.

"We've had a guy on the inside for a long time, giving us information. You destroy their computer network and you've hurt the GC for maybe a week. But you'll cripple the Trib Force's efforts to know what's going on."

"I had no idea there was someone on the inside," Gunther said.

Judd looked at his watch. "And he's supposed to fly out of here sometime today."

Westin pursed his lips. "I still like the idea of staying and doing as much harm as we can while the lights are out."

"Agreed," Gunther said.

Judd rubbed his eyes and sighed. This trip to New Babylon was supposed to have been quick, in and out, but here he was, days after he had first arrived. He had helped men escape the clutches of the GC, and some had become believers, but he couldn't help thinking about the safety of Petra.

"I understand your need to get to Petra," Westin said. "If you want to head to the airport, I'll help."

Judd hadn't talked with Chang since the day before and wondered how he was doing. He pulled out his cell phone and dialed as a rumble shattered the darkness.

"Who could be flying an airplane in this darkness?" Gunther said.

Judd's heart sank. "Rayford Steele."

Chang picked up on the second ring, and Judd asked him where he was.

"We just took off from New Babylon. And you should have seen Nicolae."

"He was at the airport?"

"Yes, and believe it or not, there's a glow about him."

"So you're headed to Petra?" Judd said.

"We had to get out of here. I haven't had a chance to tell Captain Steele about your situation. Where are you?"

Judd told him and Chang groaned. "I know that hotel. We could have waited another few minutes, I suppose, but not long enough for you to reach us. What happened at the concentration camp?"

Judd told him and Chang was overjoyed. He finally handed the phone to Rayford Steele, and Judd told the pilot what had happened over the past few days.

"Looks like you have two options, Judd," Rayford said. "You can find our contact there—his name is Otto Weser—and wait for the next airlift out, or you can hop in that truck and head across the desert. Both scenarios have their problems."

"I understand," Judd said. "Did you learn anything in New Babylon?"

"Plenty," Rayford said. "I made a contact inside the palace, met this Otto character, and we crashed a meeting of Carpathia's."

"You were actually in the room with Nicolae?"

"He didn't know we were there, but yes. We overheard him telling his people he's going to put an end to the 'Jewish problem' and he's calling a meeting of all ten heads of the global regions. They're going to meet in Baghdad to map out their strategy. And we found out Nicolae's storehouse of nuclear weapons is hidden at Al Hillah."

"The nukes the world gave up and he was supposed to destroy?"

"Right. He's moving his operation there, though the palace will still hold his staff." Rayford's phone chirped. "I've got a call from San Diego. I'd better take this. Take care, Judd. Hope to see you in Petra soon."

"Me too," Judd said.

---

Vicki knew Judd was trying to put a good face on the situation, but she could tell he was disappointed to still be in New Babylon.

"I feel like I've failed you," Judd said. "I promised I'd be careful, and I'm still in one of the most dangerous spots in the world."

"Not if this is what God wants," Vicki said. "I'm disappointed too, but look how God's used you. We've prayed that we could reach more people, and that's what happened."

"We've made the decision to find this German guy, Otto Weser. Our group and Otto's separated because of a disagreement, but maybe we'll all get out of this and get to Petra."

Vicki kept her composure until after she was off the phone with Judd. Then she ran to her cabin, buried her face in her pillow, and wept.

Two days later Vicki found herself among her friends, praying for Judd and asking God to protect him and the other believers in New Babylon. Judd had called twice and updated her on their progress. They had found Otto Weser and what Judd termed a safe place to stay and perform their operations against the GC. Judd also said they had an option of driving into the desert to hide, but that for the moment they were staying in New Babylon.

What happened next took Vicki's breath away. Mark was monitoring different news feeds and came upon Anika Janssen anchoring live from Detroit. "On the preview they mentioned something about an important arrest," Mark said.

"Where?" Vicki said.

Mark pointed at the screen and turned up the volume.

"Good evening," Anika Janssen said. "Darkness continues to plague Global Community International Headquarters in New Babylon at this hour. It is confined to the borders of the city and is believed to be an act of aggression on the part of dissidents against the New World Order.

"GC Chief of Security and Intelligence Suhail Akbar spoke with us by phone earlier from the beleaguered capital. In spite of the turmoil there, he reports good news, constituting our top story tonight."

The screen showed an outline of the New Babylon skyline and a picture of Suhail Akbar. "Yes, Anika," Akbar said, "following months of careful planning and cooperation between the various law-enforcement branches of the Global Community, we are happy to report that a combined task force of crack agents from both our Peace-keeping and Morale Monitor divisions has succeeded in apprehending one of the top Judah-ite terrorists in the world.

"The arrest was made before dawn today in San Diego after months of planning."

"San Diego!" Vicki said.

"I'd rather not go into the details of the operation," Akbar continued, "but the suspect was disarmed and arrested without incident. Her name is Chloe Steele Williams, twenty-six, a former campus radical at Stanford University in Palo Alto, California, from which she was expelled six years ago after making threats on the lives of the administration."

"Thank you, Chief Akbar. We have further learned that Mrs. Williams is the daughter of Rayford Steele, who once served as pilot for Global Community Supreme Potentate Nicolae Carpathia. He was fired some years ago for insubordination and drinking while on duty, and GC intelligence believes his resentment led to his current role as an international terrorist."

"I don't believe this," Mark said. "Those are such lies!"

"Mrs. Williams is the wife of Cameron Williams, formerly a celebrated American journalist who also worked directly for the potentate before losing his job due to differences in management style. He edits a subversive cyber and printed magazine with a limited circulation.

"Williams, his wife, and her father are international fugitives in exile, wanted for more than three dozen murders around the world. Mrs. Williams herself heads a black-market operation suspected of hijacking billions of Nicks' worth of goods around the world and selling them for obscene profits to others who cannot legally buy and sell due to their refusal to pledge loyalty to the potentate.

"The Williamses, who have amassed a fortune on the black market, have one child remaining after Mrs. Williams apparently aborted two fetuses and an older daughter died under questionable circumstances. The son, whom they have named Jesus Savior Williams, pictured here, is two years old. Acquaintances report that the Williamses believe he is the reincarnation of Jesus Christ, who will one day conquer Nicolae Carpathia and return the globe to Christianity."

The screen filled with a picture of a toddler wearing a T-shirt that read "Kill Carpathia!"

"That can't be Kenny," Vicki said.

"There are so many lies in that report," Conrad said, "I wouldn't be surprised if Carpathia wrote it himself."

"Do you think they really arrested Chloe?" Vicki said.

Mark held up a hand as the report switched to a reporter in San Diego who stood by the man who was said to be interrogating Chloe.

Colonel Jonathan "Jock" Ashmore said the arrest was very important. He nervously tugged at his uniform jacket. "Mrs. Williams has proved to be the typical terror-ist who knows when it's time to bargain. When the reality hit her that she had been positively identified and we informed her of the overwhelming charges against her, it was only a matter of minutes before she began offering various deals to save her skin."

"Are you at liberty to say what some of those might be?"

"Not entirely, though she has already pledged to enroll her son in Junior GC as soon as possible."

"I've seen enough," Vicki said. "There's no way Chloe would have talked, and there's certainly no way she would have agreed to enroll Kenny in a Junior GC program."

Vicki walked away from the video feed, shaken and confused. She pictured Chloe being tortured and questioned by her GC captors.

In a response written to Dr. Ben-Judah's Web site, Mark received the answers the people in Petra were sending out to counteract the lies of the GC.

*The only thing the news seemed to get right was Chloe's name and age and the fact that she is the daughter of Rayford and the wife of Cameron "Buck" Williams. While it's true she attended Stanford University, neither was she a campus radical nor was she expelled. She dropped out after the Rapture but had a grade point average of 3.4 and had been active in student affairs.*

*Rayford Steele did serve, while already a believer, as pilot on the staff of Nicolae Carpathia, providing invaluable information to the cause of Christ's followers everywhere. He was never fired and never charged with insubordination or drinking while on duty. He left after his second wife was killed in a plane crash.*

*The Judah-ites are anything but "the last holdouts in opposition to the New World Order." Many Jewish and Muslim factions, as well as former militia groups primar-*

*ily in the United North American States, still have refused to accept the mark of loyalty to the Supreme Potentate and must hide in fear for their lives.*

*Cameron Williams was indeed formerly a celebrated American journalist who also worked directly for the potentate, but he also quit, rather than "losing his job due to differences in management style." As for his subversive cyber and printed magazine's "limited circulation," that, of course, is a matter of opinion. The Truth is circulated to the same audience that is ministered to daily by Dr. Tsion Ben-Judah, at last count still more than a billion.*

The rest of the document corrected errors from the GC about murders, the Co-op, and Chloe's personal life.

"That clears up her past," Vicki said, "but what are they going to do with her?"

Mark pursed his lips. "If she could stay alive for another year, she'd be around for the Glorious Appearing. But I honestly don't think that'll happen."

———

Judd reeled from the news reports about Chloe and put a call in to Chang in Petra. He was surprised to hear excitement in Chang's voice when he got the return call.

"I know it's a very depressing day for the Tribulation Force around the world," Chang said, "but I have good news. I'm free."

"Right, you made it to Petra. I'm happy for you."

"No, you don't understand. The mark on my forehead. It is gone!"

# 12

JUDD fought feelings of jealousy, wishing he were in Petra with Chang, but the news that his mark was gone was incredible. Judd knew how much Carpathia's mark bothered Chang, and he couldn't imagine the embarrassment of walking into that camp of a million people with the emblem of the enemy on his forehead.

"I thought Nicolae's tattoo was permanent," Judd said. "What happened?"

"I arrived here in the afternoon, and Naomi Tiberius gave me a quick tour, including the computer center," Chang said. "It's amazing what Mr. Hassid set up. It's just like being in New Babylon without the danger."

"Everyone treating you okay?"

"Like royalty. But I'm so ashamed. I wanted to take off my baseball cap and bow every time I met someone new, but with that thing on my forehead, I could not."

"Did you meet Tsion and Chaim?"

"Yes, but not right away. They were meeting about Chloe's disappearance, and then came the news of another Tribulation Force member's death."

"Who?"

"Albie. A man Captain Steele and the others know well. The GC reported that Chloe gave up information about him, but no one believes that. And they say he committed suicide, which, again, no one believes."

Judd hadn't heard of this Albie, but if he was a member of the Trib Force, Judd knew he would be missed. "I want to hear more about your mark, but how's Captain Steele?"

"As well as can be expected. He left here not long after we arrived. He received a call from Chloe from a GC cell phone, and she gave him a coded message. I don't know all the particulars, but Captain Steele believes she was trying to tell him to get everyone in San Diego to Petra, and that's what he's trying to work out."

"Seems like the safest place to be," Judd said.

Chang described his new home. Again, Judd felt a stirring in his heart, wishing he were in Petra talking with Chang and eating manna or quail.

"How did you like the manna?" Judd said.

"It was like being fed from the table of a king. That's how a friend described it and he was right. Naomi gave me a tour on one of the ATVs. The city is so spread out that it would take days to see everything."

"Is something going on between you and Naomi?"

Chang paused. "We have a good relationship. I knew we would have to work together closely since she has become the technical leader here, but I didn't want to complicate things with . . ."

"You're falling for her, aren't you?"

"Judd, she is stunning—"

"I know. I've met her. Friendly, beautiful, and smarter than both of us."

"I've never even had a girlfriend. There were girls in high school I was interested in, but I never dared let them know."

"Do you think she feels anything for you?"

Chang chuckled. "I think so. We were drinking at the spring of water when the sun set and the skies opened and seemed to snow bits of soft bread."

Judd closed his eyes and pictured the scene. It was one of the most amazing things he had witnessed in Petra, the daily food that fell from the sky, as if God were tearing off pieces of bread and sending them floating to his children.

"Talking with Naomi is like speaking with someone I've known my whole life, but I've never met her in person. Do you understand?"

"I do."

"Anyway, I met her father, which was quite an experience, and then I met with Tsion and Chaim. We are all heartbroken about Chloe."

"They must be trying to help her escape," Judd said.

"I don't know. That will be up to Captain Steele and Mr. Williams."

"I can't imagine what Buck is going through right now. Tell me about the mark."

"Yes. I met Dr. Rosenzweig, who looks more like his

old self now than the famous Micah who stood up to the potentate. His hair's grown back and he was excited to see me. He called me 'the genius mole.'

"Then Dr. Ben-Judah approached with all kinds of people around him. I was honored he would eat a short breakfast with me. When he prayed over our meal, I thought my heart was going to burst. After our meal, I asked for some time alone with him and Dr. Ben-Judah stayed.

"I took off my cap and showed him the 30 on my forehead and the place where the Global Community biochip had been inserted. He said it was strange to see both the mark of the believer *and* the mark of Carpathia, and I told him I couldn't stand to look myself in the mirror each day."

"That mark kept you alive, Chang," Judd said.

"Yes, Tsion said it wasn't my fault, that it was forced on me, but I asked if there was any way to have it gone.

"Tsion scratched his chin and shrugged. He said he didn't know if it was possible, but that he would pray, as long as I would be content with whatever God decided."

"What happened then?"

"He called Naomi's father and Chaim back over to agree with us in prayer. I was already overcome with emotion and had begun to cry. Tsion placed his hand on my forehead, and the others grabbed my hands and touched my shoulders. I felt so loved by these men, so cared for. And then Tsion prayed. It was such a beautiful prayer that included many Scriptures.

"The tears were streaming down my face as he turned to me. He said we come together in faith believing and pray to the God to whom anything is possible, the God who spared us from the fire of the enemy.

"And then he asked, according to God's will, if God would remove any sign of the evil one from me. I went limp. It felt like my arms and legs weighed a hundred pounds each. I started sweating like an Olympic athlete. I opened my eyes and Tsion looked at me and smiled.

"Naomi's father was the first to tell me it was gone. Then I ran to his place and looked in the mirror to make sure it was true. The mark no longer mocks me, Judd."

"I'm happy for you."

"We're gearing up for at least two hundred new arrivals here in the next few days, people from San Diego. When are you coming?"

Judd told him what had happened the last few days and what he hoped would happen. It was Judd's plan to get to Petra and have Vicki join him there if possible. "As long as it's dark over here, we're continuing to try and frustrate the GC as much as we can. I guess when the time's right, we'll head that way."

---

Vicki watched news reports from the Global Community and tried not to think about what Chloe was going through. Was she in some dark, cold cell? Were they torturing her, trying to get her to give information about the Tribulation Force? Vicki guessed the GC was having a hard time getting anything out of Chloe. She was one of the most determined people Vicki had ever met.

Chloe had set the Commodity Co-op in motion and

had coordinated shipments of food and medical supplies for believers throughout the United North American States and the entire world. The GCNN reporters were right—the capture of Chloe was a tremendous success for the Global Community. But pulling information from her would be very difficult.

Vicki thought of her last conversation with Chloe. The woman had written to congratulate Vicki on her engagement. A few weeks later, Vicki had called Chloe in San Diego and talked with her about Judd's potential trip to New Babylon.

Chloe had been hesitant when Vicki told her about the trip. "Sounds like Buck to me," Chloe had said. "If there's something he can do to help the cause, he'll go there, no matter what the cost to him. But I have to admit I've done the same thing. In Greece I took some chances I wouldn't want Buck to take."

Chloe had talked about her son, Kenny, during the conversation as well. "I just hope if anything happens to me or Buck that the other one will be there to help raise Kenny. I can't imagine not seeing him grow up."

The memory sent a chill down Vicki's spine as she reread a journal entry about some of the conversation. Vicki had written a prayer at the end of the page. *God, if anything does happen to Chloe or Buck, I pray that you would make it possible for me to help in some way to raise Kenny.*

The phone rang in the main cabin and Vicki was closest. Immediately she heard background noise like someone was on an airplane. "Hello?"

"Yes, I'm looking for Zeke—I'm not sure I have the right—"

"Captain Steele?" Vicki said.

"Yes, who's this?"

Vicki told him and asked Mark to get Zeke. "Where are you?" she said.

"We're flying over the southern states now, headed for home base. We came from Petra."

"I heard about Chloe. Is it true?"

"All the information we have points to them having her," Rayford said.

"We've been praying for her—and for you and Buck and Kenny."

Rayford cleared his throat. "That means more than you can know, Vicki. I was really excited for you and Judd. Have you heard any more from him?"

Vicki told him what she knew, and Rayford told her of his conversation with Judd earlier. "We have a contact who's still in New Babylon that we'll probably need to go in and get. If Judd's not out by then, maybe he can take that flight."

"That would be wonderful."

"Plus, I'm going to talk with Zeke about something that might help you as well. Do you sense much danger from the GC there in Wisconsin?"

"It's such a remote location, they seem to have forgotten us or don't really care that we're here."

Zeke rushed in so Vicki said good-bye to Rayford. Zeke took the phone in the other room and talked for a few minutes. He returned smiling.

"What did Captain Steele want?" Vicki said.

"He asked if I was ready to come out of mothballs."

Vicki raised an eyebrow. "What does that mean?"

"You know, come out of storage. Get in the game. Go where the action is. Seems they need some help in Petra and I'm on my way."

"What are you going to do there?"

Zeke frowned. "Don't know exactly. I figure I'll be working on disguises and such, you know, fake ID cards or uniforms or maybe some tattoos. Captain Steele didn't give specifics, but I told him if they needed me, I'd be there."

"I'm happy for you," Vicki said.

"You ought to be happy for yourself."

"What do you mean?"

Zeke sat in a rickety wooden chair that strained under his weight and smiled. "Because I'm supposed to have a little company on the flight."

"Who?"

"Well, the pilot will probably be Mac McCullum or whoever they assign, but there's a certain redheaded girl from Mount Prospect who's been given the okay to be on board as well."

"Me?" Vicki choked.

"And whoever you need for the ceremony once Judd makes it back," Zeke said.

Vicki covered her mouth, then waved a hand at her face. "I have to tell Lionel. He's supposed to be Judd's best man."

Zeke laughed. "Then go tell him."

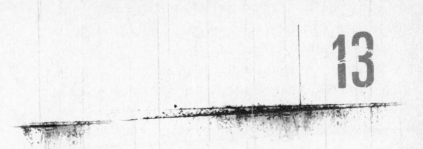

**13**

**JUDD** and a few others had moved into a hideout run by Otto Weser less than six miles from the GC palace. Westin had stayed with Gunther and the rest of the group as they tried to destroy Global Community guillotines and loyalty mark sites before the darkness ended.

After a long sleep, Judd finally met Otto. The German timberman was barrel-chested, with a wide grin and big hands. Judd asked Otto only one question and the man was off, talking a mile a minute and stopping for just enough breath to continue. He told Judd he had come to New Babylon to be part of the fulfillment of prophecy that believers would be called out of the city. Judd noticed he didn't mention anything about the deaths of Rainer's wife and the others.

"After the darkness plague hit, I knew what I had to do. For a long time I've wanted to see the palace with my own two eyes. So, when I couldn't convince anyone else to go with me, I went by myself to the compound, the courtyard, the palace—and I especially wanted to see Nicolae Carpathia's office."

"You actually went inside?" Judd said.

"Yes, and imagine my shock when I saw believers there. Four of them."

Judd quickly figured out that Otto had met Chang Wong, Rayford Steele, Abdullah Smith, and Naomi Tiberius.

"What an answer to prayer those people were. And to think, we have a connection in Petra when we need it."

When Otto took another breath, Judd said, "So you're not concerned about being here while Carpathia's goons are around?"

"Nicolae and his goons, as you call them, have left. Rayford Steele and I found out about a meeting in the palace and we went there. We actually saw Nicolae kill one of his top people. An Indian man, I think. Awful. Grabbed him with both hands and snapped his neck like a chicken bone. Then kept going with the meeting. Shows you what kind of man he is.

"Well, they reported a plane had landed, and Nicolae was personally going to inspect it. That was Rayford's plane so we had to get out of there, but before we did, we found out that Nicolae is calling together his ten kings, the leaders of all the global regions. That will happen in six months. But they're moving all leaders into the light at Al Hillah. That's where Nicolae has stored his nuclear weapons.

"Perhaps Nicolae just wants to be in the light, or

118

perhaps he knows that New Babylon will be destroyed by God. I don't know. But one thing is certain. You and I are in a very strategic place, Mr. Judd Thompson Jr."

When Otto paused, Judd seized the opportunity. "I met Rainer. He told me a little about the disagreements you had."

Otto's face went white and he sighed. "You don't know how many times I've wished I could talk with him and tell him how sorry I was. I heard he and Klaus were killed, and I hold myself personally responsible." He put his hands on his knees. "Did Rainer ever say anything about me other than the story about his wife?"

Judd reached in his pocket and pulled out the letter Rainer had given him. Tears welled in the big man's eyes. He tore open the letter and quickly read the brief note. Otto shook with emotion, then folded the letter and put it in his shirt pocket. "I will never get to tell him how sorry I am."

"Yes, you will," Judd said. "You'll see each other again and the others."

"You're right. And that day is closer now than it has ever been."

After Judd finished talking with Otto, he spent some time praying for Chloe Williams. He didn't know much about the situation, but he knew enough to sense that she was in grave danger. He prayed the Tribulation Force would be able to rescue her and get out safely and that Chloe would stay strong and not give the GC any information.

Judd thought of Petra and remembered Sam

Goldberg. It had been a while since they had talked, so he dialed the last number he had for the boy and reached the computer area at Petra.

After a few minutes, Sam was on the phone. "I've heard about your situation through Mr. Stein. He talked briefly with Captain Steele while he was here and got an update on you. We've been praying."

"How's it going with you?" Judd said.

"Let me step outside," Sam said quietly. "Most people prefer working inside at this time of day because it's hot." When he had moved outside, Sam said, "I'll be honest, Judd. I had feelings for Naomi."

"Did you talk with her?"

"Yes. She tried to let me down easy, but the truth is, my feelings haven't gone away. And now that Chang is here . . ."

"What's Chang got to do with it?"

"Naomi flew to New Babylon and has been with him almost every minute since they've been back. He's a genius with computers. I've watched him tapping into everything in New Babylon. He's not much older than me, and yet he's been given a major assignment by the Trib Force."

"You can understand that, though. The guy's been on the inside of the GC—"

"I know. And I can see why Naomi is attracted to him, but I'm still having . . ." Sam's voice trailed off. Then Judd heard him say hello to someone. "You won't believe who just walked by with a basket of manna for her sweetheart." Sam sighed. "With all the problems in the world, this one is so small."

"Sam, I'm really sorry. I'll pray that . . . well, I'll pray for you."

"I need it," Sam said.

---

With the turmoil of Judd's situation, plus learning about Chloe's capture, the last thing Vicki needed was the emotional drain of saying good-bye. But here she was again, packing the few belongings she had and getting ready to leave the friends she had made over the past few years. She carefully folded and packed the wedding dress that several of the women had made for her. It was a comfort to know Lionel would be going along and Zeke would be there too, but she hated leaving.

A few hours before the trip to catch the Trib Force plane, the group gathered in the main cabin to bid fare-well to their friends. Vicki cried when little Ryan walked up and handed her a picture of him and the Fogartys. On the back was written, *So you won't forget the joy you've brought our family.* Vicki hugged Ryan tightly and smiled through her tears at Tom and Josey.

Charlie brought Phoenix into the room, and the dog licked Vicki's face. "They say a dog is man's best friend," Charlie said, "but you've been mine, Vicki."

One by one they expressed their feelings for Vicki, Lionel, and Zeke. Darrion said she was thankful that Vicki was a person who knew how to listen. Janie, in her own way, gave tribute to Vicki and thanked her for sticking with her even when she didn't deserve it. Shelly couldn't speak. She just gave Vicki a long hug.

Mark tried to say something but couldn't. After what felt like ten minutes, but was really only one, he crossed his arms and leaned back in his chair. "I've known Vicki and Lionel as long as anyone here. We've had our disagreements, and some knock-down, drag-out fights." He looked at Vicki. "You were there when my cousin died. You've really been my family these last six years, and sometimes families get upset and bicker and . . ." He shook his head. "I don't know what to say other than . . . I love you."

Vicki, Lionel, and Mark hugged each other, the tears flowing.

Zeke blew his nose loudly and everyone laughed. "Sorry, but you guys are the ones making my nose run," he said.

When everyone had said something, Marshall Jameson stood. "It's been the treat of a lifetime getting to know you three. Zeke, you brought a servant's heart to this place. It's been an honor to serve alongside you. Lionel, you showed us what real courage is all about, and I pray God will use you in this last year as much as he's used you in our lives." Marshall paused and wiped away a tear. "And, Vicki, you have been a light. I couldn't be any happier for you and Judd, and I pray God will bless you both."

Marshall pulled out three handwritten notes. "I asked everyone to write something about you that you could take, something to remember us by. Some wrote verses that remind them of you, and others wrote personal things."

He handed them the three envelopes, then asked

everyone to gather. Vicki, Zeke, and Lionel sat while the others put their hands on them.

"Oh, God, you have given us these friends who have blessed us with their lives. And now we give them back to you, asking that you will use them mightily. Watch over them and protect them. May they always remember the love we have for them and that our love is only a fraction of your love for them."

Marshall paused. There were sniffles and sobs all around Vicki. Finally he said, " 'And now, all glory to God, who is able to keep you from stumbling, and who will bring you into his glorious presence innocent of sin and with great joy. All glory to him, who alone is God our Savior, through Jesus Christ our Lord. Yes, glory, majesty, power, and authority belong to him, in the beginning, now, and forevermore. Amen.' "

An hour later, Marshall helped Zeke drag his boxes and trunks into the underbrush near Hudson, Wisconsin. They said good-bye again and Marshall was gone.

Vicki, Zeke, and Lionel stayed out of sight until they heard the whine of the jet engine overhead. Soon, Mac McCullum had touched down and was helping Zeke pull his things to the plane.

Mac was a tall, lanky man who talked with a drawl. Vicki had heard a lot about him from Judd and others who had met him. He had flown planes for the Global Community and was presumed dead when Nicolae's expensive jet crashed in Israel. Vicki recalled how glad she felt when she heard Mac had escaped the GC before the crash.

Mr. McCullum greeted Lionel and Vicki and showed them where to put their things. As they lugged Zeke's stuff, Mac asked about Zeke's stay in Wisconsin.

"I wish you could meet everybody in Avery," Zeke said.

"No second thoughts about leaving? You must be close to these people."

"Lots of second thoughts, but I figure a guy's got to go where he's called. I was called here, and now I'm being called there. Who woulda thought a no-account like me would ever get called anywhere?"

When they were in the air, Vicki got a good look at the devastation from the heat wave. There were occasional patches of land that hadn't been affected, but most of the earth had been scorched. Cities looked like ghost towns.

Vicki asked about Chloe, and Mac told her what he knew. "We got a report in San Diego that Peacekeepers were coming our way, so we decided to get out fast. Most of us are heading to Petra, though I'm not sure if Rayford and Buck have made their final decision about a rescue."

"You mean they might not try?" Lionel said.

"Apparently they've moved Chloe to somewhere back east. We don't know where."

"Buck must be going out of his mind," Vicki said.

Mac pursed his lips. "And you should hear little Kenny crying for his mom. They're trying to take care of him, but nobody can do that like a mom can."

As Mac piloted them across the Atlantic, he told them what he knew about the Trib Force member named Albie who had been killed. "As much of this as we've gone through, it never gets easier. They're planning a little service for Albie at Petra once everybody gets there from San Diego."

Mac explained that he would drop them off at Petra, then head to Al Basrah and clear his and Albie's apartment of any clues. "I'll be taking a bigger plane from Petra 'cause I got to bring back this Otto Weser guy and his people."

"Captain Steele told me about him," Zeke said. "So you're bringing them back to Petra because of that Scripture about God's people getting out of Babylon before God destroys it?"

"Exactly."

Vicki sat forward. "Do you think Judd will be in that group you bring from New Babylon?"

"If he's not, I'll find him and hog-tie him. We gotta get you two back together."

Zeke stared at the ocean seven and a half miles below. "What must that have looked like when it was all blood?"

"You can't imagine," Mac said.

Mac turned to Lionel and said he couldn't believe how Lionel had survived his ordeal in Indiana. "And it sounds like your time in South Carolina was no cakewalk."

Lionel told them what had happened to him during his travels and said he wondered if all those believers who had helped him on his way north were still alive.

Vicki tried to keep up with the conversation, but she fell asleep to the roar of the plane's engine. A new chapter was being written in her life, and this final year would begin in Petra.

# 14

WHILE Vicki dozed, Lionel listened to Zeke and Mac talk about the different disguises the group in Petra might need for an upcoming mission. Zeke said he had found a book detailing new techniques for makeup, scars, skin and eye color, and blemishes.

Lionel was sad to leave Wisconsin, but he had been on the run so much in the past few years that this didn't feel much different. Though he loved his new friends in Wisconsin, he hadn't been there long enough to set down roots like Vicki had.

Lionel pulled out the sheet of paper Marshall had given him and read through the different messages. Some were printed from the computer, others handwritten. The one from Charlie, scrawled in pencil and slanting down one page, choked him up the most.

> *Dear Lionel,*
>     *I'm really sorry about your arm and have been pray-*

*ing for you since the accident. I hope the one Zeke made for you works good. I haven't known you as long as I've known Vicki and some of the others, but I want you to know that I've seen Jesus in you. You're always thinking of others and not yourself, always keeping people on track, and treating people like I imagine Jesus would.*

*I know Jesus wasn't black or anything, but I think you know what I mean. That's all I have to say. Thanks for being my friend.*

*Charlie*

Lionel folded the page and smiled. Charlie's line about Jesus not being black reminded him how much he had been through since the disappearances. At first, Lionel felt uneasy being the only black teenager in the group, but with the earthquake and all the plagues and death around them, his skin color wasn't an issue. They were all believers in Christ. Period.

It was what Lionel imagined an army went through. He had read stories about soldiers who disliked others because of their differences. But once the bullets started to fly, it didn't matter where the people came from or how they talked or what they looked like—they were fellow soldiers.

Lionel heard Mac say something about Carpathia's ten kings, and he began listening again.

". . . 'course, he calls 'em regional potentates, but we know what's going down, don't we?" Mac said.

"I do," Zeke said.

Mac stretched his arms. "If Otto succeeds in New Babylon, we find out where the big shindig is gonna be before it happens, and we get in there and bug the place. We're not going to try to stop prophesied events, of course, but it'll be good to know exactly what's happening."

"What happens to Carpathia's secretary?"

Lionel had wondered about this as well. That Rayford had befriended a secretary working for Carpathia was one thing. But trusting her? Lionel thought it was risky but didn't say anything.

"Krystall?" Mac said. "If I had a vote, I'd say we convince her we know what's going to happen to New Babylon and get her out of there."

"To Petra?"

Mac shook his head. "Much as we might like to do that, God has set that city aside as a city of refuge for his people only. Sad as it is, she made her decision, took her stand, and accepted the mark. Getting her out of New Babylon just keeps her from dying in that mess when God finally judges the city. She's going to die anyway, sometime between then and the Glorious Appearing, and when she does, she's not going to like what eternal life looks like."

Lionel thought of all the people he had come into contact with during the last six years who fit into that category—people who had heard the truth but decided not to believe it. Some had chosen to take Carpathia's mark. Others were still out there who hadn't chosen, but that number was dwindling every day.

He closed his eyes and prayed for the San Diego

group to get out safely. He asked God to help Buck and little Kenny and prayed that the Tribulation Force would be able to rescue Chloe. "And if they aren't able to rescue her, I pray you would give her the strength to go through whatever she's going to face.

"And, God, whatever you have for me in Petra— whether it's reaching out to people over the Internet, encouraging others, or something else—I want to do it with everything in me."

———————————

Judd awoke early and, using Otto's computer, accessed the many Global Community news feeds. He came upon one from the United North American States that disturbed him.

A female reporter stood near a large prison. "This courtyard here in Louisiana is used for two purposes. Three times each day prisoners are taken past the bronze statue of Lord Carpathia so they can worship. And to my right—" the camera panned—"are the loyalty enforcement facilitators. Everyone knows what those are used for."

Judd counted seven guillotines standing like evil guards. The GC had televised executions for a long time, so he didn't understand why the reporter was giving this background. A black SUV pulled into the courtyard and a handcuffed Chloe Williams was dragged out of the vehicle, her head banging the door.

The reporter continued talking and moved toward a group of media members. When the camera panned back to Chloe, one of the Global Community officials whirled and hit her in the forehead with the back of his hand. Then the man clamped his hand over her mouth, kneed her in the back, and tried to tape her mouth.

Chloe broke free for a moment and screamed, "Tell the truth for once! I was drugged! They—"

The man slapped the tape on her face so tightly that Judd wondered if Chloe could even breathe, let alone speak. Seeing someone he knew treated this way made Judd sick.

The reporter yelled at the GC officials, "Has she spilled any more?"

"Oh yes," the man said as Chloe shook her head. "More all the time. Of course we had to tell her there would be no trading leniency for, ah, physical favors as it were. She can only help herself by telling the truth. I'm confident we'll get there. We've already gained more knowledge about the Judah-ite underground and the illegal black-market co-op from her than from any other source we've ever had."

The man concluded by saying the daily executions would be held at 10 a.m. the next day with more than thirty executions lined up.

The camera panned back to the reporter. "Here in Louisiana prisons are notoriously hard, and none harder than Angola. International terrorist Chloe Williams will rue the day she pushed the Global Community to the point where she was sent here. The guillotine will be sweet relief compared to hard labor for the rest of her life." With a look of glee the reporter ended with, "When the life of this dissident comes to an end, we will show it to you here live."

Judd switched off the feed and buried his head in his hands. Someone touched him on the shoulder and Judd looked up.

"I'm sorry about your friend in America," Otto said. "We are all praying for her. I have an important mission this morning that may help the Trib Force find her. It's dangerous though. I have to go to the palace. Do you want to go with me?"

---

After seeing the GC coverage of Chloe Williams, Mark sent an urgent message to the Young Tribulation Force around the world, asking everyone to pray for Chloe, her family, and her friends. *And keep looking for anyone who may not have taken the mark of Carpathia.*

Everyone gathered in the main cabin in Wisconsin and prayed. Janie asked God to keep Chloe from giving any information that might hurt the Tribulation Force. Conrad prayed that no one would be captured in the rescue attempt, if there was one. Josey pulled her son to her chest and asked God to help little Kenny, who was without his mother.

Mark bit his lip. "And, God, whatever your will is, give us the courage to accept it."

---

Judd followed Otto closely as they crept into the palace of Nicolae Carpathia. It helped Judd to know that Nicolae and his top people were miles away in Al Hillah, but he still felt creepy walking the same halls and riding the same elevator as Nicolae and his aides.

There were no people in the halls. Somehow they had adjusted to the darkness and were trying to get back to work.

Otto pushed the button for the executive offices, and Judd rode the elevator up with him. Otto led him to the main office where Nicolae Carpathia's secretary, Krystall, sat talking on the phone.

"No, it's still painful, Mom," Krystall said. "I guess we're adjusting, but I can't do anything here except answer the phone. . . . No, they can evidently see fine in Al Hillah and don't have to follow his glow around anymore."

Otto pushed the door open slightly and it creaked.

Krystall sat up, her eyes wide. "I'm sorry, Mom. I need to go. Someone's here. Mmm-hmm. Bye."

"Krystall, don't be alarmed," Otto said. "I'm a friend of Rayford. I have a young man with me."

"What are you doing here?"

"I've been asked to speak to you."

"Is this about Rayford's daughter?" Krystall said.

"Yes, her location."

Krystall took a breath. "All I know is Angola Prison in Louisiana."

"Okay, I'll tell them. And the other thing is any information—"

The phone rang and Krystall jumped. "This might be the security chief, Akbar. He was supposed to call." She pointed a finger to the corner. "There's a phone over there if you want to listen."

Judd rushed to it and picked up as Krystall grabbed her own receiver. Judd held the receiver so Otto could hear too.

"This is Krystall."

"Krystall, Chief Akbar. Are you still in the dark there?"

"Yes, sir, as much as ever."

"All right. I have an update for you, if you'll take this down."

"Excuse me, sir, but how am I supposed to take it down?"

"Don't you have a system worked out yet? You could contact someone outside New Babylon and have them transcribe this message and send it out."

"Yes, sir, but—go ahead, I'll remember it."

"Good. Tell the ten heads of state that the government is up and running here in Al Hillah. We will not be deterred by these tricks of the enemy. They must know that we are in control of the situation."

"Yes, sir."

"Also, communicate to them that they should prepare for a meeting and celebration in Baghdad six months from now. Everyone is working on the preparations. The potentate wants this to be a great display with flags, banners, light shows. They have invited the singer Z-Van to be part of it, as well as other bands."

"This assumes the darkness will be gone—"

"If we figure out how to counteract this terrorist plot of darkness, we will all return to New Babylon. But no matter what happens, this meeting and celebration will take place in Baghdad."

"And where in Baghdad, may I ask?"

"At the new building—where the Iraq Museum used to be before the war."

"Yes, I know it."

"Everything will be first-class, state-of-the-art. The meetings at this venue will of course be closed, but the potentate wants some of the festivities open to the public. We'll have the media covering this as well, so we need to make accommodations for them."

"Yes, sir."

"And one more thing, Krystall. Make sure you communicate that at this meeting we will discuss the final solution to the Jewish problem."

Otto elbowed Judd and grimaced. When Krystall was finished, Otto thanked her for letting them listen. "Is there anything we can do for you?"

"Just leave quickly and quietly. I don't want anyone knowing you were here."

Otto's phone rang and he stepped into the hall.

Judd stayed in the office while Krystall fumbled through a desk drawer. "Can I help you find something?" he said.

Krystall jumped, then settled. "I'm looking for a voice recorder I had in the top drawer. I thought I'd record what I can remember of Suhail's message, then phone someone to transcribe it."

Judd moved behind the desk and quickly found the recorder.

Otto came back inside. "Krystall, one more question. Your information about Chloe Williams. Is that from inside knowledge or just from the news?"

"Both," Krystall said. "I did see the newscast, but I also heard Security and Intelligence people talking about Chloe being there. The latest information I had was that she was to be executed at 1000 hours Central Time."

# 15

**VICKI** awoke a couple of hours before they touched down in Petra, and Lionel caught her up on what he had heard from Mac and Zeke. "From what Mac says, it doesn't look good for Chloe."

"What about Judd?" Vicki said.

"If he's with this Otto guy, Mac's going to pick them up after we land in Petra."

Vicki nodded and breathed a silent prayer of thanks.

"There's something else," Lionel said. "I don't know if you picked this up from reading Scripture, but Mac said Tsion believes New Babylon is going to be destroyed."

Vicki thought of the passage in Revelation 18. It ended with the words: "She will be utterly consumed by fire, for the Lord God who judges her is mighty."

At 2 p.m. local time, Sam Goldberg met the plane and helped Zeke unload his things. Another Trib Force pilot,

Abdullah Smith, had a bigger plane ready for Mac and came for Zeke.

Vicki turned to Mac before he left. "Be careful."

"You bet," Mac said. "Like I just told Zeke, I hope to get back here before the GCNN goes on the air with Chloe—assuming everything we've heard is true."

Sam took Vicki and Lionel into the camp. The sight of Petra took Vicki's breath away. The red rocks seemed to reach into the sky. And seeing a million people spread out in the camp, knowing they were all believers who had been protected by God, gave Vicki a feeling of safety she'd never felt.

"Lionel will stay with me," Sam said. "Vicki, you will have your own place."

"I don't need—"

"It's already been settled. I talked with Mr. Stein and he said Tsion and Dr. Rosenzweig want to see you, but after this thing with the American woman is settled."

"What have you heard about Chloe?" Vicki said.

"We think the Global Community is setting a trap for the Trib Force in a place called Louisiana. I overheard Chang and Naomi talking earlier. Chang has the ability now to interfere with GC broadcasts."

"Are they going to televise Chloe's execution?" Vicki shuddered. It was a spectacle Vicki never wanted to see, but if her sister in Christ was going to be killed, Vicki wanted to witness the woman's last moments on earth.

As they walked farther, a robed figure walked toward them, the sun at his back. When they got closer, Vicki recognized Mr. Stein and hugged him.

"We've prayed for you for so long," Mr. Stein said, "and now you're here."

Vicki nodded. "Now we should pray for Judd."

---

Judd stood at a secluded spot near the New Babylon runway with about thirty other believers from Otto's group. Zvi had become so scared he would be arrested that he, Westin, Gunther, and some others decided to take their chances driving a school bus through the desert. Before they had left, Westin shook hands with Judd and smiled. "Hope I can attend your wedding at Petra, but if not, I'll be thinking about you."

Otto was now back at the palace for one last trip. As the plane circled for a landing, Otto returned, his face white.

"What's wrong?" Judd said.

"I went to thank Krystall for her help and found her body."

"She's dead? What happened?"

"I don't know. She was on the floor and the phone was buzzing. Perhaps the GC found out she was giving us information."

Judd shook his head. "Sounds like something Carpathia would do." He looked around at the sidewalks and doorways of the airport. There were dead bodies lying around. Some people were still alive, and Judd wanted to help them. They called out for food or water.

"I've got a question," Judd said. "Wasn't there supposed to be an angel or something that warned us to get out of here?"

"I guess it hasn't occurred yet," Otto said.

"Which means there must be more believers here than us," Judd said.

Otto nodded. "Yes, there are some who elected not to go with us, so they will somehow need to get out of here with the help . . ."

The plane engines drowned out the rest of Otto's words. When the plane stopped and Mac let down the stairs, the people with Otto tried to individually thank Mac, but he tried to keep them moving up the stairs.

When Mac saw Judd, he grinned and slapped Judd's back. "I dropped off a redhead in Petra. Get on the plane, boy. I'm taking you home."

Judd couldn't help laughing as he got on the plane. As Mac and Otto spoke at the bottom of the stairs, a sense of peace came over him. During his stay in New Babylon, he hadn't let himself think of the next day. He simply survived minute by minute. Now his thoughts turned to Petra and who was waiting for him.

---

Vicki joined Lionel and hundreds of thousands at the huge video display on the side of a mountain. Sam Goldberg explained that they normally didn't watch executions, but Tsion had asked everyone to be in prayer for Chloe and believed they should show the coverage.

Vicki thought of Buck, Rayford, and Kenny and wondered if they were watching. Surely they wouldn't let the little boy see such a horrible sight.

When Vicki arrived, Chloe was being led through the

gauntlet of reporters and the crowd. People cheered and clapped. The camera zoomed in on Chloe, and Vicki caught her breath. Even with the drab prison clothing she looked radiant.

The camera panned away, and Vicki noticed prisoners with the Star of David stenciled onto their clothes. These were Jews who had been starved, beaten, and tortured. They looked almost relieved to be nearing death.

The GC man in charge, Jock Ashmore, was introduced to the delight of the crowd. "We have thirty-six executions to carry out for you today," he said, "twenty-one for murder, ten for refusing to take the mark of loyalty, four for miscellaneous crimes against the state, and one for all those charges and many, many more."

The crowd went wild.

"I am happy to say that though Mrs. Chloe Steele Williams did not in the end agree to accept the mark of loyalty to our supreme potentate, she did provide us with enough detailed information on her counterparts throughout the world to help us virtually wipe out the Judah-ites outside of Petra and to put an end to the black-market co-op."

The crowd clapped and cheered again.

Vicki couldn't believe they were actually going to show all thirty-six executions live. All around her, people prayed softly. Some wept.

Vicki heard the screaming engines of a plane and looked at Lionel. They both jumped up and ran down the hill with Sam.

Judd was never happier to be back on the ground than when he stepped off the plane in Petra. As he helped the others find their way to the narrow entrance to the ancient city, he saw Sam, Lionel, and Vicki running toward him.

"What are you waiting for?" Mac said. "Go on!"

Judd waved as he ran, whooping and hollering. Sam and Lionel slowed, and Vicki reached Judd and threw her arms around him. She put her lips close to Judd's ear, and Judd could feel her hot tears on his face.

"You're back! You're finally back, and we're never going to be separated again!"

"You got that right," Judd said. "From now on, wherever I go, you go."

Judd ran alongside Vicki as Sam and Lionel took the lead. Instead of going to the big screen, Sam led them to the computer center. Chang Wong stared at a computer, and Naomi was behind him, her hands on his shoulders.

Chang and Naomi welcomed them and had them sit at a screen near the front. "The elders and some others are together in the back," Chang said. "Did you hear about what just happened?"

"I just got here," Judd said.

"The head of this whatever you call it, Jock something, was about to execute ten people in a row who had refused to take the mark. But before he could . . ." Chang paused and clicked on a computer. "I'll show you."

While the main feed continued, Judd watched a replay of what had happened. Something bright appeared in the middle of the courtyard, and an angel towered over Jock and the others. Judd guessed the angel had to be at least fifteen feet tall. His clothes were so white the crowd had to shield their eyes.

The camera shook when the angel spoke. "I come in the name of the most high God," he began. "Hearken unto my voice and hear my words. Ignore me at your peril. 'Oh, that men would give thanks to the Lord for His goodness, and for His wonderful works to the children of men!'

"For He satisfies the longing soul and fills the hungry soul with goodness. You who sit in darkness and in the shadow of death are bound in affliction because you rebelled against the words of God and despised the counsel of the Most High.

"Cry out to the Lord in your trouble, and he will save you out of your distress. He will bring you out of darkness and the shadow of death and break your chains in pieces.

"Thus says the Son of the most high God: 'I am the resurrection and the life. He who believes in Me, though he may die, he shall live. And whoever lives and believes in Me shall never die.'

"But woe to you who do not heed my warning this day. Thus says the Lord: 'If anyone worships the beast and his image, and receives his mark on his forehead or on his hand, he himself shall also drink of the wine of the wrath of God, which is poured out full strength into the cup of His indignation. He shall be tormented with fire and brimstone in the presence of the holy angels and in the presence of the Lamb.

143

" 'And the smoke of their torment ascends forever and ever; and they have no rest day or night, who worship the beast and his image, and whoever receives the mark of his name.' "

"Incredible," Vicki said, as Chang switched back to the live feed.

"I was ready to pull Chloe's execution off the air, but this is too good," Chang said. "God is even using this terrible event to reach people."

Chang and Naomi excused themselves and moved farther into the bowels of the center. Judd wished he could talk with Tsion Ben-Judah, but he knew this wasn't the time or place.

"I don't get it," Vicki said. "If there's an angel there, surely he could rescue Chloe. It doesn't seem fair."

Sam shook his head. "Why have any of us been saved or rescued? God has helped us, but others he has allowed to go through the fire. Who can know God's purposes?"

Judd put an arm around Vicki. "And we have to trust him, no matter what happens to Chloe or to us."

Though the leader of the executions had tried to tell the crowd not to worry about the angel, calling it a trick, the people looked frightened.

A short while later the executions continued with the deaths of what looked like seven true believers being beheaded at once. But just as the blades were about to come down, the screen filled with such a bright light that no one could see.

"We will not be delayed by this trick of the enemy!" Jock said and counted to three. The heavy blades dropped, and the people cheered, but no one could see the actual beheadings.

For the next half hour, the schedule continued and it seemed the angel had vanished. Judd, Lionel, Vicki, and Sam joined hands and prayed for Chloe.

When the others had all been executed, Judd put an arm around Vicki. "You don't have to watch this."

"I know, but I feel like it's the least I can do for her."

Suddenly the angel appeared again and Chloe grabbed the microphone. "A famous martyr once said he regretted he had but one life to give," Chloe began softly. "That is how I feel today. On the cross, dying for the sins of the world, my own Savior, Jesus the Christ, prayed, 'Father, forgive them, for they do not know what they do.'

"My personal preference? My choice? I wish I could stay with my family, my loved ones, my friends, until the glorious appearing of Jesus, who is coming yet again. But if this is my lot, I accept it. I want to express my undying love to my husband and to my son. And eternal thanks to my father, who led me to Christ.

"A famous missionary statesman, eventually martyred, once wrote, 'He is no fool who gives what he cannot keep to gain what he cannot lose.' He was talking about his life on earth versus eternal life with God. In my flesh I do not look forward to a death the likes of which you have already witnessed thirty-five times here today. But to tell you the truth, in my spirit, I cannot wait. For to be absent from the body is to be present with the Lord. And as Jesus himself said to his Father at his own death, 'Into Your hands I commit My spirit.'

"And now, 'according to my earnest expectation and hope that in nothing I shall be ashamed, but with all boldness, as always, so now also Christ will be magnified in my body, whether by life or by death. For to me, to live is Christ, and to die is gain. . . . For I am hard pressed between the two, having a desire to depart and be with Christ, which is far better.'

"And to my compatriots in the cause of God around the world, I say, 'Let this mind be in you which was also in Christ Jesus, who, being in the form of God, did not consider it robbery to be equal with God, but made Himself of no reputation, taking the form of a bondservant, and coming in the likeness of men. And being found in appearance as a man, He humbled Himself and became obedient to the point of death, even the death of the cross.

"'Therefore God also has highly exalted Him and given Him the name which is above every name, that at the name of Jesus every knee should bow, of those in heaven, and of those on earth, and of those under the earth, and that every tongue should confess that Jesus Christ is Lord, to the glory of God the Father.

"'Now to Him who is able to do exceedingly abundantly above all that we ask or think, according to the power that works in us . . . and to present us faultless before the presence of His glory with exceeding joy, to God our Savior, who alone is wise, be glory and majesty, dominion and power, both now and forever.' "

Vicki wiped away a tear. Judd was holding her tightly with one arm and the other he had around Lionel's shoulder.

"Buck and our precious little one," Chloe continued, "know that I love you and that I will be waiting just inside the Eastern Gate."

Chloe put the microphone down and walked to one of the guillotines. The camera followed her slowly as she knelt and laid her head under the blade. Then a glow of white light shone so bright that no one saw the blade come down and end Chloe's life on earth.

# 16

**THE FIRST** thing Vicki wanted to do after the broadcast was see Chloe's son, Kenny. She found him with Chang's sister, Ming Toy. Kenny came to Vicki right away, and she held him tightly for a long time. The boy was still asking where his mother was and when he would see her.

"Buck should be here tomorrow," Ming whispered to Vicki.

Kenny reached for Vicki's hand, and she sang him songs and helped him get to sleep that night, with the promise of exploring Petra in the morning.

When daylight came, Vicki, Judd, and Kenny walked along the rocks and watched the people gather manna.

Vicki could tell Judd was shocked by what had happened to Chloe, but they didn't want to talk about it in front of Kenny.

Later in the morning Kenny rode with Ming to meet the plane that touched down on the runway. A man staggered from the aircraft, grabbed Kenny, and held him tight. Vicki grabbed binoculars and saw it was his father, Buck.

Vicki ached to hear some kind of teaching from Tsion. She couldn't think of anything that would give more comfort than Dr. Ben-Judah, and she didn't have to wait long. As soon as Buck, Rayford, and the others reached the camp, Tsion called them all together.

Several hundred gathered at the high place, within the sound of rushing water from the stream. Zeke, Vicki, Lionel, and Judd stood with other friends from Illinois who had known Chloe personally. Kenny's arms were still wrapped around Buck's neck as Buck walked forward. When he saw Vicki and Judd, he managed a slight smile and touched her shoulder. Then he sat on a rock shelf and took in the scene.

Tsion held up his Bible and talked about his study of it the past few years. He said he could see God's finger-prints on every page. "I love this book! I love this Word! I love its author, and I love the Lord it represents. Why do I speak of the Word of God today when we have come with heavy, heavy hearts to remember two dear comrades and loved ones?

"Because both Albie and Chloe were people of the Word. Oh, how they loved God's love letter to them and to us! Albie would be the first to tell you he was not a scholar, hardly a reader. He was a man of street smarts, knowledgeable in the ways of the world, quick and shrewd and sharp. But whenever the occasion arose when he could sit under the teaching of the Bible, he took notes, he asked questions, he drank it in. The Word of God was worked out in his life. It changed him. It helped mold him into the man he was the day he died.

"And Chloe, our dear sister and one of the original members of the tiny Tribulation Force that has grown so large today. Who could know her and not love her spirit, her mind, her spunk? What a wife and mother she was! Young yet brilliant, she grew the International Commodity Co-op into an enterprise that literally kept alive millions around the globe who refused the mark of Antichrist and lost their legal right to buy and sell.

"In various safe-house locations over the past half-dozen years, I lived in close proximity to Chloe and to her family. It was common to find her reading her Bible, memorizing verses, trying them out on people. Often she would hand me her Bible and ask me to check her to see if she had a verse correct, word for word. And she always wanted to know exactly what it meant. It was not enough to know the text; she wanted it to come alive in her heart and mind and life.

"To those who will miss Chloe the most, the deepest, and the most painfully until we see her again in glory, I give you the only counsel that kept me sane when my own beloved were so cruelly taken from me. Hold to God's unchanging hand. Cling to his Word. Fall in love with the Word of God anew. Grasp his promises like a puppy sinks its teeth into your pant legs, and never let go.

"Buck, Kenny, Rayford, we do not understand. We cannot. We are finite beings. The Scripture says knowledge is so fleeting that one day it will vanish. 'For we know in part and we prophesy in part. But when that which is perfect has come,' and oh, beloved, it is coming, 'then that which is in part will be done away.

" 'When I was a child, I spoke as a child, I understood as a child, I thought as a child; but when I became a man, I put away childish things. For now we see in a mirror, dimly, but then face to face.'

"Did you hear that promise? 'But then . . .' How we can rejoice in the *but thens* of God's Word! The *then* is coming, dear ones! The *then* is coming."

Vicki wept through the rest of the service, thinking of Chloe and her family.

---

A few days later, Ming Toy and a pilot named Ree Woo were married. Not wanting to take away from the memorial service or Ming and Ree's wedding, Judd and Vicki spent a few more days waiting and preparing.

When the time came, Chang Wong linked by video with the group in Wisconsin so they could see the ceremony. Judd and Vicki had chosen a beautiful spot overlooking the spring of water. Everyone said Vicki looked lovely in her dress. When Vicki saw Judd, she tried to keep from crying but couldn't. She wished her family could have been there to share the moment. She wished she could have met Judd's mom and dad.

They had written their own vows and both wept openly as they read their words to each other. Tsion spoke for a few minutes and challenged both Judd and Vicki to give their love to each other and their lives to

God. "We do not know exactly what the next year will bring, but my prayer for you is that you would both grow in the grace of our Lord, until he comes again."

As the ceremony ended, manna fell. For the first time, Judd showed Vicki the home he had prepared.

"It's not much, but it's ours," Judd said as he picked Vicki up and carried her into the small dwelling.

**17**

**LIONEL** Washington smiled as he sat in front of a computer deep in a cave in Petra. He still couldn't believe that Judd and Vicki were married. He had been with them just after they had first met in Mount Prospect, and he would have never guessed they would wind up together. He replayed video from the ceremony a few days earlier and shook his head. *God worked this out,* he thought.

Chang Wong had set Lionel up with the computer and showed him how to access the Global Community's vast network. With a few clicks of the mouse, Lionel listened in on one of Nicolae Carpathia's secret meetings, or heard what was going on in the control room at the Global Community News Network. Chang had even given him software to control the computer with his voice, but Lionel preferred the old-fashioned way.

Lionel touched the stump of his left arm and counted the months since his accident in Indiana. He wasn't having nightmares as much, but he still found it hard to get to sleep. Sometimes he stayed up all night at the computer, trying to figure out what would happen next on God's timetable.

He had renewed his friendship with Sam Goldberg and Mr. Stein, eating manna and quail with them just about every day. But Lionel had to admit he longed for his friends back in the States. It was strange. He was in the safest place on earth, supernaturally protected by God from Carpathia and his growing armies, but Lionel longed for Wisconsin.

In a way, he felt useless and pitied. When assignments were handed out, Lionel was always given the soft jobs or nothing at all. He wanted to build things or help with chores, but he often found himself back at the computer alone.

As the yellow glow of the rising sun peeked through the opening to the cave, Lionel yawned and stretched. People would gather manna soon. Little kids would run through the camp. He loved playing with them, especially Kenny Williams, but Kenny spent most of his time with Buck now, asking questions about his mother.

Instead of heading for bed, Lionel clicked on the link for the Global Community in the United North American States. Things had gotten worse there in the past few days. The GC seemed to be taking out their frustration about the darkness in New Babylon on those without the mark. Reports of people being dragged from hiding places and executed had increased.

Lionel winced as he pulled up a report from GCNN

detailing another raid on what looked like a militia hide-out in Minnesota, fifty miles west of the Mississippi River. These people didn't have the mark of the believer or of Carpathia. They were hauled from their underground hiding place and herded onto trucks.

The camera focused on a smiling Commander Kruno Fulcire, head of the Rebel Apprehension Program. "We're very pleased with the level of cooperation from the people of this community," he said.

"How did you know they were here?" a reporter asked.

"We actually had a tip from family members of one of the unmarked. They, of course, will receive the full reward offered to those who help uncover rebels."

"Will there be more arrests and executions in this part of the country?" the reporter said.

Fulcire squinted. "I can't give that information, but we hope to have significant developments in the coming days."

Lionel sat forward and pulled up a map of the region. The site of the arrests wasn't that far from the Avery, Wisconsin, hideout. He quickly sent a warning message to Mark and the others.

———

Mark Eisman held his head in his hands while several people filed out of the main cabin in Wisconsin. Maggie Carlson put a hand on his shoulder before she left. Others weren't so kind, with mean looks and whispers.

Marshall Jameson paced in front of the computer. "I

understand your feelings, Mark. I've wanted to start a rebel radio station to tell people the truth, but some things are too dangerous."

"Why are we so concerned about staying safe?" Mark said. "Isn't it more important to get the message out?"

Conrad Graham slapped his hands on his knees. "If that's your goal, I might go along with you, but you're talking about fighting the GC. What could you possibly accomplish?"

"You saw what they did to Chloe," Mark said. "If somebody had tried to take those Peacekeepers out before they caught her, she wouldn't have lost her head."

"Reports from the Trib Force say she went outside trying to protect her family and friends," Marshall said. "But a rescue mission would have backfired. They didn't even know where she was."

Conrad stood. "I hate just sitting here as much as you do, but if you go out there, we'll be seeing your face flashed on TV."

"You guys don't need me," Mark said. "We have enough people to staff the Web site twenty-four hours a day with people left over."

"Okay, so what do you want to do?" Marshall said.

"Find those RAP people, Fulcire if I can, and give them a dose of their own medicine." Mark glanced at Conrad, then at Marshall. "If you want to know the truth, I've already packed my stuff."

Colin Dial sat in the corner. He cleared his throat and said, "What if we could find a way to get you closer to the action?" Marshall frowned but Colin held up a hand. "I don't want to see him get into trouble, but if he could get closer to the main headquarters, south of Chicago, maybe he could do some good before this is all over."

"What was the name of the lady and her son living near Chicago?" Marshall said. "The one Vicki and you guys met at the schoolhouse."

"Lenore?" Conrad said.

"That's right!" Mark said. "She was staying southwest of Chicago, wasn't she?"

"I've got her number on my cell," Conrad said, handing a phone to Mark.

Mark punched the Redial button and waited. He heard a weird noise but no dial tone. "Something's wrong with it."

Mark found Lenore's e-mail address and looked through past messages to Vicki and the group. He quickly wrote her and sent the message.

---

Vicki awoke to sunshine peeking through the lone window of her and Judd's small dwelling. They couldn't call it a house, but it wasn't a shack either. There was enough room for a nice-sized bed, a cabinet to hold their clothes, a computer desk, and a small table.

Vicki noticed Judd was gone and smiled. There was no question where he was.

She lay back and stretched. Being married was a lot different than she had thought. There had already been disagreements to work through. Her childhood image of "happily ever after" was gone. Marriage was truly a lot of work.

Vicki thought of her friends in Wisconsin. They had seen the ceremony via computer, but it wasn't the same as being there. She would have liked Shelly and Melinda and Janie to be bridesmaids, but that had been out of the question. Life wasn't normal and never would be again. But within a few months Jesus would return. Vicki had lived the past six and a half years yearning for him to come back and set things right. Now she would experience the event with her husband.

*Husband,* Vicki thought. The word made her shoulders tremble.

There was a slight knock and Judd entered. "Ready for breakfast in bed?"

Vicki chuckled. "Are you going to do this every day until Jesus comes back?"

Judd smiled, set down a pitcher of cool water, and handed her a plate filled with fresh manna. "Wouldn't be a bad job," he said, sitting cross-legged on the bed. "You sleep okay?"

Vicki nodded. "Though it took a while last night. I kept thinking about lunch today. Have you heard anything from Dr. Ben-Judah?"

"I guess we'll hear something if it's off."

Vicki had figured she would get tired of eating the same food, but each morning the honey wafers tasted great. She recalled advertisements for restaurants that claimed their donuts or croissants melted in your mouth, but the manna literally dissolved on her tongue. It was light, flaky, and tasted good any time of the day. Vicki wondered if God had put extra vitamins in the food to satisfy their hunger.

"You know, we could have made a lot of money if we'd have gotten this recipe before the Tribulation started," Vicki said. "Even people who were overweight when they came here have lost pounds eating this."

"Just shows that God's food is best," Judd said, taking a bite of a wafer. He put the plate down and wiped his hands. "I know you might be tired of hearing this, but you've made me the happiest guy in Petra."

Vicki smiled. "I never get tired of hearing that. But sometimes . . ."

"What?"

"Well, I look at Buck Williams who lost Chloe and Dr. Ben-Judah who lost his wife and children. I see their pain and almost feel guilty for feeling . . . happy."

"I know what you mean. I met a guy yesterday who lost his brother and dad to the false messiah's vipers. Every day he wakes up knowing they're never coming back."

"I met a woman a few days ago who has family in Jerusalem. She doesn't think they've taken Carpathia's mark, but there's no way to tell. She can't reach them."

"Maybe we can bring this up with Dr. Ben-Judah," Judd said.

They finished breakfast, then took a long walk to the fountain. It was one of Vicki's favorite things to do—walk hand in hand with Judd around the sprawling camp, watching people, looking at the rock formations, meeting new friends. Vicki couldn't imagine being any happier.

---

Mark rolled his clothes and a small supply of food into his sleeping bag and tied it tightly. He slipped a gun Zeke had left behind into his pocket, but Mark knew there was no way he could overpower the GC. He would have to outsmart them rather than outgun them.

As he moved his things outside, he noticed Charlie standing by the window. The crisp, fall air was cool, and he could see Charlie's breath. "You want to come inside?"

Charlie nodded and entered, pulling his hooded sweatshirt over his head. He looked at the floor and blinked.

"What's up?" Mark said.

"I heard what you're thinking about doing," Charlie said, pawing at the floor with a foot.

"And?"

"And I wish you'd stay."

"Charlie—"

"But if you won't, I want to go with you."

Mark put a hand on Charlie's shoulder. "I'm sure I could use the help—but not this time."

"You know the GC are mean people, putting Chloe in that head chopper and all. They won't stop, and if they catch you . . . I think something bad's going to happen."

"Nothing's going to happen to me," Mark said. "I hope we'll all be together at the Glorious Appearing. I want to be standing right next to you when Jesus comes back."

Charlie looked up. "You really think we'll make it to then?"

"I'm planning on it."

Charlie helped carry Mark's things to one of the abandoned cars parked in the woods, then said good-bye.

---

Lionel stared at the computer screen, trying to figure out what he had found. An e-mail sent from an aide to Kruno Fulcire to the GC supreme commander updated the progress of the raids. Much of it was straightforward, with statistics about the number of prisoners and the execution schedule. But a line at the bottom included numbers and letters that looked like gibberish.

Chang walked in and Lionel stood. "Glad you're here. Take a look at this."

Chang sat and studied the screen. "Good catch. Have you talked to your friends in Avery?"

"I e-mailed them and even made a call, but I can't get through. I saw that GCNN was predicting some kind of satellite interference for the northern part of the States."

Chang shook his head. "No way. They must be jamming that area for some reason. When did you send your e-mail?"

"About forty minutes ago," Lionel said as Chang punched information into the computer.

"Look at this," Chang said. "The GC intercepted your message. It never got to your friends."

"What? How could they—?"

Chang clicked on the e-mail from Kruno Fulcire's aide. He pointed at the bottom of the screen. "See this?

163

It's code for the higher-ups. I think they've finally broken into the Young Trib Force Web site."

"No," Lionel gasped.

"That's not the worst news. Looks like the GC has a location for your friends. If we don't alert them, they're dead."

# 18

**MARK** shook hands with Marshall and hugged the others who had returned to the main cabin. Tanya Spivey thanked him for what he had done for her, her brother, and the rest of the group from the cave. Conrad patted Mark's back. Mark noticed Josey Fogarty wiping a tear away. He hugged little Ryan and patted his head, then moved outside.

Shelly was waiting. "We haven't always seen eye to eye on things," she said.

"I've been hardheaded. I'm sorry for the stuff I did that hurt you."

Shelly nodded. "This reminds me a little of when you went with the militia. Are you sure it's the right thing to do?"

Mark sighed. "I'm a militia of one now. No, I'm not sure this is right, but I just can't stay and wonder anymore." He glanced at the people coming out of the cabin and leaned close to Shelly. "You've been a good friend to me and the others. I've been talking with Conrad. He's a great guy. Give him another chance."

Shelly nodded and gave Mark a hug. Then he was off to the small car. The two-seater was perfect for him, fast enough to escape the GC in case he got in trouble but small enough to be able to hide in a pinch.

Mark checked his phone again and dialed Lenore's number. Nothing. She hadn't answered his e-mail, but he couldn't wait. He had general directions to her area, so he would try to get as close as he could before sunup and make contact then. He put on his night-vision goggles and kept the headlights off.

He glanced in the rearview mirror and saw his friends waving. Mark wondered when he would see them again.

---

Lionel hit the redial on his phone and got the same sound. Chang said the GC could jam certain cell or satellite phones, and it was possible they were moving in on the Wisconsin group.

Judd and Vicki rushed inside the cavern with worried looks. "Naomi told us what's going on," Vicki said. "Have you gotten through?"

Lionel shook his head. "No phone, no Internet. And if the GC has control of the Web site, we can say good-bye to reaching out to people. They'll trash it as soon as they raid the hideout."

Chang hurried over and handed Lionel a printout. "I intercepted this from the United North American States. It was sent to the supreme commander about ten minutes ago."

Lionel scanned the paper. At the top was a string of letters and numbers. In the middle of the page was the message:

> We continue to have great success rooting out rebels and would like to present the potentate with something spectacular today. We believe we have discovered a nest of Judah-ites hiding in rural Wisconsin. They have gone virtually undetected the past few months. We have also been able to tap into their Web site. We hope to have these rebels in custody by morning and turn the Web site into a tool for our cause. We will have them singing "Hail Carpathia" before the morning is out.

Lionel slammed the paper on the table, picked up the phone, and dialed Wisconsin again. He still couldn't get through.

"What are we going to do?" Vicki said. "We have to warn them!"

"If I can reverse the jam on the phones we could call them," Chang said.

"Do it," Judd said.

---

Mark drove slowly down the narrow dirt road that led away from the campground. The road was little more than a path and had deep ruts from recent rains. The small car scraped bottom several times, and Mark was glad when he reached gravel.

A few minutes later he was on a paved road. He checked his map and headed west, hoping to hit a north/ south route a few miles farther. Mark settled in behind the wheel and adjusted his goggles. In this part of the country he usually saw dead animals along the road, but there were none. He did notice the barren countryside, burned-up trees, and scorched shrubs. Looking through the goggles, a stream running through the hills looked like a long, green scar.

A light flickered on the horizon to Mark's right, and he slowed. It disappeared. *Was that my imagination?* he thought. To make sure, he put the car in neutral and coasted to a stop. He watched for any movement on the horizon but saw nothing.

As he pulled back onto the road, the light flickered again, and a line of vehicles rounded the hillside. He quickly gunned the car toward the stream and looked for a place to hide. His tires spun in the soggy ground, but he managed to keep going until he reached some rocks.

As the vehicles rumbled nearer, Mark got out and scampered toward the road. He was glad he had worn dark clothing, and he hunkered down behind a tree to watch the convoy.

The line of Humvees stopped a hundred yards away. A sleek, black truck opened, and several people got out. Definitely GC. But what were they doing here? Mark was too far away to hear, so he crept forward, duckwalking and trying to stay quiet. His goggles let him zoom in on the people, and Mark gasped when he recognized Commander Kruno Fulcire.

". . . heat imaging showed they were in this area, but we need specifics," Fulcire said into a radio.

There was a pause, and then a man on the radio broke in. "We'll have those for you in just a moment, Commander."

Mark's heart raced. Specifics for what? Had the GC finally discovered their hideout?

He had to think quickly. There was no way he could start the car and race the GC back to his friends. They were sure to hear him and follow. Unless . . .

The radio crackled with a report from the satellite operator, and Mark returned to his car. He had driven several miles from the camp, but he guessed it was only a two- or three-mile trip through the forest.

Mark grabbed the phone and dialed Marshall.

Nothing.

Mark looked around the car's interior. He had ammunition, enough to keep the GC busy for a few minutes, but his main job now was to warn his friends.

He noticed the plastic gas can behind the passenger seat. Marshall had placed one in each of their vehicles in case they had to make a quick getaway and ran out of gas. Mark glanced at Fulcire and crew. He had to act fast.

---

Judd followed Vicki and Naomi through a maze of computers and workers. Since the beginning of the setup in Petra, Naomi had grown in influence as a first-rate

169

computer operator, then as a teacher. She was the daughter of one of the elders at Petra, Eleazar Tiberius. She not only had technical knowledge, but she also helped teach workers how to answer spiritual questions on Tsion's Web site, which was read by as many as a billion people every day. There were now thousands of computers and counselors spread out through the camp.

"How did Dr. Ben-Judah hear about the situation?" Vicki asked, struggling to keep pace with Naomi.

"I talked with my father, and he mentioned it to the rabbi," Naomi said. "He asked me to get you and move your meeting up from lunch."

Tsion smiled and welcomed them to his tiny living room. "Please, sit. Is there further news?"

"Chang and Lionel are working on getting in touch with our friends," Judd said.

"It's so hard when we're this far away and can't do anything," Vicki added.

Tsion clenched his teeth. "We felt the same way with Chloe. I have a feeling we are going to be doing more mourning in the days to come. Oh—" He put up a hand— "I did not mean that your friends will be harmed, but evil is rising. Antichrist and his followers are desperate."

"We understand," Judd said. "It's just that we know angels warn people. Is there any reason why God couldn't do something like that now?"

"God's ways are God's ways. I do not presume to understand why he chooses to keep some from the blade while others are taken from us. I do not understand why he chose me to lead a million people here, but I am grateful he made me part of his plan. I do not think there is any harm in asking him to act—in fact, I think he wants us to. So let us pray now that he will use some angel or human to save your friends and keep them safe."

---

Mark rushed to the stream and up a hill to a grove of charred trees. Behind him the vehicles pulled out and continued. "Come on," he whispered.

He had reached a knoll when a terrific blast shattered the night. Flames shot into the air, then another explosion. Mark had stuffed a rag in the gasoline can, lit it, and placed it under his car's gas tank.

The lead truck in the convoy stopped, and several troops jumped out, weapons ready. An officer shouted something, and the last vehicle turned sideways on the road. Mark didn't wait to see what would happen. He scrambled over the knoll, got his bearings, and headed for the camp.

He kept dialing the phone as he ran but couldn't get through. Depending on how long the GC remained occupied by the burning car, Mark had a chance of getting to his friends.

---

Vicki felt better just hearing Tsion's voice. His prayer showed a deep reverence for God, yet she could tell how much God was his friend. When Judd prayed, Vicki felt the emotion. There was something about talking with God together that touched her.

171

When they had finished, Tsion asked about their home and how their marriage was going.

Judd said they were getting along fine and asked if Tsion had any advice about what to do when they disagreed on certain issues.

"I hope you do disagree," Dr. Ben-Judah said. "You have two different perspectives. But the beauty of a relationship built on God's love is that he has brought you together to make you one. This does not mean that you won't fight about certain things, but if you did not have conflict, you would never have the opportunity to grow and learn and change. I suspect you will mature as believers more in these last six months than you have the last six years."

"Did you have fights with your wife?" Vicki said.

Tsion laughed. "We had pouting sessions at first. I would get hurt and pout for a few days. Then she would get hurt and pout for a week. She was much better at pouting than I was, let me tell you. But as we grew together, and especially after we became believers in Jesus, I saw our relationship change." He sat back and closed his eyes. "Oh, how I long to speak with her and ask her advice on things. But then I won't have to wait long for that, will I?"

"You mean when Jesus comes back to set up his kingdom, right?" Vicki said.

"Yes. I am confident that I will see my wife again and that we will have quite a reunion, along with my two children. How I long for those who have not yet believed in the message to do so. As you know, there are some

172

who have come into Petra lately who are not believers, and I want them to hear, but I also want people outside to believe a new message God has been impressing on me."

"Why don't you put it on the Web site?" Judd said.

Tsion nodded. "That is one idea I have considered, but I would like to reach even more people, those who haven't stumbled across my teaching on the Internet. I believe God has given me a message he wants even Nicolae and his followers to hear."

"Chang seems to be able to do a lot with the setup here," Vicki said. "Can't you break into international television?"

Tsion scratched his chin. "Hmm. Chang is quite resourceful. I will need to talk with the elders and Captain Steele, but that is an excellent idea."

Judd talked about the fact that he and Vicki almost felt guilty for being so happy when people were mourning.

Tsion smiled. "Joy and sorrow go hand in hand. Do not feel guilty for the good gift God has given. Enjoy each other and praise God with your love."

Judd brought up Vicki's idea about starting an orphanage after Christ's return. "In one of your messages you mentioned there could be many children who go into the kingdom who don't have parents."

"Yes, I believe that will be true," Tsion said.

Vicki blushed when Judd elbowed her. "Well, I was watching a news report about the Junior GC program the other day. There are so many young kids who've been brainwashed by Carpathia. They will need a lot of help, and I was thinking we could—Judd and I—find a place where we could take some kids in and care for them."

"The need will be so great," Tsion said. "I am thankful you are thinking ahead to such a time. The truth is, these children will probably have about a hundred years to decide."

"A hundred years?" Vicki said.

"Ask Naomi to print out the section of my teaching that deals with this. I think you will find it quite helpful."

Before they left, Tsion led them again in prayer for their friends. Vicki thought of little Ryan and the others in Wisconsin and prayed that they would be kept safe.

# 19

**MARK** ran through the forest and realized he didn't recognize anything. He heard the faint crackling of fire behind him and guessed the convoy was still inspecting the explosion. Mark needed to find something familiar—like the road. If he didn't, the GC could locate his friends before he did.

Mark turned to his right. The goggles bounced on his face as he jogged, so he took them off. Without them, he could barely see. He finally put them back on and slowed, making sure he didn't trip over dead branches or dips in the ground.

A thousand thoughts flashed through his mind. His friends had no idea of the danger. He imagined the GC breaking into each cabin and hauling people out. Charlie would be so scared. Mark knew Tom Fogarty kept a gun in his cabin, but what good would it do?

Mark picked up his pace, the night-vision goggles bouncing crazily. It had been a long time since the group had even thought about a GC raid. When they had first arrived, Marshall had conducted surprise drills, but that had been so long ago Mark doubted anyone would remember what to do.

His legs ached from the pounding. He wanted to stop and rest but knew he had to keep going, keep moving toward his friends. He was their only chance of survival.

If he stopped, they died. Simple as that.

Mark felt a rage that pushed him on. He hated Nicolae Carpathia and everything the Global Community stood for. The man had brought such death and destruction to the world, and people still followed him. Mark recalled a different version of "Hail Carpathia" that Judd had sung:

> *Hey, Carpathia, you're not the risen king;*
> *Hey, Carpathia, you don't rule anything.*
> *We'll worship God until we die*
> *And fight against you, Nicolae.*
> *Hey, Carpathia, you're not the risen king.*

Mark chanted the words softly as he ran, moving his feet to the words. He had never been much of a singer, and his cousin John had made fun of him in church once. Mark smiled at the memory. John had been killed at sea by a giant wave, and Mark had never really gotten over John's death. Sure, he had gone on with his life and tried to help others come to know God, but John was always in the back of his mind. What would have happened if he had stayed with the group, instead of heading east and getting drafted by the GC?

There were so many what-ifs in Mark's world. The biggest was what would have happened if he had believed the message *before* the Rapture. He wouldn't have seen all the destruction, plagues, and deaths of friends.

His heart beat wildly and he gasped for air. He searched his mind for some verse of Scripture or words from a song to keep him going, but nothing came.

"God, I don't know why this is happening, and maybe you wanted me to go out tonight because you knew the GC were coming," Mark prayed. "But whatever the reason, you put me here. Now help me reach my friends before it's too late."

---

Lionel clicked on the computer's world-time function and saw it was 3 a.m. in Wisconsin. If the GC carried out their plans, they would catch his friends in the middle of a Bible study, trying to get the Web site running again, or worse, sleeping.

Lionel had never seen anyone work as hard as Chang at trying to override systems, but finally Chang threw up his hands. "I'm sorry, Lionel."

A report from Commander Fulcire had sparked a bit of hope. "Explosion nearby—may be an attack," the report said. But a few minutes later another report dashed Lionel's hopes. "False alarm. Explosion linked to dead Judah-ite's car. Someone may know we're coming, which means we're on the right track. Proceeding to target."

"It's in God's hands now," Chang said.

Lionel shook his head. "I wish there was something more we could do."

Chang put a hand on Lionel's shoulder. "When I was in New Babylon, many times I felt like there was nothing I could do. But I realized the greatest thing any of us can do is pray and ask God to work out his will. You see, God really is *for* us. He wants to help us through difficulties. I used to think he should just take us out of them or solve them for us. But sometimes I think he shows himself greater by walking through our troubles with us. So let's invite him to have his perfect way in your friends' lives and in our lives too."

Lionel nodded, then bowed his head. He prayed first for Mark.

---

A verse finally came to Mark, but it wasn't the one he wanted to think of. *"The greatest love is shown when people lay down their lives for their friends."*

Mark didn't want to lay down his life, though he had seen that done many times in the past six years. He thought of Natalie Bishop who had worked for the GC, Pete Davidson who had led the GC away from the kids, and Chloe Williams.

Mark had watched Chloe's execution with a mix of fascination and horror. The appearance of the angel at the event had raised many questions. Had he spoken with Chloe? Was that where she got the strength to be so bold at the end? And why didn't the angel rescue Chloe and the other believers who were executed?

Mark's right leg stuck in a hole, and he felt a sharp pain behind his knee. He stumbled forward, then fell back, grabbing his leg and screaming. He pulled his foot from the hole and rolled to his left side, holding his leg and rocking.

When he tried to stand he fell. He couldn't imagine taking another step, let alone running the rest of the way.

Something rumbled and the convoy approached. Mark lifted his head and realized he was sitting next to the dirt road leading to the cabins. The ground vibrated as the first Humvee approached, and Mark held his breath. "Keep going," he whispered, putting his head back and closing his eyes.

Mark expected to hear brakes squeal, but the vehicles roared past. *They missed the entrance!* Mark thought. *Maybe they're not after us.*

When the last Humvee passed, Mark struggled to stand. He managed to put his weight on his left leg, but his right felt like a knife was sticking through it. He hopped up to the road and nearly passed out from the pain.

With short steps and hops he started toward the cabins, finding that putting his hand behind his right knee helped. He took off his belt and buckled it around his leg. The pressure seemed to work.

He kept going as quickly as possible. When he reached the trees surrounding the cabins, he left the dirt road and yelled for his friends.

Mark heard a noise to his right—something running. He set the night-vision goggles to macro and saw two eyes rushing for him.

179

Then he heard it. The most wonderful sound in the world!

Phoenix's bark!

"Come here, boy," Mark said, sitting on the ground and gathering the dog in. "Go on back now and make some noise."

He patted Phoenix's back and sent the barking dog away. Mark limped farther and saw a light in the distance from the main cabin. The door opened and someone called Phoenix.

"Help!" Mark hollered.

"Mark?" It was Marshall. "What are you doing?"

"Please, we don't have much time! Come get me."

Marshall and Conrad carried him to the main cabin.

"GC, they passed me on the road. They're coming here."

"How do you know?" Conrad said.

"I don't have time to convince you. Just get everybody out of here."

Conrad nodded and hurried outside.

Marshall sat Mark on a chair and inspected his leg. "You might have torn some ligaments. We're going to need to look at it—"

"We can look at it later," Mark said. "Do we have enough vehicles?"

"We should. What happened to the car you took?"

Mark told him.

Marshall scratched his chin. "We have the 15-passenger, another minivan, and some smaller—"

"Get them ready," Mark said.

Tom Fogarty rushed inside. "I have Josey and Ryan in the van. Everybody else is gathering."

Marshall handed him the keys. "Start it up while I help Mark to the—"

"No," Mark interrupted. "I'm going alone."

"That's crazy!" Marshall said.

"Go! I'm going to torch this place."

"What if it's a false alarm?" Tom said.

"It's not," Mark said. "It might already be too late. Now if you value your wife and son, go."

Tom rushed outside.

"When you get to the main road, go west," Mark said. "And keep your lights off. I'll follow as soon as I'm finished."

Marshall hesitated and Mark pushed him toward the door. "Call Petra. Once you get far enough away from here, a cell might open up. Chang might be able to block the satellites they're using to find us."

"We'll head for Lenore's place," Marshall said. "We'll meet you there." He gave Mark keys to a different car and hurried into the night.

Mark watched Charlie turn and wave. Janie and Shelly smiled at him.

When they finally pulled out, Mark grabbed lighter fluid and poured it on their computers. Anything that might lead the GC to someone inside the Tribulation Force or Young Tribulation Force had to be destroyed. He lit a match in the main cabin, took a deep breath, and threw it on the fluid. With a loud *whomp*, the fire began.

Mark hopped to the next cabin, tossing lighter fluid

and a lit match inside. He knew this would attract the GC, but it had to be done.

Each step was painful, but Mark managed to make it to the end of the row of cabins, lighting fires and getting away. He hobbled back past the main cabin as the fire whistled and cracked. Mark found his car, a diesel, and it chugged to life. He pulled out, the fire lighting up the forest behind him. He pulled onto the path and gunned the engine.

He came to a stop at the main road and pounded his fist on the steering wheel. "Take that, Fulcire!" he whooped.

Mark turned the wheel to the right and started to pull out but stopped. He couldn't leave now. The GC would come back and see the fire, then go after his friends. Maybe there was something more he could do.

He turned around and headed back into the trees. He would figure out some way to delay the GC. Anything for his friends.

# 20

**LIONEL** prayed for those in Wisconsin as Chang clicked his way through the Global Community network.

When Chang got through to GC satellite operations, he gasped. "They've got images of the hideout in Wisconsin!"

The screen showed a wide shot and a glow coming from the ground. Chang zoomed closer. "There's a fire."

Lionel's heart sank. "We're too late."

"Maybe not. I know the GC likes to burn people out, but if they knew this was Young Tribulation Force headquarters, they wouldn't have burned it before they got all the evidence." Chang clicked on another computer and turned. "The latest message from Fulcire is a request for location, not a report that they've caught the rebels."

Lionel glanced at the satellite image. "So you're saying our people might have figured it out and torched the place?"

"It's possible," Chang said. "And if so, they're on the run. Which means we need to lock this thing up so the GC can't track them."

"You can do that?"

Chang smiled. "We can do lots of things." His fingers flashed over the keyboard like lightning as he went deep inside the satellite operation. "They won't even know what hit them."

Five minutes later, Chang clicked his mouse a final time and sat back. "Want to know what they're seeing right now?"

Lionel nodded.

Chang clicked on the satellite image and crossed his arms. A huge, yellow smiley face appeared. Underneath was written, *Temporarily out of service. Thanks for your patience.*

"Awesome," Lionel said.

"Now let's listen in on the satellite control room," Chang said. He clicked a few more keys and brought up audio of people shouting and cursing.

A female worker tried to figure out what had gone wrong. "I don't understand it, sir. One minute I had a bead on these rebels, and then the image was gone."

"Sir, Commander Fulcire is calling!" someone yelled.

The man cleared his throat and punched the speakerphone.

"This is great," Lionel said.

"Commander, we're having some technical difficulties, but my technician said she's tracking your convoy and you've gone past the location. It should be easy for you to locate now. There's a fully engaged fire there."

"We're heading back that way and can see the flames. Can you give me exact coordinates?"

The man replied with a list of numbers Lionel didn't understand. "But with this fire, there's a chance the rebels are on the run."

"Do a heat imaging of the area to see if you can locate any vehicles or people getting away."

"We can't, sir. As I said, we're having some technical difficulties."

"Do you know how long we've been working on this?" Fulcire shouted. "Don't give me technical difficulties. I want answers or heads are going to roll!"

"Yes, sir, we're working on it, sir," the man said. He hollered at the others, trying to motivate them to fix the problem. Everyone seemed angry at the yellow smiley face.

Chang clicked the keyboard again and smiled. "I can't wait to hear what they'll say when they see this."

The smiley face changed to a frowning face. Underneath it were the words, *We're so sorry you're having trouble. Keep a positive attitude and maybe you won't lose your heads.*

Lionel thanked God for David Hassid, who had originally designed this computer center. While Chang worked his magic, trying to keep his friends safe, others answered questions from believers and nonbelievers around the world. It was estimated that a billion people every day got information from Tsion Ben-Judah's Web site, and the many mentors around Chang and Lionel were hard at work with Tsion's cyberaudience twenty-four hours a day.

"Let's just hope this buys our people enough time to get out of there," Chang said.

---

Mark parked the car behind some trees away from the cabins and stumbled to a hiding place. His knee throbbed. The lower part of his leg tingled since the belt had cut off his blood circulation. He sat on the ground, his back to a tree, and tried to stretch his leg, but it only brought more pain.

The fire and smoke glowed against the black sky. Ashes rose overhead, and trees near the cabins caught fire. Branches and needles crackled.

Mark heard a rumbling and noticed the convoy on the main road. Instead of taking the dirt road, which Mark was sure they couldn't see, the convoy went down an embankment and cut across an open field. They finally found the dirt road and drove through the trees to within fifty yards of the burning cabins.

Mark crawled closer to the vehicles while GC officers jumped out to inspect the cabins. The lead vehicle, a smaller black truck, parked closest to the main cabin, and a tall man got out, cursing.

*Fulcire,* Mark thought.

"Check every cabin and the perimeter behind them," Fulcire shouted. "I want these rebels now!"

As the officers ran, Mark got an idea. Everyone was so intent on following orders that no one paid attention to the vehicles.

He pulled himself up and staggered to the last

Humvee. After making sure no one was inside, he quietly opened the driver's door. His heart beat like a freight train when a light went on and a *ding, ding, ding* sounded. He quickly found a button on the doorframe and pressed it, turning off the light and the sound.

Mark grabbed the keys dangling from the ignition, pulled them out, and stuck them in his pants pocket. *One down,* he thought.

———

Vicki sat on the bed reading the printout Naomi had given her, fascinated with the words of Dr. Ben-Judah. This section dealt with the one thousand year millennial kingdom of Jesus. She giggled.

Judd turned from his computer. "What's so funny?"

"I was just thinking about my life before the Rapture. I would never have dreamed I would be so excited about reading stuff about the Bible."

"All we've been through has a way of changing your mind about a lot of things," Judd said. "What's in there?"

"Tons. For example, Tsion believes that in the one thousand year kingdom, God's going to lift the effects of original sin."

"How?"

"Well, he says it's going to be a lot like the Garden of Eden. All the people who rebelled against God and the bad angels will be gone."

"And not on vacation." Judd smirked.

Vicki continued, "God's going to bind Satan so he can't tempt people, and Christ—with the help of angels and believers—will basically enforce God's laws. Everybody will have their own home. There won't be war—"

"That verse about turning swords into farm plows or something . . ."

"Yeah, Tsion includes that here. It's from Isaiah 2. 'The Lord will settle international disputes. All the nations will beat their swords into plowshares and their spears into pruning hooks. All wars will stop, and military training will come to an end.' "

"I can't imagine a world without war, can you?"

"We won't have to imagine it. It'll be reality soon."

"What else does he say?"

Vicki turned a page. "Here it is. According to Isaiah 65, Tsion says people will live as long as those before the days of Noah. That means a believer who is born near the beginning of the kingdom could live almost a thousand years."

"No way."

"Another verse says a person will still be considered young at the age of one hundred."

"Sounds ideal."

"Just think about it," Vicki said, putting the pages down. "No more drug addicts. No more thieves and murderers. The stuff on TV won't be so violent. Everybody's going to know about God because Jesus will be the true King."

"I still can't get my mind around it," Judd said.

"The people who enter into the kingdom in their natural bodies, hopefully like you and me, will still be able to die. There's just so much to learn about—and think, we only have a few months until the whole thing starts."

"The best thing is, we're going to get to see our friends and family. You'll finally get to meet my mom and dad—and my little brother and sister."

"I can't wait," Vicki said.

---

Mark moved to the next Humvee, but this time he threw the keys as far as he could into the trees. As he crept toward the next vehicle, someone approached from the other side and Mark hit the dirt, the pain in his leg almost making him cry out.

"We're searching now, but my guess is they're not here." There was no question that this was Fulcire. "What's our intel on their movement?" After a pause, Fulcire cursed and yelled, "Can't you people do anything right!?"

Mark breathed a sigh of relief when the man walked toward the main cabin. The front window was open in the next Humvee so he quickly reached inside, snatched the keys, and tossed them into the woods. This time they pinged off a tree.

Fulcire turned. "People! People! I heard something in the woods to the east. Everybody over there—now!!!"

Mark stayed low to the ground, watching officers move away from the burning cabins. *Perfect*, he thought. *One more set of keys and I'm outta here.*

Mark sneaked to the lead vehicle and pulled himself alongside the driver's window. The tinted glass kept him from seeing inside. He carefully opened the door, and an alarm pierced the night.

"Somebody's messing with the vehicles!" a man shouted.

Mark reached for the keys, but they weren't in the ignition. He pulled the handgun from his pocket and shot out the left front and rear tires as he limped toward the last Humvee. He pulled the keys from his pocket, opened the door, and struggled into the driver's seat. The Humvee roared to life while officers streamed from the woods.

Mark slammed the gearshift in reverse and backed away as the first volley of gunfire hit the Humvee. *Bulletproof glass*, Mark thought. *Lucky me.* In spite of the pain in his leg, he jammed his foot on the accelerator and rocketed down the dirt road, bullets clinking off metal, dust and rocks thrown in the air. In his side mirror he saw flashes of fire from the soldiers' weapons.

Mark focused on the road and turned on his lights. As he neared the main road, he glanced back and saw the frantic officers trying to find their keys. He smiled, knowing he was free.

But he wasn't.

As soon as he turned onto the main road, a bus careened in front of him, cutting him off. Mark jerked the wheel to the right, plunging into a ditch. The Humvee shook and rattled. A sharp pain shot through his right leg, and Mark nearly lost control. As the Humvee jumped out of the ditch, the driver of the bus swerved. Another ditch, this one deeper than the last, loomed in front of him. Mark struggled to keep the vehicle on the road, dodging to his left and hitting the bus, then lurching down the hill into dead trees. He slammed on his brakes with his left foot and watched the bus zip past. Peace-keepers ran forward, shooting at his tires.

Mark whipped the Humvee around and headed east. He was going sixty miles per hour when a Peacekeeper with a rifle opened fire, exploding a front tire. He lost control and veered left as a back tire shredded.

The Humvee, tires smoking now, ran off the road and slammed into a burned tree, knocking it down and sending Mark into the windshield.

Dazed, Mark shook his head and tried to see how badly he was hurt. He felt his forehead and pulled back a handful of blood. He felt like someone had hit him in the face with a baseball bat.

*Gotta get out of here,* he thought, reaching for the door handle.

The door opened by itself, or so it seemed. Mark swung his legs around and leaned into the barrels of several Global Community guns.

"We have him, Commander," one said into a radio. The man grabbed Mark's gun and threw it away. Then he twisted Mark's hands behind him and cuffed them.

Mark went limp and collapsed.

# 21

**MARK** awoke in the back of the bus, handcuffed and aching. His right leg felt like it was hanging on by a thread. His belt was still buckled tightly around his knee. His eyes stung, and he realized blood had trickled down his forehead while he was unconscious. He leaned forward to the seat in front of him and rubbed his eyes for relief.

The Peacekeepers weren't happy. They had expected to fill the bus with rebels. A Humvee followed, and Mark figured Commander Fulcire was in it.

Mark sat back and tried to get comfortable. His shoulders throbbed, and his hands had fallen asleep. He tried to pray and remembered a verse Marshall Jameson had talked about during one of their meetings—the one about the Holy Spirit praying for believers with groans that can't be expressed. At the time Mark hadn't understood the concept, but now he was living it. Though he couldn't form the words, God knew what was going on.

Mark had often thought about what he would do if he ever got caught by the GC. If he kept his mouth shut, he couldn't go wrong. The moment he talked, they would offer things—food, water, or sleep. But Mark was desperate to know if his friends had truly made it to safety. If he knew that, he could keep going as long as it took.

Mark knew of others who had been captured. Chloe Williams had no doubt been questioned by the GC, and while news reports said she had given lots of information, no one believed it. He shuddered at the thought of facing the guillotine. If he was going to die as bravely as Chloe, he knew he would have to have God's help.

*I'm not going to die*, Mark thought. *My friends are going to find me and get me out of here. Period.*

A Peacekeeper glanced at Mark. The soldier looked a couple of years older than him, and Mark wondered if he had heard that within six months Jesus would return to crush the Global Community. *He's coming back soon*, Mark thought. *Sooner than you think.*

The soldier sneered and keyed a microphone attached to his uniform. "He's awake, sir."

"Condition?" It sounded like Commander Fulcire.

"Looks a little dazed," the soldier said. "Still breathing."

"Give him some water. Nothing else."

The soldier unscrewed the cap from a bottle of water and held it out. Mark opened his mouth, and the man poured a few drops in. Then he poured so fast that Mark choked, coughing and sputtering.

The soldier laughed. "Get enough, Judah-ite?"

Mark caught his breath.

The soldier sat across the aisle and leaned close. "You ready for what they're going to do to you? No mark, no head. But since you caused trouble back there, I think they're going to make it even more painful for you."

Mark wondered how the GC had found out about their hideout. Had they tapped into their phones? Or infiltrated the Web site? Had someone tipped them off?

*I guess it doesn't matter now*, he thought.

Mark didn't want to talk, but he had to know about his friends. "Seems like a lot of people for just one guy." His throat felt scratchy and raw.

The soldier smiled. "No way you were working alone. We've got the others in custody. They'll face the same fate as you." He leaned closer and whispered, "They say the blade sticks sometimes. It can cut you a few inches, and they have to raise it back up and let it go again. If you talk, they give you a clean one that gets it over quick."

Mark thought about Jesus—how he had endured mocking and torture. Before the soldier could say anything else, Mark slumped against the seat and fell asleep.

---

While Vicki read more of Tsion Ben-Judah's printout, Judd jogged to the tech center for an update. He spotted Rayford Steele, Chloe's father, and watched him walk toward the meeting place. Over the past few months, Rayford had reorganized the Tribulation Force. Mr. Whalum, who had flown Lionel and Judd to South

Carolina, had taken over the Co-op and helped plan the movement of supplies throughout the world.

Rayford had agreed with a daring plan by Chang to bug an upcoming meeting in Baghdad, where Nicolae's ten kings were supposed to appear. Judd had asked Chang if he and Vicki could be part of the tech crew, but Judd knew Rayford would have the final say. Judd didn't know much about the plan, just that Chang hoped to use hidden cameras and microphones. There was even talk of Zeke making special disguises for everyone.

As Judd entered the tech center, Lionel waved frantically.

Judd rushed over and found Chang watching satellite video of a fire. Lionel explained that it was the Wisconsin hideout, and Judd gulped.

"Darrion just got through on the phone and is going to call us back any minute," Lionel said.

"Did they all get out?" Judd said.

Lionel shrugged. "Let's hope so."

Chang went to the kids' Web site and explained how the GC was able to break in and discover where the Young Trib Force was headquartered. Judd felt sick when he saw Nicolae Carpathia's picture on their Web site. The GC had not only removed any reference to Jesus, the Bible, and Tsion Ben-Judah, they had already posted several articles about the great Nicolae.

*If you've been to this Web site before, you'll notice a number of changes,* one post read. *We have to admit we were wrong about the Global Community and especially Potentate Carpathia. If you haven't taken the mark offered by the GC, do*

*it now. It's painless and it'll help them keep order and peace.
After all, that's what we all want.*

The article was signed *Vicki B.*

"We worked so hard on that," Judd said. "All that data, all the articles . . . everything's gone?"

Chang frowned. "Unless you have originals, I'm afraid so."

The phone rang and Chang put the call on speaker-phone. It was Darrion.

"Where are you guys?" Lionel said.

"Illinois. We finally got the cell phone working just across the Illinois border and got in touch with Lenore. She and the others in her group had to move, and we're heading there tonight."

"What's your location now?" Chang said.

"We found an old farmhouse that wasn't destroyed in the fire," Darrion said. "As long as the GC doesn't use their satellite stuff to find us, we're okay."

"I've taken care of that," Chang said.

"Did everyone get out?" Lionel said.

"Everybody but Mark. He stayed and we haven't heard from him."

Judd bit his lip. "How did you guys find out the GC were coming?"

"Mark limped into camp telling us we had to get out. Marshall thinks he ran into the GC along the road."

"Where was he going?" Lionel said.

"There was a big fight and Mark decided to leave," Darrion said. "Everybody was upset with him, but I guess if he hadn't left, the GC might have found us."

Lionel asked about Charlie and several other members of the group. Darrion told them they had escaped with Phoenix, but all of their supplies, computer equipment, and clothes were still in the cabins.

"The cabins don't exist," Judd said. He told her about the fire.

"You guys settle in and stay safe," Chang said. "I'll jam their satellite until you make it to Lenore's."

---

Mark noticed the sun rising to his left. They were heading south toward Chicago. Maybe they were taking him to the new GC headquarters he had heard about. Or a prison where they televised executions.

Mark tried to put the thought out of his mind. He had memorized a lot of Scripture, so why couldn't he remember anything now?

As he sat in the rumbling bus, emotion overtook him. Tears dripped from his nose onto the seat. He tried holding them back, but that only made things worse. Sobs racked his chest, and he thought he would die.

"Please, God," he prayed, "give me the strength to go through whatever is going to happen. I know I won't be able to make it without you."

---

Vicki's heart raced when Judd told her what had happened to their friends and that the cabins had burned. The news about Mark sent a wave of panic through her.

They rushed to the tech center, where Chang was at a computer on the other side of the room working on jamming the satellite. Lionel was at another computer in the back and waved at them.

"Just got into the GC's database," Lionel said. Vicki was amazed at how fast Lionel could type one-handed, his fingers rushing back and forth among the keys. "Chang showed me how to see anything Fulcire sends to his superiors. We can't hear phone conversations, but we'll see any written info." He clicked on a previous message and something beeped. "New message."

*This confirms phone conversation that there will be a press briefing this afternoon,* Fulcire wrote. *We'll go over the raid in Minnesota and the capture of this new rebel. We do not have a name yet, but I assure you we will by the time of the briefing. Though he's young, we think we've caught one of the big fish in this so-called Young Tribulation Force.*

Vicki put a hand to her mouth and whispered, "Mark."

"I wish we could send out a message to have people pray," Judd said.

"We could do it on Tsion's Web site," Lionel said.

"Can you make that happen?" Judd said.

"Just tell me what you want it to say, and I'll have Chang post it."

Vicki gagged when she saw the kids' Web site. She thought of all the articles the kids had carefully created. Mark had rewritten most of Tsion Ben-Judah's messages especially for young readers. Now it was all gone.

199

Vicki, Judd, and Lionel spent a few minutes praying for Mark and asking God to protect him. "Let Mark know that you love him and that you're there for him," Vicki prayed.

## 22

**MARK** scooted close to the side of the bus and propped his head against the wall. The emotion had passed, and now he just felt tired and sore. The cuffs cut into his wrists, and he wished the Peacekeeper would loosen them.

Mark tried to think of something to take his mind off the pain. His first thought was Vicki, and he smiled. She had looked so pretty on the video feed from Petra. Beautiful. He had known early that Vicki was attracted to Judd. Mark's own feelings hadn't stirred until much later. He loved the sound of her voice, the way she took chances to help people. There was something fearless about her, something pure and noble.

"You gotta forgive me, Vicki," Mark whispered. He felt bad about yelling at her at the Dials' hideout in Wisconsin. He had told her she had to leave or he would, but the truth was, deep down, Mark was simply confused about his feelings. Now he knew he felt jealous of Judd and had lashed out at her in anger.

Later, when he and Vicki had talked, he had almost told her how he felt. Almost let her know that he wanted to be more than friends. Mark took a deep breath and tried to hold back the tears. It was okay that she didn't know, almost better.

The bus rumbled on as the sun rose higher. Peacekeepers slumped in their seats, trying to catch a few minutes of sleep. A man Mark hadn't seen before walked down the aisle. He wasn't wearing a GC uniform. The bus driver stared straight ahead, not noticing the man.

As the man neared, Mark looked closer at his long robe that reached the floor. He passed the Peacekeeper in the seat next to Mark, stopped, and looked directly into Mark's eyes.

"Who are you?" Mark croaked.

The man's eyes seemed full of compassion, as if at any moment he would weep. He gave a slight smile. "A messenger."

"Okay." Mark hesitated. "So what's the message?"

The man gathered his robe and sat. "Lean forward," he said. The pressure on Mark's shoulders suddenly relaxed. The handcuffs fell, and the man placed them on the seat.

Mark rubbed his wrists and put his head back. His neck muscles, which had been so tense, loosened. The feeling was heavenly. "I think I could sleep for a hundred years. How did you do that?"

The man smiled. "It's not important for you to know the how, just the why."

"All right, why?"

"Your heavenly Father knows your needs. He has heard the cry of your heart and has sent me."

Mark sat up. "Is this a rescue? Are you taking me out of here and past all these Peacekeepers?"

The man looked at the floor. "This is the message I was sent to give you. 'When you go through deep waters and great trouble, I will be with you. When you go through rivers of difficulty, you will not drown! When you walk through the fire of oppression, you will not be burned up; the flames will not consume you.' "

"Who are you talking to?" the bus driver said, looking in his mirror.

The man nudged Mark. "Don't worry. He can't see me. At least, not yet."

Mark ignored the driver and lowered his voice. "What does that verse mean? That you're not going to get me out of here?"

"The Father has not promised to snatch you away from trouble. But he has promised to be with you every step. You have served him well, Mark. You will serve him yet."

Mark moved his leg and noticed he had feeling below the knee. He quickly untied the belt and removed it. No pain. "Did you do that?"

The man put an arm around Mark's shoulder. "In Proverbs it says, 'An unreliable messenger stumbles into trouble, but a reliable messenger brings healing.' "

Mark flexed his leg. The torn ligaments were healed and without surgery—at least normal surgery. It was all he could do to sit still. "What do you mean, I'll serve him? I don't even know where these guys are taking me. How am I going to serve God from some GC jail?"

The angel—for Mark knew this was what he was—closed his eyes and spoke. It was like a whisper to Mark's heart. " 'Have you never heard or understood? Don't you know that the Lord is the everlasting God, the Creator of all the earth? He never grows faint or weary. No one can measure the depths of his understanding. He gives power to those who are tired and worn out; he offers strength to the weak. Even youths will become exhausted, and young men will give up. But those who wait on the Lord will find new strength. They will fly high on wings like eagles. They will run and not grow weary. They will walk and not faint.' "

Mark was overwhelmed by the words and felt a sense of hope. "I have to know if my friends are okay. Can you tell me?"

The angel stood. "Your actions and the actions of friends far away enabled them to escape. They are safe."

"Thank you."

The man turned. He was only inches away from a Peacekeeper, but the GC soldier kept sleeping.

Mark wondered if the angel had caused the others to sleep. "Do you have to go?"

"We will see each other again before the end." He leaned toward Mark and with a twinkle in his eye said, " 'The Lord is my strength, my shield from every danger. I trust in him with all my heart. He helps me, and my heart is filled with joy. I burst out in songs of thanksgiving.' "

The angel turned and walked toward the bus driver. Mark pulled himself up for one more glimpse, but the angel was gone.

The bus driver slammed on his brakes and shouted, "Hey, take care of your prisoner! He's gotten his handcuffs off!"

"How did you get out of those?" a Peacekeeper said, pouncing on Mark.

Mark just smiled and held out his hands. He remembered Vicki's favorite chorus that the group had sung at the first hideout in Wisconsin and began singing.

Laughing, crying, and singing to God.

It was a song of joy and thanksgiving.

---

Lionel watched news reports from the United North American States alone. Using codes Chang had given him, he was able to tap into a live feed from an unnamed prison.

The female reporter began with footage of the night before when a camera crew had caught the action in Minnesota. As far as Lionel could tell, these were militia members and not believers, though the reporter labeled them "suspected Judah-ites."

"Another raid early this morning brought the arrest of a high-level member of what the Global Community called a rebel youth movement responsible for many deaths and destruction of Global Community property."

"We're looking forward to interrogating our prisoner," Commander Fulcire said with a wink.

"Why aren't you going to execute him for not taking the mark?" the reporter said.

"Normally we would, but we believe this prisoner has valuable information. What we have here is a troubled young man who has been brainwashed to believe our lord Carpathia is evil. I'm not making excuses for his crimes, but if we can go inside his head and get information about other members of this dangerous group, we'll be that much closer to the kind of world peace we've been striving for the last few years."

The camera cut to a shot of Mark being led off a bus, handcuffed and shackled at the ankles. He saw the camera and started to say something, but the Peacekeeper behind him hit him on the head with the butt of his rifle and Mark fell.

Lionel closed his eyes and gritted his teeth. The reporter parroted the GC's lies. *If they knew the truth about Mark and the others in the Young Trib Force . . .* He shook his head. *No, if they knew the truth, they'd still report lies because they're under the control of the biggest liar of them all.*

The woman concluded her report and threw it back to the anchor at the Global Community News Network. Lionel kept watching the live feed, wondering if she would say anything once she was off the air.

"How did that come off?" the woman said. "Did you get a shot of the guy yelling about Jesus?"

"Yeah," someone said from behind the camera. "But we cut the audio out of his Jesus line. The producer didn't want anyone saying that name."

Though GC officials tried everything to get Mark to give
his name and information, he kept silent. He didn't want
to be traced to Nicolae High School and his friends in the
Young Trib Force.

After they processed him, Mark spent hours waiting in
an interrogation room. He finally got so tired that he put
his head on the table and went to sleep.

His dreams the past few years had been filled with
nightmares of GC raids and fires, huge, dragonlike creatures chasing him, and the one repeating dream of being
caught by Nicolae himself. But this time he dreamed of
golden streets filled with light, love, and laughter.

Mark awoke to a slamming door and looked at the
clock. Had he really been asleep six hours, or had they
changed the clock?

Commander Fulcire placed a plate of food on the
table and sat. Chinese. One of Mark's favorites. He tried
not to look hungry, but his stomach growled.

"I heard you wouldn't tell us your name," Fulcire said.
He took a mouthful of fried rice, chomped into an egg
roll, and wiped his mouth. "I know you think we're evil,
but we can be quite nice to people who give information."

Mark was determined not to say anything that would
hurt his friends, and he didn't want to talk at all, but he
couldn't resist this chance. "My mom always taught me
not to talk with my mouth full."

"She did? And what was your mother's name?"

Mark stared at him.

"Let me tell you something about this facility. There are isolated cells where you'd be alone, and there are general population cells where we put you with other . . . how should I say this? . . . criminals like yourself. These aren't nice people. They don't believe in much of anything other than their own survival. We put a nice young man like you in with them, and who knows what awful things could happen."

Mark sat back and thought of what the angel had said. God was going to use him in some way.

"Tell us your name or you'll go into one of those cells."

Mark stared straight ahead.

"Suit yourself," Fulcire said. He finished the meal, scraping every piece of rice from the plate, and walked out of the room.

When he was gone, Mark bent over and tried to lick some of the sauce from the plate, but that only fueled his hunger.

A round man in a green sweater walked in with another plate of food. He glanced through the window on the door, put the plate in front of Mark, and took Mark's handcuffs off.

"You need to hurry and eat that," the man said. "They could be here to get you any minute."

Mark grabbed a plastic fork and pushed some fried rice into his mouth. He was so hungry he almost inhaled the food. The man seemed fascinated with how quickly Mark could eat.

"Why are you helping me?" Mark said.

The man shook his head. "Can't stand the way they treat people. I don't care if you don't have Carpathia's mark, you're a human being." He held out a hand. Mark shook it and kept eating.

"Fulcire is a decent man. He just wants to know some information so we can process—"

"So he can process my neck with the blade," Mark said.

"We're getting information from the others who were staying with you."

Mark smiled. "You didn't catch anyone because there wasn't anyone to catch."

"I'm just trying to help. I don't want to see you suffer any more than you have to. If there's something you'd like to talk about, tell the guard you want to talk to me—"

The door opened and Fulcire barged in. "Cummings, what do you think you're doing?"

"I'm sorry, sir. I was just—"

Fulcire swatted the half-eaten plate of food from the table, and rice flew onto the walls and floor. "Get him out of here!"

A guard rushed in, seized Mark, and took him through a series of doors. Another guard released Mark's feet and pushed him toward a row of cells. The room stank, and Mark thought he would throw up at the smell. The guards took him to the largest cell where at least five people slept on cots pushed against the walls. They handed Mark an energy bar, shoved him inside, and slammed the door.

Two large men stood and approached him. One was bald, and Mark guessed he weighed three hundred pounds. The other was a smaller black man with a stubbly beard.

The bigger one pulled something sharp from his pocket and held it out. "Give me that food or we'll cut you!"

**23**

**JUDD** and Vicki sat in their home, wondering what Mark was going through. They had seen the video report Lionel had recorded and read the messages Commander Fulcire had written. No doubt the GC was gloating about this new arrest.

Judd felt confident that Mark wouldn't tell the GC anything important, and even if he did, their friends were headed to safety. The two prayed for Mark again, asking God to help Mark be strong.

"Do you think they'll torture him?" Vicki said.

"They'll do anything to get information." Judd took Vicki's hand. "You know how this is going to end."

Vicki nodded and tears welled in her eyes. "I hate this. We all know it can happen after watching Chloe. I still remember the feelings I had when they caught Pete. You hope something miraculous happens, you pray that God will step in, but deep down you know your friend is as good as gone."

Judd sighed. "I can't imagine what Buck is going through after losing Chloe."

"I talked with Priscilla Sebastian earlier. She's watching Kenny when he's not with Buck or Rayford. She said Buck basically spends his waking hours taking care of Kenny or writing."

"Makes sense. Staying busy probably keeps him sane."

"I've volunteered to watch Kenny whenever they need a break."

"He really likes you," Judd said. "You'd make a good mom."

Vicki grinned. "I don't know. It seems like such a huge responsibility." She paused. "But if that's what God has for us, to be parents, I'm up for the challenge."

Judd touched her shoulder. "I've been thinking about all that time before the Rapture. My parents wanted me to become a godly man—I didn't even know what that meant, didn't care. I think I want the chance to pass God's love on to other people, kids. And maybe they're not ours. Maybe they're kids without parents like you're talking about."

Vicki smiled and hugged him. "Sometimes I see my mom's face in my dreams. She loved me so much, and I didn't even know it."

"I remember catching my mom praying for me one night. I've never told anybody about it. I was coming home late from some party that I shouldn't have gone to, and I slipped in without anybody hearing me. I thought they'd all be asleep, but when I passed my parents' bedroom, I saw my mom in her reading chair, the light on behind her."

"What was she doing?" Vicki said.

"Crying. And she was whispering a prayer—I heard my name. I always felt bad that I didn't tell her I was home. I just went to my bedroom."

Vicki groaned. "It makes me so sad to think what I was like before all this. It's almost like I wasn't alive—I was just a shell looking for something to numb myself even more, so I drank or smoked or did stuff to help me not feel anything."

Judd nodded. "I guess if you don't have God, you don't want to feel anything because it's so scary. You're all alone."

"Yeah, and that's what makes being a believer so great. You can finally be alive. I think about the verse that says the evil one comes to steal and kill and destroy but Jesus came to give real life."

"That's what I want. Even though life can bring a lot of pain and can really be awful, I'll take living it with God's help rather than being a spiritual zombie."

---

Mark nervously handed the larger man his energy bar. "I'm not really that hungry."

The man tore it open, broke it in half, and gave some to the bearded man. They ate, then retreated to their bunks.

Mark looked for an empty cot but found none, so he went to the corner and sat on the floor.

A young man, Mark guessed he was in his thirties, slept nearby. The man opened his eyes. "What'd they get you for?"

Mark shrugged. "Guess I didn't want to cooperate with their rules."

The man lifted his head and stared at Mark. "Hey, you don't have Carpathia's tattoo."

"Don't like tattoos. Especially the GC kind."

The man smiled, showing missing teeth. "Same here. I dodged it for as long as I could, then got caught and thrown in here yesterday. Sure seemed like the GC was in a hurry with something big. I guess they'll make us take the thing or chop us sometime today."

"What did you do wrong?"

"Sure are nosy, kid," the bearded man said from across the room.

"Lay off him, LeRoy." He turned back to Mark. "I'm Steve. We were doing a little relocation of goods when the GC found us."

"Problem was, it was the GC's goods we were relocatin'," LeRoy said.

"What do you mean?" Mark said.

"We got caught taking some electronic equipment we wanted to sell," Steve said. "Some stuff out of a GC warehouse a few miles from here. That was LeRoy's idea that I said was too risky—"

"We'd have gotten away with it if you could have kept your big mouth shut," LeRoy said. "This is the last place I wanted to wind up."

"He was in before for murder," Steve said. "Got loose during the big earthquake. Been on the run since."

Mark looked at LeRoy, remembering Lionel's story about his uncle being killed by a man named LeRoy. "What's your last name?"

"Banks. What about it?"

*That's it! This is the same guy!* "Nothing," Mark said. "The name just sounded familiar."

"Well, you can forget it because I'm gettin' out of here and away from this deadwood of a partner you're talkin' to. He's going soft on me anyway, talking about that Ben-Judah guy."

Mark looked at Steve. "You've been reading Dr. Ben-Judah's Web site?"

Steve nodded. "Had a lady talk to me about God and tell me I should read it. I did, but I didn't understand it."

Mark glanced at the men in the next cell. "Are there others here who don't have Carpathia's mark?"

"I don't know. Ask 'em," Steve said.

Mark stared down the row of darkened cells. He had no idea how long he had before the GC came back for him. "Excuse me," he began nervously. "I don't mean to wake you, but how many of you—?"

"Shut up!"

"We're trying to sleep, stupid!"

Others cursed him and threw things at the cell bars.

Mark took a breath and kept going. "Just give me a minute and answer this. How many of you in here don't have the mark of Carpathia?"

"Shut your yap, jerk!"

Steve hurried over to Mark. "You'd better watch yourself. These guys'll turn on you fast."

"I don't know how much time I have left in here. I have an important message, and if I don't talk now they may never hear what I have to say."

"Your funeral," Steve said.

Mark continued. "If you haven't taken the mark of Carpathia, I want you to listen. You still have a chance to believe the truth."

A handful of men rolled from under their blankets and looked at him.

"What do you mean, the truth?" Steve said.

"I think some of you are ready for what I'm about to say. God's been working on you."

"I'm going to work on *you* if you don't shut up," someone said. "LeRoy, take care of this kid."

"Shut up and let him talk," LeRoy said. "I got a feeling he won't be here much longer."

Mark nodded at LeRoy and turned to face the men. "When the disappearances happened, did any of you lose friends or family members?"

"Of course we did," a man said. "Everybody did."

"Okay. Now think about those people. Were any of them religious? Did they talk a lot about God and go to church?"

"My mother-in-law vanished and it made me religious," a man said. "I thanked God for a whole year!"

The others laughed.

Mark studied the unmarked men. "The reason those people vanished is because God came back for his true children. They were immediately taken to heaven, which is where they are today. That means every one of us in here didn't know God. Anybody who was left behind missed the truth."

He took a step to his right. "You might have gone to church or grown up hearing stories from the Bible. I

216

know a lot of people who lived good lives but were left behind. The truth is, everyone still on earth never asked God to forgive them, and they never turned away from the bad stuff they'd done."

Mark lowered his voice and explained the prophecies about Antichrist and how each of the plagues the world had seen had been predicted thousands of years earlier. Then he spoke of the prophecies concerning the Jewish Messiah who would come not just to save Jewish people but all who believed in him.

"That man's name is Jesus," Mark said. "He was God in the flesh, and he lived a perfect life and died in your place on the cross."

"Why would God have to die to let us go to heaven?" a man said.

Mark paused, trying to think of a way to explain. "God is the great judge of every person, and because he's holy, he can't let anyone into heaven who's not perfect. Is there any one of you who's done everything right?"

"My wife always thought she was perfect," a man said, and the others laughed.

"Everybody falls short of God's standard," Mark said. "We're all guilty and deserve to be separated from him forever. But instead of punishing us, the judge *himself* became a prisoner, lived a perfect life, and then took our sentence."

"What's this got to do with us?" LeRoy said. "This ain't church."

Mark focused on the few men standing who had no mark. "God is offering each of you a key to unlock the cell that's holding you. That cell is sin. It traps us and keeps us from following God. In the end it will kill our souls if we don't ask to be forgiven."

Someone in the back moved and a cot creaked. That was the only sound Mark heard.

"What about those of us who took that mark?" a man said from a few cells away. "I didn't want to take it, but they made me."

Mark pursed his lips. "I don't know what to say. The Bible says anyone who takes the mark of Antichrist is condemned."

A clamor rose so loud that Mark thought the guards would come. He retreated to his corner and prayed for wisdom.

When things calmed, Steve tapped him on the shoulder. "Some of the guys want to know what to do. Will you tell us?"

Mark looked up and saw those without Carpathia's mark standing with their faces pressed against cell bars. A door opened down the hall, and Mark heard footsteps.

"Okay, listen carefully," Mark said. "I'm going to tell you. Then you have to pass it on to the others."

Steve frowned. "I don't know if I can—"

"There's no time! Even if you don't believe this or pray the prayer, you have to promise me you'll tell the others."

"I guess I can try."

"Good. You pray something like this from your heart: 'God, I know that I've sinned, and I'm sorry for that sin. I believe you sent Jesus, your only Son, to die in my place, and then he rose again three days later. . . .' "

Footsteps stopped in front of his cell. Someone unlocked the door.

"I ask you right now to forgive me, come into my life, and change me from the inside out. And help me not to give in to the evil one."

"Rebel," the guard yelled, "on your feet!"

"Do you have it?" Mark whispered.

Steve nodded. "I think so."

"Rebel!"

"One more thing," Mark said. "Afterward, you should be able to see something on their foreheads—that is, if you pray too."

"All right, we'll have to come in and get you," the guard said, taking a step toward Mark.

"And remember, tell them not to take Carpathia's—"

The guard jerked Mark to his feet by an arm, almost ripping it from its socket. Mark yelped and grabbed his shoulder as he was dragged from the cell. He looked back at Steve. "If they pray, God will give them the strength to face the blade." He turned to the others watching in stunned silence. "Give your lives to God right now! Don't wait!"

With that the guard threw Mark up against the wall. "There's only one god and it's Potentate Carpathia!" He kneed Mark, doubling him over, then put a gag in his mouth and pushed him through the door.

Mark glanced back but couldn't see Steve or any of the others. "God, I don't know if I gave them enough, but I pray you'd use what I said in their hearts," Mark prayed. "Help Steve, and give them the faith to see the truth and call out to you."

# 24

**MARK** was led into a room that had a table, three chairs, and a huge mirror on one wall. He guessed Commander Fulcire was watching from the other side but was surprised when the man entered and sat across the table from him.

Though Mark's leg wasn't hurting, his head and stomach ached from the guard's treatment.

"I was told you weren't cooperating in the cell," Fulcire said.

Mark stared at him.

Fulcire tossed a folder onto the table. Mark's mug shot was on top. "Your name is Mark Eisman. You attended Nicolae High in Mount Prospect. I suspect you were part of the underground that began the rebel newspaper at that school. You were known to be a friend of Vicki Byrne, the same Vicki Byrne who killed her principal. Also known to the Global Community as Vicki B. She's been quite a burr under our saddle."

Mark was shocked.

Commander Fulcire ran a hand over the file and pulled out a page printed from the Young Trib Force's Web site. "We've pieced together some of your movements. The old schoolhouse, the fire in Wisconsin, the Stahley hideaway. Tell me, is the young girl—Darrion, I think her name was—still with your group, or did you leave her behind like you did the others?"

"What others?" Mark said.

Fulcire raised his eyebrows. "That got your attention, eh?" He pulled a picture of Natalie Bishop out of the pile and held it up. "This face ring a bell? Would you like to see what she looked like as she pleaded for her life? As she told us everything she knew about you?" He held up a gruesome photo of Natalie just after her execution.

"You're a monster," Mark mumbled.

"Excuse me? I didn't hear that last comment."

Mark clenched his teeth and tried to keep quiet, but his anger boiled over. "You will pay for the way you've treated followers of God."

"You mean followers of the false god. And I think the one who is about to pay is you."

"She was a sweet girl. You had no right to—"

"That 'sweet girl' helped several prisoners escape, gave vital Global Community information to our enemies, and was a wolf in sheep's clothing. But she became quite talkative near the end."

"Right, which is exactly what you're going to say about me, though I'm not going to give you any more information than she did."

Fulcire pursed his lips. "We can do this the easy way or the hard way. I suppose you prefer the more difficult path. Makes you feel like you're doing something noble, suffering like your so-called Messiah."

Fulcire nodded toward the door, and a guard walked behind Mark's chair. Mark braced himself for a blow to the head or body, but none came.

"There are ways to get the information we need," Fulcire said. "We don't have time to starve you. Things must move along a little quicker than that. We want to know about the others who were with you in the cabins."

Mark smiled. "I knew you hadn't caught them."

"So there were others . . ."

"Hundreds," Mark said. "And they all escaped by balloon."

Fulcire scowled and looked at the guard. Suddenly Mark felt pain in his right arm. The guard had stabbed him with a needle.

"This little concoction will be swimming through your bloodstream in a few minutes," Fulcire said. "We'll continue our discussion then, and I promise you will be more forthcoming."

Mark closed his eyes and shook his head. "It's working already. My head . . . it feels so light."

Fulcire squinted and leaned over the table.

"I'll tell you now," Mark gasped. "It wasn't a balloon. They took the yellow brick road to Oz."

Fulcire stood and glanced at the guard. The two walked out without speaking.

"Don't go yet," Mark pleaded, laughing. "I have more to tell you about the flying monkeys and the Tin Man."

As the door slammed, Mark's laughter turned to tears. The drug gave him a strange sensation.

"'The Lord is my shepherd; I have everything I need,' " Mark whispered. " 'He lets me rest in green meadows; he leads me beside peaceful streams. He renews my strength. He guides me along right paths, bringing honor to his name. Even when I walk through the dark valley of death, I will not be afraid, for you are close beside me. Your rod and your staff protect and comfort me. . . .' "

---

Judd was excited to meet with Rayford Steele and talk about the mission to Baghdad. Judd had seen Rayford around Petra but hadn't talked with him face-to-face.

Judd didn't expect to play a big part in the Baghdad operation, but he and Vicki definitely wanted to be there. He had tinkered with electronics when he was younger, and he was sure he could help. And with Zeke's ability to change people's appearances, there was no way the GC would ever know who he and Vicki really were.

Rayford met Judd and Vicki at the tech center and moved to one of the high places where Tsion and his elders had their meetings. Rayford had aged a few years since Judd had first seen him, and though his hair was turning a little gray, he was still in good shape.

"We've been praying for you and Buck and Kenny," Vicki said as they sat.

"That means a lot to us," Rayford said. "We know

every day that passes brings us closer to seeing her again, but it's hard. If we didn't have the hope of heaven, I don't know what we'd do."

"You spoke with her before she died, right?" Judd said.

Rayford nodded. "I guess the GC was trying to trick her by having her call one of our secure numbers, but it backfired on them."

"How's that?" Vicki said.

"Well, after she gave me a message for Buck and Kenny, she told me she had been jogging near the San Diego hideout—which couldn't have been true. Chloe would never have been caught outside like that."

"What do you think she was doing?" Judd said.

"Trying to draw the GC away," Rayford said. "They were close to finding the others, and she was on watch that night."

"So how did her call backfire on the GC?" Vicki said.

"She mentioned something about a vacation our family had taken. I couldn't understand why talking about that was so important, and then I realized she was trying to tell me something. She said if she had one dream it would be that 'we could all go there right now, as soon as possible.'"

"She was talking about the others in the hideout?" Judd said.

"Yes. I didn't figure it out until later when Mac asked questions about that vacation. One of the places we went was Red Rocks, west of Denver. Mac made the connection about the red rocks of Petra, and we figured she meant we should get everybody over here pronto."

"Chloe was one of the smartest people I ever met," Vicki said.

Rayford smiled. "She said the same about you. Chloe told me once that you reminded her of her, just a few years younger."

Vicki blushed. "That's the best compliment I've ever received."

"Which makes what I'm about to say even more difficult," Rayford said. He took a breath. "We're not going to be using you in the Baghdad operation."

Judd gulped and looked away. "Can I ask why?"

"It was my decision. Chang and I have handpicked the team and feel we have the right amount of people. The GC has seen Vicki's picture, and we can assume they've seen yours as well. We don't need unnecessary risks."

"But *you're* going, aren't you?" Judd said.

"That's right."

"And you were on Carpathia's staff. That has to be a lot more dangerous than—"

Vicki put a hand on Judd's arm.

Captain Steele looked at the ground.

"I'm sorry," Judd said. "I don't mean to question your authority. We'll abide by whatever decision you make. And we'd be glad to help out here any way we can."

"I like that attitude."

After Rayford left, Judd and Vicki walked back to their home and talked about the situation. "I think we have to face the fact that Captain Steele is always going to think we're still just crazy teenagers," Judd said.

"I don't think he feels that way. Think of all the other

people he didn't include in this operation. Our time will come."

"I just think we're going to be left out of the really good assignments."

"Which ones?" Vicki said.

Judd opened the door to their home and followed Vicki inside. He clicked on the computer screen and brought up a map of Israel. "This is the area where the Battle of Armageddon is going to be fought. And this is the spot where Jesus is supposed to come back."

"I know all that," Vicki said. "What's it got to do with us?"

"I want to be there, right in the middle of things and see it with my own eyes. I want to help fight the GC or at least support those who are trying to defend Jerusalem."

"And what about me?"

"I want you right there beside me." Judd took Vicki in his arms. "It'll be the greatest moment in the history of the world, and you and I are going to see it."

"One problem. How are we going to get there?"

Judd pushed Vicki a few inches away and looked at her. "I'll take care of that, but not a word about this to anybody. It's going to be our secret."

---

A few minutes after they gave Mark the shot, he felt woozy. *This must be what a numbskull feels like,* he thought.

He sat up and noticed someone standing in the corner by the one-way mirror. Mark leaned close and squinted. It was the angel from the bus.

"You're back?" Mark said.

The angel smiled and nodded. "You didn't finish the verses. The rest of the Psalm you were quoting."

"Oh, that," Mark said. "Where was I?"

"'You prepare a feast for me in the presence of my enemies. You welcome me as a guest, anointing my head with oil. My cup overflows with blessings.'"

Mark nodded and picked up the end of the verse. "'Surely your goodness and unfailing love will pursue me all the days of my life, and I will live in the house of the Lord forever.'"

"That is what you can look forward to, my friend," the angel said.

Mark leaned back in his chair. "This stuff they gave me, will it make me talk?"

"You don't have to do anything you don't want to do. God will give you the strength to resist, no matter what they put into your veins. After all, as one of your hymn writers has said, 'The body they may kill; God's truth abideth still: His kingdom is forever.'"

"So I just shut my mouth and keep quiet?"

"Be creative."

Mark smiled. "Yeah, I'll try."

"They are almost ready to return. Before they do, I must tell you there was great rejoicing today."

"For what?"

"Because of you, because of the message, and because a few have gone from the kingdom of darkness to the kingdom of light."

"Steve," Mark whispered. "He told the others what I said?"

"He did, and they all believed in the only begotten Son of the Father, Jesus, the name that is above every name."

"How many?" Mark said.

Footsteps echoed down the hall.

"The ones who were appointed to believe have done so. You need not be concerned about the number. And now I will leave you."

"Please don't," Mark said. "Can't you stay and help me . . . do whatever I'm supposed to do?"

"If you truly need me, I'll be here," the angel said.

With that, the door opened and Commander Fulcire walked in with another man Mark hadn't seen before. When the door closed, Mark noticed the angel was gone.

Commander Fulcire looked closely at Mark and sat with a huge sandwich and onion rings. Barbecue sauce dripped from the bread, and Mark's stomach growled.

Fulcire took a bite of the sandwich and licked his fingers. "You know, it's amazing what the cooks here can do. A little information and we'll serve you a heaping plateful of some delicious food."

"I'm worried about your cholesterol," Mark said. "You really need to cut down on the fatty foods."

The other man sat near Fulcire and eyed Mark. "Let's start with something easy," he said.

"Who are you?" Mark said.

"Deputy Commander Lockerbie," the man said. "You're Mark Eisman, right?"

"If that's who you want me to be, that's who I am."

"It's not a question of who we want you to be but a quest for reality. Are you Mark Eisman?"

"Yes."

The man noted his answer and continued. "Are you part of the so-called Young Tribulation Force?"

"Yeah, I head up intramural sports."

"What was that?" Fulcire said.

"You know, basketball, football, badminton—that kind of thing. We tried to get a bowling team together, but we couldn't find an alley—"

"That's enough, Mr. Eisman," Fulcire said.

"Yeah, it was enough for us to go after a softball team. Had a hard time getting jerseys made up and an even harder time finding someone to play against."

"Enough!" Fulcire said.

"Have you ever participated in disloyal acts to the potentate?" Lockerbie said.

"No, not since I became a believer in him."

"Have you ever stolen anything to aid in your rebel acts?"

"Well, there was that satellite truck. I'm real sorry about that. I was going to fill it up with gas and return it, but I couldn't find you guys."

Lockerbie and Fulcire were not laughing, but Mark was having a good time. He looked past the men and saw his friend standing in the corner, chuckling.

"How am I doing so far?" Mark said to the angel.

Fulcire thought he was talking to him. "You won't be laughing when we take you to the blade."

"Probably not, but at least I'll know where I'm headed after my head's gone. You can kill my body, but you can't take my soul."

When Fulcire looked at the list of questions, Mark shook his head. "Look, Commander, I'm not going to tell you any more about my group because I don't know anything more. You probably want supply routes and locations of safe houses and that kind of stuff, and I'm just not going to give it up. So why don't we call this thing a bust? You sharpen your blade, and we can be done."

Lockerbie asked a few more questions, but Mark wouldn't say a word.

Finally Fulcire slammed his fist on the table and yelled, "Solitary!"

Mark was surprised he had gotten away without anyone trying to torture him. Would that come later? When he made it to his room, he collapsed on his cot and fell into a deep sleep. He dreamed of streets paved with gold.

# 25

EARLY the next morning in Petra, Lionel made contact with Darrion and the others in Illinois and discovered they had found Lenore and her friends. Lionel wrote down their information and promised he would give them an update on Mark as soon as he heard anything.

"Jim Dekker, Colin Dial, and Conrad are talking about a rescue," Darrion said.

"I wouldn't recommend it," Lionel said. "If the info we're getting from Fulcire's computer is right, Mark is deep in the jail there. It would take a magician to get in and out."

Darrion said she would talk with the others and said good-bye.

Lionel had been glued to the computer for a long time, so he decided to take a walk. He found Sam Goldberg and Mr. Stein and explained the situation. The two were visibly upset and knelt where they were and prayed.

"Sovereign Lord, we ask you to send your ministering angels to encourage Mark right now," Mr. Stein prayed. "Prepare him for whatever you have planned."

After they had prayed, Sam took Lionel to meet his friend Lev Taubman and his mother. They had become believers shortly after family members had died in a rebellion.

"Lev has been in touch with some friends in Jerusalem," Sam said.

"Believers?" Lionel said.

Lev shook his head. "But they have not taken the mark of Carpathia. They say they are going to fight with rebel forces against Carpathia. They want to save Jerusalem."

"That'll be like a peewee football team trying to win against an NFL team," Lionel said.

"What?" Sam said.

"They're going to lose the battle, and they'll probably all be killed."

"I know that," Sam said. "But Lev and I think we might be able to reach some of them for God. We want to go to Jerusalem before the big battle and tell them the truth."

After hearing their plan, Lionel thought he should tell Judd and Vicki about this new development.

---

Mark sat alone in the darkness and waited. He could have played the interrogation a little better and made them think he was giving them solid information, but he was tired of playing.

His cell was down the hall and around the corner from the other prisoners. He felt something crawling on him and stood and flailed his arms. He settled on the cot and pulled a lone blanket around his shoulders.

Through the hall came singing, but Mark couldn't make out the words. Then another voice joined in and another. There had to be at least half a dozen people singing now.

Mark put his ear to the door. He heard the word *Jesus* in the song, slid to the floor, and closed his eyes. He thought of little Ryan, the Fogartys' son. How many times had Mark helped put him down for a nap singing "Jesus Loves Me"? That was one of Ryan's favorites, and he always asked Mark to sing it again and again.

A soft glow filled the room, and Mark greeted the angel. The being looked at him kindly and sat. Mark couldn't believe he was so comfortable with this heavenly visitor.

"What was that singing?" Mark said.

"I was teaching your friends a new song," the angel said.

"Were they scared of you?"

"No. And they learned the words quickly."

"What about the unbelievers? They must have been afraid."

The angel smiled. "They managed to fall into a deep sleep."

"That happens a lot with you, doesn't it?" Mark said. "Those guards on the bus did the same thing when you came around."

The angel smiled again.

"What song did you teach them?"

The angel closed his eyes and began singing in a low, pleasing voice.

*"What can wash away my sin?*
*Nothing but the blood of Jesus;*
*What can make me whole again?*
*Nothing but the blood of Jesus.*
*Oh! precious is the flow*
*That makes me white as snow;*
*No other fount I know,*
*Nothing but the blood of Jesus."*

"That's good. You should get a band together and go on the road."

"We lift our voices in praise every day, but I must say, the words of the hymn writers are unique."

"What do you mean?" Mark said.

"Humans write about redemption, salvation, the power in the blood of Jesus. We angels know nothing about such things, other than what we observe. We cannot be 'saved,' as you would call it. We had one chance to follow or rebel and that was it."

"You mean when Satan was cast out of heaven?" Mark said.

"Correct. One third of the host of heaven followed Lucifer, and the others remained faithful to the Almighty. But all humans have fallen. All of them have sinned and fallen short of the glory of God."

"I guess I've never really thought about it that way. So why did we get a second chance and you didn't?"

The angel took a breath, as if he were smelling a sweet flower for the first time. "The grace of God," he whispered. "We look at it and are encouraged. We see it at work and are in awe of the plan of the Lord. He became one of you, a kinsman redeemer—a person who was in every way like you, except that this person was without sin. Jesus, who was God, became human. . . . I was there, you know."

"Where?"

"Bethlehem, on the hills overlooking the town. You should have seen those shepherds when we started singing." The angel paused. "But I tell you too much."

"No, please don't stop," Mark said.

The angel put his hands on his knees. "We didn't know what to think, the Son of God coming to earth as a helpless baby. That he would submit to such a life, then give himself as a sacrifice on Golgotha." The angel shuddered. "Such an ugly death."

"You were there?"

"The Son could have called on us at any moment, and we would have taken him from that place." He held out a fist. "We would have struck down those Romans like toy soldiers. But he didn't call on us. He took the shame and the beatings and the nails." He shook his head. "How can you understand? How can any being comprehend such love?"

Mark bit his lip. "Can you teach me the song? I went to church, but I don't really remember it."

The angel spoke the words again, then picked up the melody and Mark sang along. When he heard the words, Mark found he could memorize them immediately. Tears rimmed his eyes as he reached the next verse.

*"Now by this I'll overcome—*
*Nothing but the blood of Jesus;*
*Now by this I'll reach my home—*
*Nothing but the blood of Jesus.*
*Oh! precious is the flow*
*That makes me white as snow;*
*No other fount I know,*
*Nothing but the blood of Jesus."*

Footsteps approached and the angel stood, his nostrils flaring.

"Is this it?" Mark said.

"I'm not sure. From what I can tell, there may be one more test of your will. But stand strong, my friend. You are a child of the King, and you will soon be home."

The door opened and Mark scooted to avoid it.

Deputy Commander Lockerbie walked through with another guard. "This way, Eisman."

They led Mark through a series of hallways. He had no idea what time it was, but when the deputy commander took him outside, the cool, brisk air hit him in the face and Mark breathed deeply. The moon shone brightly in the cloudless sky.

Across the courtyard was a row of wooden tables, dwarfed by several guillotines. Mark had seen this setup on live feeds from GC prisons around the world. Some of the highest rated programs on television were rebel executions. Mark hadn't watched many of these, but the ones he had seen had turned his stomach.

In spite of the cool weather, flies buzzed around them. The smell was overpowering. Several huge trash bins stood alongside the main building.

The deputy commander excused the guard and turned to Mark. "This is where it happens. Unless you cooperate, tomorrow you'll be out here."

"This is where I'll wind up no matter what I say and you know it."

"Not necessarily. You give us information on pilots, supply routes, locations of hiding places, information like that, and we'll make things easier." Lockerbie had a kind face, not unlike Mark's cousin John. In fact, the two looked remarkably alike. "We have information that your group has been in contact with the mole inside the palace in New Babylon. Do you know anything about that?"

"Look, I can help in a lot of ways, but if the palace has a mole, I'd suggest you get an exterminator or a trap. I don't know much about catching small animals."

"Not that kind of mole. You know what I'm talking about."

"You get nothing from me," Mark said.

The deputy commander turned Mark around and keys jangled. Soon Mark's hands were free. He rubbed his wrists to get the circulation going again. "Why'd you do that?"

Lockerbie sighed. "Not all of us in here are the

monsters you think we are. We do have some compassion."

"You mean like a nice meal before you slice my neck?"

"No, I can see that you live. Simply take the mark and we'll put you in a cell of your own. After this all dies down you can be moved and have more privileges. I'll even find a Bible for you."

"Right, like I really believe you're going to come through on all that."

Lockerbie dug into his pocket and frowned. "They would have *my* head if they knew I was doing this, but I had a younger brother. He was killed in the outbreak of poison gas. You remind me of him." He handed Mark a cell phone. "I'm going to let you stay out here for a while. You won't be able to run. There's razor wire all around, and the guards are armed. But think about your life and what it's worth. Call someone you know, someone who cares for you. I'll be back in a few minutes."

Mark took the phone and studied it as the deputy commander slipped inside. *What an obvious trick! The GC wants me to call my friends—any number they can trace. The phone might even have a bug in it so they can listen.*

Mark ambled over to a wooden table and glanced at a guard high in a tower. The ground was wet with dew. He sat on the table and studied a guillotine. The contraption disgusted him and he turned away.

Who could he call? No way was he going to dial Conrad, Shelly, or the others. He also didn't want to call Petra. Though he longed to talk with Judd, Lionel, or

Vicki, he didn't want to mess up and have them give information the GC wanted.

Then he got an idea. A truly inspired idea.

*The angel will like this one,* Mark thought.

---

Lionel hit the Record button while he watched the latest news from the United North American States. He had asked Naomi to get Judd and Vicki.

An anchorwoman named April Wojekowski held one hand to her ear as she searched for words. "I'm told that you're one of the rebels captured by Commander Fulcire in last night's raid, is that correct?"

"You got that right," a young man said.

The voice sounded familiar. *Could it be Mark?*

"That commander is a tough bird. He's been asking me lots of questions, and I've been giving him lots of answers."

*It is Mark!*

"Is that so?" Wojekowski said.

"Yeah, they gave me one phone call, and I thought I'd make it to the media so you could have the story."

"And what story is that?"

"I was part of a group called the Young Tribulation Force that started an underground Web site. We wanted people to know about the Global Community because we thought it was bad. Now, after talking with Commander Fulcire and the others here, I know the truth."

"So the commander has set you straight?"

"Right."

241

Lionel's heart sank. Was Mark giving the GC information? Had they somehow brainwashed him? Judd and Vicki ran in and Lionel put a finger to his lips. "Mark's on the phone with GCNN."

---

Mark had slowly moved behind the huge trash bins, being careful the guard in the tower didn't notice him. He hid, choking at the awful smell, hoping this would be the last place anyone would look.

He had gotten the GCNN phone number from the directory of the deputy commander's cell phone. He hadn't expected to actually get on the air, but when it happened he prayed God would keep him calm.

"What have you told Commander Fulcire that you'd like to share with us?" Wojekowski said.

The door to the courtyard banged open, and several guards poured out.

Mark held the phone close, took a deep breath, and spoke softly. "Actually, I haven't even shared this with the commander, so you'll be the first to know." He imagined the woman looking into the camera and sitting a little taller in her chair. "To all those who have read our Web site, or who were interested in knowing why the disappearances happened, or why we've had all these natural disasters, like the darkness in New Babylon, I'd like to point them to Dr. Tsion Ben-Judah's Web site." Mark gave the address quickly before the woman cut him off.

"So the commander hasn't really changed your mind about being against Potentate Carpathia?"

Footsteps getting closer. Voices yelling.

"Being in here and seeing how they treat prisoners makes me all the more determined to live my last breath for Jesus Christ," Mark said.

"Behind the garbage bins!" a guard shouted.

"Judd, Vicki, Lionel, Conrad—and anybody who's listening—I'm not alone in here! I'm all right. And I'll see you on the other side!"

The phone clicked and Mark wondered if his friends had heard his last few words.

Someone shoved a gun barrel into Mark's back and he stood. Deputy Commander Lockerbie snatched the phone away and led him back to his cell.

# 26

THE NEXT few minutes were agony for Judd and the others watching from Petra. Judd put himself in Mark's place and pictured the GC leading him straight to the guillotine.

It was Vicki's idea to pray, and Naomi Tiberius ran for her father, an elder at Petra. She returned with him and Chaim Rosenzweig.

"Dear ones," Chaim said softly, "let us join together."

For the next hour the group gave thanks to God for Mark—for all the things he had done to help people come to know Jesus and for the good friend he had been.

"Father, we ask that you give special comfort and strength to Mark right now," Chaim prayed. "Stir his heart and give him a peace that passes all understanding."

When Eleazar Tiberius spoke, his voice boomed in the tech center, and many of the workers stopped what they were doing and gathered around. Judd didn't even know most of them, but he could tell they sensed one of their brothers was in trouble.

"Sovereign Lord, we knew when this period of Tribulation began that many would die for your sake," Mr. Tiberius prayed. "And though we would ask for a miracle, it may be your will that Mark passes through this fire rather than being taken out of it. So I ask you to bring to his mind what the psalmist said: 'Lord, give to me your unfailing love, the salvation that you promised me. Then I will have an answer for those who taunt me, for I trust in your word. Do not snatch your word of truth from me, for my only hope is in your laws.'"

Vicki wept as she prayed. "Father, you know how much Mark and I disagreed, but I never doubted that he wanted to follow you as much as anyone. Whatever's happening to him right now, help him remember all of his friends and how much we love him."

"Yes, Father," Chang prayed. "Because of you and your love, none of us is ever alone. We thank you for friendships and the chance to join in the sufferings of our brother Mark. If we could take his place, we would do that, but you have called him to face this final task and you would not choose someone who would fail you. We give you thanks and pray you would hold Mark up even now."

---

Mark came back to consciousness, not knowing how long he had been in his darkened cell. He groped his way across the floor until he reached the cot. He felt his head and found a lump the size of a Ping-Pong ball. His back ached, and he wondered how many guards had joined in the capture.

He wished his angel friend would return. He would have to ask his name this time. How good of God to send a final companion.

Verses flooded Mark's mind, especially from the Psalms. Then he recalled Jesus in the Garden of Gethsemane and his prayer to God to 'take this cup of suffering away from me.' Jesus' mental anguish had been so intense that the Bible said he had sweat great drops of blood. Suddenly Mark could understand that a little better.

"God, thanks for letting me go through this. I wouldn't have chosen it, but if this is what you want me to do, I want to be faithful."

Mark thought of Jesus' crucifixion. He had been tortured and killed. Dying on the cross took hours of agony. Mark's would be over in seconds—at least that's what he hoped.

"What are you thinking, my friend?" someone said.

Mark looked up. It was the angel, standing in a corner, shining with a heavenly light. "You mean you can't read my mind?" Mark said.

"Only the Almighty can see into your heart. We can only guess."

"I'm just trying to think straight," Mark said. "Could I ask your name?"

"You may call me Caleb."

"Have you done this many times?"

Caleb nodded. "There have been more in the past few months than ever."

"Does anybody . . . I mean, when it comes time to . . . you know . . ."

"God's people have always acted with great courage. Some weep at the end, others sing, and some quote Scripture. It is different every time, and yet there are remarkable similarities."

"Like what?"

"The looks on their faces. The hope that shines through. Those who are doing the killing look like shells, but the ones being executed are truly alive. It happened that way recently with Chloe Williams. She was able to speak of the living Christ before her death."

"You visited Chloe?"

Caleb put a hand over his chest. "Her heart was breaking over leaving her husband and son, but she expressed her desire to be with Jesus."

"Will you do the same thing you did in the courtyard when Chloe was executed? You know, the bright shimmering thing we saw on TV?"

Caleb smiled. "Each event is different. If there is need for me to be there and speak, I will." He tilted his head slightly to the left and gazed at Mark. "Thus says the Son of the most high God: 'I am the resurrection and the life. He who believes in Me, though he may die, yet shall he live. And whoever lives and believes in Me shall never die.' Be comforted by these words."

Mark raised his eyebrows. "Thank you. I hope I won't let you down."

The angel stepped closer. "I know you won't because you are one of his."

Mark took a deep breath. His throat caught and he had trouble speaking. "Well, I don't know how to thank you for coming and helping me get through this. I suppose you have other things you could be doing—angel stuff."

Footsteps echoed down the hallway.

Caleb smiled again. " 'Peace I leave with you,' says your Lord Christ. 'My peace I give you, not as the world gives, give I unto you. Let not your heart be troubled, neither let it be afraid.' "

And Caleb was gone.

Commander Fulcire stepped into the room, accompanied by several guards. Mark thought it odd the deputy commander wasn't there.

When Mark stepped from the prison, the first rays of light peeked over the horizon. A long, thin cloud tinged with yellow hung in the sky. The way the sun hit it made it look almost golden. A jet sped high in the sky leaving a white trail. It intersected the cloud and came out the other side. Mark couldn't help thinking the whole thing looked like a cross.

Mark expected the same kind of fanfare as Chloe, news trucks lined up, the works. But there weren't even people manning the tables at this hour. A few guards huddled together, trying to keep warm.

Fulcire pushed Mark to the first guillotine and turned. "Bring out the others."

After a few moments, six men were led from the jail. Mark recognized Steve at the front of the group with the mark of the believer on his forehead. The others all had the same mark.

Commander Fulcire pulled a cell phone from his pocket and dialed a number.

Steve smiled and stood close to Mark. "I was afraid you'd be gone before they brought us out here."

"Me too," Mark said. "You must have remembered all I said."

"It's funny. I knew everything you told me, even believed it. I knew God was doing all the stuff around us, but I always thought I was too far gone to turn around."

"We want to thank you," another man said to Mark. "I think God brought you to us."

Mark nodded. "I think you're right." He looked at Steve. "But why did they single you guys out this morning?"

Steve's eyes twinkled. "We all said we didn't want you to be alone. We told the guards we would never bow down to Carpathia or take his mark, and if they were going to use these—" he nodded toward the guillotines— "that we wanted to be with you."

Mark shook his head and bit his lip to keep from crying. "You didn't have to do that."

"You didn't have to come to us, and you didn't have to risk telling us your message," another man whispered. "But you did."

"That reminds me of a verse in the Bible, a couple actually," Mark said. "Paul says something about being thankful to God every time he thinks of the people he's writing. He says, 'I always pray for you, and I make my requests with a heart full of joy because you have been my partners in spreading the Good News about Christ from the time you first heard it until now.'

"You guys haven't been believers long, but you have been faithful to what God called you. The next verse says, 'And I am sure that God, who began the good work within you, will continue his work until it is finally finished on that day when Christ Jesus comes back again.' That day is coming real soon, but we're going to see him sooner.

"When Jesus hung on the cross, just before he died, he said to a man next to him, 'Today you will be with me in paradise.' Well, I believe that the moment we leave this life, we're going to see him, and you'll see that the little bit of suffering we had to go through here will really be worth it."

"A man came to us and taught us a song," another man said.

"That was an angel," Mark said.

The men's eyes widened.

"I didn't see any wings," Steve said.

Commander Fulcire stepped forward and faced Mark. "You have some kind of feeling for these prisoners?"

"They're my brothers," Mark choked.

"Quaint. Well, I'll give you one more chance. What you say now could save the life of your 'brothers,' as you call them. I will allow them to go back to their cells and live if you'll tell us what we want to know."

Mark wanted to tell Commander Fulcire the truth a final time. He wanted to scream at him that Jesus was coming back and would conquer the armies of the Antichrist. Instead, Mark felt compassion for the man who had followed the devil.

251

"I feel sorry for you," Mark whispered.

Fulcire laughed. *"You* feel sorry for *me?"*

"One day every person on earth will admit that Jesus Christ is Lord. He is the true Potentate and the Creator of the universe."

"So you don't want to save your friends?"

"One day soon, New Babylon is going to be destroyed."

"Impossible."

"And the armies of your leader will go to battle against God's people."

"I hope to be there," Fulcire said.

"You and those like you who wear the uniform of the Global Community will be struck down."

"With all the weaponry and firepower at our disposal? Not likely."

Mark looked at the guards with Fulcire. "Do anything you can to stay away from the last battle. Get sick. Run away. But don't be near Israel in six months."

The guards scoffed. Fulcire motioned, and two guards led Steve to the guillotine. "Last chance to save this man's life," the commander said.

Steve looked back at Mark. "I've already been saved. Can you guys sing one more time?"

The others began the song Caleb had taught them. As they sang the verse, "'This is all my hope and peace, Nothing but the blood of Jesus; This is all my righteousness, Nothing but the blood of Jesus,' " the blade fell and Steve died.

One by one the guards led the others in front of Mark to the guillotine. The guards tried to stop them from singing, and several men went to the guillotine with missing teeth, but they kept singing to the end.

Fulcire saved Mark for last. As the guards picked up the body of the man before him and moved it, the commander pushed Mark toward the blood-caked machine. "Look around you, Eisman. No masses of people to preach to. No flashing lights of supposed angels. You die alone, and you die now."

Mark felt a sense of peace flowing, like the prayers of his friends were lifting him. Faces flashed in his mind—Judd's, Vicki's, Lionel's, Ryan's, and many others. He had fought the good fight. He hadn't done everything perfectly, and he had done some stupid things, but God had used him.

He knelt on the blood-soaked ground. *Holy ground,* he thought. *Ground soaked by the blood of the martyrs.*

Caleb's song came to him and he sang it softly. "'Now by this I'll overcome—Nothing but the blood of Jesus, Now by this I'll reach my home—Nothing but the blood of Jesus. Oh! precious is the flow that makes me white as snow; No other fount I know, Nothing but the blood of Jesus.' "

With his eyes fixed on the ground, Mark breathed a final prayer knowing that at any second he would be in the presence of God.

"Into your hands I commit my spirit," he whispered.

"Good riddance, Judah-ite," Fulcire said.

A lever tripped.

Something clunked, and Mark felt the machine shudder as the blade plunged.

A millisecond before it hit his neck, Mark thought he heard rustling wings and singing.

Then a flash of light.

And he was in heaven.

# 27

**FOR THE** next several days Judd moved around Petra in a fog. He kept replaying first meeting Mark and John at Nicolae High and all the things they had been through. Though Vicki talked openly about Mark's death, Judd found it difficult. He knew that frustrated Vicki, but it was taking him longer to accept the truth. Mark was gone.

As Vicki played with Kenny in their house, Judd took a walk to one of the high places and sat. He asked God to help him understand what had happened. Within minutes, an ovation arose in the distance. As Judd made his way carefully down the mountainside, he heard the voice of Tsion Ben-Judah echo off the rock walls.

Judd had heard from Lionel that Tsion planned to go live on international television with Chang's help. Judd wondered what Carpathia and his goons would think of that. Tsion was speaking to not only a million in Petra but billions worldwide.

When Judd arrived at the massive gathering, Tsion was already well into his message. He explained that the truth of God's Word was confirmed by the judgments and plagues. From the disappearances to the hail and fire, the burning mountain that fell into the sea, to the demonic locusts—all these and more were proof that God's Word was true.

". . . Two more judgments await before the glorious appearing of our Lord and Savior, Jesus the Christ," Tsion was saying to the people and a nearby camera. "Hear me! The Euphrates River will become as dry land! Scoff today but be amazed when it happens, and remember it was foretold. The last judgment will be an earthquake that levels the entire globe. This judgment will bring hail so huge it will kill millions.

"I am asked every day, how can people see all these things and still choose Antichrist over Christ? It is the puzzle of the ages. For many of you, it is already too late to change your mind. You may now see that you have chosen the wrong side in this war. But if you pledged your allegiance to the enemy of God by taking his mark of loyalty, it is too late for you.

"If you have not taken the mark yet, it may *still* be too late, because you waited so long. You pushed the patience of God past the breaking point.

"But there may be a chance for you. You will know only if you pray to receive Christ, tell God you recognize that you are a sinner and separated from him, and that you acknowledge that your only hope is in the blood of Christ, shed on the cross for you.

"Remember this: If you do not turn to Christ and are not saved from the coming judgment, this awful earth you endure right now is as good as your life will ever get. If you do turn to Christ and your heart has not already been hardened, this world is the worst you'll see for the rest of eternity.

"For those of you who are already my brothers and sisters in Christ around the world, I urge you to be faithful unto death, for Jesus himself said, 'Do not fear any of those things which you are about to suffer. Indeed, the devil is about to throw some of you into prison, that you may be tested. . . . Be faithful until death, and I will give you the crown of life.'

"What a promise! Christ himself will give you the crown of life. It shall be a thrill to see Jesus come yet again, but oh, what a privilege to die for his sake."

Judd sat on a rock and thought about Mark. He had earned the crown of life! Even now he could be in the presence of Jesus, worshiping and praising God. Judd missed the next few moments of Tsion's message, then focused on the man's words as he spoke of things to come.

"Now I must tell you there is also bad news," Tsion said. "The wrath of the evil one will reach a fever pitch from now until the end. There will be increasing demands for all people to worship him and take his mark. To you who share my faith and are willing to be faithful unto death, remember the promise in James 5:8 that 'the coming of the Lord is at hand.'

"Oh, believer, share your faith and live your life

boldly in such a way that others can receive Christ by faith and be saved. Think of it, friend. You could pray to be led to those who have not yet heard the truth. You may be the one who leads the very last soul to Christ.

"Second Peter 3:10-14 says that 'the day of the Lord will come as a thief in the night, in which the heavens will pass away with a great noise, and the elements will melt with fervent heat; both the earth and the works that are in it will be burned up.

" 'Therefore, since all these things will be dissolved, what manner of persons ought you to be in holy conduct and godliness, looking for and hastening the coming of the day of God, because of which the heavens will be dissolved, being on fire, and the elements will melt with fervent heat? Nevertheless we, according to His promise, look for new heavens and a new earth in which righteousness dwells.

" 'Therefore, beloved, looking forward to these things, be diligent to be found by Him in peace, without spot and blameless.'

"I urge you to imitate our Lord and Savior and say with him, 'I must be about My Father's business.' "

As Tsion continued, Judd felt a new resolve to serve God. No matter what it cost him, no matter where he had to go, he wanted to be about God's business.

Tsion urged viewers to visit his Web site for more information and to decide for Christ. "The most wonderful news I can share with you today is that God has prompted us to use the brilliant minds and technology we have been blessed with here. Anyone who communicates with us via the Internet will get a personal response with everything you need to know about how to receive Christ.

"Yes, I know the ruler of this world has outlawed even visiting our site, but we can assure you that it is secure and that your visit cannot be traced. We have thousands of Internet counselors who can answer any question and lead you to Christ.

"We also have teams of rescuers who can transport you here if you are being persecuted for the sake of Christ. This is a dangerous time, and many will be killed. Many of our own loved ones have lost their lives in the pursuit of righteousness. But we will do what we can until the end to keep fighting for what is right. For in the end, we win, and we will be with Jesus."

Tsion's words warmed Judd's heart, and as he walked home he prayed for the people who would see the broadcast and who hadn't accepted the mark of Carpathia. He believed everything Tsion had said, but there was still an ache in his heart about Mark.

———————

Lionel saw Judd a few days after Tsion had spoken and called him over. "You don't think Mark's death is your fault, do you?"

Judd winced. "I know I couldn't have done anything to save him, but I don't understand why he was so stupid."

"He saved the others. That wasn't stupid."

"Not that. The way Mark was, going with the militia, doing stuff without thinking about the consequences."

"You mean you're upset because he was so much like you?" Lionel said.

Judd stared at him.

"I'm serious," Lionel said. "Mark was always doing stuff without talking with others, getting an idea and running with it. Sometimes it worked out. Sometimes it didn't."

Judd shook his head. "Maybe I'm mad because he didn't change."

"And maybe this whole Baghdad thing—that you didn't get to go with Captain Steele—has something to do—"

"It's not that," Judd snapped. He turned away and looked at a row of screens with people typing messages. "You know what really ticks me off? That God let it happen in the first place."

"Okay, so that's who you're really mad at."

"Why does he allow his followers to die like that? Thousands have been executed by the GC. Thousands! And God just sits there or stands or whatever."

"Remember when my uncle André died?" Lionel said. "I thought I had a good chance to tell him the truth. I was ticked off at God for a long time about that."

"How'd you resolve it?"

Lionel scratched his head and patted the stump of his left arm. "Same way I resolved this. There are some things I'm just not going to understand. God lets some things happen that don't make sense, at least to me. But I guess part of faith is believing that God is still on the throne and that none of this is taking him by surprise."

Judd sat and heaved a sigh. "When I was little one of my uncles died. He was a strong Christian and used to take me on sailing trips on Lake Michigan. I couldn't understand how God could let such a good guy get cancer and die. I still don't see any sense in it, even though I believe God's there and really does care."

"I like to think that God was so near to Mark at the end," Lionel said, "that Mark could have gone through anything. It's clear from the communication from Fulcire that Mark didn't give them a thing."

"Though the reporters said he blabbed everything."

Lionel clicked on the computer and pulled up messages from readers to Tsion Ben-Judah's Web site. Tsion had allowed Lionel and the others to put a section for the Young Trib Force there, and Vicki had written a tribute to Mark.

"Mark worked so hard on different parts of the Web site," Lionel said, "and there are people who are believers today because of what he did. And if he were here right now, I think he'd want us to keep doing everything we can to reach out to people."

"That's my goal too, but there's something else that's come up since his death."

"What's that?"

Judd lowered his voice. "Vicki and I want to be in Jerusalem when the final war starts."

"You're crazy."

"We want to make life miserable for those GC troops that'll try to overrun the city and then be there when Jesus comes back and wins the battle with only a few words."

"You're both going to get killed."

"So, if that's what God wants . . ."

"Don't let your anger at Fulcire and his goons make you go off the deep end. When the GC get here, they're going to unleash everything they have. If you're in the way—"

"I have to be in the way," Judd snapped.

Lionel rubbed his neck. "You haven't seen the video from Baghdad yet, have you?"

"I wasn't invited to see it."

Lionel caught Chang's attention and asked if he could show Judd a clip of the conference. Chang showed Lionel where to find the file, and Lionel pulled it up on the screen. "This is the creepiest thing I've seen from Carpathia. And if he's going to be in Jerusalem when the end comes, it's one place I don't want to be, and I don't want you to be. I hope seeing this will help you change your mind. If Vicki's going with you—"

"Just show me the video," Judd said.

"All right, but let me set it up. Captain Steele and the others put bugs in the conference room where they knew Nicolae and his cabinet would meet. Before his heads of state got there, Carpathia hinted to his top people that something big was up."

"More beheadings of believers?"

"No, though that's happening. He said he wanted to introduce his people to a trio who would help accomplish their goals. Leon Fortunato and the others begged to hear more, but Carpathia wouldn't tell them. Then when they had their big meeting . . . well, let me just show you." Lionel fast-forwarded the video. "I'm showing you this so you know what kind of evil you're dealing with. Are you ready?"

Judd nodded and prepared himself for the worst.

# 28

VICKI walked into the tech center and spotted Judd looking over Lionel's shoulder. Judd still hadn't been able to talk much about Mark, but she was trying to be patient.

"Hello, Mrs. Thompson," Chang said with a smile.

Vicki couldn't get used to hearing the words *Mrs. Thompson*. It made her feel old. "Please call me Vicki."

Judd waved Vicki over and explained what they were watching. He seemed more excited than he had for days as he told her what was happening on the screen. Lionel started the video over, and Vicki stared at the surprisingly clear footage.

Vicki had seen news reports about the arrival of the ten regional potentates to Baghdad and the resulting parades, light shows, and stage shows performed in their honor. Stands filled with people cheered each regional potentate. It was more than Vicki could stand to watch the unholy mockery.

Leon Fortunato had introduced Nicolae, and the crowd had interrupted him many times with huge ovations. Most chilling was Carpathia's pledge to eliminate those who opposed peace, as he put it, within half a year.

*Interesting timing,* Vicki thought.

"This meeting took place the morning after Carpathia's big speech about killing their enemies," Lionel said. "Nobody saw this except for the people in that room in Baghdad and those who were handpicked by Rayford Steele here in Petra."

"Amazing," Vicki said as she studied the video. She saw a nervous Leon Fortunato and several potentates, including the one from the United North American States. She also noticed Suhail Akbar, chief of Security and Intelligence.

"You can see they're each wearing clothing from their region," Judd said, pointing to the African and South American potentates who wore colorful outfits.

"Who are those three?" Vicki said. "They look like statues."

Lionel nodded. "Just wait. You'll see."

The three didn't move an inch. They seemed to be staring at the wall in front of them and didn't even react when Carpathia walked into the room.

Vicki shuddered. "They give me the creeps."

"Let me jump to the place where Carpathia begins." Lionel found the spot, and Judd scooted a chair close so Vicki could sit.

Nicolae thanked the group for coming and told them

he was the boss. He reminded them that three potentates from the group had died untimely deaths. His message was clear: Either follow me or die.

"Questions?" Nicolae said. "I thought not. Let us proceed."

"This is where it gets good," Lionel said. "I mean, not good, but . . . you know what I mean."

"Ladies and gentlemen," Carpathia said, "the time has come for me to take you into my confidence. We must all be on the same page in order to win the ultimate battle. Look into my eyes and listen, because what you hear today is truth and you will have no trouble believing every word of it. I am eternal. I am from everlasting to everlasting. I was there at the beginning, and I will remain through eternity future."

Nicolae stood and began to slowly circle the table.

"It's as if they're in a trance," Vicki said. "Like they're scared to even look at him."

"Here is the problem," Carpathia continued. "The one who calls himself God is not God. I will concede that he preceded me. When I evolved out of the primordial ooze and water, he was already there. But plainly, he had come about in the same manner I did. Simply because he preceded me, he wanted me to think he created me and all the other beings like him in the vast heavens. I knew better. Many of us did."

Vicki looked at Judd and shook her head. "I can't believe he's really saying this."

Carpathia talked as if he were explaining a math problem to a group of second graders. "He tried to tell us we were created as ministering servants. We had a job to do. He said he had created humans in his own image and that we were to serve them. Had I been there first, I could have told *him* that I had created *him* and that it was *he* who would serve me by ministering to my other creations.

"But he did not create anything! We, all of us—you, me, the other heavenly hosts, men and women—all came from that same primordial soup. But no! Not according to him! He was there with another evolved being like myself, and he claimed that one as his favored son. He was the special one, the chosen one, the only begotten one.

"I knew from the beginning it was a lie and that I—all of us—was being used. I was a bright and shining angel. I had ambition. I had ideas. But that was threatening to the older one. He called himself the creator God, the originator of life. He took the favored position. He demanded that the whole earth worship and obey him. I had the audacity to ask why. Why not me?"

"Because you're the father of lies," Judd said under his breath.

Carpathia admitted he had started a rebellion against God. "About a third of the other evolved beings agreed with me and took my side, promised to remain loyal. The other two-thirds were weaklings, easily swayed. They took the side of the so-called father and his so-called son."

"Is he talking about the angels?" Judd said.

"He has to be," Vicki said. "In Revelation it talks about a third of the stars being cast down to earth with Lucifer."

Carpathia continued, saying he would go back to heaven where he was before he was cast out. "We have been mortal enemies ever since, that father and that son and I. He even persuaded the evolved humans that he created them! But that could not be true, because if he had, they would not have free will. And if he created me, I would not have been able to rebel. It only makes sense.

"Once I figured that out, I began enjoying my role as the outcast. I found humans, the ones he liked to call his own, the easiest to sway. The woman with the fruit! She did not want to obey. It took nothing, mere suggestion, to get her to do what she really wanted. That happened not far from right here, by the way."

Carpathia walked around the group, lecturing them and giving his spin on the Bible. This was the gospel of the Antichrist, and the people in the room seemed to drink it in.

"And the first human siblings—they were easy! The younger was devoted to the one who called himself the only true God, but the other . . . ah, the other wanted only what I wanted. A little something for himself. Before you know it, I am proving beyond doubt that these creatures are not really products of the older angel's creativity. Within a few generations I have them so confused, so selfish, so full of themselves that the old man no longer wants to claim they were made in his image.

"They get drunk; they fight; they blaspheme. They are stubborn; they are unfaithful. They kill each other. The only ones I cannot get through to are Noah and his kin. Of course, the great creator decides the rest of history depends on them and wipes out everyone else with a flood. I eventually got to Noah, but he had already started repopulating the earth.

"Yes, I will admit it. The father and the son have been formidable foes over the generations. They have their favorites—the Jews, of all people. The Jews are the apples of the elder's eye, but therein lies his weakness. He has such a soft spot for them that they will be his undoing.

"My forces and I almost had them wiped out not so many generations ago, but father and son intervened, gave them back their own land, and foiled us again. Fate has toyed with us many times, my friends, but in the end we shall prevail.

"Father and son thought they were doing the world a favor by putting their intentions in writing. The whole plan is there, from sending the son to die and resurrect— which I proved I could do as well—to foretelling this entire period. Yes, many millions bought into this great lie. Up to now I would have to acknowledge that the other side has had the advantage.

"But two great truths will be their undoing. First, I know the truth. They are not greater or better than I or anyone else. They came from the same place we all did. And second, they must not have realized that I can read. I read their book! I know what they are up to! I know what happens next, and I even know where!

"Let them turn the lights off in the great city that I loved so much! Ah, how beautiful it was when it was the center for commerce and government, and the great ships and planes brought in goods from all over the globe. So it is dark now. And so what if it is eventually destroyed? I will build it back up, because I am more powerful than father and son combined.

"Let them shake the earth until it is level and drop hundred-pound chunks of ice from the skies. I will win in the end because I have read their battle plan. The old man plans to send the son to set up the kingdom he predicted more than three hundred times in his book, and he even tells where he will land! Ladies and gentlemen, we will have a surprise waiting for him."

Lionel stopped the recording. "See what I mean?"

"He actually thinks he can beat God," Judd said. "Incredible."

Lionel went forward on the recording and hit Play.

"We rally everyone—all of our tanks and planes and weapons and armies—in the Plain of Megiddo," Nicolae said. "It is in the Plain of Esdraelon in northern Israel, about twenty miles southeast of Haifa and sixty miles north of Jerusalem. At the appointed time we will dispatch one-third of our forces to overrun the stronghold at Petra.

"The rest of our forces will march on the so-called Eternal City and blast through those infernal walls, destroying all the Jews. And that is where we shall be, joined by our victorious forces from Petra, in full force to surprise the son when he arrives."

Vicki sat, stunned at the shameless way Nicolae was talking about Jesus.

Carpathia's next plan was to use the nuclear weapons stored at Al Hillah. "Needless to say, we do not want or need to destroy the planet. We simply want your soldiers to have more than what they need to wipe out the Jews and destroy the son I have so long opposed. So once I tell you how we will get your military leaders on board, your next assignment will be to get them to Al Hillah, where our Security and Intelligence director, Mr. Suhail Akbar, will see that they are more than fully equipped."

When the Russian potentate asked how to persuade troops that were discouraged, sick, and injured, Nicole rose. "The time has come to introduce you to three of my most trusted aides. No doubt you have been wondering about the three at the end of the table."

"Wondering why they seem not to have so much as blinked since we sat down," the British potentate said.

Carpathia laughed. "These three are not of this world. They use these shells only when necessary. Indeed, these are spirit beings who have been with me from the beginning. They were among the first who believed in me and saw the lie the father and son were trying to perpetrate in heaven and on earth."

Nicolae and Leon walked to the end of the table.

Lionel sat straight in his chair. "I hope you two have strong stomachs."

"What's going to happen?" Judd said.

"Wait a minute," Vicki said. "Revelation says something about this."

Lionel smiled. "Chapter 16, verses 13 and 14. Good job, Vicki. Dr. Ben-Judah recognized it the first time he saw it too."

"What's that say?" Judd asked.

Lionel stopped the video and pulled up the verses. " 'And I saw three unclean spirits like frogs coming out of the mouth of the dragon, out of the mouth of the beast, and out of the mouth of the false prophet. For they are spirits of demons, performing signs, which go out to the kings of the earth and of the whole world, to gather them to the battle of that great day of God Almighty.' "

Lionel started the video again.

Nicolae and Leon leaned toward the robotlike creatures and opened their mouths. Out came ugly, slimy, froglike beasts that leaped into the mouths of the three, one from Leon and two from Nicolae.

The three creatures suddenly opened their eyes wide and looked around the room. A camera angle switched, showing their faces, and the three sat back, smiling and nodding to the potentates around the table.

"Please meet Ashtaroth, Baal, and Cankerworm. They are the most convincing and persuasive spirits it has ever been my pleasure to know. I am going to ask now that we, all of us, gather round them and lay hands on them, commissioning them for this momentous task."

"This is so sick," Vicki said.

"Everything Carpathia does mocks God," Judd said.

With the potentates and the others touching the three, Nicolae said, "And now go, you three, to the ends of the earth to gather them to the final conflict in Jerusalem, where we shall once and for all destroy the father and his so-called Messiah. Persuade everyone everywhere that the victory is ours, that we are right, and that together we can destroy the son before he takes over this world. Once he is gone, we will be the undisputed, unopposed leaders of the world.

"I confer upon you the power to perform signs and heal the sick and raise the dead, if need be, to convince the world that victory is ours. And now go in power. . . ."

A huge bolt of lightning flashed on-screen, and the recording went black. When the image returned, Ashtaroth, Baal, and Cankerworm were gone, and Lionel quickly turned the volume down before a noisy peal of thunder erupted.

Nicolae beamed at his audience. Vicki wondered if showing this video would convince some people who Nicolae really was, but she knew most of the world was blind to the truth.

"Farewell, one and all," Nicolae said. "I will see you in six months in the Plain of Megiddo on that great day when victory shall be in sight."

Vicki shuddered as Judd muttered, "I'll be there, Nicky. And I'll see you thrown into hell."

## 29

**OVER** the next several weeks, Judd noticed a flurry of
activity in Petra. Nicolae's war plans were in full effect,
and his persecution increased. There were more
beheadings and more torture of prisoners, and the hunt
for Judah-ites continued. News had come of a GC raid in
France. A chateau filled with suspected Judah-ites had
been discovered, and all the occupants had been
beheaded.

Darrion and the others in Illinois wrote that they had
moved with Lenore into a hiding place run by a man who
had been discovered by Chloe Williams.

"His name is Enoch Dumas," Darrion said over a
scratchy phone line. "He was head of a group living in
downtown Chicago. That's where Chloe found them and
then brought them into the Strong Building."

"Where are they now?" Judd said.

"They split up after they left the Strong Building. Now

Enoch and a bunch of his friends are here in Palos Hills. It's a pretty rough group. Lots of former prostitutes and druggies. Sweet people, actually. They know what it means to be forgiven."

Judd explained the persecution they had seen over the past few weeks. "Is it safe there?"

"We're in the basement of an abandoned house. Others are scattered through the neighborhood. There are more than seventy, and Enoch says we'll probably reach a hundred before Jesus comes back."

"You should be careful of newcomers. Never know what the GC will try."

"I know, but what can we do, turn them away? People actually go out and try to find more converts every day. Enoch says we're trying to 'get more drowning people onto the life raft.' "

"Do you have meetings?"

Darrion chuckled. "Yeah, and they're nothing like the Young Trib Force meetings. People come in here, sing, and tell their stories. One man yesterday told how he had kept from taking Carpathia's mark. Not because he was a believer—he was just scared of getting a disease through the tattoo. His name is Adrian, and a GC Peacekeeper found him one day in a stairwell of some old apartment building. Before the Peacekeeper could react, Adrian hit him over the head with a pipe. Knocked him out cold."

"What did Adrian do then?"

"He went through the Peacekeeper's pockets looking for Nicks or food. You have to understand what it's like on the streets now. There's so much crime, but the GC only seems to be interested in getting people without Carpathia's mark."

"They don't report it on GCNN, but we've heard how bad it's getting."

"Well, guess what Adrian finds in the Peacekeeper's pocket? A pamphlet explaining the gospel. We think the Peacekeeper found it in some church or on a believer. Anyway, this Carpathia follower was actually a missionary because Adrian took the pamphlet, read it, and gave his heart to God."

"Incredible."

"He was so glad to find our group, not just because we have food and can give him protection, but to be near other believers. He didn't know he had the mark of the believer until he got here."

Darrion told him more stories, and Judd asked about Shelly, Conrad, and the others.

"We're doing pretty well. Mark's death shook all of us. I don't know that any of us have gotten over it."

"I know the feeling," Judd said. "But we'll see him again. You know that."

"I can't wait to see my mom and dad and Ryan Daley too."

The mention of Ryan took Judd's breath away.

When he hung up with Darrion he went outside and watched people gather their evening meal. It had been years since Ryan had been with them. He had missed so much of the Tribulation. What would Ryan be like when they saw him again? Would they really be able to recognize him? Would he be the same age as when he died, or would God somehow change his body to be older but still recognizable?

No matter what Ryan looked like—or Mark or Pete or John or the others who had died—Judd knew there was a great reunion ahead.

———————————

Vicki stayed busy over the weeks becoming an Internet counselor for young people. After intense sessions with the elders, Chang Wong, and Naomi Tiberius, Vicki took her place beside people of all nationalities who answered questions from around the world. She was excited that some of those she counseled were actually airlifted into Petra by Trib Force pilots.

Vicki knew the suffering and persecution would end, but as she heard the stories of hurting and wounded people, she longed for the return of Jesus even more. She couldn't wait to see him and hear his voice. She knew from reading the Scriptures that there were more prophecies concerning Jesus' seconding than his first. And this time he wouldn't come as the lowly, humble servant but as the mighty, conquering king ready to defeat his enemies.

Vicki was amazed to see the questions that came into the Web site. She even received one from a woman who was clearly not interested in knowing God but in finding out when the plague of darkness would be lifted from New Babylon.

"How could she believe that we have answers from the Bible but not believe the truth about God?" Vicki asked Judd as they ate one night.

"She's blind," Judd said. "These people know there's something to the claims of the Bible, but they follow Carpathia anyway. Those troops know how many soldiers God wiped out, but they still follow orders."

There was a slight knock on the door, and Judd opened it to find Sam Goldberg. Sam sat and had some wafers and quail. Judd and Vicki had been secretly talking with him about a possible trip to Israel before the start of the last great battle.

"Have you found anyone yet?" Judd asked.

"My friend Lev Taubman is from Jerusalem," Sam said quietly. "He wants to go back there badly, but his mother won't hear of it."

"Does he know any hiding places, any members of the resistance?" Vicki said.

"There is a man my father was acquainted with," Sam said. "Very old. His name is Shivte. Lev says he and his sons would never take the mark of Carpathia, but they are not believers either."

"You think they're still in Jerusalem?"

"Lev is sure of it because he received a message from another friend saying Shivte's wife has become a true believer. And with what I hear about . . ." Sam stopped and stared at them.

"What is it?" Vicki said.

"I'm not sure I should tell you what I heard about Dr. Ben-Judah."

"What, that he's teaching an elite group of Captain Steele's military people?" Judd said. "We know that."

"Did you know he has officially turned over his

administrative and teaching duties for Petra to Dr.
Rosenzweig?" Sam said.

*"What?"* Judd and Vicki said in unison.

"I can't tell you where I heard this, but I believe Tsion
wants to be part of the fighting force in Jerusalem. He's
been training to use a weapon."

"I don't believe it," Vicki said.

Sam leaned closer. "This is what I have heard. Tsion
believes the Bible teaches that a third of the remaining
Jews will turn to Messiah before the end. That means that
many will still need to be reached, and Tsion thinks if he
can get to Jerusalem, he can reach them."

Judd scratched the stubble of his beard. "It makes
sense, I guess."

"Now I don't feel so bad wanting to get to Jerusalem
to see Jesus return," Vicki said.

"Where does Tsion get that more Jews will come to
Messiah?" Judd said.

"It's in Zechariah 13. Verses 8 and 9."

Vicki grabbed a Bible, flipped toward the end of the
Old Testament. " '"And it shall come to pass in all the
land," says the Lord, "That two-thirds in it shall be cut
off and die, but one-third shall be left in it: I will bring
the one-third through the fire, will refine them as silver
is refined, and test them as gold is tested. They will call
on My name, and I will answer them. I will say, 'This is
My people'; and each one will say, 'The Lord is my
God.' "' "

As Vicki read the verses, something stirred inside her.
If there were more Jews who would accept Jesus as

Messiah, they had to be hiding. If she and Judd could help find them and prepare them in some way for the message . . . She looked at Judd and could tell he was thinking the same thing.

---

Lionel ate breakfast with Zeke Zuckermandel at least once a week and caught up on the latest with the Tribulation Force. Zeke was fun to talk with, and the two relived their days in Illinois and Wisconsin.

"You about ready to come out of that place with all the fancy computers and get yourself dirty?" Zeke said.

"What do you mean?" Lionel said.

"Just that I'm getting a band of people together to help out during the war."

"Tell me about it."

Zeke leaned forward and drew a finger through the sand. "This here is Petra with all the rocks and stuff. Here's the desert in front of us and around us, and all the way over here is Israel. Now, most people are mixed up about the Battle of Armageddon."

"How so?"

"This comes straight from Tsion himself. This valley of Armageddon is really just the staging area for Carpathia's armies. You know, where they set up, eat, prepare, that kinda thing. The actual wars are gonna take place here at Petra—" he pointed to the circle in the sand—"although you have to believe God won't let the armies have a victory here, and over here in Jerusalem. Tsion says people should call this 'the War of the Great

Day of God the Almighty.' But I can see how sayin' it's
Armageddon's just plain easier."

"I'm still confused about what's going to happen
when," Lionel said.

"Tsion says there are going to be something like eight
things happening after the Euphrates River goes dry."

"What's so important about that?"

"Well, you ever see an army try to get across a river
that's running? When it dries up, the kings and armies
east of here will have a clear shot at us. They can come
into this valley—it's called Megiddo—and be ready for
the trap."

"What trap?"

"Well, Tsion says this is exactly what God wants. It'll
look like there's no way anyone can stand up to the
strength of all those tanks and missiles and troops, but
God's gonna zap 'em."

"What else happens?"

"Once the river goes dry and the armies get together,
Babylon will be destroyed. God's gonna do that real
quick, and then comes the fall of Jerusalem. I'm kinda
hazy about how that happens, but finally Jesus will
appear on a white horse with a big army of his own. He'll
be mad at old Nicolae, and there's gonna be a lot of
blood, you can bet on that. There's gonna be a battle
close to here, though Petra will be safe. And then Jesus
will show up at the Mount of Olives."

"Wish I could be there," Lionel said.

"You and me both. But there's plenty to do here. As a
matter of fact, I'm looking for some volunteers."

"Is this the getting myself dirty part?"

Zeke smiled. "You got it. I need people to go out and pick up weapons, uniforms, ammo—just about anything you think we could use."

"Sounds dangerous."

"Could be. But my guess is the GC won't have any power over believers who are living here in Petra. God's gonna protect us."

"You don't know that for sure."

"Right. Not 100 percent, but I'm willing to chance it. How about you?"

---

Judd went to the airstrip in late December and met with Mac McCullum. Mac, Abdullah Smith, and Ree Woo had become the main pilots for the Tribulation Force, and they had recruited other pilots to help fly believers to Petra from all over the world. Mac had tons of stories of miraculous things God had done to keep believers safe, but this was a short meeting.

"Found what you were looking for in Morocco," Mac said, handing Judd a small box. "Hope the little lady enjoys it."

Judd thanked him and raced back to their empty house. Vicki had finished her work at the tech center for the day and was spending some time with little Kenny.

Judd quickly went behind their house to a rock outcropping where he had seen a small bush. After he dug the plant up by its roots and put it in a pot, he placed it on the nightstand. He cut strips of cloth and draped them around the bush, then set the wrapped box on one of the sturdy branches.

He watched for Vicki for nearly an hour. When he saw her coming, he hid in a corner of the room and waited.

"Judd?" Vicki called as she came close. "Mr. Thompson? Are you home?" She walked inside and saw the bush. "What in the world?"

Judd started humming a Christmas tune.

Vicki caught her breath. "What's going on?"

"Just because we're in the middle of the Tribulation doesn't mean we can't celebrate, right?"

"It's December 25th! I forgot all about it."

Judd pointed at the tiny, crudely wrapped present in the bush. Vicki just stared at it, her mouth open. Judd handed her the box and she opened it slowly, the fading sunlight twinkling off the stone in the middle of the ring.

She couldn't say anything for a moment. Then, "It must have cost a fortune."

"I didn't have a chance to get you a ring when we were married. Mac found a jeweler on one of his flights, and he got a bargain. The jeweler thinks it'll last at least a thousand years."

Vicki smiled. "I hope we get to find out if he's right."

**LIONEL** awoke from another nightmare and wiped sweat from his forehead. On some nights he dreamed about dogs chasing him, barking and biting at something trapped under a rock. Other nights Lionel dreamed of a dragon chasing his friends toward a cliff. At the edge of the cliff was a huge army.

This time he had dreamed of Judd and Vicki being caught by the Global Community. He knew it had something to do with their leaving the day before. Lionel had promised he wouldn't say anything to Chang or anyone else about their secret departure. Judd had been sure Captain Steele would have stopped them.

When Judd had discovered that Westin Jakes, Z-Van's former pilot, had caught an airlift out of the desert near New Babylon and was again flying for the Tribulation Force, Judd had asked a favor. Lionel had seen them off to the airstrip and waved good-bye, not knowing if he would ever see his friends again.

285

Lionel got a glass of water and looked out the screenless window at the lightening sky. The sight of Petra in the morning never ceased to move him. The red-rocked city seemed to glow at both sunup and sundown.

Lionel quietly went to the tech center. He kept in contact with his friends in Illinois and e-mailed a new friend in New Babylon, of all places. Through Tsion's Web site Lionel had met a young German woman named Steffi. She was with a group that had stayed in the still-darkened city. She reported that nothing much had changed. People were still screaming and chewing their tongues, and the believers were able to move through the city undetected.

*Lionel, is there a way I could call your phone and talk about our airlift out of here?* Steffi wrote. *I know that our main connection is through Otto Weser and you probably don't have much to do with that, but it would calm my nerves if I could talk.*

Lionel wrote back, giving Steffi a number and a time. As soon as he sent the message, another message popped up.

*Lionel,*

*We finally made it to Shivte's house a little after four this morning and wanted you to know we're okay. We're supposed to meet with some of the resistance fighters later.*

*The flight out of Petra was a little scary, but Westin found the landing strip. Then we hooked up with one of Shivte's sons and made the drive into Jerusalem without being spotted by the GC.*

*Westin told us the most amazing story about getting out of New Babylon. He and his friends found an abandoned terrorist training camp and holed up there for a while. Westin got a flight out through the Trib Force, but Judd's friend Zvi and some of the others decided to go back into New Babylon.*

*Thanks for praying for us, and don't worry. We're not planning to do any fighting, just trying to reach out to Jewish people who haven't accepted their Messiah.*

*Take care and we'll call you soon.*

*Love,*
*Vicki*

Lionel shook his head. Most people would try to stay as safe as they could during the final battle. But after all Judd and Vicki had been through, they still wanted to reach people with the message of God's love and forgiveness.

---

Judd shook hands with Shivte in the dimly lit home and introduced Vicki. The elderly man shuffled to the kitchen table of their small home. He and his sons were stocky men and soft-spoken. None of them had the mark of the believer.

Shivte asked one of his sons to get his wife, then motioned for Judd and Vicki to sit. "You should know that it was my wife who arranged this," he said. "And I only agreed to help you come here on the condition that you would not try to get us to change our beliefs."

Judd pursed his lips. "As I wrote from Petra, we don't want to get in the way. We just want to support the resistance effort in any way we can."

"My son will show you to one of the underground hideouts," Shivte said. "There are military people there who can show you what is needed."

Shivte offered them some meager rations, which Judd and Vicki politely refused. "We brought some supplies with us," Judd said. "It would please us if you would take them."

Shivte nodded. "We're grateful."

Shivte's wife came through the doorway, smiling. She was a large woman with heavy lines in her face, and Judd thought she looked a lot like his grandmother. When she spotted the mark of the believer on their foreheads, Judd thought she would weep. She hugged them both and thanked them for bringing food.

"How I would have liked to have experienced Petra, if only for a few days," the woman said. "I can only imagine the teaching and fellowship you enjoyed there." She glanced at her husband. "But there are more pressing matters here. You can see that I have not yet convinced the most important people in my life of the truth."

Shivte stood and waved a hand at her. "I'm not staying to hear this."

"Will you go get the people now?" she said.

Shivte nodded and left the house.

"Who is he going to get?" Judd said.

"You'll see," Shivte's wife said.

"How did you become a believer?" Vicki said.

"I didn't plan on it," she said. "My husband and sons said they would not take Carpathia's mark, but we had to have food. So I volunteered to take it so I could buy and sell. The idea of worshiping that statue . . . well, I couldn't imagine it, but we had to survive."

"How close did you come to taking it?" Judd said.

"I was at the Temple Mount, in line. I thought it was the only way to save my family. But then I saw a disturbance and slipped out of line. A man of God was shot—his name was Micah—but the bullets didn't kill him. After that, I had to know more about this message. I have a young friend, the one who wrote your friend Sam, and he helped me find Tsion Ben-Judah's Web site."

"And your husband and sons?" Vicki said.

"We have agreed not to talk about it. They are devout Jews, and they will resist Carpathia to the end, but they are not ready for Messiah. How I pray for them every day that somehow the message will get through."

Footsteps sounded on the street outside. Shivte's wife stood and motioned for Judd and Vicki to follow her to the door. "I was talking with a friend about you two and where you would stay. We have very little room here. One conversation led to another, and finally I discovered that—"

The door opened and a man and a woman walked through. In the dim light, Judd couldn't see their faces. When they moved closer, his mouth dropped open. "I don't believe it!"

The two hugged Judd tightly and wept. Judd turned to Vicki. "Remember Nada and Kasim? These are their parents, Jamal and Lina Ameer."

Lina reached out and hugged Vicki. "So this is the person Judd was in love with. You're very beautiful, my dear."

Vicki blushed. "I'm very sorry about your son and daughter. Our group back in the States prayed for you almost every day."

"We appreciate that more than you can know," Jamal said.

"We couldn't believe it when we heard you were coming," Lina said. "We'd love to hear what God has done since we last talked. How is Lionel?"

They sat at the table and Judd explained about Lionel's injury and how they had gotten back to the States. The two were saddened to hear about Lionel's arm but were glad he was safe in Petra.

Judd asked if they knew anything about the rebel fighters, and Jamal pulled out a crude map. "There are underground tunnels through here. Many people have hidden in them since the GC took over. We have weapons and ammunition, even some computers to help us track the movement of the GC One World Unity Army's troops. We can go through there as we head to our apartment. You will stay with us."

Shivte closed the door quietly and put a finger to his lips. "We must hide. The GC are going house to house down the street."

Judd and Vicki followed the others to a hiding place under the stairs.

"Does this happen often?" Vicki whispered to Jamal.

"All the time," Jamal said.

Lionel took Steffi's call and listened to her story. It was much like others he had heard from people who had already come out of New Babylon. Her father wanted to be in Carpathia's city to fulfill prophecy, but things had become so horrible there with the plague of darkness that Steffi couldn't imagine staying any longer.

"Fortunately, I think you'll be out of there pretty soon," Lionel said. "The seven-year anniversary of Carpathia's peace treaty with Israel is coming up in only a few days."

"I've longed for the coming of Jesus," Steffi said. "I've been afraid the plague of darkness will lift and the GC will catch my father."

"Does he spend a lot of time in GC areas?" Lionel said.

"The palace, the prison—wherever he thinks he can find information or a possible person who doesn't have the mark of the believer. I've told him he should be more careful. . . ."

Lionel pulled the phone away from his ear. Something odd was happening in Chang Wong's area. "Hang on a second, Steffi."

Chang was standing and pointing to his computer screen. "It's happened!"

Others came running.

"What's happened?" Lionel said, but Chang didn't hear him.

"What's going on?" Steffi said.

"It might be something with the Euphrates River," Lionel said. "Chang's been watching sensors planted there by the GC—"

Before Lionel could finish his sentence, Chang turned to Naomi Tiberius and said, "There was water in the Euphrates a minute ago, and now it is dry as a bone. You can bet tomorrow it will be on the news—someone standing in the dry, cracking riverbed, showing that you can walk across without fear of mud or quicksand."

"That is amazing," Naomi said. "I mean, I knew it was coming, but isn't it just like God to do it all at once? And isn't that a 1,500-mile river?"

"It used to be."

Lionel explained what he had heard to Steffi, and she gave an excited shout. "This means the Lord's return is that much closer."

Lionel finished the conversation and joined Chang and the others.

Later a Trib Force scout plane reported vast weapons and troop movement toward the dried-up river. Lionel figured Carpathia had been reading the Bible but was too stupid to understand how the book ended.

---

Vicki was excited about Jamal and Lina's spacious apartment. The two offered to give Judd and Vicki their bedroom, but instead they put down sleeping bags from Petra in the living room.

The next few weeks Judd and Vicki spent time getting to know the complex series of passageways underneath Jerusalem. It would be their job to supply ammunition to the rebel forces seeking to keep the GC away.

"We respect your wish to not be involved in the actual

fighting," Jamal said, "but your job will be just as critical to defending Jerusalem."

After dinner one evening, Lina showed Vicki pictures of their family and pointed out Kasim and Nada. "I miss them both very much, but it won't be long before we're together again."

"It might be sooner than we think," Jamal said. "Judd just showed me an intercepted message from a top Global Community officer."

"What did it say?" Vicki said.

"Basically, it warned all Peacekeepers and Morale Monitors throughout the world to prepare for a new assignment in the Middle East. We think it will only be a few days before hundreds of thousands join the GC One World Unity Army."

"Which means people without Carpathia's mark will be able to come out of hiding," Vicki said.

"As long as they're careful," Judd said. "Citizens can still kill people without the mark and get a reward. But it looks like the end is close."

---

Lionel was talking with Sam Goldberg when he noticed Rayford Steele running toward the helipad. Lionel and Sam walked to a rock outcropping as droves of people headed for a clearing.

"What's going on?" Lionel said.

"Maybe it's the evacuation of New Babylon," Sam said. "I heard that pilots from here will fly the rescue mission as soon as word comes that believers are to move out."

"They'd need something bigger than a helicopter, don't you think?" Lionel said.

Many people near the chopper wept. Sam climbed down and ran to the edge of the crowd, then returned. "They're saying good-bye to Dr. Ben-Judah. He's going to Jerusalem."

A few moments later, Tsion and Buck Williams moved through the crowd. Tsion pulled what looked to Lionel like a handkerchief from his pocket and waved it as Buck climbed aboard the chopper.

"People! People!" Tsion shouted. "I am overwhelmed at your kindness. Pray for me, won't you, that I will be privileged to usher many more into the kingdom. We are just days away now from the battle, and you know what that means. Be waiting and watching. Be ready for the Glorious Appearing! If I am not back before then, we will be reunited soon thereafter.

"You will be in my thoughts and prayers, and I know I go with yours. Thank you again! You are in good hands with Chaim Rosenzweig, and so I bid you farewell!" Tsion kept waving at the people as the helicopter lifted off.

"Wish we could be going to Jerusalem," Sam said.

"You're part of Zeke's brigade," Lionel said. "There'll be plenty of action here."

Lionel sprinted toward the tech center. He couldn't wait to tell Judd and Vicki that Tsion was heading their way.

**31**

**JUDD'S** head spun with Lionel's news of Tsion's departure from Petra. Then Chang Wong reported that hundreds of thousands of troops would arrive in the valley of Megiddo the following day. Everything was happening so fast.

"That's going to be a nightmare to feed and equip all those soldiers," Vicki said.

"The Global Community's been preparing for this a long time," Jamal said. "They'll find a way to mass their troops."

With the help of others, Judd and Vicki placed ammunition boxes in strategic places throughout the tunnels. When the fighting began in Jerusalem, they would be able to get ammo to rebels within minutes.

"They keep talking about a guerilla war," Vicki said. "What's that mean?"

"Lots of little wars throughout the city," Judd said.

"Basically the rebels know they have no chance of beating this army head-on, so they're going to spread out and try to make it as difficult as possible for the GC."

Rebel leaders barked orders, and young men and women prepared for battle. Teams of workers went into the street to set up barricades.

"Chopper's landing at the Temple Mount," one man yelled as he ran through the tunnel to get more Uzis and grenades.

Judd grabbed the man by the arm. "Is it a GC chopper?"

"Didn't look like it, but I didn't stay long. There's an angry mob out there."

"You think that's Tsion?" Vicki said.

"Has to be," Judd said.

It took Judd a few minutes to get his bearings once he and Vicki had climbed out of their hiding place. Making sure there were no Global Community forces nearby, they headed for the Temple Mount.

Judd was surprised to see old men praying at the Wailing Wall, something they hadn't been allowed to do for a long time. "I haven't seen so many unmarked people since Masada."

"These people must have been in hiding for years," Vicki said. "But you can tell they're scared."

"They're scared, but you have to understand. This is their city. They'll do anything to defend it."

"Even if it's going to fall?" Vicki said. "You know Tsion believes it will."

Judd took Vicki's hand, and they ran to the place

where Judd had seen the two witnesses, Eli and Moishe.
He wished they would come back now and preach.

Suddenly there was a commotion when a man with a
gun at his side pushed his way through the crowd at the
Wailing Wall. He wore loose-fitting canvas-type clothing
and a jacket. On his head was the traditional covering of
the Jews, a yarmulke. "Men of Israel, hear me!" he
bellowed. "I am one of you! I come with news!"

"It's Tsion!" Judd whispered. "Come on!"

They pushed their way to the edge of the gathering,
then climbed higher for a better look. Men yelled at
Tsion, but Judd couldn't tell what they were saying.

Finally, Tsion said, "What you need is Messiah!"

Some cheered, many laughed, and even more grumbled. Judd caught sight of Buck Williams.

"Many of you know me! I am Tsion Ben-Judah. I
became persona non grata when I broadcast my findings
after being commissioned to study the prophecies
concerning Messiah. My family was slaughtered. I was
exiled. A bounty remains on my head."

"Then why are you here, man? Do you not know the
Global Community devils are coming back?"

"I do not fear them, because Messiah is coming too!
Do not scoff! Do not turn your backs on me! Listen to
our own Scriptures. What do you think this means?" He
read Zechariah 12:8-10: " 'In that day the Lord will
defend the inhabitants of Jerusalem; the one who is
feeble among them in that day shall be like David, and
the house of David shall be like God, like the Angel of
the Lord before them. It shall be in that day that I will

seek to destroy all the nations that come against Jerusalem.

" 'And I will pour on the house of David and on the inhabitants of Jerusalem the Spirit of grace and supplication; then they will look on Me whom they pierced. Yes, they will mourn for Him as one mourns for his only son, and grieve for Him as one grieves for a firstborn.' "

Judd felt tears coming to his eyes and glanced at Vicki. She was overwhelmed with emotion too.

"You tell us what it means!" someone yelled.

"God is saying he will make the weakest among us as strong as David," Tsion said. "And he will destroy the nations that come against us. My dear friends, that is all the other nations of the earth!"

"We know. Carpathia has made it no secret!"

"But God says we will finally look upon 'Me whom they pierced,' and that we will mourn him as we would mourn the loss of a firstborn son. Messiah was pierced! And God refers to the pierced one as 'Me'! Messiah is also God.

"Beloved, my exhaustive study of the hundreds of prophecies concerning Messiah brought me to the only logical conclusion. Messiah was born of a virgin in Bethlehem. He lived without sin. He was falsely accused. He was slain without cause. He died and was buried and was raised after three days. Those prophecies alone point to Jesus of Nazareth as Messiah. He is the one who is coming to fight for Israel. He will avenge all the wrongs that have been perpetrated upon us over the centuries.

"The time is short. The day of salvation is here. You

may not have time to study this for yourselves. Messiah is God's promise to us. Jesus is the fulfillment of that promise. He is coming. Let him find you ready!"

People shouted at Tsion, clearly offended. Some walked away, but others seemed to want to hear more. Even with all the noise and confusion the crowd grew, and Judd was worried Peacekeepers or Morale Monitors might show up.

Tsion kept talking, quoting Scripture, and explaining it. He spoke of the armies gathering to destroy them, but he urged the people not to be afraid of them but to be ready for the Messiah.

"If you want to know how to be prepared for him," Tsion yelled, "gather here to my left and my associate will tell you. Please! Come now! Don't delay! Now is the accepted time. Today is the day of salvation."

Vicki looked at Judd. "Does he mean Buck?"

Judd nodded in amazement. Buck wasn't Jewish and was a reporter, not a preacher.

But to Judd's astonishment, Buck began speaking after a short pause. "When Jewish people such as yourselves come to see that Jesus is your long-sought Messiah, you are not converting from one religion to another, no matter what anyone tells you. You have found your Messiah, that is all. Some would say you have been completed, fulfilled. Everything you have studied and been told all your life is the foundation for your acceptance of Messiah and what he has done for you."

Tsion bowed his head in prayer as Buck told the men how to accept God's gift of salvation through Jesus. "He comes not only to avenge Jerusalem but to save your soul, to forgive your sins, to grant you eternal life with God."

---

Lionel stared at the computer screen, now split into two sections. On one side he watched troop movement into the valley outside Jerusalem. On the other he monitored GCNN's coverage of the pending battle. For the last several days, reporters had talked about the Euphrates River drying up.

Now they focused on Nicolae Carpathia riding a huge, black horse. The man held a long sword and grinned from ear to ear. "We have the absolute latest in technology and power at our fingertips," Carpathia shouted. "My months of strategy are over, and we have a foolproof plan. That frees me to encourage the troops, to be flown to the battle sites, to mount up, to be a visual reminder that victory is in sight and will soon be in hand.

"It will not be long, my brothers and sisters in the Global Community, until we shall reign victorious. I shall return to rebuild my throne as conquering king. The world shall finally be as one! It is not too early to rejoice!"

---

Vicki couldn't believe that she was seeing prophecy fulfilled before her eyes. As Buck prayed with people pressing toward him, Tsion Ben-Judah told others the truth about Jesus, and more Jews streamed in to hear the message. The people who had rejected Jesus for so long now believed he was their Messiah.

Crowds surged around Tsion and Buck. Soon thousands wept aloud and fell to their knees, asking God's forgiveness.

Tsion continued his message, telling the throng that the armies gathered nearby would face another terror from God, a mighty earthquake. He said hail weighing as much as one hundred pounds would fall to the earth, crushing people.

"Do you know what will happen here, right here in Jerusalem?" Tsion said. "It will be the only city in the world spared the devastating destruction of the greatest earthquake ever known to man. The Bible says, 'Now the great city'—that's Jerusalem—'was divided into three parts, and the cities of the nations fell.'

"That, my brothers, is good news. Jerusalem will be made more beautiful, more efficient. It will be prepared for its role as the new capital in Messiah's thousand-year kingdom."

---

Lionel wrote a quick report to the rest of the Young Trib Force and hoped they would see it. There was so much activity in the tech center that Lionel had to put on headphones to hear the latest from GCNN. With a click of a button, he viewed a camera mounted at the top of Petra. Below the edges of the rock walls, platoons of soldiers prepared their weapons. He clicked on GCNN, which showed an aerial picture of Nicolae's army, and shook his head. *A few thousand soldiers against that?*

His phone rang and he was surprised to hear Steffi on the other end. Her voice trembled with fear. "We've been watching the coverage about the battle. I'm afraid we've waited too long to get out of here."

Lionel explained what he knew about the rescue effort and told Steffi that Mac McCullum would fly there. "Where are you now?"

"Outside of our hiding place on the—" Steffi stopped, then gasped.

"What is it?" Lionel said.

"Something so bright that the darkness is gone!" she said. "It's big. Very big."

Before Lionel could ask another question, a piercing male voice sounded through the phone. " 'Babylon the great is fallen, is fallen, and has become a dwelling place of demons, a prison for every foul spirit, and a cage for every unclean and hated bird! . . .' "

Lionel raised a fist in the air. "Steffi, that's the angel! I'll go tell Mr. McCullum. He'll come get you!"

But before Lionel could hang up, another voice said, " 'Come out of her, my people, lest you share in her sins, and lest you receive of her plagues. For her sins have reached to heaven, and God has remembered her iniquities.' "

As soon as Lionel hung up, he raced to find Mac. He finally found him at his airplane, firing up the engines.

Mac had heard the report from someone else and was on his way to New Babylon. "Got room for one more, if you'd like to come along," he said.

Lionel climbed on board while Mac called for another

plane to help evacuate believers. "With these two planes, I figure we should be able to bring up to two hundred people out of there. I hope that's enough."

They landed near the palace and Lionel gasped. People who had been living in darkness wandered about the runway, limping and staggering, not knowing what to do.

As soon as the plane stopped, Lionel helped Mac get the stairs down. More than 150 believers cheered outside. The other plane landed and took half of the believers who carried their belongings in sacks and boxes. Loading took only a few minutes, and they were ready to go.

Lionel looked at the faces of people as they boarded, wondering which one was Judd's friend Zvi. Lionel saw a blonde young lady with an older woman and approached her. "Steffi?"

"Lionel?"

The two hugged, and Steffi introduced Lionel to her mom.

"No time for chitchat," Mac said. "Let's get out of here."

Soon the planes raced down the runways. Before the wheels of Mac's plane were off the ground, Lionel noticed a volley of missiles being launched from just outside the city. As the planes rose higher, black smoke engulfed the once gleaming city. Mac circled as missile after missile hit the heart of New Babylon, destroying the entire city in less than one hour.

---

As darkness fell, Judd and Vicki broke away from Tsion's preaching and scurried underground. The news of Babylon's fall had reached them through Tsion's Web site. Believers in the underground passage were excited about Judd and Vicki's news that thousands of Jews were turning to Christ, but unbelievers scoffed.

"If Babylon has fallen," Vicki said, "that means there are only two prophetic events left."

"The seventh Bowl Judgment and the Glorious Appearing," Judd said.

Vicki nodded. "And if that's true, should we stay here and feed ammo to a losing cause or try to convince as many people as possible that they need Christ?"

"I don't want to let the resistance down, but a lot of people are hungry for the message. After all, once these people die, we won't have another chance."

Judd thought about Vicki's idea while he found something for them to eat. A supply area had pita bread and peanut butter, but that was about it.

When he returned, Vicki was talking with a female Jewish rebel without Carpathia's mark. *Reaching more people is what this is all about,* Judd thought.

When she finished with the woman—who did not pray—Vicki seemed even more animated. "There are so many like her all around us. If we can get to them tonight before—"

A noise interrupted her. Several rebel leaders rushed into the tunnel. Walls vibrated, and lights clinked against ancient stone walls. At first Judd thought it was an earthquake. Then he realized the truth.

It was the rumble of Carpathia's army.

# 32

VICKI held tightly to Judd as the Global Community's Unity Army rumbled through the streets of Jerusalem. She hoped they were simply putting their tanks and soldiers into place, but Carpathia's army could attack at any moment.

Vicki had felt a sense of adventure coming to the Old City. Jamal and Lina, Judd's friends from a previous trip to Israel, had taken them in. They had also met an old man named Shivte and his wife. These rebels were trying to hold off the GC army—something Vicki believed was part of biblical prophecy.

But the closer the GC army came and the more the walls of the underground tunnel shook, the less excited she became about being here. They could have stayed in Petra. Instead, they were in the crosshairs of the GC.

Vicki reminded herself that Jesus would soon be back to wipe out this army. And she and Judd had been overwhelmed when thousands had become believers earlier near the Temple Mount. Rabbi Tsion Ben-Judah had given the message of Jesus. Still, the thundering army sent a shiver through her.

Judd scurried to talk with one of their leaders and came back a few minutes later. "He thinks we won't see action until morning. He wants us to get some rest. Let's head back to Jamal's place."

They took a tunnel heading east, passing rebels armed with Uzis and hand grenades. Vicki had become as familiar with these tunnels over the past few months as she had with their hideout in Wisconsin. Secret passageways snaked underneath streets and buildings. Lights clanked on the stone walls as GC tanks and transport trucks rolled overhead.

A few believers spoke with rebels about Jesus when they passed, trying to convince them of the truth, but many fighters didn't want to hear about the gospel.

"We don't want your blasphemy!" one rebel yelled at a believer. "Stay away from us!"

Judd peeked through the tunnel opening and motioned Vicki forward.

By the time they made it safely to Jamal's apartment, darkness had fallen. Neither Jamal nor Lina was home. While Judd checked the computer for the latest troop movement news, Vicki pulled the curtain back on the window. "You don't have to check the computer—look out the window," she said.

They were high enough to see outside the walls of the Old City. Tanks and large vehicles were in place. Streetlights cast eerie shadows on the monstrous army.

"Our people are going up against *that*?" Judd said.

"It's not just our people—God's fighting against the army," Vicki said.

"What does Tsion say about Jerusalem? Doesn't the Bible predict it's going to fall?"

Vicki nodded and closed the curtain. "Chang said in his last e-mail that Tsion was coming here to help bring his fellow Jews into the kingdom before it was too late. Tsion believes the Unity Army will capture many rebels and conquer Jerusalem."

"Are you scared?"

Vicki hugged Judd. "I keep remembering what you said about sticking together no matter what. And if we're attacked by the GC, at least we'll die together."

"I'd rather be alive to see Jesus when he comes back, but you're right. From here on out, we stick close."

---

Lionel Washington sat on his bed in Petra, scanning the list of names in his prayer diary. Many of them were highlighted in yellow and had the word *home* written after their name. Ryan Daley. Pete Davidson. Mark Eisman. Chloe Williams. *It won't be long until I see all of these people*, he thought.

He wasn't as sure about his other friends on the list. Rayford Steele. Buck Williams. Tsion Ben-Judah. Lionel knew from Chang Wong that Buck and Tsion were in Jerusalem. And Rayford Steele had returned to Petra in a chopper and was probably spending time with his grandson, Kenny. But what would happen in the morning?

Would Jesus come back before the GC attacked? Already the Unity Army had Petra surrounded.

*What if Tsion is wrong about Petra? What if Jerusalem stands and Petra falls?*

Lionel pushed the questions from his mind and prayed over each name. It had been more than seven years since the disappearances and the moment he had finally cried out to God. He had come far in those seven years, and now he was near the end.

Lionel didn't know the exact time of Jesus' return, but surely it would happen in the next day or two. What that moment would be like was anyone's guess, and Lionel couldn't wait.

Zeke called him on the radio. The burly man had asked Lionel to be part of a team that gathered weapons, ammunition, and even uniforms from fallen GC troops. "I'm out here taking a look at the edge of the camp. You should see this."

"When do you want me down there?" Lionel said.

"Before daybreak, unless the attack comes earlier, which I don't think will happen. Get a little sleep. Then head out."

Lionel had felt left out of some of the best assignments since coming to Petra and was glad Zeke had included him in this one. Now that he was close to actually going to the front line, Lionel felt unsure. Would God protect them?

He lay back on his bed and tried to fall asleep by thinking of all the people he had met in the past seven years. Carl Meninger came to mind. What a great story he had—becoming a believer while working for the Global Community. Carl was now a vital part of the Tribulation Force in South Carolina and had seen hundreds of people believe the truth about God since Lionel and Judd had last seen him.

Lionel recalled others. Conrad Graham and Darrion Stahley, who were in Illinois, awaiting the return of Jesus with a group of inner-city believers. The stories they sent via e-mail were exciting and a little scary.

Lionel and the others had grieved the loss of the Young Trib Force Web site to the Global Community, but Chang Wong had worked his magic and was able to automatically direct anyone who logged on to Tsion Ben-Judah's Web site to a section run by the kids.

*Kids,* Lionel thought. *We haven't been kids since this whole thing started.* The disappearances had forced them to grow up fast.

Lionel tossed and turned on his cot for more than an hour.

Finally, he got up, dressed, and went to find Zeke.

---

Conrad Graham watched the sun move toward the horizon from a basement window of an abandoned house in Palos Hills, Illinois. He and the other members of the Wisconsin group had finally settled into several homes near Enoch Dumas, the shepherd of a growing group of Christ followers from many different backgrounds. Enoch spoke with a Spanish accent, which Conrad loved. One night a Latino woman who had lived in an abandoned laser-tag park told her story. The next night it was an African-American man who admitted to everything from grave robbing to murder. Kids from the street and drug addicts all had stories of how God had reached out to them.

Conrad had been able to stay with Enoch himself and considered it as big a privilege as being in Petra. They had the chance to bring people to God every day. Though many had cautioned them to be more careful, Enoch and his followers wouldn't pass up a chance to help people receive Christ.

Conrad's mattress lay in Enoch's musty basement. The past few nights had been cold, so Conrad had given his best blanket to Shelly, who lived about three blocks away. It was shortly after Mark's death that Shelly and Conrad had renewed their friendship. Something Mark had said to Shelly caused her to give Conrad another chance after a bad disagreement in Wisconsin. They weren't going to get married anytime soon, but the fact that they could be friends gave Conrad hope.

"Don't suppose we'll get much shut-eye tonight, eh?" Enoch said, walking into the room.

"I've waited years for this," Conrad said. "No way I'm going to sleep through it."

Enoch nodded. "I know what you mean. But I don't think it'll happen until morning."

"Why is that? Doesn't the Bible say no one knows when Christ will return?"

"True. But eight in the morning our time will be the seven-year anniversary of the signing of the treaty between Carpathia and Israel. To the minute."

Enoch's love of the Bible was contagious. Since coming to the group, Conrad found himself reading more, taking notes, and seeing the Bible come alive in new ways.

"You think it's going to happen at eight tomorrow morning?" Conrad said.

"Don't know for sure, but it's as good a guess as anyone's."

Enoch flipped on a small radio and tuned to the latest news. New Babylon, the gleaming jewel of Nicolae Carpathia, had been wiped out in less than an hour. Though the GC had tried to put a positive spin on the worldwide chaos, Conrad knew from reading e-mails from Chang Wong in Petra that there were more suicides now than ever before.

The news reporter quickly turned to the Middle East where Nicolae Carpathia readied his troops. A vast army was nearing Jerusalem and had spread across the nearby desert to Petra. "An almost innumerable legion of tanks, artillery, and soldiers has assembled here to wage what should be a very quick end to a pesky enemy."

The reporter played a clip of Carpathia giving orders. It was clear that Carpathia wanted to level Petra and over-run Jerusalem.

"The only logical response to such an overwhelming military campaign is surrender," the reporter said, "but no one who has studied the history of the Judah-ites and Israelis over the last seven years believes that will happen."

"The one who should be surrendering is Carpathia," Enoch said. "God's going to make that clear real soon."

"I can't wait," Conrad said.

Judd found sleep impossible and stayed up watching the GC troops. He heard Vicki's breathing from the other room and was grateful she was getting some rest.

Judd felt concerned for Jamal and Lina, wondering what had happened to them. The last he had seen them, they were trying to convince several Israelis about Jesus.

At nearly 3 a.m. they crept inside, surprised to see Judd awake. "You won't believe who we saw at Shivte's home," Lina said, wide-eyed. "Tsion Ben-Judah. He was there with an American—"

"Buck Williams?" Judd said. He had seen the two together earlier at the Temple Mount.

"Yes! To see the teacher in person was such an honor," Lina said.

"And to see his commitment to the fight is even better," Jamal said. "He is not just here to give us moral support. He has a gun and is ready to use it."

Lina smiled and shook her fists like a child. "But we haven't told you the best news. Shivte and his sons were at the Wailing Wall this evening. They heard Dr. Ben-Judah and have believed in Messiah! All that praying we did for them, and now they are true believers."

It was all Judd could do not to rush to Shivte's house to see Buck and Tsion, but he didn't want to wake Vicki and there was no way he was going to leave without her.

When Lina left the room, Jamal spoke softly. "Shivte's sons told me they believe the GC will come from the northwest and try to get through the Damascus Gate. We'll leave for there within the hour."

"Couldn't the GC come through just about any gate?" Judd said.

"Perhaps, but the Damascus Gate is where they need us most. I think you should leave your wife here and come with me."

Judd shook his head. "No, we've both promised—"

"This is no place for women. There will be much bloodshed. The GC is bent upon the destruction of every rebel living here in the Old City."

"Vicki and I feel God has brought us here for a reason," Judd said. "I can't leave her behind."

Jamal patted Judd's shoulder. "I understand, and I wish you success. When my wife returns, don't tell her where I've gone. Come to the Damascus Gate as soon as possible." He slipped out the door.

Jamal was gone a few moments when Lina returned with a sackful of supplies. She looked at Judd, then at the door, and burst into tears. "Tell me where he's gone! I've lost a son and a daughter to the GC! I will be with my husband at this critical hour."

"She's right," Vicki said, walking into the room.

Judd nodded. "Let's get our things. We're going to the Damascus Gate."

# 33

**JUDD** ducked the first time he heard gunfire. It took only a few minutes to get used to the automatic weapons and the screams of those who had been hit. He and Vicki, along with their friend Lina, rushed to the end of a tunnel near the Damascus Gate and watched.

Rebels ran everywhere, shouting news of the battle. The Yad Vashem Historical Museum to the Holocaust victims had been destroyed. Hebrew University, the Jewish National Library, and Israel Museum were on fire. Unity Army troops were close, and many rebels were either dead or captured.

*Are these rumors or facts?* Judd thought.

Vicki clung to him tightly as they came upon open ammunition boxes. Judd pushed the empty boxes away and handed ammo to Vicki as a runner hurried by. Rebels poured into the underground.

"Have you seen my husband?" Lina said to the runner.

The man ignored her, yelling instructions to other rebels.

Jamal raced inside and saw his wife. He gave Judd an icy stare. Before Judd could explain, Jamal grabbed his arm. "We're holding here. But the Dung Gate is under attack. Go."

Judd knew the Dung Gate was to the south. What the Unity Army had planned, he couldn't guess. Were they going for the Temple Mount? Would Carpathia try to set up his headquarters in that holy place?

Another report came—the Unity Army was trying to break through the Wailing Wall!

Judd glanced at Vicki, who strained under the weight of the bullets and grenades she carried. "You ready for this?" he said.

Vicki bit her lip and nodded.

---

Lionel looked out at the desert in the predawn light. The sand had transformed into miles and miles of soldiers, horses, and weaponry. At least 200,000 troops on horse-back were in position.

He found Zeke holding a strange-looking weapon and listening for radio contact from their leader.

"What's with the horses?" Lionel said. "All those tanks and advanced weapons and they put cavalry in front?"

"Doesn't make a lick of sense to me, but I'm glad they did it," Zeke said. "We're gonna try to spook some of the horses and riders with these babies—" he patted his weapon—"and see if we can't stir things up."

"What is that?"

"It's called a DEW, short for directed energy weapon. Sends out a beam of energy that burns like fire."

Lionel winced. "I've seen one, but not that big. Can it reach the troops from here?"

"You bet," Zeke said. "We've also got fifty-calibers along the perimeter. Those will cause more damage, but they're still nothing compared to what the GC has."

A helicopter rose in the distance, and Zeke said it was Rayford Steele scouting the area. Suddenly a flash of light and a smoky cloud billowed from the Unity Army.

"We've got incoming," someone said on Zeke's radio.

"That missile's headed straight for Rayford," Zeke muttered.

———————

As soon as Judd and Vicki arrived at the Dung Gate, another fight broke out, so they followed a group of rebels heading north. Like waves on an angry sea they surged forward, and finally Judd said they should abandon the tunnels. Judd tried to check in with Jamal by phone but couldn't get through.

Several rebels hooted and threw fists into the air as they passed on the street.

"Where are you going?" Judd yelled.

"Herod's Gate!" one said, his eyes flashing with anger.

"Judd, those men don't have the mark of the believer," Vicki said. "If they're gunned down, that's the end for them."

"I know," Judd said, "but there's no way they'll stop to listen now."

Hundreds of rebels moved toward Herod's Gate. Judd was out of breath when Vicki caught his arm. "I have an idea," she said, sprinting to the side as gunfire erupted.

*What in the world is she thinking?* Judd thought.

———

Lionel closed his eyes and said a quick prayer. Rayford Steele had made it through seven years of plagues and now this. Zeke whooped and Lionel opened his eyes. "What happened?"

"Missile went right through the chopper and came out the other side," Zeke yelled, laughing. "Looks like they might have hit some of their own troops. How do you like that? God's letting the GC take themselves out of this war."

An order came to open fire with the DEWs, and Zeke aimed his weapon. Lionel picked up binoculars and watched the perfect line of horses fall apart. Horses galloped in all directions, some knocking each other to the ground.

"Yahoo!" Zeke hollered. "Look at 'em go!"

———

Vicki knelt by a wounded soldier who had been shot in the leg. Judd dropped his ammo and tied a tourniquet above the wound.

A few years earlier, God had caused a cross to form on believers' foreheads, a supernatural sign that they were true followers of Christ. This man had neither the mark of Carpathia nor the mark of God.

"Take my weapon," the man groaned. "They need more fighters."

"We want to help you," Vicki said. "The Global Community is going to be defeated by God's power—"

"Leave me alone!" the man screamed, using his gun to help him stand. "I have to get back to my brothers!"

Vicki and Judd tried to stop him, but the man limped off with the crowd. Her heart ached for him and the others fighting against the overwhelming army.

Someone put a hand on her shoulder and she turned. A man carrying a gun stood behind her.

"Dr. Ben-Judah!" Vicki gasped.

"No time to talk," Tsion said, out of breath. It was strange seeing the teacher in battle dress, carrying a gun. "Keep reaching out—many still need to hear the message."

"No one wants to listen," Vicki said, but Tsion was already gone, pushed along by the crowd.

A man grabbed Tsion by the shoulders and yelled, "Hail to Ben-Judah, fearless leader of the remnant!" Another man raised Tsion off the ground and soon he was on their shoulders, people shouting his praises. As the crowd rounded the corner, Tsion was above their heads, bobbing like a parade balloon.

"This is crazy," Judd said over the noise.

"This is great," Vicki said.

They moved forward, looking for more wounded. A short time later shots fired down the street as the Unity Army came over Herod's Gate. Judd raced a few yards ahead, then came back to report that the rebels had fallen and were retreating. Judd and Vicki ducked into a doorway.

"You think Dr. Ben-Judah will be protected?" Judd said.

"I hope so," Vicki said.

"We've got to get out of here before the Unity Army comes," Judd said.

They slipped into the street and ran with the crowd.

---

Judd found an entrance to the tunnels and plunged down with others searching for ammunition or a place to hide. Some younger soldiers cowered in a corner, shaking and whimpering.

A man with the mark of the believer walked up to Judd and Vicki. He was armed with an Uzi and had a string of grenades strapped around his belt. "Any news of Messiah?"

"Not yet," Judd said, "but he's coming."

A Jewish woman in her twenties wiped tears from her eyes. She wore fatigues and black boots and reminded Judd of Nada, Jamal's daughter.

"Why are you talking about legends at a time like this?" the woman said. She did not have the mark of the believer.

Vicki approached her. "Surely you've heard that a Messiah is coming."

"Yes, I've heard that all my life, but I've always thought it was a myth created by people who didn't want to deal with reality. And reality now is that we're all going to die. A fairy tale is not going to change that."

"It's no fairy tale," Vicki said, "any more than the

320

disappearances and the earthquake and everything else
that's happened during the past seven years. Jesus is
coming back—at any moment—and you need to be
ready."

"I'm ready to die for my country. I want to rid the
earth of Nicolae Carpathia, but I won't turn my back on
my religion. Get away from me."

"Please, just listen to—"

"Go!"

Judd felt bad for Vicki and even worse for the woman
who seemed closed to the truth.

Another rebel nearby waved a hand, so Vicki and Judd
walked over. "I heard what you said," the young man
said. "And I heard Dr. Ben-Judah last night. I almost
prayed, but I was with my father and he cursed the man."

"We can help you," Judd said. "What do you need to
know?"

The man looked around the darkened hallway.
Several people listened. "I always thought the talk about
Jesus was blasphemy. A story made up to make people
hate Jews. Now I think I might have been wrong. I've
been wondering if he could be the Messiah."

"We all rejected him," Judd said. "Everyone who's
living now missed him. But the good news is you can be
forgiven."

Judd and Vicki shared Bible verses showing that Jesus
fulfilled Old Testament prophecies. Some in the hallway
scoffed and kept going, but others stayed.

"Paul was a famous Jewish person from the first
century," Judd said. "He studied under the best teachers

321

and even persecuted followers of Jesus. Then something happened and this is what he wrote."

Judd held out a small Bible for the man. He read aloud, " 'I am not ashamed of this Good News about Christ. It is the power of God at work, saving everyone who believes—Jews first and also Gentiles.' "

Judd flipped a few pages and read from Romans chapter 15. " 'Remember that Christ came as a servant to the Jews to show that God is true to the promises he made to their ancestors.' Jesus came and fulfilled everything predicted about him—that he would suffer and die a cruel death, that he would save his people, that he would—"

"But what about the verses that say Messiah will be a king," the young rebel said, "a ruler of the people who will establish righteousness?"

Vicki smiled. "Jesus is a descendent of King David. He is going to sit on David's throne, just like the prophecies said. And he's going to do it when he returns to conquer Satan and those who serve him."

"It seems so . . . foreign to me," the man said.

"There's a verse in Corinthians that says we can't find God through human wisdom," Vicki said. "That God used the cross and the foolishness of preaching to draw people to himself. And that's what we're saying to you, as foolish as it might sound. Jesus died so your sins could be forgiven. He gave his life and paid the penalty so you could be a true child of God. And he offers you the chance to believe in him right now."

"We believe Jesus could come back any second," Judd said. He looked around at the others who had gathered.

"Don't wait any longer to give your lives to him and serve him."

"What do we have to do?" a man said.

Judd nodded at Vicki and she understood. "Pray with me," she said. "Give your lives to God right now."

Judd glanced around the tunnel and saw several people bow their heads.

"Dear God, I'm sorry for rejecting you and the Son you sent to die for me. I do believe that Jesus is the Messiah and that he gave himself for me on the cross. I believe he rose again and made a way for me to spend eternity with you. I ask you right now to come into my life, forgive me, and make me a new person. Show me what you want me to do before Jesus returns. In his name I pray. Amen."

The people looked up as a new group of rebels ran through the tunnel. The rebel Vicki had first spoken with stood.

"What's that on your forehead?" a man said.

"You have something on yours too," the young rebel said.

Judd looked through tears at the scene. What would have happened to these people if he and Vicki hadn't come to Jerusalem? And what would happen to them now?

# 34

**JUDD** helped Vicki gather the new believers and prayed with them, asking God to help them spread the message of Christ's return even in the middle of the war. A few rebels ran through the tunnel passing on rumors that the Unity Army was retreating in confusion. Others said it was a trick.

"The rabbi said it is true," a newcomer said. "Something from Zechariah about God striking horses and riders."

"Where is the rabbi?" Judd said.

"I didn't see him. I was just told about—"

"Where do you *think* he is?" Judd interrupted.

"Someone said he was near Herod's Gate, but don't go unless you want to hear more about Messiah."

Judd grabbed Vicki's arm, and they climbed out of the tunnel into the street. The silence was eerie. No gunfire, no hum of GC vehicles or crash of battering rams against gates.

As they ran for Herod's Gate, the unmistakable voice of Nicolae Carpathia blasted over a giant bullhorn. "Attention, people of Jerusalem! This is your supreme potentate!"

A crowd shouted ahead of them, and Judd and Vicki kept moving.

"Please listen, citizens," Carpathia said. "I come in peace."

More shouting.

"Come, let us reason together!" Carpathia paused. "I come to offer pardon. I am willing to compromise. I wish you no ill. If you are willing to serve me and be obedient, you shall eat the good of the land; but if you refuse and rebel, you shall be devoured by the sword. I will rid myself of my adversaries and take vengeance on my enemies. I will turn my hand against you and thoroughly purge you.

"But it does not have to be this way, citizens of the Global Community. If you will lay down your arms and welcome me into your city, I will guarantee your peace and safety."

Judd and Vicki had made it to the edge of the crowd at Herod's Gate and looked for Tsion.

"This will be your sign to me," Carpathia said. "If at the count of three I hear silence for fifteen seconds, I will assume you are willing to accede to my requests. A single gunshot into the air during that time will be your signal that you would rather oppose me. But I warn you, half of Jerusalem is in captivity already. The entire city could be overthrown easily within an hour. The choice is yours at the count of three."

Judd wished he had a gun, but before Carpathia could even count to one, thousands of weapons fired.

When the shooting stopped, Judd noticed someone moving on a wall above the crowd. It was Tsion Ben-Judah!

"It is not too late!" Tsion said. "Make your stand for Messiah now! Repent, choose, and be saved!"

As Tsion spoke, the mark of the true believer appeared on forehead after forehead. Even at this late hour, God was working in people's hearts.

Judd looked at Vicki, who stared at the scene, fascinated. Suddenly Judd felt they should get to safety. Was it God telling him or his own fears? He wasn't about to take a chance, so he pulled her away from the gathering and to the entrance of another tunnel.

---

Lionel watched Unity Army riders get their horses under control. The vast army had moved toward Petra like an endless swarm of bees and had overcome whatever had spooked the horses.

Sam Goldberg scrambled up an incline toward Lionel and knelt beside him. "You ready for this?"

"How can I be?" Lionel said. "This is David versus Goliath times a million."

"Yeah, but you know who won that fight." Sam shook his head. "I'm not sure why we're out here, though. Can you imagine going into the middle of that army and trying to bring back anything?"

The order came for another round of DEWs, which

Sam called ray guns. The Unity Army's front line fell back, and troops shifted and rippled like a human ocean. Lionel wondered if the GC would respond with an attack, but nothing came.

"Where's Mr. Stein?" Lionel said.

"Praying with some of the elders," Sam said. "He's upset he couldn't be in Jerusalem."

"I know how he feels."

"What, this isn't enough excitement for you?"

———————————————————

Judd sat by Vicki, listening to the battle above them and wondering if he had been wrong about not fighting with these brave men and women. After all, Jesus was coming back any minute—or at least within the next day. He was as sure of that as the mark on his forehead.

Sitting in the tunnel near a stairwell, it was all he could do to resist grabbing a rifle and heading up. But his promise to Vicki meant that if he went to the fight, she would have to go as well, and Judd didn't want that.

Finally the noise died a little and Vicki spoke. "I think we should go up. Maybe there are people who need more ammo or need to hear the message."

Judd nodded. "Okay, stay here and I'll check it out."

He flew up the stairs and carefully opened the door. The sight turned his stomach. Weapons and bodies of rebels littered the street. He inched out and closed the door to see if the Unity Army was near.

A *kerthunk* sounded some distance away, and Judd instinctively ducked. A shell struck the building behind him, sending debris flying. He stayed on the ground, coughing and waving a hand.

When the dust cleared, he saw a hole the size of a small car in the wall behind him.

The hole was right next to the stairwell.

"Vicki!" Judd screamed.

---

Lionel took a walk along the edge of the Petra defensive line, passing a man holding a DEW in one hand and a small television in the other. Lionel stopped and squinted at the screen.

"You want to see?" the man said, holding the screen higher.

Lionel thanked him and sat.

"This is a GCNN report about the war," the man said. The screen showed an aerial view of the One World Unity Army shot before sundown. The reporter explained that one-third of Carpathia's forces had surrounded Petra and that rebel leader Tsion Ben-Judah was hiding there.

"They don't have a clue," Lionel muttered.

"The other two-thirds of the Unity Army is poised to overtake the city of Jerusalem," the reporter said. "Potentate Carpathia himself reports that nearly half the city has been occupied and that it is just a matter of time before the Old City is overrun."

The report switched to a press conference with Carpathia recorded earlier. "We are confident that these are the last two rebel enclaves in the world," he said, "and that once they have been thoroughly defeated and our enemies scattered, we will realize what we have so long dreamed of: an entire world of peace and harmony. There is no place in a true global community for rebellion. If our government was anything but benevolent or did not have the attitude of 'citizen first,' there might be cause for dissention. But all we have ever attempted to do was create a utopia for society.

"It is most unfortunate that it comes to this, that we have to resort to bloodshed to achieve our goals. But we will do what we have to do."

A reporter asked about the huge army fighting against so few.

Carpathia said no effort in the cause of world peace was wasted. Then he chuckled when another reporter asked if the GC was afraid of the rebels' God.

"I do not worry about fairy tales," Carpathia answered, "but even if they did have supernatural help, they would be no match for our fighting machine. . . ."

Lionel gritted his teeth. "You're going down, Nicolae."

"Why not win this war all at once?" a reporter said. "What's the delay?"

"I am a man of peace. I always believe first in diplomacy and negotiation. The window of opportunity for settling this peacefully is always open. I had hoped that the enemies of peace would be persuaded by our size and would come to the bargaining table. But our patience is running out. They seem markedly uninterested in any reasonable solution, and we are prepared to use any means necessary. So it is just a matter of time now."

Lionel thanked the rebel for letting him watch and

asked Zeke if he could spare him for a few minutes. Lionel wanted to see the reaction of the remnant.

———————————

Judd didn't care if the Unity Army was coming—he had to get to Vicki. The door to the stairwell was blocked by stones, so he went through the hole opened by the shell. He checked the street and saw a few rebels but no GC. *Must have been a stray shot,* he thought.

It was hard to breathe inside. He called for Vicki, but there was no answer. Finding the way blocked, he dashed back outside and yelled at a few passing rebels. "My wife is trapped! Can you help me?"

"I'm headed to Herod's Gate," one said. "Can't stop."

"Please," Judd said. "It'll only take a minute."

"In another minute the Unity Army might be over the wall!" The men ran on.

Finally, Judd saw a believer, and the husky man helped Judd move debris in front of the door. When they had cleared it, Judd tried the doorknob but it wouldn't open.

"Stand back," the man said. He raised his gun and blew the knob to pieces. Judd pried the door open and turned to thank the man, but he was already running away. "I hope you find your wife," he called, raising a fist. "I'll see you after Messiah comes."

Judd raced through the dust to the bottom of the steps. The tunnel wasn't as damaged as the wall outside, but there were still huge stones on the floor.

"Over here," Vicki said, coughing. She lay on the floor with a stone on her leg. "I tried to move it."

THE YOUNG TRIB FORCE

Judd's heart beat furiously as he struggled to free
Vicki. The stone wouldn't budge. He snagged a gun
propped against the wall and used it to pry the stone up a
few inches, but Vicki's leg was still pinned. He was afraid
the stone would fall and injure her worse if he tipped it
farther. His arms ached as he yelled for help.

A young rebel came toward them from the other side
of the tunnel. He put his gun under the stone, and
together he and Judd lifted it enough for Vicki to scoot
out. The stone crashed to the floor with a tremendous
*thud!*

"Thank you," Vicki said, holding her leg.

Kneeling, the young man took out a knife, slit Vicki's
pant leg at the bottom, and tore it until he reached her
kneecap. Judd gasped at the gash in her leg. The wound
was to the bone, and blood gushed out.

The young man unzipped a pocket on his jacket and
pulled out some gauze and antiseptic. He poured it on
the wound, and Vicki yelped in pain. When he had
wrapped her leg, he said, "It doesn't look like it's broken,
but someone should look at it soon."

"I'll take her to our friend's apartment right now,"
Judd said.

"You don't believe in Messiah," Vicki said, putting a
hand on the man's arm.

The young man frowned. "Judah-ites," he muttered.

"Jesus is coming soon. You need to be ready."

"The Unity Army is coming sooner," the man said,
grabbing his gun and racing up the stairs.

Judd picked Vicki up and climbed the stairs. "We'll

make it to Jamal's place quicker through the street than the tunnel."

He struggled up the last steps, then was outside. Vicki buried her head in his chest as they passed rebel bodies. The sun was high in the sky now.

"How does it feel?" Judd said, looking at the bloody bandage.

"I'm okay. It's just throbbing."

"We'll get some medicine back at—" Judd stopped in the street and stared.

"What's wrong?" Vicki said.

"Over there, the guy at the edge of the curb. Is that . . . ?"

"Judd, it is! Oh, Judd, it's Tsion!"

Judd walked over to the body and put Vicki down gently. Tsion's eyes were closed, his hands together at the waist. Someone had smoothed his hair and closed his jacket over a chest wound.

Vicki wept softly, saying the man's name over and over.

"Vick, we have to go. Someone's coming."

Several rebels passed. One slowed and studied the body. "Is that who I think it is?"

Judd nodded. "The rabbi."

The man yelled at his friends, who returned. "This is our leader. We must take him."

"Take him where?" another said.

"Anywhere but here. If the Unity Army finds him, they'll give the body to Carpathia."

"We'll build a shrine for him!" another said.

"No," Judd said, "he wouldn't want that."

But two of them picked up Tsion's body and hustled down the street.

Judd gathered Vicki in his arms and neared Herod's Gate.

"They're coming!" someone shouted. Then a terrific explosion rocked the area. Judd ran the other way, looking for an escape.

# 35

**LIONEL** glanced at his sweat-soaked watch. It was a little after one in the afternoon, and the sun had heated the desert up past one hundred degrees. Shells had fallen on Petra in the past few minutes, and though Lionel hadn't seen anyone killed or injured, the bombs had landed. Had God lifted his protection?

The million-plus inside Petra were clearly antsy as they streamed toward the meeting place. Lionel saw Mr. Stein and asked what was happening.

"Dr. Rosenzweig is about to speak," Mr. Stein said.

---

Judd had gotten turned around by the advancing Unity Army and ended up on a street he didn't recognize. All this time in Jerusalem, planning and memorizing its layout, and now he was lost. The Old City was only a third of a mile square. This shouldn't have happened. And

Vicki was losing lots of blood. She hadn't complained about her injury, but he could tell she was in pain.

She lifted her head from his shoulder, and her red hair fell across her face. "How much farther?"

Judd couldn't help thinking how beautiful Vicki was. Before the disappearances he had been attracted to girls who wore all the right clothes. Vicki had told him the only pair of designer jeans she ever owned had been bought at the thrift store near her trailer. Vicki's inner beauty shone through now, and he couldn't imagine anyone more attractive.

"Almost there," Judd assured her, though he had no idea where they were. He stopped in a doorway and gently placed her in the shadows to catch his breath and get his bearings. "I'll be right back."

She caught his arm. "Don't leave."

"Just going to make sure there's nobody around that corner. Hang tough."

Judd raced to the end of the street, flexing his arms and stretching his back. Vicki was light, but his arms felt like Jell-O after carrying her for so many blocks.

He reached the end of the street and sneaked a peek around the corner. He recognized a storefront café half a block away. Jamal's apartment was only three or four blocks from it. He heaved a sigh of relief and turned.

Footsteps. Boots on pavement. Someone barking orders.

Had the Unity Army come this far? Or was it the rebels? Judd rushed down a stairwell and peered over the railing. He had to get back to Vicki.

Lionel watched the huge crowd at Petra quiet for Chaim
Rosenzweig. The man introduced a sermon given by Dr.
Shadrach Meshach Lockridge. The image of the famous
black preacher was projected off two white walls of
smooth stone. Lionel found some shade in front of a big
rock and sat. This preaching reminded him of home,
especially when he and his family would visit relatives
down South.

Though the sermon took his mind off the advancing
army, he knew this was designed to reach unbelievers in
the camp. Lionel closed his eyes and listened. Something
made him want to pray for Judd and Vicki.

---

Judd held his breath while a platoon of rebels passed
Vicki's position and headed toward him. He rushed up
the steps, and a rebel aimed his gun at him.

"No, I'm with you!" Judd shouted.

The man lowered the gun and scowled as the group
kept moving. "Get out of here! Unity Army's on its way."

Judd sprinted back to Vicki and gasped when he saw
her limp form draped across the top step.

"What happened?" Judd whispered as he made it to
her side.

Vicki opened her eyes. "Didn't know if those were
ours or theirs, so I played dead."

"Good girl. You had me fooled."

"Where are we?"

"Jamal's place is not far. We're going to be okay, and

pretty soon Jesus is going to come through those clouds and we're both going to see him face-to-face."

"Can't wait."

Judd pulled her right arm around his shoulder to help her stand, but before he could pick her up, more foot-steps sounded behind them. There was no time to move, so Judd tried the door of the building.

Locked.

"This way!" someone yelled from the street.

Judd and Vicki huddled in the shadows, hoping it wouldn't be the Unity Army. Soon he heard their squawking radios and GC leaders giving commands.

As the troops came into view someone said, "We don't want them escaping through the Lion's Gate to the east. After the shelling starts, we'll push them north toward Herod's Gate. They've held it since yesterday, but they'll have to open it to get through and we'll have them trapped."

The platoon passed quickly without noticing Judd and Vicki. With each heartbeat, more blood oozed from Vicki's wounded leg.

"As soon as they're around the corner, we're out of here," Judd whispered.

"What time is it?" Vicki asked, her head lolling to one side.

Judd didn't want to move to see his watch. "It's after two thirty."

"Wrong. It's time for Jesus to come back."

"Amen to that," Judd said.

A bomb exploded. Gunfire erupted. Choppers filled the sky. The platoon hurried around the corner.

Judd stood, picked Vicki up, and headed for Jamal's apartment. He cast a glance at the sky and said a simple prayer: "Come, Lord Jesus."

---

Lionel's heart was stirred by the video of the black preacher and the response of people in Petra. He wanted to stay until the end of the message, but he wanted to be at the battle line even more.

He quickly returned to his assigned position and looked for Zeke. Sam told him Zeke was meeting with a Trib Force member. In the past half hour, the ragtag Petra army had fired their DEWs and some bigger guns at Carpathia's vast army.

"Bet those guys are hot in those black uniforms," Lionel said.

"I wonder if those tanks are air-conditioned," Sam said, smiling.

"GC casualties," someone said from ahead. He turned and looked at Lionel and Sam. "You two part of Zeke's crew?"

"Yeah," Lionel said.

"Then you're up," the man said. "Four casualties—must be scouts—straight ahead."

"Got it," Lionel said. He grabbed a couple of duffel bags and handed one to Sam. "Let's go."

While some of Zeke's crew rushed across the sand, Lionel and Sam moved cautiously. Their job was to harvest weapons, IDs, and uniforms.

Sam reached the bodies first and tugged at the

uniforms. Lionel seized weapons and put them in his duffel bag, keeping a wary eye on the line of horsemen not far away.

"Judah-ite!" a Unity Army soldier yelled. "Leave those weapons or die."

Lionel stood, clutching the bag in his right hand.

"What happened to your arm?" Another soldier laughed. "Get it caught in the lies of your leader, Ben-Judah?"

Lionel stared at him. Zeke had made Lionel a new arm, but he had left it behind for this mission. He knew it was better to say nothing, but he couldn't pass up the opportunity. He remembered two verses from Matthew and began reciting them. " 'Immediately after those horrible days end, the sun will be darkened, the moon will not give light, the stars will fall from the sky, and the powers of heaven will be shaken. And then at last, the sign of the coming of the Son of Man will—' "

"Blah, blah, blah," the first soldier said. "So you think you can beat us with a few energy weapons? Is that what your God told you? Your God is wrong. We could simply keep moving and trample all of you without even firing a shot." He leveled a gun at Lionel. "No, your God is wrong. Dead wrong."

"Don't shoot!" Sam shouted.

The soldier fired his weapon.

---

Judd ran as fast as he could carrying Vicki, wishing he had stayed in the tunnels. He stuck close to the buildings, moving quietly.

"Just around this corner and we'll be able to see it," he whispered, saying it as much for himself as for Vicki.

Vicki's injured leg dangled and blood dripped. Judd didn't slow as he rounded the corner. What he saw took his breath away.

Several Unity Army soldiers stood near bodies of rebels. A soldier fired a shot at Vicki and Judd, grazing a stone just above Judd's head.

"Hands up!"

"We're unarmed," Judd yelled, trying to put Vicki down carefully. "My wife was hurt in one of the blasts near—"

"Shut up!" an officer said. He motioned at another soldier, and the second man moved toward them, his weapon raised.

Vicki turned to Judd. "Go. It's your only chance."

"Shut up!" the officer repeated.

"Make it to the tunnel," Vicki whispered. "Go."

Judd pursed his lips. "We promised each other we'd stick together. I'm not leaving you now."

"They're unmarked, sir," the soldier said, circling Judd.

Vicki collapsed and Judd tried to help her, but the soldier hit him in the back of the head with the butt of his rifle. Judd nearly passed out.

"Take them to the holding area," the officer said. "If they bat an eyelash, shoot them."

---

Lionel heard the gunshot as he closed his eyes and flinched. He expected to be lying on the ground with a bullet hole in his chest, but the shot whizzed past him—or *through* him. He turned to see a penny-sized hole in the sand directly behind him, then glanced back at the shooter.

*If that bullet landed there, how did it miss me?* Lionel thought.

"Lionel, Sam, get outta there," someone said behind them. It was Zeke, standing on the crest of a dune.

The soldier fired again while Lionel and Sam turned and walked away.

"Their weapons won't do a thing here," Zeke said. "Just wastin' their ammo."

"We'll roll over you and smash you into this desert," the officer yelled.

"Yeah, I'm sure that's what you think," Zeke said, helping Lionel and Sam back to the line. "Your guy's a loser. Ours is the true Lord."

Lionel was shaking when he made it back to the line. He found a small hole in the front of his shirt and one the same size in the back.

# 36

**CONRAD** Graham awoke a little after 6 a.m. in Palos Hills, Illinois, wiped the sleep from his eyes, and hit the light button on his watch. He had wanted to stay up the whole night, but fatigue had set in a little after 2 a.m. He had been praying for his friends, praying against the Unity Army of Carpathia, and praying for those who still hadn't believed in Jesus.

*They'll believe soon, one way or the other,* he thought.

Enoch Dumas slept on the musty mattress in the corner, and his heavy breathing filled the room. Conrad picked up the jacket he had draped over himself and quietly tiptoed upstairs. He had told Shelly he would meet her at six thirty.

As Conrad stepped into the morning chill and darkness, he thought about his brother, Taylor. Taylor had hated everything Carpathia stood for and lost his life trying to work against the GC. However, Taylor had been killed without ever trusting God.

That fact had haunted Conrad the past few years. No matter how many people he helped understand the truth or how many people he prayed with, there was always a shadow of regret. He would never meet Taylor again, never hear his laugh or relive old times.

Shelly met Conrad at the door of the old house where she lived with several others from the Young Tribulation Force. She gave him a hug and said she hadn't slept the whole night. "Darrion and I just kept looking at the sky and asking God to come back before daybreak, but nothing's happened."

Conrad whispered what Enoch had said the night before, and they went downstairs. Several candles lit the meeting room, and Conrad smiled at the familiar people. Darrion. Ty and his sister, Tanya. Janie. Melinda.

Charlie walked into the room yawning, followed by Phoenix, who padded up to Conrad and licked his hand. "How's Mr. Enoch doing?" Charlie asked Conrad.

"Sleeping right now," Conrad said. "Before he fell asleep he told me to remind everybody that we're meeting at the mall at eight."

"I wouldn't miss that," Charlie said.

"What time is it over there?" Melinda said.

"I think it's early afternoon in Jerusalem," Shelly said. "Two or three? I wonder how Judd and Vicki are."

Darrion switched off a handheld television. "GCNN reports total victory in the Old City, if you can believe anything they say."

"Is that where Judd and Vicki are?" Charlie said.

Shelly put a hand on Charlie's shoulder. "They'll be okay. Judd and Vicki know how to take care of themselves."

Charlie sighed. "I've been praying for them all night."

"Maybe we should do that now," Janie said. "Everybody, grab hands."

Conrad bowed his head and thanked God that Jesus was coming back. "Please make it today, Lord."

---

Vicki cradled Judd's head in her lap as her tears fell on his face. He had struggled to carry her and then fell when they reached the transport truck.

There were few believers on the truck, mostly rebels with chalky white skin. Vicki guessed they had lived underground the past few years since Carpathia's mark had been required.

One believer had helped her scoot near Judd. "Your friend is knocked out. He should be coming around soon."

But Judd didn't awaken during the ride or when the truck reached the remains of Teddy Kollek Stadium. The GC had set up a command post there and brought many of their prisoners to the infield area. The once beautiful structure now had a gaping hole in one side where the prisoners were led. No one was in handcuffs. There were too many of them, and besides, anyone who tried to run was shot.

The believer who had helped Vicki carried her from the truck as GC soldiers dropped Judd on a grassy area. The believer placed Vicki beside Judd.

People filled the stadium infield, and the scene was like some horror movie. Those bloodied from battle stared through vacant eyes. Unity Army troops watched for any reason to shoot.

Vicki looked around the stadium, remembering the sight from Tsion Ben-Judah's televised meetings a few years earlier. Tsion had spoken to thousands of Jewish evangelists who had traveled the world spreading the message of Jesus. The two witnesses, Moishe and Eli, had walked through this very infield. And Nicolae Carpathia had made an appearance onstage. Now, like the rest of the world, Teddy Kollek Stadium was crumbling.

A uniformed man with several bars on his shoulders approached a group of soldiers who snapped to attention.

"Yes, sir, Commander Fulcire," one of the soldiers said.

Vicki focused on the commander's face. This was the same man who had chased the kids in Wisconsin and executed Mark and Natalie Bishop.

The commander had been the top dog back in the United North American States. Now, at the moment of the biggest battle in history, Fulcire was on guard duty.

Vicki felt Judd's neck for a pulse. It was there. He was still breathing. "Hang in there," she whispered, her hair touching Judd's face. "It won't be long until we see our Lord face-to-face."

---

Conrad and the others in the Young Trib Force gathered with Enoch's group behind the shopping mall just before eight in the morning. People listened to Enoch's teaching, looking at the sky, some frowning.

Conrad wondered whether or not it was safe for this many people to gather in broad daylight. It was true that the GC had scaled back their Peacekeepers in the area. Most had been shipped to the Middle East. But citizens loyal to Nicolae Carpathia received cash for every unmarked citizen they captured or killed, and Conrad felt antsy. When Enoch suggested they move to the inner court of the empty mall, he felt better.

Enoch took a flurry of questions from the group.

Charlie started it all by asking, "When's it gonna happen?"

Enoch said he believed today was the day, then was interrupted by a woman in the back holding a tiny TV. "Look like somebody done took over the GC's airwaves again. That Micah guy runnin' things at Petra is gonna speak about what comes next."

Darrion and some others pulled out their little TVs.

"Should we listen, Brother Enoch?" the woman said. "Will you be offended?"

"Hardly," Enoch said, taking out his own TV. "What could be better than this? Dr. Rosenzweig is a scholar's scholar. Let's have church."

"Why don't we line up the TVs on that bench and turn up the volume so everyone can hear?" Conrad said.

"Wonder what old Nicolae thinks of this broadcast," Darrion said.

Dr. Rosenzweig was just beginning when they turned up the volume. He sat at a table with a Bible open before him.

347

"I speak to you tonight probably for the last time before the Glorious Appearing of our Lord and Savior, Jesus Christ the Messiah," Chaim said. "He could very well come during this message, and nothing would give me greater pleasure. When he comes there will be no more need for us to fight Antichrist and his False Prophet. The work will have been done for us by the King of kings.

"But as he did not return seven years to the minute from the signing of the covenant between Antichrist and Israel, many are troubled and confused."

Chaim continued, saying he believed Jesus would return before midnight, Israel Time. Then he spoke to those who had not accepted Jesus as Messiah.

Conrad moved closer to the tiny screens when a Web site address appeared beneath Dr. Rosenzweig. Anyone making a decision for Christ was asked to let Chaim know about it.

Dr. Rosenzweig read from Matthew 24 and explained what he believed would come next. "This *is* the last day of the Tribulation that was prophesied thousands of years ago! Today is the seventh anniversary of the unholy and quickly broken covenant between Antichrist and Israel. What is next? The sun, wherever it is in the sky where you are, will cease to shine. If the moon is out where you are, it will go dark as well because it is merely a reflection of the sun. Do not fear. Do not be afraid. Do not panic. Take comfort in the truth of the Word of God and put your faith in Christ, the Messiah."

Conrad was thrilled when Chaim turned to Zechariah

and read prophecy written hundreds of years before Jesus' birth.

Then the man leaned forward, looked into the camera, and spoke. "One of our first-century Jews, Peter, said, 'Anyone who calls on the name of the Lord will be saved.' I cannot choose more appropriate words than his when I speak to fellow Jews, saying, 'People of Israel, listen! God publicly endorsed Jesus of Nazareth by doing wonderful miracles, wonders, and signs through him, as you well know. But you followed God's prearranged plan. With the help of lawless Gentiles, you nailed him to the cross and murdered him. However, God released him from the horrors of death and raised him back to life again, for death could not keep him in its grip.

" 'King David said this about him: "I know the Lord is always with me. I will not be shaken, for he is right beside me. No wonder my heart is filled with joy, and my mouth shouts his praises! My body rests in hope. For you will not leave my soul among the dead or allow your Holy One to rot in the grave. You have shown me the way of life, and you will give me wonderful joy in your presence."

" 'Dear brothers, think about this! David wasn't referring to himself when he spoke these words I have quoted, for he died and was buried, and his tomb is still here among us. But he was a prophet, and he knew God had promised with an oath that one of David's own descendants would sit on David's throne as the Messiah. David was looking into the future and predicting the Messiah's resurrection. He was saying that the Messiah would not be left among the dead and that his body would not rot in the grave.

" 'This prophecy was speaking of Jesus, whom God raised from the dead, and we all are witnesses of this. Now he sits on the throne of highest honor in heaven, at God's right hand. And the Father, as he had promised, gave him the Holy Spirit to pour out upon us, just as you see and hear today.

" 'So let it be clearly known by everyone in Israel that God has made this Jesus whom you crucified to be both Lord and Messiah!'

"Beloved," Chaim raced on, "the Bible tells us that 'Peter's words convicted them deeply, and they said to him and to the other apostles, "Brothers, what should we do?" '

"Do you find yourself asking the same today? I say to you as Peter said to them, 'Each of you must turn from your sins and turn to God, and be baptized in the name of Jesus Christ for the forgiveness of your sins. Then you will receive the gift of the Holy Spirit. This promise is to you and to your children, and even to the Gentiles—all who have been called by the Lord our God.'

"Oh, children of Israel around the globe, I am being signaled that our enemy is close to wresting back control of this network. Should I be cut off, trust me, you already know enough to put your faith in Christ as the Messiah."

Chaim closed by reading a prophecy from Isaiah 53 given more than seven hundred years before the birth of Christ.

Conrad wondered how many watching had responded to the man's appeal.

## 37

**LIONEL** watched in awe as the sun dipped toward the horizon. He had never seen such a sight. Throughout the day, the sky had been clear. Now, fluffy marshmallow-like clouds seemed to appear, one after another, moving quickly above him.

After the incident in the desert, Sam and Lionel asked Zeke for a break and Zeke agreed. Sam and Lionel moved back into camp and ate their evening meal. When Mr. Stein joined them, Sam explained all that had happened.

Mr. Stein saw the fear in Sam's eyes. "The Lord has protected us these past few years," he said, smiling. "Why would you think it would be different now?"

"We've never gone up against that before," Sam said, pointing to the vast army.

"But look at that," Mr. Stein said, gesturing to the sky. The clouds had formed a canopy above them, and the reflection of the orange sun took their breath away. "Your outlook needs an up-look. Any God who could create that masterpiece should be trusted with your life, don't you think?"

Lionel looked at the Unity Army. All day they had advanced at a snail's pace. Now the army covered the desert like the clouds covered the sky, a perfect mirror. Only one was beautiful and the other hideous.

———————

Vicki held Judd until the fatigue stiffened her whole body. She lay down beside him, an arm draped over him. The rising and falling of his chest let her know he was still alive.

The sun's orange glow reflected in the clouds above, clouds she hadn't seen earlier. She wished Judd would wake up so they could share this.

She tried to shut out the conversation of the GC soldiers around them. Many mocked the prisoners, saying they were Jesus freaks or Ben-Judah freaks or cursing them. "I don't know why they had us take prisoners in the first place," one said. "We should have killed them all where they stood."

Later, when a group of soldiers moved toward Vicki, she propped herself up on an elbow. Her leg ached from the deep wound, and she worried it would get infected.

Commander Fulcire picked out prisoners to be taken away. He turned and waved a hand at Judd. "And that one too."

"What!?" Vicki shouted. "Why are you moving him?"

Fulcire glared at Vicki. "We're burning the dead for health reasons—"

"He's not dead!" Vicki yelled.

Fulcire cocked his head and stared at her.

"Please, God," Vicki prayed silently, "help Judd wake up."

"Do I know you?" Fulcire said, squinting.

"This is my husband," Vicki said, ignoring the question and looking away. "I won't let you take him."

Two soldiers approached Judd. "Your husband is dead, rebel," one soldier said, taking Judd's arms. The other moved to his legs and stooped.

Vicki breathed another prayer as she fell on Judd's torso and screamed in pain.

Judd's eyes fluttered and he moaned.

Fulcire moved closer as the two men tried to pick Judd up. The commander held up a hand, so the soldiers dropped Judd.

"Ah, back from the dead, are we?" Fulcire crooned. He knelt beside Vicki. "Something looks familiar about you. You're from the United North American States, right?"

Vicki hugged Judd and ignored the man. She decided she wouldn't speak again unless she had to. If this guy figured out who she was, her life was over.

Fulcire stood. "Take them both to interrogation."

Vicki didn't protest when the men helped them to their feet. Judd was still groggy, but he made eye contact with Vicki and put a hand to the back of his head.

"We're going to be okay," Vicki said. "Look at the clouds."

Judd glanced skyward, and his mouth opened in an O. "He should be here by now, don't you think?"

"Soon," Vicki said.

Conrad glanced at his watch. It was about noon in the Midwest, and the people asked Enoch to teach them more. Conrad listened intently and looked at the sky. Something was happening with the clouds.

Enoch explained that twenty-one judgments had come from heaven in three sets of seven. These showed God's mercy on one hand, calling people to repentance, but also God's anger at evil. According to the Bible, the judgments were poured out by angels from bowls or vials.

Enoch went through each of the seven bowls, judgments that came in the form of sores on people's bodies, the sea turning to blood, rivers and springs turning to blood, the sun becoming hot enough to burn people alive, New Babylon's darkness, and the drying up of the Euphrates River.

"The seventh bowl judgment, the one we still await, will be poured out upon the *air* so that lightning and thunder and other celestial calamities announce the greatest earthquake in history. It will be so great it will cause Jerusalem to break into three pieces in preparation for changes during Christ's millennial kingdom. It will also be accompanied by a great outpouring of hundred-pound hailstones.

"And what will the general response be from the very ones God is trying to reach and persuade? Revelation 16:21 tells us that 'they cursed God because of the hailstorm, which was a very terrible plague.' "

"And this is what's coming next?" an older man said.

"In advance of the Glorious Appearing," Enoch said. "Yes."

Conrad thought of Judd and Vicki in Jerusalem. If they were still there and still alive, the ground would soon be shaking beneath them.

---

Judd was dropped on his back near the Unity Army command post outside what was left of Teddy Kollek Stadium. It took him a few seconds to catch his breath. Soldiers plopped Vicki down beside him, and he tried to help her get into a comfortable position.

"Are you okay?" Vicki said.

"There's a knot on the back of my head and I have a headache the size of Cleveland, but I think I'm okay. What happened?"

Vicki filled him in. "I think Fulcire knows who I am. I mean, he may not have figured it all out, but he remembered something about me."

"Let's tell him we were over here on vacation and just happened to get caught up in the war."

"And what do we tell him about not taking Carpathia's mark?"

Judd bit the inside of his cheek. "We have a skin condition?"

Vicki shook her head. "I'm glad one of us has a sense of humor right now."

There were several other prisoners on the sidewalk outside the stadium. Some looked like they had been beaten and were waiting for another round of questioning.

Listening to the soldiers, Judd picked up information that Nicolae Carpathia was in Jerusalem but would soon be heading to Petra. Rebels currently held the Temple Mount, but the Unity Army was going after them. The GC now controlled most of the Old City. Something was brewing to the south and northeast, a revolt of some sort among Unity Army troops, but Judd couldn't figure out what that was about.

A GCNN reporter with a camera crew shuffled by taking shots of the prisoners. Judd and Vicki turned their heads as they passed.

"This is something, isn't it?" Vicki said. "To be in the middle of Carpathia's army on the last day of the world."

"If this is the last day," Judd said.

"What do you mean?"

"What if Tsion was wrong? Even Jesus said no one knows the hour when he's going to return."

"True, but I think he was talking about the Rapture when he said that. From Daniel 9:27 we know that the Glorious Appearing happens seven years after—" Vicki stopped as Commander Fulcire returned and spoke in hushed tones to another officer.

The officer hustled to Vicki, held out a small electronic device, and mashed her fingers across a square pad.

"He knows," Vicki whispered.

The commander returned with a smile, holding the device. He turned it around, and Judd tried not to react. Vicki's picture, along with her personal information, flashed on the screen. She was one of the most wanted young people in the world.

"So, Vicki B—" Fulcire grinned—"we finally meet. Who would have thought I'd have to come all the way to Israel to find you? What a lucky break."

"Your luck is about to run out," Vicki mumbled.

"I'm sorry. What was that?" Fulcire said, kicking at Vicki's injured leg.

Judd wanted to kill Fulcire, but he scooted closer to Vicki, trying to protect her. She writhed in pain, and Judd noticed blood seeping from her bandage.

"You've been with the rebels," Fulcire said. "We've wiped out most of them, but some are still in hiding. I want to know where."

"Even if I knew, I'd never tell you," Vicki said through clenched teeth.

"That's the same thing all you Judah-ites say. That friend of yours back in the States, Mark something. He said he would never tell us a thing, but the prospect of the blade—how should I say it?—loosened his tongue."

"You monster," Vicki said.

"Mark didn't tell you anything," Judd yelled.

Fulcire glanced at Judd and smiled. He motioned for a soldier.

"What are you doing?" Vicki said.

"Maybe you won't tell us what we know if we threaten *you*, but what about this husband of yours?"

"No!" Vicki screamed.

"It's okay," Judd said, standing. "This is all going to be over soon. You and your army are going back to dust—"

A soldier hit Judd on the knee with the butt of his

rifle, and Judd fell with a sickening thud. Something cracked in his leg as he tumbled to the ground.

The soldier pointed his rifle at Judd's head and looked at Fulcire.

"Do you have anything to tell us now?" Fulcire said to Vicki.

"You know where our leaders are," Vicki cried. "They're all at Petra."

"We know the rebels use tunnels," Fulcire said. "I'd rather not blow up all these buildings to find them. Lord Carpathia will need them. Show us where the rebels are."

---

Vicki looked at Judd. If she didn't give Fulcire the information he wanted, Judd would die. If she did give the information, rebels would die.

"Don't do it," Judd said, gasping at the pain.

The soldier hovering over Judd kicked him, and blood spurted from his mouth. Judd's head hit the concrete hard, and Vicki fell on top of him.

"They're going to kill us anyway," Judd managed to say. "Don't tell them anything."

"I won't let them hurt you," Vicki said.

The soldier raised his gun again, and Vicki held up a hand. "Stop! I'll tell you what you want, but you have to stop."

Fulcire waved the soldier away and knelt near Vicki. "I'm waiting."

"No," Judd groaned.

"I'll take you there," Vicki said.

Lionel went home and closed the door. He had been so excited about the return of Christ, but the oncoming army sent shivers down his spine every time he looked at the desert. The sun had dipped below the horizon now, and a full moon peeked out from behind the increasing clouds.

A roar rose outside and Lionel's heart fell. Had he missed the return of Jesus? No, there would be signs in the heavens—maybe that's what the clouds were!

He hurried outside to see tens of thousands gathering their evening meal applaud people riding on ATVs. Rayford Steele was being carried by someone from the Tribulation Force. Lionel had heard earlier that Rayford had been injured or possibly killed in an accident. People waved and screamed encouragement as the former pilot for Nicolae Carpathia passed.

Lionel joined several people who had gathered to pray. The Unity Army was less than a football field away from Zeke and the others at the front lines. *The battle has already been won,* Lionel thought. *God said he was going to take care of these people and either I'm going to believe it or not!*

Lionel rushed toward Rayford Steele's home. He had to talk with someone he knew. As he approached, he heard voices inside and recognized Chaim Rosenzweig's. Lionel was about to knock when a cell phone chirped.

"Yeah, Sebastian, it's Ray. . . . I'm okay, a little banged up, but okay. What's the latest on Buck? . . . No, go ahead and tell me. . . ." There was a long pause. "Does Mac know how it happened?" Another pause. "Okay, thanks for letting me know."

"Is it Buck?" Chaim said, his voice shaky.

"Yeah. Mac found his body in Jerusalem. He was torn up pretty bad."

"I cannot believe Buck and Tsion are both dead," Chaim said.

Lionel staggered away from the door. *Both dead?* He sprinted down the hillside to find Sam, praying for Judd and Vicki as he ran.

# 38

VICKI huddled close to Judd in the back of the truck as they entered a gate at the Old City. Bodies lay strewn about the road, and the truck shimmied as it rolled over dead rebels. The rebels' clothes lay torn and in some cases ripped apart, which made Vicki wonder if the GC hadn't gone through their clothing for valuables. She closed her eyes at the horrific scene.

"Vicki, you can't do this," Judd whispered. "I won't let you."

"Trust me," she said. "I won't give them anything."

"Then what are we doing?"

Vicki glanced up. The canvas canopy over the truck had been pulled back, and they could see the sky. Clouds parted, showing the full moon. "I'll think of something."

The truck ground to a halt, its brakes squealing. Vicki's leg ached with a pain she had never experienced. Judd's leg was nearly useless. She doubted he could walk.

"Out!" Commander Fulcire shouted.

A soldier on the ground helped Vicki down, but he pushed Judd off so he landed hard, crying out in pain.

"I swear if you hurt him any more, I'll tell you nothing!" Vicki yelled.

Fulcire seized Judd by an arm and pulled him up. "He's okay. Just a couple of scratches, eh, young man? Now show us an entrance, and no warning your compatriots that we're coming."

Vicki walked slowly away from the truck, looking at buildings and street signs.

"Stop here," Fulcire said. He walked around Judd and faced Vicki. "We know there are tunnels—show us or we add you to the dead."

Judd nudged Vicki and pointed up. A light shot across the night sky in front of the moon. Vicki gasped and Fulcire looked up as well.

"Guards, take him!" Fulcire said.

But as soon as they moved toward Judd, the moon went black. The streets disappeared under a dark blanket. Several soldiers screamed.

"It's just like in New Babylon," one said. "It's another plague! And you know what happened to that city!"

"Shut up!" Fulcire ordered. "Try the truck lights."

"Come on," Vicki whispered to Judd. "Let's get out of here."

But before they could move, the lights on the truck blazed, lighting up the street. The soldiers sighed with relief.

Fulcire radioed someone and received a report from

Teddy Kollek Stadium that their lights were all working and there was nothing to worry about. He turned to Judd and Vicki.

"Do you see that, Commander?" Vicki said, pointing at the sky. "That's part of the prophecy. God said the sun and moon will be dark on this day. He's going to punish the world for its evil. This is happening around the world, and you'd better get ready for the next thing he's going to do."

Scores of verses from the Old and New Testaments flooded Vicki's mind. All spoke of the wrath of God poured out on the earth. She wanted to spill the verses out one after another.

The commander smirked. "The moon goes behind a cloud and she claims it's a miracle of God."

Soldiers laughed, but not very hard, Vicki thought. They had seen enough in the last few years to make them wary.

"We've heard your prophecies of gloom and doom," Fulcire snapped. "Show us the entrance to—"

"You may have heard enough, but obviously you haven't seen enough," Vicki shot back. Her words appeared to stun him.

"Babylon the great has fallen, just like God said it would," she continued. "And soon you will see the Son of Man coming in the clouds with great power and glory. He'll be on a white horse, and he will make war with you and will overcome you and your armies."

"Yes, Jesus will show up by and by, pie in the sky, and then we'll all die," Fulcire mocked. "But you won't be around to see him, will you, Judah-ite?" He pulled a

pistol from a holster around his waist and aimed it at
Judd's head. "Now point the way to one of the tunnels, or
I'll send your precious husband to be with Jesus where he
can ride all the white horsies."

Vicki looked at Judd, his face lit by the truck's lights. It
struck her as strange that it would end this way. They had
survived seven years of disasters, only to be killed a few
hours—maybe a few minutes—before the return of
Christ.

"I love you," Judd whispered. There didn't seem to be
a hint of fear in his voice. "I'll always love you."

"Your choice," Fulcire said, cocking the pistol.

———————————

Conrad had jumped to his feet and cried out with the
others when the early afternoon sun disappeared from
the sky in Palos Hills, Illinois. The temperature dropped,
and the world turned pitch dark.

But it was the roaring, whistling sound that spooked
everyone the most. It sounded like a jet coming in for a
landing, engines screaming. Conrad looked up and saw a
fiery trail behind something—maybe a spaceship,
airplane, or falling star. He didn't know what it was, but
he wasn't about to stay and find out. He grabbed Shelly's
hand, and they ran for cover.

"Don't be afraid!" Enoch yelled. "This was prophesied. It's all part of God's plan."

The object crashed on the other side of the mall, and
everyone rushed to it. Streetlights popped on as Conrad
and Shelly ran, hand in hand. They found a ten-foot-wide

hole in the road, smoke billowing, and heat so intense they couldn't get close.

Tom and Josey Fogarty darted across the street, heading for safety with their little boy, Ryan.

"Here comes another one!" Ty Spivey shouted.

The falling object roared overhead. Flames licked at its edges as it plunged to earth, and people screamed. Conrad took Shelly's hand again, and they bolted toward the Fogartys.

"You can come to our house," Shelly said to Conrad.

"I believe we're protected!" Enoch yelled behind them. "None of the judgments from heaven harmed God's people! We bear his mark, his seal! He will protect us!"

But Conrad and Shelly continued to run, with the screaming meteor falling. When a terrific explosion lit the darkness, Conrad looked back. This meteor—at least twice as big as the first—slammed into one of the large stores at the mall.

"Wonder how the GC is going to spin this," Shelly said.

"They'll probably tell everybody they shouldn't be afraid," Conrad said. "After all, it's just the sky falling on them."

---

Lionel reached the defense perimeter of Petra as the moon darkened and GC troops lit flashlights and high-tech lanterns. When the first streaks of light crossed the sky, the Petra rebels *ooh*ed and *aah*ed. Then the first meteor fell several hundred yards from Lionel's position, and the Unity Army panicked. Horses reared and soldiers screamed orders.

The next meteor slammed into a mass of tanks and transport vehicles, causing a huge explosion. Soldiers flew into the air. The front lines of the army withdrew—how far Lionel couldn't tell.

Rocks nearby shook with the crashing of each meteor. While the Unity Army was struck again and again, Petra remained safe.

Someone turned on large searchlights near the camp and pointed them straight up. The light allowed Lionel to see the edges of the Unity Army and the clouds above that bubbled and churned like boiling macaroni. There was a flash in the distance. Then came a low rumble.

Something big was happening. Lionel felt chills. He wondered if Judd and Vicki were seeing the same thing. Or if Judd and Vicki were even alive.

----

Vicki covered her eyes as Commander Fulcire leveled the pistol at Judd. She heard a whooshing sound, and something approached overhead. Several men yelled and Vicki looked again, surprised to see Commander Fulcire with his gun at his side, staring into the darkened sky.

"Incoming!" someone shouted from the truck.

The soldiers hit the dirt before a fiery sphere hurtled to earth. The impact shook the ground, and Judd nearly fell down from the shock.

Radios blared, soldiers ran, and everyone seemed confused.

"What's going on?" Judd whispered.

"God's show is starting," Vicki said.

Fulcire motioned to a nearby soldier. "Get these two back in the truck!"

The soldier hustled Judd and Vicki to the back of the vehicle and told them to climb inside. Vicki tried to help Judd, but he had trouble lifting his injured leg. Judd grasped a handle on the side and tried to pull himself up, but before he could, another meteor flew overhead and the soldier hit the ground. In the confusion, darkness, and roar of the explosion, Vicki grabbed Judd's hand and pulled him to the side of the truck, out of sight. The soldier whimpered on the ground.

"Get down and crawl under," Vicki said. "They might not see us."

They scrambled underneath and watched soldiers rush for safety. But where could they go? The meteors looked like they were as big as cars, so the craters they left behind had to be huge.

"Did you know this was coming?" Judd whispered.

Vicki nodded and inched closer to the edge of the truck so she could see the sky. "In Isaiah, I think. There's also supposed to be a sign in the heavens."

"What kind of sign?"

"I don't know what form it will take, but that's supposed to happen before Jesus comes back."

"Maybe the clouds are the sign."

"Could be."

Judd pointed across the street. "You know there's an entrance to the tunnels about half a block away?"

"I wasn't going to tell them."

"You were just going to let me die?" Judd was smiling.

"That's what you said to do. And that part about loving me forever was nice."

"Everybody in the truck!" Commander Fulcire yelled. "Now!"

"Sir, the prisoners . . . they're not here!" a soldier at the back said.

The soldier tried to defend himself, but Fulcire wouldn't listen. A gun fired and the soldier fell, his face looking straight at Judd and Vicki. A red stain pooled around his body.

Vicki clamped a hand over her mouth to keep from screaming. Soon, more meteors fell, and it appeared that Fulcire was more interested in getting to safety than finding Judd and Vicki.

The soldiers piled into the truck, and Judd and Vicki rolled to their left into the darkness. The truck sped through the gate as they limped to the entrance to the tunnel. Seconds later a meteor slammed into the earth, just past the gate, shattering windows. Judd and Vicki went inside, gingerly climbing to the next floor where they could see the scene. Fulcire's truck had tried to stop before a huge crater, but it teetered on the edge. Fulcire shouted commands as he climbed out the passenger-side window.

Soldiers began jumping from the rear, in spite of Fulcire's orders. The commander made it out of the truck's cab and climbed on top. But when several more soldiers leaped out the back, the truck tipped forward.

Fulcire grabbed for something to hold on to, but the truck's top was too slick. He tried to jump to a concrete walkway but didn't make it. His screams echoed as he and the truck plunged down.

Lightning flashed, casting eerie bursts of light on the Old City.

"What do you want to do?" Vicki said.

"Let's see how far we can get through the tunnels," Judd said. "Maybe we'll find someone who can help us."

"I don't want to be in here when Jesus comes," Vicki said.

"Me either, but with this busted leg, they'll catch us outside."

Vicki found Judd a place to rest. "This time let me find someone and bring them back to help," she said. "Stay right here."

# 39

**LIONEL** sat with Sam on Petra's perimeter and watched God's light show. Lightning flashed through the deepening clouds, thick streaks of gold firing overhead. He remembered watching a tornado years before the Tribulation began, but that didn't compare with this.

Lightning increased, with hundreds and thousands of bolts crashing to the desert floor every second. It was like the end to a terrific fireworks display, only this one was a million times brighter and stronger. Thunder shook the ground, and Lionel tried to cover his ears.

Sam pulled out his tiny television and cupped a hand around the screen so they could see it. The Global Community News Network treated God's light show as a nonstory. Instead, their coverage focused on the war effort. Unity generals reported troops heading toward the Valley of Megiddo.

Nicolae Carpathia was shown getting onto a huge

horse. "I am pleased with the reports from the South and from the Northeast. And now we are about to embark on one of our most strategic initiatives. A third of our entire fighting force will advance upon the rebel stronghold cowering in Petra. Intelligence tells us that a paltry defensive unit has rung the city round about, but they are hopelessly outnumbered and have already offered to surrender."

"Did you know we were ready to surrender?" Sam said.

Lionel shook his head. "I'm glad we're on the side of the one causing this lightning and thunder."

Carpathia answered questions, lying about his contact with leaders in Petra. "We made peaceful overtures to the leadership, offering amnesty for any who would voluntarily leave the stronghold and take the mark of loyalty. Our understanding is that many wished to make this move, only to be slaughtered by the leadership. Many will recall that it was this very leadership who assassinated me, serving only to give me the opportunity to prove my divinity by raising myself from the dead.

"Well, this time around, there will be no negotiating. Loyalists to our New World Order have either been murdered or have escaped, so intelligence tells us Petra is now inhabited solely by rebels to our cause, murderers and blasphemers who have thumbed their noses at every attempt to reason with them."

Carpathia waved a sword for the camera and continued. "I shall personally lead this effort, with the able assistance, of course, of my generals. We shall rally the troops as soon as we arrive, and the siege should take only a matter of minutes."

Carpathia raced off on the horse, and a reporter called after him, "All the best to you, holy one! And may you bless yourself and bring honor to your name with this effort!"

"Won't be long now," Lionel said.

---

Conrad and Shelly huddled together on the front porch of the house where Shelly was staying. Conrad had a Bible open and could read by the lightning strikes. Enoch had shown Conrad many verses about what was to come.

Conrad turned toward the end of the Old Testament to Zephaniah and read some verses to Shelly. " 'That terrible day of the Lord is near. Swiftly it comes—a day when strong men will cry bitterly.

" 'It is a day when the Lord's anger will be poured out. It is a day of terrible distress and anguish, a day of ruin and desolation, a day of darkness and gloom, of clouds, blackness, trumpet calls, and battle cries. Down go the walled cities and strongest battlements!

" 'Because you have sinned against the Lord, I will make you as helpless as a blind man searching for a path. Your blood will be poured out into the dust, and your bodies will lie there rotting on the ground.' "

He closed the Bible, and Shelly scooted closer. Houses crackled and burned not far away. The acrid, smoky smell of the meteors filled the air.

"What do you think all that means?" Shelly said.

"I guess it means your life is worthless if you fight against God," Conrad said. "He's going to win every time."

Suddenly the lightning and thunder stopped. The sky was pitch-black, and Conrad wondered how long God would wait. Soon Jesus would return—but would he be seen just in Jerusalem or everywhere?

Conrad put an arm around Shelly. "Enoch says he's going to find a way to get to Israel as soon as possible. He's even going to try and raise money for his people to go there."

"I'd do anything to see Jesus start setting up his kingdom," Shelly said. "Let's go together."

Conrad smiled, pulling her close. "We could stay with Judd and Vicki."

---

Vicki limped through the deserted tunnel, listening for rebels. The pain in her leg had gotten worse, and it was difficult to walk. She tripped and fell over a dead rebel, and her wound opened again.

She found medical supplies and bandages and stumbled back to Judd. She guessed his leg was broken, so there was nothing she could do except put a blanket over him and try to make him comfortable.

When she got her own bandage off, the sight turned her stomach. The rock had torn away her skin, and the deep gash was now a sickly color. She poured in some antiseptic and thought she was going to pass out from the pain. After rebandaging the wound, she crawled up the stairs and peeked outside. The thundering of the guns had stopped. A few scattered shots were fired every now and then, but the battle seemed to be over. The GC had overtaken Jerusalem just like the Bible said.

She returned to Judd and lay down beside him. She remembered the words of her Little League coach: "Leave everything on the field."

She smiled, thinking they had done just that—they'd used all their energy to help people. Whatever happened next would happen without their help.

---

Lionel and Sam sat in the stillness of Petra, darkness covering the land. Rebels with weapons seemed restless, waiting for something to happen. Sam gave Lionel a canteen of water, and he took a long drink.

"Carpathia's on the move," Lionel said. "We might see him tonight."

"I'd like to see him get thrown into the lake of fire where he belongs," Sam said. "I can't wait until—" He stopped in midsentence.

Lionel had tilted his head back and taken another drink from the canteen. Suddenly a light flashed in the sky and something buzzed, like the sound of a light saber in one of those old *Star Wars* movies. Sam pointed, mouth agape, and Lionel pulled the canteen from his mouth, water spilling.

A yellow streak of light—like lightning, only it wasn't—pulsed in the sky. It started near the horizon and went straight up miles into the sky. Two-thirds of the way up, another yellow streak intersected the first one, forming a huge cross.

Lionel was so overcome he dropped the canteen. He could only imagine what was going through the minds of the Unity Army soldiers.

------

Conrad shielded his eyes from the blazing cross and couldn't help smiling. A warm feeling surged through his body. He and Shelly stood and stared in awe.

"He's really coming back," Shelly whispered, full of emotion. "This is the sign of the Son of Man Dr. Ben-Judah wrote about."

"Amazing," was all Conrad could say.

"Let's find Enoch," Shelly said.

On the way, Conrad stopped outside a house and peered in the front window. A huge television stood against the far wall. People inside screamed and pointed. On the screen was the yellow cross, blazing for the whole world to see.

------

Judd opened his eyes and noticed a glare shining through a tiny hole in the brick wall. A bomb must have exploded, he thought, and created the crack there. He glanced down and noticed Vicki on his chest.

She shifted slightly and looked up at him. "You're awake. How do you feel?"

Judd put a hand in front of his face. "Fine except for that annoying light coming from over there." He gestured at the wall. "You think the Unity Army's put up floodlights?"

"If they have, they're yellow," Vicki said. "Listen."

Judd sat up quietly, straining to hear a hum coming from outside. "It's weird that we'd hear it down—"

"Shh," she said. "Can you feel it vibrating?"

Judd listened a few more seconds. "It almost sounds like the light in the aquarium back home. Only a million times louder."

Vicki's gaze darted left and right.

"What is it?" Judd said.

"I don't know. Maybe we've missed it," Vicki said.

"Jesus?"

"Yeah, maybe he's already come back and we were down here. Or maybe . . ."

"What?"

She rolled to her knees and stood, peeking out of the crack in the wall. "There was supposed to be a sign in the sky. . . ."

"No way I'm going to miss this," Judd said, racing her up the stairs.

They plunged through the door and into the street, not caring that the GC was nearby. The sight in the sky took their breath away. Judd put an arm around Vicki and hugged her.

"A cross," she whispered. "Of course!"

Judd couldn't take his eyes from the yellow pulsing light. He wondered what was happening at the Temple Mount right now and in the desert with Carpathia's army. Could the GC sense their end was near?

"Wait a minute," Vicki said. "What are you doing? You have a broken leg and you just . . ."

Judd stared at her. "And you—we just ran up those stairs, but . . ." He put all his weight on his bad leg. No pain. He wasn't even sore. "I thought for sure it was broken."

Vicki felt the back of his head. "There was a big knot here. What happened?"

Judd's eyes grew wide as he pulled Vicki's pant leg up and unwrapped her bandage.

"What are you doing?" she said. "I want to keep it covered so it won't get infected."

"You were limping on this, right?"

"Yeah, but—"

Vicki's mouth dropped open. Her leg looked perfectly normal. No skin tears, no blood, no scars. Not even a scratch.

"We've both been healed!" Judd said.

They jumped and giggled like schoolchildren. Judd felt ten pounds lighter.

"What do we do?" Vicki said, unable to stop smiling.

"Jesus is supposed to come back to the Mount of Olives, right?"

She nodded. "And he's going to split it in two."

"Okay, there's got to be another mount close by where we can see everything."

"Mount Scopus," Vicki said.

"Mount Scopus it is," Judd said. "Let's go."

---

Lionel picked up the canteen and screwed on the lid as he watched the cross. It was a symbol of how far God would go to show his love.

Lionel felt pressure on his left arm, and the one Zeke had made for him pushed forward.

Sam yelled and pointed, startled by something on Lionel's clothes.

Lionel brushed his hand against his shirt, thinking there might be an insect on him. "What is it?"

Sam stared at Lionel's left arm. Lionel raised it. His arm had returned. Two hands.

A miracle!

Lionel raised both hands toward the cross and fell to the sand, overcome with thanksgiving.

**40**

**JUDD** and Vicki ran through Jerusalem with the pulsing, flashing cross lighting their way. Judd knew the Unity Army controlled the city, but he didn't care. His Lord was coming, and Judd wanted to see him.

They rounded a corner and noticed several dead bodies. To Judd's amazement, one of them moved. He and Vicki rushed to the man.

When he saw the mark on Judd's and Vicki's foreheads, he smiled. "I was shot and fell here. I pretended I was dead—and nearly was. But just now I felt something strange." He pointed to his chest. "Look. The hole where the bullet went through isn't there."

"We were healed too," Vicki said. She explained where they were going.

"I'll go with you and show you a way around the Unity Army," the man said. "My name is Ehud."

The three raced into the night, wondering what they

would find around the next corner. What would God do to top what he had already done?

---

Lionel was so excited about his arm that he didn't notice what was happening behind him.

Zeke rushed up and yelled, "You two fall back. They're coming!"

"What?" Lionel said.

But it was too late. The cross in the sky had set something in motion with the Unity Army, and Lionel heard hoofbeats on the sand. He glanced back as horses galloped toward them.

"Big Dog One to all units," someone said over a radio Zeke had on his shoulder. "Hold your fire. Wait. On my command."

"What's he thinking?" Zeke said. Then he hollered at the rebels in front of him, "You heard him—hold your fire!"

The men grumbled, pointing at the oncoming army, a death machine rolling across the desert. The radio crackled with protests.

"Hold, hold, hold!" Big Dog One shouted.

"Permission to speak my mind, sir," someone said.

"Denied. Follow orders."

Lionel backed up while he and Sam watched the human tornado heading straight for them. The front line closed the gap in seconds. In the eerie, yellow light, horsemen pointed rifles. Others wielded swords that glinted yellow off their sharpened edges.

Suddenly, a shot. Then all riders opened fire. Bullets pinged off rocks. Lionel shouted for Zeke to get down, but the man stood tall. The army rushed through the line of rebels, and the lead rider raised his sharpened sword and plunged it down at Zeke.

Lionel put his head in his hands. When he had the courage to look, he saw Zeke still standing. How could the lead rider have missed?

Sam stood, smiling and waving, daring the army to hurt him. He jumped on a rock, both hands in the air, yelling at the top of his lungs.

A rider flicked his sword out and took a swipe at Sam as he passed. If Lionel hadn't seen it, he wouldn't have believed it. It was as if the blade went straight through his friend's body. Sam didn't crumble in pain and blood didn't spurt from his wound, because there was no wound.

Others stood against the gunfire, unhurt by bullets that simply passed through them.

"Come on up!" Sam called to Lionel. "Either these guys are really bad shots, or God's up to something!"

Lionel climbed onto the rock as another wave of riders approached. A man fired at Lionel at close range. When Lionel didn't move, he fired again. The soldier looked at his weapon and paused. Riders swept into him, knocking him from his horse.

Lionel reached down and helped the soldier up.

The man pulled out a pistol and fired again. "Blanks. They're all blanks."

"No," Lionel said, "it's just that your bullets don't work here."

The man turned to run but was caught in the stampede. Horses couldn't take the steep landscape, and those at the front stalled and turned back. Others kept coming, creating a horse traffic jam.

In the chaos, Lionel and Sam climbed down and joined the rebels who calmly walked through the enemy throng.

Zeke found them and slapped Lionel on the back. "We're heading back to the others. Gonna wait on Jesus with our friends up top rather than down here with the GC."

Sam gave a fake cough and waved a hand in front of his face. "Yeah, these guys are kicking up too much dust."

---

Conrad and Shelly made it to Enoch's house with others from different hiding places. Charlie had taken Phoenix to Enoch's basement, and the dog was barking his head off.

"You sense it too, don't you, boy?" Conrad said to the shaking dog.

Charlie pulled Phoenix onto his lap and that seemed to help. "You think he knows Jesus is coming?"

"Wouldn't doubt it," Conrad said. "If dogs can sense an earthquake, I'll bet they can sense the King of kings."

"You think he'll get to see Ryan Daley again?" Charlie said. "He's the one who found Phoenix in the first place."

"I hope so."

"What about animals in Jesus' kingdom? Dr. Ben-Judah taught that people could live a long time, even hundreds of years. What does that mean for animals like Phoenix?"

"Well, this is a guess, but I think dogs will live a lot longer, just like people. Dogs and other animals don't have souls, but it does say in the Bible that the wolf and the lamb are going to lie down together."

"And isn't there supposed to be less effects of sin, you know, diseases and sickness and all that?" Charlie said.

"True. Plant life is supposed to grow like crazy, so I wouldn't be surprised if old Phoenix here grew old with the rest of us."

Charlie smiled. "I can't wait to see his reunion with Ryan."

---

Vicki followed closely behind Judd and Ehud as they made their way through Jerusalem. They rushed down the Via Dolorosa, hit Carpathia Way, and headed for the Damascus Gate. When they found a few Unity Army soldiers there, Ehud led Judd and Vicki east to a breach in the wall and they climbed over.

The cross stayed behind them, lighting the way. Vicki wondered if this was the same kind of light given off by the star announcing Jesus' birth.

They stayed off the main roads, circling the Old City at a safe distance. After they passed a museum, Ehud motioned them northeast to a road renamed Fortunato Boulevard. Vicki chuckled because every block sported a likeness of Leon, the Most High Reverend Father of Carpathianism. Each banner showed him in a different outfit, and in the glowing yellow light, he looked even more ridiculous.

"How much farther?" Judd said.

"Mount Scopus is right this way," Ehud said.

"What if the troops are there?" Vicki said.

"If I'm right, they'll have moved past it, but if not, I know a place where we'll be safe."

---

Lionel wanted to go to the tech center to see the latest from Chang on Jewish conversions and hear any word from Judd and Vicki, but the stream of people climbing up the side of the mountain changed that. Thousands made their way to the top of a mount overlooking the valley.

"Where's everyone going?" Lionel asked an elderly man who had stopped to catch his breath.

The man pointed up. "The elders . . . they asked us to stay in our groups . . . one hundred groups of a thousand. . . . We'll be going up to the north, over there."

Sam got on one side of the man, Lionel on the other, and they helped him keep up with the others. Lionel was amazed at how orderly everyone was. No one pushed or shoved.

When they reached the top, they helped the man find his place and moved to the edge of the mount. The view of the cross and the Global Community troops was incredible.

"Carpathia's supposed to be out there somewhere," Sam said. "They should be attacking pretty soon."

"Bring it on," Lionel said. "Just means Jesus will come that much sooner."

---

Conrad and Charlie joined the others gathered in Enoch's backyard. The man usually didn't go outside during the day, but no one seemed afraid. Everyone focused on the sky, wanting to know if they could tell when Jesus returned.

Enoch kept his voice low. "Well, the Bible says the whole world will know when he comes. Revelation 1:7 says, 'Look! He comes with the clouds of heaven. And everyone will see him—even those who pierced him.' "

"How's he gonna 'complish that?" a young man said. "Holy Land's on the other side of the world."

"Don't you think they're seeing what we're seeing now?" Enoch said.

"I guess, but like when the moon is out, people over there see the other side of it, right?"

"They could be seeing the other side of this cross too. We have no idea how massive it is."

"Or if there's more than one," Darrion said.

"How's that?" Enoch said.

"God can do what he wants, right?" she said.

And they all chimed in, some asking questions, others nodding or saying, "Amen."

"He could put ten crosses in the sky to make sure everybody sees one," someone said.

"But there's only one Jesus," another said.

"Yeah, but he can show up anywhere he wants at the

same time. Just like he was only one man but he died for everybody, he can appear to everybody too."

"Now you're talking," Enoch said.

"Is he gonna kill a bunch of people here, like he is over there?" Charlie said.

"I'm afraid he is. If they're working for the Antichrist, they're in serious trouble."

---

Judd noticed signs for a hospital and a university as he followed Ehud and Vicki toward Mount Scopus. He hoped they would make it to the top before the return of Christ.

He wondered about his friends—Jamal, Lina, and the others he had come to know over the past few months. Had they all been killed? Would he see them again? He pushed the thoughts from his mind and kept going.

"Stop, rebels!" someone yelled behind them.

Judd turned, catching a glimpse of a Unity Army patrol. They rode in an uncovered vehicle, and a soldier aimed a gun at them.

Judd shielded Vicki, and Ehud put up his hands. "You guys run," Judd whispered.

The vehicle drove closer.

"Don't you remember our promise?" Vicki said. "We stick together."

"I'm with you two," Ehud said.

A soldier threw a cigarette on the ground and cursed. "Let's kill them now and get it over with."

"You know our orders," another said.

"Yes, but who's going to know?" the first said. "Just three more heads to chop off later."

A tall man bounded from the vehicle and motioned to the others. "Load them up."

"Where are you taking us?" Judd said as he jumped into the back of the vehicle.

"To the Temple Mount," a soldier said. "You can watch the rest of the rebels die."

As the vehicle pulled out, Judd looked at the pulsing cross in the sky. "Come, Lord Jesus," he whispered.

**41**

**JUDD** thought the Unity soldier might be lying to them about going to the Temple Mount, but that's where they were taken. Along the way, citizens came out of their homes to applaud the soldiers.

They passed several makeshift jails—some inside buildings, others inside barbed-wire fences. It was to one of these outside holding areas that Judd and Vicki were taken. Soldiers took Ehud inside a row of buildings.

"The King is coming!" Ehud shouted as he was led away. "I'll see you when he returns."

Screams came from inside the buildings.

"What is that place?" Vicki said.

Before Judd could answer, a woman behind them spoke. "That's where they torture us, trying to get information about rebels inside the Temple."

The woman, who did not have the mark of the

believer, told them about the battles she'd been in and how valiantly the rebels had fought, even against over-whelming odds.

Vicki looked at Judd, and he winked at her. They were thinking the same thing. God had brought them here to reach out to people before the return of Christ.

---

Lionel stared at the sky and noticed movement on a ledge above. Chaim Rosenzweig and the elders stood where most of the remnant could see them.

"Brothers and sisters in the Messiah," Chaim said. "We gather here in this historic place, this holy city of refuge provided by the Lord God himself. We stand on the precipice of all time with the shadow of history behind us and eternity itself before us, putting all our faith and trust in the rock-solid goodness and strength and majesty of our Savior.

"May the Lord appear as I speak. Oh, the glory of that moment! We stand gazing into the heavens where the promised sign of the Son of Man radiates before us, thundering through the ages the truth that his death on the cross cleanses us from all sin.

"Within the next few minutes, you may see the enemy of God advancing on this fortified city. I say to you with all the confidence the Father has put in my soul, fear not, for your salvation draweth nigh.

"Now many have asked what is to happen when Antichrist comes against God's chosen people and the Son intervenes. The Bible says he will slay our enemy with a weapon that comes from his mouth. Revelation 1:16 calls it 'a sharp two-edged sword.' Revelation 2:16 quotes him saying that he 'will come to you suddenly and fight against them with the sword of my mouth.' Revelation 19:15 says that 'from his mouth came a sharp sword, and with it he struck down the nations.' And Revelation 19:21 says the army 'was killed by the sharp sword that came out of the mouth of the one riding the white horse.'

"Now let me clarify. I do not believe the Son of God is going to sit on his horse in the clouds with a gigantic sword hanging from his mouth. He is not going to shake his head and slay the millions of Armageddon troops with it. This is clearly a symbolic reference, and if you are a student of the Bible, you know what is meant by a sharp, double-edged sword.

"Hebrews 4:12 says the Word of God 'is full of living power. It is sharper than the sharpest knife, cutting deep into our innermost thoughts and desires. It exposes us for what we really are.'

"The weapon our Lord and Messiah will use to win the battle and slay the enemy? The Word of God itself! And while the reference to it as a sword may be symbolic, I hold that the description of the result of it is literal. The Word of God is sharp and powerful enough to slay the enemy, literally tearing them asunder."

Lionel felt chills as a million people cheered and applauded. With the cross in the sky, God's remnant around him, and the enemy collected in the valley, Lionel couldn't help but feel the emotion. When someone began singing "A Mighty Fortress Is Our God," he could barely choke out the words.

As the song echoed down the mountainside, Lionel noticed a motorcade thundering toward them across the desert. Jets screamed overhead, and it looked like Carpathia was ready for the attack.

A Humvee pulled up a steep slope, and someone got out. A light flashed on the man who drew his sword and raised it above his head.

"That's gotta be Carpathia," Sam said.

Singing stopped and everyone looked down on the showy sight. The remnant reacted strongly when Nicolae said, "If there really is a God of Abraham, Isaac, and Jacob, and if he truly has a Son worthy of facing me in combat, I shall destroy him too!"

People gasped.

Nicolae challenged God, daring him to come against his army. It was insane, and yet Carpathia continued. "Be prepared to advance upon Petra on my command. Leave no man, woman, or child alive. The victory is mine, says your living lord and risen king!"

"Let's pray," someone said near Lionel. He bowed his head and prayed. "God, you are the supreme ruler, and you've promised to return and defeat your enemies. I pray you would do that right now."

A murmur of voices rose against the rock walls. Prayers of a million people floated in the air as people joined hands and cried out to God.

Then, with a loud scream, Carpathia ordered his troops to attack. The army surged toward the hill below

Lionel and the others. Jet engines roared overhead.
Machine guns rattled, cannons fired, grenades and rockets
launched, and the remnant in Petra simply stared.

Seconds after the attack came, the pulsing cross in the
sky disappeared. Darkness covered the land. A strange
clacking sound drifted up from the desert, and Lionel
realized the GC's weapons weren't firing. No light came
from vehicles or flash-lights.

Thousands around Lionel whispered prayers, pleading
for Jesus to return.

---

When the lights went out, Vicki grabbed Judd's arm and
stood. They felt their way to the edge of the barbed-wire
fence and listened to the anxious voices of the Unity
Army officers. The woman Vicki had talked with had
prayed with her and asked God's forgiveness for not
seeing Jesus as her Messiah. The woman immediately
began talking with other prisoners.

"Is this some kind of—?" Judd began, but he stopped.
Light.

Intense white light from heaven covered everything.

It was so bright that GC officers cried out even more
than from the darkness.

Vicki glanced up at the thick cloud cover and gasped
as it scrolled back. *This is it!* she thought. *This is what
we've been waiting for!* But nothing came from her mouth.
She and Judd fell to their knees in awe.

As heaven opened, a white horse appeared. On it sat
Jesus, the Messiah, Creator of the universe, Son of God.

Vicki's eyes were riveted on her Savior—right in front of her, his eyes flashing, his head held high. He wore a white robe that stretched to his feet. On the robe were the words: *KING OF KINGS AND LORD OF LORDS.* Around his chest was a golden band. In his right hand were seven stars, and his face shone like the sun. People—a crowd so big it was impossible to count—followed him on white horses.

An angel stepped forward, held out its arms, and beckoned to the birds saying, "Come! Gather together for the great banquet God has prepared. Come and eat the flesh of kings, captains, and strong warriors; of horses and their riders; and of all humanity, both free and slave, small and great."

Then Jesus spoke with a voice that shook the earth. "I am the Alpha and the Omega—the beginning and the end."

*Is everyone else seeing this?* Vicki wondered. *Is everyone on earth hearing what we're hearing?*

---

Lionel was thrilled at the voice of Jesus. So this was why Bruce Barnes, Tsion Ben-Judah, and others called it the Glorious Appearing.

Lionel wanted to reach out and thank the Lord for restoring his arm, for hearing his prayers, for saving him from his sins, for his love and justice—for everything!

When Jesus spoke his first words, Lionel glanced at the Unity Army as thousands of soldiers fell like a sea of dominoes. At first, it looked like their bodies sank into the sand, but as Lionel looked closer he noticed bodies ripping open and blood pouring out.

"I am the living one who died. Look, I am alive forever and ever!" Jesus said. "And I hold the keys of death and the grave."

---

Judd felt like he was in a dream. He had seen people play the part of Jesus, but the real Jesus didn't look or sound like them at all. His voice spoke peace to every part of Judd's heart.

"I am the Son of Man, the Son of God, the Amen—the faithful and true witness, the ruler of God's creation. I am the Lion of the tribe of Judah, the heir to David's throne, the one who conquered to open the scroll and break its seven seals."

Judd glanced at the soldiers around him. They stared, mouths open.

"I am the Lamb that was slain and yet who lives. I am the Shepherd who leads his sheep to the springs of life-giving water. I am the God who will wipe away all your tears. I am your Salvation and Power. I am the Christ who has come for the Accuser, who accused our brothers and sisters before our God day and night, the one who has been thrown down to earth."

Believers looked on in awe and worship while God's enemies whimpered.

---

Conrad couldn't take his eyes off Jesus. The moment he had waited for since he had asked God to forgive him had finally come. He fell to his knees and soaked in the Lord's presence.

But how was Jesus doing this? How was he appearing to him in Illinois *and* in the Holy Land? And for that matter, Conrad thought, to people around the globe?

"I am the Word of God," Jesus said. "I am Jesus. I am both the source of David and the heir to his throne. I am the bright morning star."

Everyone in Enoch's group remained quiet and listened. Conrad heard soft weeping from Shelly, and he put his arm around her. A commotion next door distracted Conrad for a second when a door opened and neighbors burst from their homes. The light from Christ blinded them, and they ran through the yard, bumping into each other.

"I see him, Mama," little Tolan said, reaching toward the sky.

"That's right," his mother, Lenore, said. "And he sees each one of us down here."

"Where did he get that horse?" Tolan asked.

Lenore smiled and put a finger to her lips, watching Jesus in the sky.

Conrad thought it was a good question. And they had plenty of time to get answers. A thousand years, in fact.

# 42

**VICKI** stared at the heavenly scene, overwhelmed by the sight of Christ. She knew, deep down, that this is what she had been waiting for all her life, not just since she had become a believer. All the drinking and partying, the sneaking out on her parents, all the nights alone—abandoned by her so-called friends—the tears, the sorrow. Jesus was the answer to all her questions, and he was the source of love and everything good. His plan, his life was what she had always needed.

She noticed the people behind Jesus and realized that somewhere back there was her family. Ryan Daley was there too and Pete Davidson and Mark. The list went on and on, and she couldn't wait to see her friends, but that would be later. Right now she focused on the Messiah.

"I am able, once and forever, to save everyone who comes to God through me. I live forever to plead with God on their behalf. I come from above and am above all. My

Father has delivered all things to me. God has put all things under my authority, and he gave me this authority for the benefit of the church. I am the anchor of your soul, strong and trustworthy. I am the Lord's Christ."

Vicki had read that Jesus appeared with a sword from his mouth and assumed this sword would be the Word of God. Was Jesus killing his enemies at Petra? What was going on there?

---

Lionel tore his eyes from Jesus and picked up the high-powered binoculars on the ground. He had to see what was happening on the desert floor.

"I am the vine; you are the branches," Jesus said, his voice booming off the rocks above Lionel. "Those who remain in me, and I in them, will produce much fruit. For apart from me you can do nothing. Anyone who parts from me is thrown away like a useless branch and withers. Such branches are gathered into a pile to be burned.

"I am God's Messenger and High Priest, appeared in the flesh, righteous by the Spirit, seen by angels, announced to the nations, believed on in the world, taken up into heaven.

"I am the Son whom God has promised everything to as an inheritance, and through whom he made the universe and everything in it. I reflect God's own glory, and everything about me represents God exactly. I sustain the universe by the mighty power of my command. After I died to cleanse you from the stain of sin, I sat down in the place of honor at the right hand of the majestic God of heaven. I am far greater than the angels, just as the name God gave me is far greater than their names."

Lionel scanned the battlefield and was amazed at the amount of blood. Some soldiers saw their fallen comrades and were so upset they turned their guns on themselves. Others dug into the blood-soaked sand, trying to find a place to hide from the white light of God.

The army—at least those still alive—ran away from Jesus. But where were they going? Where could anyone go from the gaze of almighty God?

Lionel remembered comforting words from the Psalms: "I can never escape from your Spirit! I can never get away from your presence!" Now that verse took on new meaning. Where could any enemy go to get away from God's judgment?

As the rest of the living fled, Lionel scanned the perimeter of Petra. For miles he saw dead and dying soldiers, holes in the sand where trucks and tanks lay buried, dead horses, and a few skeleton-like people walking in a daze. Above this awful scene circled a huge flock of birds. They flew to the bodies and began eating.

In the lull that followed, someone began singing, "Praise God from whom all blessings flow. . . ." It was Mr. Stein, standing with Chaim and the elders. Soon a million others joined their song of praise.

———

Conrad had imagined this moment a thousand times. He had pictured Jesus riding on a horse the size of an airplane, running about ten feet off the ground, his hair

trailing in the wind. He'd also dreamed of a hundred-
foot-tall Jesus walking toward Jerusalem, smashing things
like monsters did in horror movies. But Conrad had
never imagined anything like this. It was as if Jesus had
come for Conrad alone and was looking straight at him.

"Just fellowship with your Savior," Enoch said quietly.

Jesus said, "Keep your eyes on me, on whom your
faith depends from start to finish. I was willing to die a
shameful death on the cross because of the joy I knew
would be mine afterward. Now I am seated in the place
of highest honor beside God's throne in heaven.

"Now God commands everyone everywhere to turn
away from idols and turn to him. For he has set a day for
judging the world with justice by the man he has
appointed, and he proved to everyone who this is by raising me from the dead.

"I am Jesus Christ, the one who pleases God
completely. I am the sacrifice for your sins. I take away not
only your sins but the sins of all the world. God raised me
to life. And you are witnesses of this fact! I am the Word
that became human and lived here on earth among you. I
am full of unfailing love and faithfulness. And you have
seen my glory, the glory of the only Son of the Father.

"Though I am God, I did not demand and cling to my
rights as God. I made myself nothing; I took the humble
position of a slave and appeared in human form. And in
human form I obediently humbled myself even further
by dying a criminal's death on a cross.

"Because of this, Conrad, God raised me up to the
heights of heaven and gave me a name that is above every

other name, so that at the name of Jesus every knee will bow, in heaven and on earth and under the earth, and every tongue will confess that Jesus Christ is Lord, to the glory of God the Father."

People around Conrad wept.

"Did you hear that?" Enoch said. "He used my name."

"He used *my* name too," Conrad said, still unable to believe it.

"He called me by name," Josey Fogarty said.

Charlie rushed to Conrad and Shelly. "He talked to me too!"

---

Vicki glanced at Judd, and by the look on his face she could tell he had heard his name too. When Jesus had used her name, she almost blushed, almost felt guilty. Then she realized this was going on with each believer.

"Vicki," Jesus said, "you know my love and kindness, that though I was very rich, yet for your sake I became poor, so that by my poverty I could make you rich.

"I have rescued you from the one who rules in the kingdom of darkness, and I have brought you into the Kingdom of God's dear Son. I have purchased your freedom with my blood and have forgiven all your sins.

"I am the one through whom God created everything in heaven and earth. I made the things you can see and the things you can't see—kings, kingdoms, rulers, and authorities. Everything has been created through me and for me. I existed before everything else began, and I hold all creation together.

"I am the head of the church, which is my body. I am the first of all who will rise from the dead, so I am first in everything. For God in all his fullness was pleased to live in me, and by me God reconciled everything to himself. I made peace with everything in heaven and on earth by means of my blood on the cross."

Vicki leaned against a post holding the barbed wire and whispered, "Jesus, I don't deserve the things you've done for me."

"And you, Vicki, were once so far away from God. You were his enemy, separated from him by your evil thoughts and actions, yet now I have brought you back as his friend. I have done this through my death on the cross in my own human body. As a result, I have brought you into the very presence of God, and you are holy and blameless as you stand before him without a single fault."

---

After Jesus stopped speaking, Lionel walked with Sam and found Mr. Stein. They both had many questions, and Mr. Stein tried to answer them.

"Didn't Dr. Rosenzweig say the remnant was supposed to go to Jerusalem, back to their home city?" Sam said.

"He did," Mr. Stein said.

"But how?" Lionel said. "There's no way to transport a million people."

"Ah, have you forgotten whose battle this is?" Mr. Stein said, pointing at Jesus. "If God wants us in Israel, he will make a way. Now the elders have asked us to head down the mountain—"

Mr. Stein stopped when Jesus spoke again in a loud voice. "Someday, O Israel, I will gather the few of you who are left. I will bring you together again like sheep in a fold, like a flock in its pasture. Yes, your land will again be filled with noisy crowds!

"I, your leader, will break out and lead you out of exile. I will bring you through the gates of your cities of captivity, back to your own land. I, your king, will lead you; I, the Lord, will guide you."

People rushed down the mountainside. Mr. Stein kept up with Lionel and Sam, scurrying along the rocks and pathways made over the past few months.

Lionel paused, looking up at Petra, wondering if they were leaving it forever. In the distance dust clouds rose from the crowds. Were the people driving ATVs? Had God provided a way to Jerusalem? He turned to Mr. Stein.

"We're not going to Jerusalem yet," Mr. Stein said. "The Lord is taking us to the next battle—there will be three more, according to Dr. Rosenzweig."

As they reached the desert floor, people around them laughed and talked about following Jesus. Were they going to walk? Many of the remnant were small children, and others were elderly.

Lionel stared at the dust and shook his head. He had just seen thousands of the enemy killed by Jesus' words, and he was concerned about a sixty-mile trip?

Sam had wandered ahead and now ran back. "Come on. Run with us."

"What do you mean?" Lionel said, but Sam pulled at his arm, making Lionel go faster. Lionel glanced up at Jesus who looked back and smiled, seeming to urge him on.

Lionel broke into a jog, and soon he was sprinting along with Sam, jumping over GC bodies and weapons, his feet barely touching the ground. He was moving faster than a human was supposed to run.

Lionel had done a research project in middle school about how fast humans could run. He had come up with a maximum speed of 27 miles per hour for sprinters, and an average speed of between 15 to 20 mph for those running distances of any kind.

But there was no way he was going 15 miles per hour now. Or even 30. Objects on the ground were a blur! And it wasn't only healthy young people going fast—it was all ages. Youngsters just out of diapers ran next to Lionel. And Mr. Stein was not far away, grinning and laughing. God was providing the speed. All Lionel had to do was work his legs.

"It's like riding a bike for two!" Mr. Stein called. "The Lord is the one doing the pedaling. We just have to get on and follow!"

The sensation of running three and maybe four times as fast as a human had ever run made Lionel laugh out loud. His feet moved faster, but his strides, instead of being a yard, took in ten feet with each step. The amazing thing was, Lionel didn't feel out of breath. His strength kept coming like the manna that fell every day.

Thirty minutes later, Lionel and his friends neared the

town of Bozrah. The rest of the million inside Petra had arrived as well, drawn to the scene by Jesus himself.

Unity Army troops stood before them, looking haggard and tired. Huge sweat stains fouled their uniforms while the people from Petra looked like they had just returned from lunch at an air-conditioned restaurant.

"What happens now?" Lionel said.

Mr. Stein motioned to the depleted army. "I think they're foolish enough to attack."

# 43

**LIONEL** couldn't believe it when the Unity Army moved forward and unleashed everything they had on the unarmed men, women, and children. Soldiers at the front aimed guns and fired, while troops behind launched missiles, rockets, and mortars. The noise was deafening and the flash of fire was blinding, but every time a missile or rocket hit, even in the midst of the people, no one was hurt.

Lionel looked to his Savior. Over the roar of the battle, Jesus' voice could be heard clearly. "Come hear and listen, O nations of the earth. Let the world and everything in it hear my words. For the Lord is enraged against the nations. His fury is against all their armies. He will completely destroy them, bringing about their slaughter."

As soon as Jesus spoke, soldiers and horses exploded. Lionel grabbed a pair of binoculars and looked closer. He focused on a soldier firing his weapon toward the remnant. The man's eyes grew wide, and he lowered his gun. Then his face bloated and turned red, as if his blood were boiling. The next second, the man's body blew into a million pieces, as did those around him.

"Their dead will be left unburied, and the stench of rotting bodies will fill the land. The mountains will flow with their blood. The heavens above will melt away and disappear like a rolled-up scroll. The stars will fall from the sky, just as withered leaves and fruit fall from a tree."

Lionel again focused on the nearest soldiers. They threw down their weapons and dropped to their knees. Some shoved fists in the air at Christ, cursing him before they died. Instead of exploding, these were sliced in two, and their insides poured onto the desert floor. When those behind them saw, they turned to run, but the same thing happened to them. They were cut in two where they stood, and their blood gushed.

"When my sword has finished its work in the heavens, then watch," Jesus said. "It will fall upon Edom, the nation I have completely destroyed. The sword of the Lord is drenched with blood. It is covered with fat as though it had been used for killing lambs and goats and rams for sacrifice. Yes, the Lord will offer a great sacrifice in the rich city of Bozrah. He will make a mighty slaughter in Edom. The land will be soaked with blood and the soil enriched with fat."

Now the army fell like red sticks. Lionel couldn't tell whether Christ's judgment was coming from the air or from the earth as men and women who had pledged their lives to Carpathia were cut down.

An aircraft of some sort screamed in and landed at the other side of the slaughtered army. It was a jet helicopter, and someone mentioned it was for Nicolae.

The firing stopped. Except for the chopper, everything was deathly still. The craft lifted off and headed north, leaving the remnant to stare out on the valley of blood.

Sam touched Lionel's shoulder. "Look! The Lord Jesus is coming down."

The King of kings landed and dismounted from his white horse. He walked through the battlefield, the hem of his robe turning red from the blood of the enemy.

The army of heaven that hovered above him began to speak in unison. "Who is this who comes from Edom, from the city of Bozrah, with his clothing stained red? Who is this in royal robes, marching in the greatness of his strength?"

Jesus answered, "It is I, the Lord, announcing your salvation! It is I, the Lord, who is mighty to save!"

"Why are your clothes so red, as if you have been treading out grapes?" they asked.

"I have trodden the winepress alone; no one was there to help me," Jesus said. "In my anger I have trampled my enemies as if they were grapes. In my fury I have trampled my foes. It is their blood that has stained my clothes. For the time has come for me to avenge my people, to ransom them from their oppressors.

"I looked, but no one came to help my people. I was amazed and appalled at what I saw. So I executed vengeance alone; unaided, I passed down judgment. I crushed the nations in my anger and made them stagger and fall to the ground."

The conversation continued back and forth until Jesus turned toward the remnant in Bozrah. "When you see Jerusalem surrounded by armies, then you will know that the time of its destruction has arrived. Then those in Judea must flee to the hills. Let those in Jerusalem escape, and those outside the city should not enter it for shelter.

"For those will be the days of God's vengeance, and the prophetic words of the Scriptures will be fulfilled. . . . So when all these things begin to happen, stand straight and look up, for your salvation is near!"

---

Judd watched Jesus sink from view, then looked at Vicki. The light of Jesus was still there and, he assumed, could be seen all over the world. But they couldn't see the Lord anymore.

"What do you think's happening?" Judd said.

"Not sure," Vicki said. "But there's no doubt he'll be heading this way soon. If Tsion was right, Jesus will overcome the enemy as he reaches Mount Megiddo. Then he's coming here."

"But Jerusalem's going to fall, right?" Judd said.

Vicki nodded. "I'm just not sure what that means. The GC will take the Temple Mount, but whether they kill everybody or not . . ."

Judd glanced at the guards standing nearby. These soldiers had been as fascinated with the return of Jesus as anyone.

"What's that guy over there doing?" Vicki whispered.

A soldier had run in from the direction of the Temple

Mount and now spoke with a higher ranking official. They gestured toward the prisoners, and Judd strained to hear their conversation.

". . . and we've now surrounded the entire city," the soldier said. "Our forces are massed from west of the Dead Sea to the Valley of Megiddo."

"We're in good shape then," the officer said.

"Except for the casualties in Edom—"

"Stop!" The officer drew close and warned the soldier not to talk about any loss of life on the Unity Army side.

"Sorry, sir," the soldier said. "But you need to know about the unrest."

"What are you talking about?"

"Our troops are hungry. There are rumors that there are no reinforcements—"

"They're wrong!" the officer shouted, his face turning red with rage. "And don't count our southern troops out yet."

"—and you know how long it's been since we've been paid."

"A Unity Army soldier doesn't perform this work for the pay. We serve in the interests of peace, and that is our payment. We ultimately serve the risen Lord Carpathia."

"Yes, of course, sir. Still, you can understand why they're upset. And now, with having to take prisoners . . ."

The two men looked at the holding area.

"I don't like the way they're looking at us," Vicki said.

Judd put an arm around her. "It's okay. Jesus will be here soon." But inside, Judd agreed with her. He didn't like the looks of this either.

413

For the next few hours, Lionel and a million others followed Jesus, who was again riding his horse. The people ran through the desert at lightning speed, watching Jesus ahead of them and the heavenly army above.

Lionel's heart leaped when Jesus spoke, his voice sounding as if he were standing right next to him. "I am the King who comes in the name of the Lord. I mediate the new covenant between God and people. I personally carried away your sins in my own body on the cross so you can be dead to sin and live for what is right.

"I am the true bread of God who came down from heaven and gives life to the world. So let us celebrate the festival, not by eating the old bread of wickedness and evil, but by eating the new bread of my purity and truth."

Lionel had read the Bible for many years and recognized the things Jesus was saying as words taken directly from Scripture. Still, hearing Jesus speak thrilled him. Just when Lionel thought things couldn't get any better, Jesus spoke directly to him.

"Lionel, I came to bring truth to the world. All who love the truth recognize that what I say is true. I assure you, I can do nothing by myself. I do only what I see the Father doing. Whatever the Father does, I also do. I am the stone that the builders rejected and have now become the cornerstone."

All Lionel could do was say, "Thank you" each time Jesus spoke to him. He couldn't think of anything else, and it seemed to make Jesus smile.

"Where are we going?" Lionel said to Sam.

"Wherever Jesus leads," Sam said. "I don't pretend to know what's going to happen, but if we follow the Lord, we will be in just the right place at the right time."

Lionel couldn't get over the sight of old men and women running so fast. In Petra these people had walked slowly, hunched over, some using canes, others walking from rock to rock, careful of their footing. Now they were upright, running faster than Olympic athletes.

They continued north, following Jesus, listening to his words. A portion of Carpathia's army fell dead as Jesus passed them.

"Lionel, take my yoke upon you," Jesus said. "Let me teach you, because I am humble and gentle, and you will find rest for your soul. For my yoke fits perfectly, and the burden I give you is light."

As the group moved farther, the Unity Army seemed to be dug in and waiting. The GC no doubt believed they would have a great victory.

The remnant bypassed Israel, far to their left, and headed toward Megiddo, or the Valley of Armageddon. At one point, Jesus said, "I give you eternal life, Lionel, and you will never perish. No one will snatch you away from me, for my Father has given you to me, and he is more powerful than anyone else. So no one can take you from me. The Father and I are one.

"I am leaving you with a gift—peace of mind and heart. And the peace I give isn't like the peace the world gives. So don't be troubled or afraid."

Lionel recalled the verse that said, "If God is for us, who can ever be against us?" He had never felt the truth of it so clearly.

Jesus seemed to go ahead of them faster, leaving the remnant behind. Lionel and the others slowed, then stopped north of Jerusalem. No one seemed tired, but it was clear that Jesus wanted them to stay.

"Looks like we won't need to do any more work for Zeke," Sam said.

"I have to tell you," Lionel said, "I didn't like our jobs very much."

"What do you think you'll be doing once the kingdom begins?"

Lionel shrugged. "Whatever needs to be done, I guess. I'm not picky."

Sam looked away. Lionel asked if something was wrong, and Sam nodded. "I was just thinking about my father. You're going to see your family again. I'll see my mom, but not my dad."

Lionel put an arm around him. "I understand. I had an uncle who I tried to talk to after the Rapture. He knew the truth, but he died before he could pray."

"How do you know for sure?" Sam said. "Were you with him?"

"No, Judd and I found him—"

"Then he could have asked God's forgiveness."

"You don't know my uncle André," Lionel said.

Lionel fell silent as Jesus spoke again. "No one has ever seen God. I, his only Son, who am myself God, am near to the Father's heart; I have told you about him. I am called the Son of the Most High. And the Lord God will give me the throne of my ancestor David."

Another voice came from heaven. "Look at my Servant, whom I have chosen. He is my Beloved, and I am very pleased with him. I will put my Spirit upon him, and he will proclaim justice to the nations."

Sam's eyes grew wide. "You think that was God the Father?"

"I can't imagine who else," Lionel said.

Jesus answered: "The law was given through Moses; God's unfailing love and faithfulness come through me. Now, Lionel, may the God of peace, who brought me from the dead, equip you with all you need for doing his will. May he produce in you all that is pleasing to him. Amen."

On the last word, the people fell to their knees, praising God. Lionel kept his head down, thanking God and worshiping him.

Then the noise of battle wafted over the desert. Jesus spoke, and even from this distance Lionel heard soldiers wailing.

A few minutes later, another great flock of birds appeared in the sky. Lionel guessed this was not good news for Nicolae and his army.

## 44

**THE TEMPERATURE** dropped quickly around Lionel and the others, then returned to normal. News reached them of a great hailstorm—with chunks of ice weighing a hundred pounds or more—that had fallen on the massacred Unity Army. Water mingled with blood, creating a red, gooey liquid that was four feet deep in some places.

Fresh from battle, Jesus addressed the remnant. "You belong to God, my dear children. You have already won your fight with these false prophets, because the Spirit who lives in you is greater than the spirit who lives in the world. These people belong to this world, so they speak from the world's viewpoint, and the world listens to them. But you belong to God; that is why those who know God listen to you. That is how you know if someone has the Spirit of truth or the spirit of deception.

"Dear friends, continue to love one another, for love comes from God. Anyone who loves is born of God and

419

knows God. But anyone who does not love does not
know God—for God is love. God showed how much he
loved you by sending his only Son into the world so that
you might have eternal life through him. This is real love.
It is not that you loved God, but that he loved you and
sent me as a sacrifice to take away your sins.

"Lionel, since God loved you that much, you surely
ought to love each other."

As Jesus spoke, people slowly turned toward Jerusalem. Jesus moved ahead of them, his horse galloping
onward until Lionel lost sight of him.

---

Judd watched the soldiers huddle together to stay warm
through the icy blast. When things warmed, a number of
citizens strolled through the thousands of soldiers. Rebels
still held the Temple Mount as far as Judd could tell, but
the Unity Army seemed content to let them have it for
now. A radio crackled with news that the potentate was
on his way, and soldiers snapped to attention.

Soon loudspeakers boomed Nicolae's voice through
the area. "As we approach what many have referred to as
the Eternal City, I am pleased to announce that following
our victory here, this shall become the new Global
Community headquarters. My palace shall be rebuilt on
the site of the ruins of the temple, the destruction of
which is on our agenda."

Carpathia continued, predicting a total takeover of
Jerusalem. Judd couldn't believe it when the man referred
to Jesus as "this one who flits about in the air quoting

ancient fairy-tale texts." Nicolae predicted Jesus would die. "He is no match for the risen lord of this world and for the fighting force in place to face him. It does not even trouble me to make public our plan, as it has already succeeded. This city and these despicable people have long been his chosen ones, so we have forced him to show himself, to declare himself, to vainly try to defend them or be shown for the fraud and coward that he is. Either he attempts to come to their rescue or they will see him for who he really is and reject him as an impostor. Or he will foolishly come against my immovable force and me and prove once and for all who is the better man."

Though Judd expected this speech of Nicolae's to encourage the troops, the soldiers nearby seemed unaffected. No yelling, screaming, or shouting Nicolae's support.

"My pledge to you, loyal citizens of the Global Community," Carpathia said, "is that come the end of this battle, no opponent of my leadership and regime will remain standing, yea, not one will be left alive. The only living beings on planet Earth will be trustworthy citizens, lovers of peace and harmony and tranquility, which I offer with love for all from the depths of my being.

"I am but ten miles west of Jerusalem as we speak, and I will be dismissing my cabinet and generals so they may be about the business of waging this conflict under my command. The Most High Reverend of Carpathianism, Dr. Leon Fortunato himself, will serve as my chauffeur for my triumphal entry. Citizens are already lining the roadway to greet me, and I thank you for your support."

A few minutes later, drums and trumpets sounded in the distance. Vicki, who had buried her head in Judd's chest, looked up. "Carpathia has mocked everything God's done. This is his version of the triumphal entry."

"Let him enjoy it," Judd muttered. "He doesn't have much longer."

A young officer spoke to his superior. "Sir, we could present these prisoners to the potentate for execution. Those without the mark could be beheaded in front of him as a sacrifice."

The commanding officer glanced at the prisoners, then waved a hand. "That can come after the victory."

"They're going after the rebels at the Temple Mount," Vicki said. "Sounds like Carpathia's gonna lead the charge."

"Let him come," Judd said, sneaking a peek at the sky. Jesus and his heavenly army were nowhere in sight.

---

Lionel and Sam joined the others on a hill overlooking Jerusalem. The sky cleared as Carpathia paraded through Jerusalem.

Someone pulled out a handheld TV and caught GCNN's coverage of Nicolae riding a stallion, his sword raised in the air. He swung it, and the troops around him whooped. "Follow me to the Western Wall and make way for the battering ram and missile launchers! Upon my command, open fire!"

Lionel couldn't help thinking of Judd and Vicki. Though he knew they would see each other again soon, he hated the thought of them being killed in Jerusalem. "Lord Jesus, protect my friends until we see each other again."

Since Jesus had appeared, Lionel's attitude toward prayer had taken on a new dimension. Instead of just saying, "Amen," Lionel looked up and listened for an answer.

---

Vicki heard the oncoming army and shuddered. The others in the holding area moved toward the barbed wire.

"Don't get any ideas," a soldier said, waving an Uzi at them. "I'll mow all of you down."

Some civilians stood on a wall behind them pointing and cheering as hundreds of horses clip-clopped their way toward the Temple Mount.

"Here he comes!" a woman shouted, then broke into a not-so-stirring rendition of "Hail Carpathia."

The woman stopped when Nicolae shouted orders. Mounted soldiers urged their horses forward but they reared and bucked, spinning into each other. Some ran headlong into the wall. One horse and rider headed straight for the barbed-wire enclosure. The armed guard fell under the horse's hooves while the animal flung itself into the makeshift prison.

Quickly, the prisoners climbed over the downed wire, only to be met by three Unity Army soldiers holding guns. Vicki and Judd took a step back, still inside the prison.

"No!" Vicki screamed as the soldiers aimed their guns.

But before they could shoot, skin dripped from their arms and their eyes melted. The once-healthy soldiers were now simply uniforms full of bones. Seconds later the same thing happened to the horses. Their flesh and eyes and tongues dripped away like candle wax.

Vicki was too stunned to move. She had read verses in Revelation that said this was going to happen. She had even seen people die from the horsemen of terror and stung by the demon locusts, but she had never seen anything so gruesome. Without a shot fired or a missile launched, the Unity Army melted into the street.

"Look over there," Judd said.

Leon had his face in his hands and knelt. Nicolae Carpathia, God's archenemy, ordered Leon Fortunato to his feet. "Get up, Leon! Get up! We are not defeated! We have a million more soldiers and we shall prevail!"

Leon just whimpered and wailed.

Carpathia cursed God and lifted his sword to the sky. Then he paused, seeing something in the heavens.

Vicki glanced up when God's temple opened and a flood of brilliant light surrounded her.

Judd pulled Vicki toward a nearby wall as lightning flashed, thunder roared, and the earth shifted.

In seconds the earth buckled and swayed. Carpathia's soldiers were swallowed through great cracks in the earth.

---

Conrad held on to Shelly while they rode out the huge earthquake together. Somehow the Global Community

News Network managed to stay on the air and showed satellite pictures of the earth bathed in a light that originated from Jesus. In North America, a huge dust cloud hovered over Arizona, and reports that the Grand Canyon had been filled in and was now level brought *ooh*s and *aah*s from their friends. Even more incredible was the shot over Nepal showing that Mount Everest and the mountain ranges surrounding it had crumbled and were now as flat as every other place on earth. Islands disappeared into the sea. Everything had been leveled except for the city of Jerusalem.

Someone gasped and pointed up. Conrad glanced skyward and saw Jesus, who spoke in a loud voice. "Speak tenderly to Jerusalem. Tell her that her sad days are gone and that her sins are pardoned. Yes, the Lord has punished her in full for all her sins.

"Fill the valleys and level the hills. Straighten out the curves and smooth off the rough spots. Then the glory of the Lord will be revealed, and all people will see it together. The Lord has spoken!

"Watch, for the day of the Lord has come when your possessions will be plundered right in front of you! On that day I gathered all the nations to fight against Jerusalem. Half the population was taken away into captivity, and half was left among the ruins of the city. I went out and fought against those nations, as I have fought in times past.

"And I sent a plague on all the nations that fought against Jerusalem. Their people became like walking corpses, their flesh rotting away. Their eyes shriveled in their sockets, and their tongues decayed in their mouths. On that day they were terrified, stricken by me with great panic.

"I made Jerusalem and Judah like an intoxicating drink to all the nearby nations that sent their armies to besiege Jerusalem. On that day I made Jerusalem a heavy stone, a burden for the world. None of the nations who tried to lift it escaped unscathed.

"I caused every horse to panic and every rider to lose his nerve. I watched over the people of Judah, but I blinded the horses of her enemies.

"I defended the people of Jerusalem; the weakest among them will be as mighty as King David! And the royal descendants will be like God, like the angel of the Lord who goes before them! I destroyed all the nations that came against Jerusalem.

"Therefore, a curse consumed the earth and its people. They were left desolate, destroyed by fire. Few were left alive.

"Throughout the earth the story is the same—like the stray olives left on the tree or the few grapes left on the vine after harvest, only a remnant is left.

"That group called on my name, and I answered them. I said, 'These are my people,' and they said, 'The Lord is our God.' "

---

Lionel followed the others to the east side of the Old City. Only a small portion of Carpathia's army remained alive, and most of them had been injured. Piles of human bones stood several feet high in some places. Many of the living staggered toward shelter as Jesus sat on his white horse. A host of his army was behind him looking on at the one-sided victory.

"It's going to be hard to get used to everything being flat," Sam said.

Lionel smiled and looked at the sky. "There's going to be a lot of things around here that *won't* be hard to get used to."

**45**

**JUDD** was proud of Vicki for having the idea of finding their new friend Ehud and releasing him. They crept through the narrow street, avoiding the surviving Unity Army soldiers, and found several dozen Jewish believers chained together in a basement of a two-story building. Ehud called to them and said many of the prisoners had been starved and tortured, but they all looked fine now. Judd noticed bones of a guard near a vending machine and fished through the man's pockets until he heard keys rattle.

While Vicki loosed the prisoners, Judd smashed the vending machine and handed out food. Vicki wanted to look for more prisoners, but Judd thought it wouldn't be safe with the Unity Army still around.

"How long before we see the Messiah return to the Mount of Olives?" a skinny prisoner said to the others.

When no one answered Vicki said, "It has to be soon.

It looks like he's already taken care of most of Carpathia's troops."

Ehud ran away with the other prisoners while Judd and Vicki moved through a gate and toward a hillside. Judd thought she looked as happy as he had seen her in months.

"Why is the Mount of Olives so important?" Judd said.

Vicki started to answer. Then her jaw dropped. "Look, the remnant is moving this way."

———

Lionel left Sam and the rest of the remnant and jogged toward Jerusalem. When he reached the wall of the city, he climbed on top and scanned the area. Bodies lay strewn about the streets. Dead rebels were scattered among the bones of Unity Army soldiers. Surviving soldiers regrouped for another attack on the Temple Mount.

He wondered where the bodies of Dr. Ben-Judah and Buck Williams were. Perhaps Buck and Tsion were mixed in with the other dead in front of him.

Lionel scampered down from the wall and raced back to his friends. He was thrilled that he would be face-to-face with Jesus again soon.

———

Conrad and Shelly helped Enoch move his furniture from the basement to the first floor of his house. Enoch said there would be no more hiding now that the Lord had returned. Shelly called for them from upstairs, where they found Nicolae Carpathia and Leon Fortunato on television, surrounded by advisors, generals, and a swarm of reporters.

"You'd think he'd have enough sense to get out of there," Enoch said.

"Denial's not just a dried-up river in Egypt," Conrad said.

"That was bad," Shelly said, punching Conrad on the shoulder.

Carpathia waved his arms and barked orders at troops. Conrad turned up the volume in time to hear Nicolae say, "This city shall become my throne. The temple will be flattened and the way made for my palace, the most magnificent structure ever erected. We have captured half the enemy here, and we will dispose of the other half in due time.

"The final stage of our conquest is nearly ready to be executed, and we will soon be rid of this nuisance from above."

---

Lionel looked up and saw Jesus hovering over the remnant. He spoke words of comfort and compassion, and when Lionel fell to his knees, Jesus spoke directly to him. "It has pleased God to tell his people that the riches and glory of Christ are for you, Lionel. Christ lives in you, and this is your assurance that you will share in his glory. I am a mighty Savior from the royal line of God's servant David. The truth is, I existed before Abraham was even born!"

The remnant burst into praises to Jesus, drowning out the sound of the marching band that played "Hail Carpathia" in the distance.

Lionel moved along the edges of the crowd, watching Jesus.

Behind him a familiar voice said, "He's blinded to the truth about himself and God. He's leading every one of those soldiers to certain death."

Lionel turned and saw Judd and Vicki. He put his left arm behind his back and yelled for them.

Their faces lit up when they saw Lionel, and they rushed toward him.

"Wait. I have a surprise," Lionel said, pulling his left arm from behind his back. Vicki and Judd were amazed at what God had done, and they hugged Lionel.

"Can you believe we're actually here?" Vicki said. "I've dreamed of this moment since we met in Bruce Barnes' office at New Hope Village Church."

"And we're together." Lionel began to tell them about his experience running from Petra to Jerusalem, but when Jesus nudged his horse forward to the Mount of Olives, he stopped. The remnant stood and Carpathia headed toward them, his sword held high, the rest of his army trailing.

Jesus dismounted as Carpathia shouted the command to attack. As soldiers fired and horses galloped forward, Jesus' voice sounded like a trumpet. "I AM THE ONE WHO ALWAYS IS."

Immediately the Mount of Olives split in two. The newly formed chasm left Carpathia and his army on one side, Jesus and the remnant on the other. The firing and galloping stopped. Soldiers screamed in agony, and their bodies burst open.

Jesus spoke to those still held prisoner in Jerusalem. "You will flee through this valley, for it will reach across to Azal. Yes, you will flee as you did from the earthquake in the days of King Uzziah of Judah. Then the Lord your God will come, and all his holy ones with me."

People inside Jerusalem shouted, and Vicki put a hand to her mouth. "Look," she whispered.

Out of the gates came prisoners, some with chains still on their feet. Their bodies were thin and many had scars, but they ran toward the valley created when the mount had split. The earth rumbled, and Lionel stared as the whole city of Jerusalem rose higher and higher into the air until it stood thirty yards above everything.

Judd tapped Lionel's shoulder and pointed toward two figures running for their lives. "That's Nicolae and Leon, but what's that bright thing bouncing ahead of them?"

Lionel shrugged. "They say that Satan disguises himself as an angel of light. Maybe that's old Lucifer."

Unity Army soldiers chased the freed captives through the new valley. But when Jesus spoke, the soldiers fell dead.

"Life-giving waters will flow out from Jerusalem," Jesus said, "half toward the Dead Sea and half toward the Mediterranean, flowing continuously both in summer and in winter. And the Lord will be king over all the earth. Today there will be one Lord—his name alone will be worshiped.

433

"All the land from Geba, north of Judah, to Rimmon, south of Jerusalem, has become one vast plain. But Jerusalem has been raised up in its original place and inhabited all the way from the Benjamin Gate over to the site of the old gate, then to the Corner Gate, and from the Tower of Hananel to the king's wine-presses. And Jerusalem will be filled, safe at last, never again to be cursed and destroyed."

---

Tears came to Vicki's eyes when Jesus mounted his horse and rode on. Every word he spoke devoured his enemies.

"This is the day of God's vengeance, and the prophetic words of the Scriptures have been fulfilled. The arrogance of all people will be brought low. Their pride will lie in the dust. The Lord alone will be exalted!"

Voices from heaven shouted, "The whole world has now become the Kingdom of our Lord and of his Christ, and he will reign forever and ever.

"We give thanks to you, Lord God Almighty, the one who is and who always was, for now you have assumed your great power and have begun to reign. The nations were angry with you, but now the time of your wrath has come. It is time to judge the dead and reward your servants. You will reward your prophets and your holy people, all who fear your name, from the least to the greatest. And you will destroy all who have caused destruction on the earth."

As Vicki followed the people, she expected to see dead bodies about the streets and fallen weapons and equipment. Instead, as the remnant sang and danced and praised God, she saw clean streets and no bodies. And something else strange—all the walls had been leveled.

"There is only one God and one Mediator who can reconcile God and people, I, the man Christ Jesus. I gave my life to purchase freedom for everyone."

People lined up for miles behind Jesus, and finally they all were inside the city. Hovering over them were the hosts of heaven, still on horseback. Judd grabbed Vicki's arm, she grabbed Lionel, and they moved to a ledge overlooking the crowd.

Jesus had dismounted and stretched out his arms. "O Jerusalem, Jerusalem," the Lord cried, "the city that kills the prophets and stones God's messengers! How often I have wanted to gather your children together as a hen protects her chicks beneath her wings, but you wouldn't let me. And now look, your house is left to you empty. And you will never see me again until you say, 'Bless the one who comes in the name of the Lord!' "

Vicki had held her breath for so long, but now she couldn't help bursting forth, "Bless the one who comes in the name of the Lord!"

Everyone else had shouted the same thing at the same time, and Jesus beamed.

---

Judd looked around at people from different backgrounds who spoke different languages. He put his head in his hands and whispered, "Thank you, Jesus. Thank you for letting us be here at this moment."

When he looked up, five heavenly beings stood behind Jesus. Vicki nudged Judd and said, "The second one from the left is the one we saw in Wisconsin."

People around them spoke the angels' names. Nahum, Christopher, and Caleb had been angels of mercy, delivering some from certain death. The two other angels near Jesus were Gabriel and Michael.

Judd looked into Jesus' eyes, and something stirred in his heart. Jesus said, "Come to me, my child."

Judd's mouth dropped open, and he put a hand to his chest. "Me?"

Jesus nodded.

Judd looked at Vicki. She and Lionel moved forward with him. The whole throng moved toward Jesus as he spoke to a million people individually. Incredible!

"Come to me, Judd, and I will give you rest."

Judd kept moving, wanting to run into the arms of Jesus like a child, but he couldn't stop thinking about his sin. He had been so selfish and felt dirty, as if Jesus might reject him.

But the Lord reached out with his scarred hands. "Come," he said softly.

Judd looked into Jesus' eyes—burning like fire and so loving. He ran into the arms of Christ and was gathered in.

"Judd, Judd, how I have looked forward to and longed for this day. I knew your name before the foundation of the world. I have prepared a place for you, and if it were not so, I would have told you."

Judd tried to speak but couldn't.

Jesus gently pushed Judd back and looked him full in

the face. Judd was only inches away from the King of kings. "I was there when you were born. I was there the night at the youth group when you decided you would go your own way."

"Forgive me . . . ," Judd choked.

---

Vicki stared into the eyes of love and wept.

"Vicki, I was there when you cried yourself to sleep. When your uncle caused you so much pain. I was there when your mother and father chose me and you rejected me."

"I'm so sorry. . . ."

"I was there when you were left behind. I was there when you first met Judd. And I was waiting when you heard the truth and finally came to me."

Vicki cocked her head, and a tear ran down her cheek. "Oh, Lord, how can I thank you?"

"I have loved you with an everlasting love. I am the lover of your soul. You were meant to be with me for eternity, and now you shall be."

Then Jesus put one hand on Vicki's shoulder and the other atop her head. "I pray that from my Father's glorious, unlimited resources he will give you mighty inner strength through his Holy Spirit. And I pray that I will be more and more at home in your heart as you trust in me. May your roots go deep into the soil of God's marvelous love. And may you have the power to understand, as all God's people should, how wide, how long, how high, and how deep his love really is. May you experience my love, though it is so great you will never fully understand it. Then you will be filled with the fullness of life and power that comes from God.

"Now glory be to God! By his mighty power at work within us, he is able to accomplish infinitely more than we would ever dare to ask or hope. May he be given glory in the church and in me forever and ever though endless ages. Amen."

# 46

**IT HAD** happened so quickly, Vicki thought. And for everyone—a million people had experienced a personal encounter with Jesus.

Vicki moved back to her place and took Judd's hand. He and Lionel worshiped God in silence and with tears. But no one seemed ashamed of the emotion. They were all in the presence of the one who had loved them enough to die for them.

The next few minutes were a blur as Vicki thought of her encounter with Jesus. The Lord spoke, praying to God the Father for the people.

Gabriel also spoke finally, saying, "The Lord is faithful; he will make you strong and guard you from the evil one."

At the mention of the evil one, the archangel Michael brought forth Nicolae Carpathia, Leon Fortunato, and the three Carpathia look-alikes—Ashtaroth, Baal, and

Cankerworm—Vicki had seen on video a few months earlier. These were demonic creatures bent on deceiving the nations.

Gabriel leaned down to the three and said, "As a fulfillment of age-old scriptural prophecy, you kneel this day before Jesus the Christ, the Son of the living God, who, though he was God, did not demand and cling to his rights as God. He made himself nothing; he took the humble position of a slave and appeared in human form.

"And in human form he obediently humbled himself even further by dying a criminal's death on a cross."

"Yes!" the three squealed. "Yes! We know! We know!" And they bowed their deformed bodies.

Gabriel continued: "Because of this, God raised him up to the heights of heaven and gave him a name that is above every other name, so that at the name of Jesus every knee will bow, in heaven and on earth and under the earth, and every tongue will confess that Jesus Christ is Lord, to the glory of God the Father."

"Jesus Christ is Lord!" they hissed. "Jesus Christ is Lord! It is true! True! We acknowledge it! We acknowledge him!"

Jesus leaned forward. " 'As surely as I live,' says the Sovereign Lord, 'I take no pleasure in the death of wicked people. I only want them to turn from their wicked ways so they can live.' "

"We repent! We will turn! We will turn! We worship you, O Jesus, Son of God. You are Lord!"

"But for you it is too late," Jesus said with sorrow in his voice. "You were once angelic beings, in heaven with

God. Yet you were cast down because of your own prideful decisions. Rather than resist the evil one, you chose to serve him."

"We were wrong! Wrong! We acknowledge you as Lord!"

"Like my Father, with whom I am one, I take no pleasure in the death of wicked people, but that is justice, and that is your sentence."

The three look-alikes screamed in pain, their snake-like bodies shedding their clothes. Then they burst into flames and were finally carried away by the wind.

Now it was Leon's turn. He wailed and sobbed, casting away his robe and shoes. "Oh, my Lord and my God! I have been so blind, so wrong, so wicked!"

"Do you know who I am?" Jesus said. "Who I truly am?"

"Yes! Yes! I have always known, Lord! You are the Messiah, the Son of the living God!"

"You would blaspheme by quoting my servant Simon, whom I blessed," Jesus said, "because my Father in heaven revealed this to him? He did not learn this from any human being."

"No, Lord! Your Father revealed it to me too!"

"I tell you the truth, woe to you for not making that discovery while there was yet time. Rather, you rejected me and my Father's plan for the world. You pitted your will against mine and became the False Prophet, committing the greatest sin known under heaven: rejecting me as the only way to God the Father and spending seven years deceiving the world."

"Jesus is Lord! Jesus is Lord! Don't kill me! I beg you! Please!"

"Death is too good for you. How many souls are separated from me forever because of you and the words that came from your mouth?"

"I'm sorry! Forgive me! I renounce all the works of Satan and Antichrist! I pledge my allegiance to you!"

"You are sentenced to eternity in the lake of fire."

"Oh, God, no!"

"Silence!" Gabriel said, and Leon crawled away sobbing.

Vicki had prayed for Leon's and Nicolae's demise, but she couldn't help feeling sorry for both of them. They had defied God and persecuted his people. Now they would pay.

Michael grabbed the elbow of a defiant Carpathia and spun him around. "Kneel before your Lord!"

Carpathia sneered and wrenched away from Michael.

Jesus said, "Lucifer, leave this man!"

With that, the air seemed to go out of Nicolae. His hands and fingers became bony. He looked like a helium-filled balloon a week after the party, all shriveled and shrunken. When Gabriel ordered him to kneel, the potentate got on all fours.

As Nicolae lowered his head, Jesus said, "You became a willing tool of the devil himself. You were a rebel against the things of God and his kingdom. You caused more suffering than anyone in the history of the world. God bestowed upon you gifts of intelligence, beauty, wisdom, and personality, and you had the opportunity to make the most of these in the face of the most pivotal events in the annals of creation.

"Yet you used every gift for personal gain. You led millions to worship you and your father, Satan. You were the cunning destroyer of my followers and accomplished more to damn the souls of men and women than anyone else in your time.

"Ultimately your plans and your regime have failed. And now, who do you say that I am?"

Silence. Then a weak voice said, "You *are* the Christ, the Son of the living God, who died for the sins of the world and rose again the third day as the Scriptures predicted."

"And what does that say about you and what you made of your life?"

"I confess that my life was a waste," Nicolae whispered. "Worthless. A mistake. I rebelled against the God of the universe, whom I now know loved me."

With sadness Jesus said, "You are responsible for the fate of billions. You and your False Prophet, with whom you shed the blood of the innocents—my followers, the prophets, and my servants who believed in me—shall be cast alive into the lake of fire."

Gabriel stepped forward and said, "Then I saw the beast gathering the kings of the earth and their armies in order to fight against the one sitting on the horse and his army.

"And the beast was captured, and with him the false prophet who did mighty miracles on behalf of the beast—miracles that deceived all who had accepted the mark of the beast and who worshiped his statue.

"Both the beast and his false prophet were thrown alive into the lake of fire that burns with sulfur."

When Gabriel moved, a hole a yard in diameter opened in the ground, and a stinky smell burst forth. Flames erupted from the hole, and the crowd backed away. Michael walked Nicolae and Leon forward. Leon cried like a baby and tried to get away, but Michael pushed him into the fire, his cries fading as he fell. Then Michael pushed Nicolae in, and the man's screams echoed throughout Jerusalem. The hole closed, and the Beast and the False Prophet were gone.

Gabriel addressed the people. "Jesus is the true light, who gives light to everyone. But although the world was made through him, the world didn't recognize him when he came. Even in his own land and among his own people, he was not accepted. But to all who believed him and accepted him, he gave the right to become children of God. They are reborn! This is not a physical birth resulting from human passion or plan—this rebirth comes from God.

"So the Word became human and lived here on earth among us. He was full of unfailing love and faithfulness. And we have seen his glory, the glory of the only Son of the Father. Amen."

Vicki hugged Judd and thought about all they had seen and heard. That Nicolae and Leon were gone was a relief, but what about Satan himself?

The answer came a few minutes later when Gabriel said, "But now you belong to Christ Jesus. Though you once were far away from God, now you have been brought near to him because of the blood of Christ. For Christ himself has made peace, and he has brought this Good News of peace to you Gentiles who were far away from him, and to you Jews who were near. Now all of you, both Jews and Gentiles, may come to the Father through the same Holy Spirit because of what Christ has done for you.

"So now you Gentiles are no longer strangers and foreigners. You are citizens along with all of God's holy people. You are members of God's family. You are his house, built on the foundation of the apostles and the prophets. And the cornerstone is Jesus Christ himself. You who believe are carefully joined together, becoming a holy temple for the Lord. Through him you Gentiles are also joined together as part of this dwelling where God lives by his Spirit.

"Since you have been raised to new life with Christ, set your sights on the realities of heaven, where Christ sits at God's right hand in the place of honor and power.

"Let heaven fill your thoughts. Do not think only about things down here on earth. For you died when Christ died, and your real life is hidden with Christ in God. And when Christ, who is your real life, is revealed to the whole world, you will share in all his glory.

"Be careful! Watch out for attacks from the Devil, your great enemy. He prowls around like a roaring lion, looking for some victim to devour. Take a firm stand against him, and be strong in your faith. Remember that Christians all over the world are going through the same kind of suffering you are. In his kindness God called you to his eternal glory by means of Jesus Christ. After you have suffered a little while, he will restore, support, and strengthen you, and he will place you on a firm foundation. All power is his forever and ever. Amen."

The crowd shouted "Amen!" and the multitude began worshiping and singing as Gabriel shouted, "Then I saw an angel come down from heaven with the key to the bottomless pit and a heavy chain in his hand."

The crowd cheered.

"He seized the dragon—that old serpent, the Devil, Satan—and bound him in chains for a thousand years."

People screamed, their hands raised.

"The angel threw him into the bottomless pit, which he then shut and locked so Satan could not deceive the nations anymore until the thousand years were finished."

Now the people seemed to quiet, then gasped in fear as the archangel Michael came forward with an enormous lion. Gabriel quieted them by saying, "But you belong to God, my dear children. You have already won your fight with these false prophets, because the Spirit who lives in you is greater than the spirit who lives in the world."

The lion's roar shook the buildings around them. Vicki dipped her head and clamped her hands over her ears. When she looked again, the lion had transformed into a giant snake and coiled himself around Michael's arms and legs. Michael wrestled it to the ground, but then it turned into a dragonlike monster. Michael pulled a heavy chain from thin air and subdued the flame-snorting creature.

Finally, the dragon calmed and became an angel

brighter than any behind Jesus. The chain slid to the ground in a pile, and the being argued with Michael.

Jesus took control and said, "Kneel at my feet."

"I will do no such thing!" Lucifer hissed.

"Kneel."

Lucifer hunched his shoulders but knelt.

"I have fought against you from shortly after your creation," Jesus said.

"My *creation!* I was no more created than you! And who are you to have *anything* against *me?!*"

"You shall be silent."

It looked like Lucifer tried to stand and speak, but he could do neither.

Jesus continued, "For all your lies about having evolved, you are a created being."

The creature shook his head.

"Only God has the power to create, and you were our creation. You were in Eden, the garden of God, before it was a paradise for Adam and Eve. You were there as an exalted servant when Eden was a beautiful rock garden."

Jesus gave Satan's history as the being writhed silently. "You have opposed my Father and me from before the creation of man. A third of the angels in heaven and most of the population of the earth followed your model of rebellion and pride. This will earn for them and for you separation from almighty God in the everlasting fire prepared for you and your angels."

Jesus accused Lucifer of deceiving Eve, putting murder into Cain's heart, causing the suffering of mankind,

447

blinding the minds of millions who did not believe in the gospel, and many more sins.

When Jesus finished detailing Satan's crimes, Lucifer gasped through clenched teeth, unable to speak.

Gabriel leaned over the angel of light and shouted, "Acknowledge Jesus as Lord!"

Satan clenched his fists and shook his head.

Jesus looked left where another hole opened and black smoke billowed. Michael moved to Satan with the chain. Satan fought him as a dragon, then a snake, and finally a lion. Michael struggled to chain the animal, picked him up under one arm, and flew into the smoky hole.

The crowd cheered but quieted when Jesus raised a hand. "Glory and honor to God forever and ever. He is the eternal King, the unseen one who never dies; he alone is God. Just as sin ruled over all people and brought them to death, now God's wonderful kindness rules instead, giving you right standing with God and resulting in eternal life though Jesus Christ your Lord. I stand before you this day as the King of Israel, he who comes in the name of the Lord."

From the clouds came praises and singing. Then Michael flew out of the hole holding a key. Satan and the chain were gone.

Jesus led his horse to the Temple Mount, where Vicki knew he would take his place on King David's throne. The crowds slowly scattered, many of them going back to their homes.

Vicki took Lionel's hand in one hand and Judd's in the other, and they walked through the streets, now filled with green plants and trees. It was a brand-new world.

**JUDD** and Vicki took Lionel to Jamal and Lina's apartment and were surprised to find them preparing a huge meal. The two had escaped the Unity Army and had hidden near the Siloam Pool. They had fresh fruit, vegetables, and meat from a nearby market.

When they prayed for the meal, thanking God, Jesus answered. In fact, each time Judd spoke with the Lord, he spoke to Judd personally.

Their talk over the meal centered on Jesus and how his presence had changed things. Wild animals seemed tame and walked through the streets without attacking other animals. And the fruits and vegetables were said to ripen on the vine right in front of those who picked it.

Lina and Jamal said they couldn't wait to see their children who had died, but they understood it might be some time before that happened.

"Why's that?" Lionel said.

"You know how there was a gap between the Rapture and the beginning of the Tribulation?" Vicki said, taking a bite of steak. "It's the same with the Glorious Appearing and the beginning of the Millennium."

"How do you figure that?" Judd said.

"It's in Daniel's prophecy," Vicki said. "Something like seventy-five days. I can show you after dinner."

Jamal and Lina seemed impressed with Vicki's knowledge and wanted to know more. Vicki explained what she knew of prophecies from Daniel 12 and Ezekiel 40.

"So you're saying this seventy-five days is preparation time for Jesus?" Jamal said.

"Yes, at least that's what Tsion Ben-Judah taught," Vicki said.

"It only took six days for God to create the world," Lionel said. "Think of what this world is going to look like after seventy-five."

"So much has been destroyed through the judgments," Vicki said. "Tsion said God wants the earth to be like it was back in the Garden of Eden."

The conversation turned to when they would see those who had died during the Tribulation, and Lionel raised a hand. "I've been studying this one. From what Tsion wrote and what I read in the Scriptures, we'll be seeing people like your kids—" he nodded to Jamal and Lina—"at the same time the Old Testament saints are resurrected. Old Testament people like Moses and David and Daniel will rule with Christ during the next one thousand years along with martyrs who died during the Tribulation."

"What about Christians who died before the Rapture?" Lina said.

"They were resurrected at the time of the Rapture," Lionel said. "They were part of the heavenly army behind Jesus."

Vicki looked away. "Which means my mom and dad were there. It all seems so unbelievable, and yet we saw it today."

"But my son and daughter, Kasim and Nada, they will be resurrected when?" Jamal said.

"Soon," Lionel said.

---

Conrad was so curious about what had happened to Global Community workers that he drove to a GC police station a few miles from Enoch's house. What he saw amazed him. All employees of Carpathia had died—presumably at the time Jesus spoke. Enoch taught that all unbelievers still alive would die soon.

Conrad, Shelly, and other members of the Young Trib Force had decided they would head toward Mount Prospect rather than toward Chicago with Enoch, but that changed when Enoch stood before the young people. He had just returned from a drive through Chicago.

"I know you've heard Jesus' voice just like I have," Enoch began. "I've been asking him what we should do, especially since prophecy seems to ignore America. I thought we might try to rebuild this as a Christian nation, but the Lord made it clear he wants us with him."

"What did he say?" Darrion said.

"He said, 'Fear not, Enoch, for you have rightly deduced that you and your flock are to be with me.' He said he would transport us, that we shouldn't be worried."

"When?" Janie said.

"That's what I asked." Enoch chuckled. "And Jesus said, 'Enoch, if God cares so wonderfully for flowers that are here today and gone tomorrow, won't he more surely care for you? You have so little faith! So don't worry about having enough food or drink or clothing. Your heavenly Father already knows all your needs, and he will give you all you need from day to day. So don't worry about tomorrow."

Enoch's eyes twinkled. "So we're going to Israel. I don't know how. I don't know exactly when, but I do know God is going to make a way."

---

When Vicki awoke the next morning one thought sprung to her mind. She was to go to the Valley of Jehoshaphat—the one created when Jesus set foot on the Mount of Olives. She nudged Judd awake and they dressed.

"I don't think we—"

"—should eat," Judd finished. "We should just go right to the valley. That's what the Lord seems to be saying to me too."

Jamal, Lina, and Lionel felt the same way.

*Incredible*, Vicki thought. *Jesus is speaking to us, leading us, and showing us exactly what to do. And he's doing it for everyone!*

Conrad and Shelly had taken a walk with Phoenix and now sat on a stone bench in the courtyard of the nearby mall. They had talked about Jesus the whole day, and when they weren't talking about him, they were talking with him or he was talking to them.

Shelly held Phoenix on her lap, scratching under his collar. The dog's eyes closed with contentment, and Shelly leaned over to Conrad. "He's asleep now. You can kiss me if you'd like."

Conrad smiled. Since Jesus had come, everyone had worked together, and no one argued or squabbled over petty things. He and Shelly had discussed their problems and worked things out, but now there seemed to be a new depth to their love.

Conrad leaned forward, closed his eyes, and kissed Shelly. When he opened his eyes, he saw that things were different. Instead of sitting on a stone bench in Palos Hills, Illinois, they were sitting on the sand in Israel in some kind of valley. And there were millions of people passing by them. Phoenix, still on Shelly's lap, opened his eyes, wagged his tail, and leaped to the ground.

The sky above filled with angels and the heavenly army. Conrad shielded his eyes—the light was so intense.

"Do you believe this?" Shelly gasped.

Conrad shook his head and smiled. "That was a great kiss."

They both laughed and stood.

Then the voice of Jesus spoke to Conrad's heart, and from the look on Shelly's face, he was speaking to her too. "Conrad, when you see my throne, join those on my right, your left."

"Okay, Lord," Conrad said.

---

Jesus sat upon a throne on a platform before all the people. The sight of millions of people moving to the left and the right of Jesus made Lionel gasp. When Jesus told Lionel where to go, he obeyed and moved toward a smaller group. Most were headed to Jesus' left, and people there looked frightened.

"Worship the King of kings and Lord of lords!" Gabriel shouted, and everyone fell to their knees.

"Jesus Christ is Lord!" Lionel said along with millions of others.

Gabriel motioned for everyone to stand. "John the revelator wrote: 'I saw under the altar the souls of all who had been martyred for the word of God and for being faithful in their witness.

" 'They called loudly to the Lord and said, "O Sovereign Lord, holy and true, how long will it be before you judge the people who belong to this world for what they have done to us? When will you avenge our blood against these people?"

" 'Then a white robe was given to each of them. And they were told to rest a little longer until the full number of the servants of Jesus had been martyred.'

"People of the earth, hearken your ears to me! The time has been accomplished to avenge the blood of the martyrs against those living on the earth! For the Son of

Man has come in the glory of his Father with his angels, and he will now reward each according to his works! As it is written, ' "At that time, when I restore the prosperity of Judah and Jerusalem," says the Lord, "I will gather the armies of the world into the valley of Jehoshaphat. There I will judge them for harming my people, for scattering my inheritance among the nations, and for dividing up my land.

" '"They cast lots to decide which of my people would be their slaves. They traded young boys for prostitutes and little girls for enough wine to get drunk." ' "

A commotion rose from Jesus' left, and the group fell down and wailed, "Jesus Christ is Lord! Jesus Christ is Lord!" A man dressed in black with long hair tried to stand. *Z-Van!*

Calmly, the Lord spoke. "Lionel, come, you who are blessed by my Father, inherit the Kingdom prepared for you from the foundation of the world. For I was hungry, and you fed me. I was thirsty, and you gave me a drink. I was a stranger, and you invited me into your home. I was naked, and you gave me clothing. I was sick, and you cared for me. I was in prison, and you visited me."

"Lord, when did I see you hungry and feed you or thirsty and give you something to drink?" Lionel said. "Or see you as a stranger or see you in prison?"

"I assure you, Lionel," Jesus said, "when you did it to one of the least of these my brothers and sisters, you were doing it to me!"

Lionel nodded. "Thank you."

Jesus walked to the edge of the platform. With

emotion in his voice he said, "Away with you, you cursed ones, into the eternal fire prepared for the Devil and his demons! For I was hungry, and you didn't feed me. I was thirsty, and you didn't give me anything to drink. I was a stranger, and you didn't invite me into your home. I was naked, and you gave me no clothing. I was sick and in prison, and you didn't visit me."

Millions protested. "When did we see you hungry or thirsty or a stranger or naked . . . ?" The noise of their pleadings reached a crescendo.

Then Jesus said, "I assure you, when you refused to help the least of these my brothers and sisters, you were refusing to help me. And you will go away into eternal punishment, but the righteous will go into eternal life."

After a time, Gabriel stepped forward and silenced the crowd. "Your time has come!"

Jesus lifted a hand, and a huge hole opened in the earth to his left and swallowed the millions who had never received Jesus as their Savior and Lord. Then the earth closed again.

---

Vicki was overcome with sadness at the destruction of the people. Jesus spoke to her softly. "I know your heart, Vicki. Now accept my peace. The peace I give isn't like the peace the world gives. So don't be troubled or afraid. Listen now as my servant comforts you."

For the next few minutes, Gabriel spoke, giving Scripture, explaining the unexplainable—the love of God, the grace of Christ. Jesus spoke as well, and after Gabriel told everyone to sit, he smiled and said in a loud voice, "Blessed and holy are those who share in the first resurrection. For them the second death holds no power, but they will be priests of God and of Christ and will reign with him a thousand years.

"The mighty God, the Lord, has spoken; he has summoned all humanity from east to west! From Mount Zion, the perfection of beauty, God shines in glorious radiance. Our God approaches with the noise of thunder. Fire devours everything in his way, and a great storm rages around him. Heaven and earth will be his witnesses as he judges his people.

Jesus stood. "Bring my faithful people to me—those who made a covenant with me by giving sacrifices."

From everywhere came the souls of those who had died in faith, the "believing dead," as Tsion had called them. All these wore clean, white robes and gathered around Jesus' throne. Vicki searched the faces for anyone she knew, but there were so many!

Jesus began by honoring Old Testament saints, people Vicki had heard about when she was small and went to vacation Bible school. As Jesus called them forward, he embraced them and they knelt at his feet. "Well done, good and faithful servant," Jesus said to each.

Noah, Samuel, Ruth, Gideon, and many more approached Jesus. The ceremony must have gone on for days, Vicki realized, but Jesus had given everyone his strength and patience.

When Abraham stepped forward, Jesus said, "By faith you obeyed when God called you to leave home and go to another land that God would give you as your inheritance. You went without knowing where you were going. And even when you reached the land God promised you, you lived there by faith—for you were like a foreigner, living in a tent. And so did Isaac and Jacob, to whom God gave the same promise. You did this because you were confidently looking forward to a city with eternal foundations, a city designed and built by God."

Abraham's wife, Sarah, was right behind him and later Jacob and Joseph. Vicki was thrilled at the sight, but her heart ached to see her friends, those who had died during the Tribulation and those who had been taken from her in the Rapture.

She took Judd's hand and squeezed it gently. "Can't wait to meet your parents," she whispered.

# 48

**THE HONORING** of Old Testament saints was complete, and Judd couldn't believe it had been days since it had first begun. He didn't feel tired, hungry, or anything other than worshipful toward Jesus. He thanked God again and again for letting him be a part of this.

"You're welcome, Judd," Jesus said. "But the best is yet to come."

Judd had dreamed of talking with Old Testament heroes, but now Gabriel stood and said, "John the revelator wrote, 'I saw the souls of those who had not worshiped the beast or his statue, nor accepted his mark on their forehead or their hands. They came to life again, and they reigned with Christ for a thousand years.'"

This ceremony didn't happen like the Old Testament saints. Somehow the Lord arranged it so that only people who knew a Tribulation saint saw that person getting their reward. One of the first Judd noticed was Bruce

Barnes, the pastor who had helped him, Vicki, and Lionel understand the truth.

Vicki stood and pointed at a white-robed man. "It's Bruce!" Before Judd or Vicki could yell at him, Mark Eisman stepped forward. Tears streamed down Judd's face as Mark received his reward. Then came Mark's cousin John Preston. Then Perryn Madeleine, the young man who had been beheaded in France. Then Pete Davidson, the biker Judd had helped during the earthquake.

---

Vicki wept as Natalie Bishop knelt in front of Jesus. The Lord honored her by mentioning that she had sacrificed her own life to save her friends. Natalie had worked inside the Global Community and had been eventually beheaded.

Vicki could hardly contain her joy as Chaya Stein and her mother stepped forward. Mr. Stein was not far away from Vicki. He stood, praising God, tears streaming.

Hattie Durham appeared and embraced Jesus. When she knelt at his feet, Jesus placed a sparkling tiara on her head. "My daughter, you were martyred for your testimony of me in the face of the Antichrist and the False Prophet, and so you will bear this crown for eternity. Well done, good and faithful servant."

Phoenix barked when Ryan Daley, an original Young Trib Force member, approached. The dog ran up to Ryan and licked his face. Ryan knelt at Jesus' feet. As Jesus gathered Ryan into his arms, the Lord reached out and gently patted Phoenix's head.

When Vicki looked again, Ryan had moved away, and Chloe Williams took his place. Behind her were Buck Williams and Tsion Ben-Judah. Caleb, the angel who had appeared to Vicki and the others in Wisconsin, stepped from behind the throne and embraced Chloe.

Jesus said to Chloe, "You too suffered the guillotine for my name's sake, speaking boldly for me to the end. Wear this crown for eternity."

To Buck, Jesus said, "You and your wife gave up a son for my sake, but he shall be returned to you, and you shall be recompensed a hundredfold. You will enjoy the love of the children of others during the millennial kingdom."

When Tsion Ben-Judah stepped forward, Jesus praised him for "your bold worldwide proclamation of me as the Messiah your people had for so long sought, the loss of your family—which shall be restored to you—your faithful preaching of my gospel to millions around the world, and your defense of Jerusalem until the moment of your death. Untold millions joined me in the kingdom because of your witness to the end."

---

Lionel set out to find Ryan Daley as soon as he saw him approach Jesus. He jumped up and tried to see over the throng, but suddenly the honoring of these martyrs and saints was over.

Jesus stood at the front edge of the platform and spread his arms. "I will declare the decree. The Lord has said to me, 'You are my Son. Today I have become your

Father. Only ask, and I will give you the nations as your inheritance, the ends of the earth as your possession. You will break them with an iron rod and smash them like clay pots.'

"Now then, you kings, act wisely! Be warned, you rulers of the earth! Serve the Lord with reverent fear, and rejoice with trembling. Submit to God's royal Son, or he will become angry, and you will be destroyed in the midst of your pursuits—for his anger can flare up in an instant. But what joy for all who find protection in him!

"I welcome you, one and all, to the kingdom I have prepared for you. Lionel, welcome."

"I praise you, Lord," Lionel said.

And then the noise of reunions began. People swarmed through the crowd looking for anyone to hug. Some grabbed strangers and embraced. Others who found friends or relatives leaped into the air, hugging each other tightly.

Someone touched Lionel on the shoulder and he turned. A familiar face looked back at him, and for a moment Lionel didn't know who it was. Finally he recognized the man and shouted, "Uncle André!"

Lionel's uncle smiled and turned his head shyly. "Bet you didn't expect to see me here."

"B-b-but . . . Judd and I . . . we found your body," Lionel stammered. "What happened?"

"All that stuff you said—I took it to heart. Just before I died, I cried out to the Lord to save me, and he did. I'm glad you never gave up on me."

Judd fell to his knees as Bruce Barnes and Ryan Daley walked arm in arm toward him and Vicki. Phoenix trailed not far behind, his tail wagging and his body trembling with delight. In the background, Judd saw Dan and Nina Ben-Judah embracing their father and Mrs. Ben-Judah close by.

Ryan knelt and hugged Judd. Then Vicki joined them, and they laughed and cried at the same time.

The joy Judd felt was so real he couldn't stop crying. He shook his head. "Ryan, I'm so sorry for—"

"No!" Ryan exclaimed. "There is no sorrow here. You've been forgiven. I've been forgiven. We've all received God's grace."

Bruce Barnes joined the little group. "We've been so proud of what you've done. There are many souls here because of your faithfulness to give the message."

"It's because of you that we even found the message," Judd said to Bruce.

Bruce nodded and his eyes widened. "Excuse me. I see my wife and children."

Lionel pulled his uncle André into the group and introduced everyone. When Ryan saw Lionel, Judd thought Ryan would jump out of his skin. They hugged and danced and slapped high fives.

Judd turned and looked toward the throne. Jesus watched, drinking in the excitement and fervor of the reunions. "Thank you," Judd whispered.

"You're welcome, Judd," Jesus said. "I delight in

giving you the desires of your heart." He looked slightly to his left. "There are others who wish to greet you."

Judd turned and saw his mother, father, brother, and sister. Beside them were people he had never seen before. He rushed to his mom and hugged her, then his dad.

"I was on a plane—I took a credit card—," Judd started but couldn't finish.

"It's okay, Son," his father said, hugging him tightly.

Marc and Marcie beamed at Judd, then looked at Vicki. "Are you his wife?"

"Yes," Judd said. "Let me introduce you."

But before he could, Vicki let out a squeal.

---

Vicki flew to her mother and father and embraced them. Then she hugged her little sister, Jeanni, and twirled her around. "Mom, Dad, I want you to meet Judd Thompson."

Mrs. Byrne smiled. "Thank you for watching out for our little girl."

Judd dipped his head. "She's the joy of my life." He looked at Mr. Byrne. "If I could have, I would have asked your permission before we were married."

"You have our blessing and our thanks," Mr. Byrne said. "I couldn't have picked a better son-in-law."

Vicki quickly introduced her family to Judd's, and it felt like they had known each other all their lives.

Later Vicki found Pete Davidson and Natalie Bishop, and she had a chance to talk more with Ryan Daley. She saw Darrion Stahley walking with her mother and father. Manny Aguilara and his sister, Anita. Josey Fogarty with her sons, Ben and Brad, and people she had known in high school who had disappeared.

Chad Harris, the young man Vicki had met in Iowa, smiled and gave her a hug. Judd and Chad talked for a long time. Vicki spotted Cheryl Tifanne visiting her son, Ryan Victor, and spoke with her about her last months in Wisconsin. Vicki met Tom and Luke Gowin, two believers from South Carolina who had lost their lives. Judd seemed overjoyed to introduce a handsome young man named Pavel Rudja to Vicki. She later learned that Pavel had been in a wheelchair for most of his life.

As families headed toward homes and living quarters, Judd talked about their future. He mentioned Vicki's idea about taking in children with no families.

Vicki stopped, noticing several children standing alone. A light caught her eye and she glanced at Jesus.

"Let the little children come to me," Jesus said. "Don't stop them. For the Kingdom of heaven belongs to such as these."

"Am I supposed to—?"

"I have already put this desire in your heart, Vicki," Jesus said.

Vicki walked up to a redheaded girl who was moving a finger through the sand. She couldn't have been older than seven.

"What's your name?" Vicki asked.

"Anne," the girl said.

"Where's your family?"

"I don't have any. They're gone."

Vicki looked at Judd and extended a hand to the girl.

The three walked toward a boy sitting on a rock, and Vicki smiled at Anne.

"You have a family now," Vicki said.

*In that day the wolf and the lamb will live together;*
*the leopard and the goat will be at peace.*
*Calves and yearlings will be safe among lions,*
*and a little child will lead them all.*

ISAIAH 11:6

# ABOUT THE AUTHORS

**Jerry B. Jenkins** (www.jerryjenkins.com) is the writer of the Left Behind series. He owns the Jerry B. Jenkins Christian Writers Guild, (www.ChristianWritersGuild.com), an organization dedicated to mentoring aspiring authors, as well as Jenkins Entertainment, a filmmaking company (www.Jenkins-Entertainment.com). Former vice president of publishing for the Moody Bible Institute of Chicago, he also served many years as editor of *Moody* magazine and is now Moody's writer-at-large.

His writing has appeared in publications as varied as *Time* magazine, *Reader's Digest*, *Parade*, *Guideposts*, in-flight magazines, and dozens of other periodicals. Jenkins's biographies include books with Billy Graham, Hank Aaron, Bill Gaither, Luis Palau, Walter Payton, Orel Hershiser, and Nolan Ryan, among many others. His books appear regularly on the *New York Times*, *USA Today*, *Wall Street Journal*, and *Publishers Weekly* best-seller lists.

He holds two honorary doctorates, one from Bethel College (Indiana) and one from Trinity International University. Jerry and his wife, Dianna, live in Colorado and have three grown sons and three grandchildren.

---

**Dr. Tim LaHaye** (www.timlahaye.com), who conceived the idea of fictionalizing an account of the Rapture and the Tribulation, is a noted author, minister, and nationally recognized speaker on Bible prophecy. He is the founder of both Tim LaHaye Ministries and The PreTrib Research Center.

He also recently cofounded the Tim LaHaye School

of Prophecy at Liberty University. Dr. LaHaye speaks at many of the major Bible prophecy conferences in the U.S. and Canada, where his prophecy books are very popular.

Dr. LaHaye earned a doctor of ministry degree from Western Theological Seminary and an honorary doctor of literature degree from Liberty University. For twenty-five years he pastored one of the nation's outstanding churches in San Diego, which grew to three locations. During that time he founded two accredited Christian high schools, a Christian school system of ten schools, and Christian Heritage College.

There are almost 13 million copies of Dr. LaHaye's fifty nonfiction books that have been published in over thirty-seven foreign languages. He has written books on a wide variety of subjects, such as family life, temperaments, and Bible prophecy. His current fiction works, the Left Behind series, written with Jerry B. Jenkins, continue to appear on the best-seller lists of the Christian Booksellers Association, *Publishers Weekly, Wall Street Journal, USA Today,* and the *New York Times.* LaHaye's second fiction series of prophetic novels consists of *Babylon Rising* and *The Secret on Ararat,* both of which hit the *New York Times* best-seller list and will soon be followed by *Europa Challenge.* This series of four action thrillers, unlike *Left Behind,* does not start with the Rapture but could take place today and goes up to the Rapture.

He is the father of four grown children and grandfather of nine. Snow skiing, waterskiing, motorcycling, golfing, vacationing with family, and jogging are among his leisure activities.

areUthirsty.com

well . . . are you?